Gabrielle Lord is [...] of Australia's foremost writers. Her popular psychological thrillers are informed by a detailed knowledge of forensic procedures, combined with an unrivalled gift for story-telling. She is the author of eleven novels—*Bones, Tooth and Claw, Salt, Jumbo, The Sharp End, Feeding the Demons, Whipping Boy, Fortress, Death Delights, Baby Did a Bad Bad Thing* and most recently *Lethal Factor*. Her stories and articles have appeared widely in the national press and been published in anthologies. Winner of the 2002 Ned Kelly award for best crime novel for *Death Delights* and joint winner of the 2003 Davitt crime fiction prize for *Baby Did a Bad Bad Thing*, Gabrielle has also written for film and TV and is currently completing her next novel. She lives in Sydney.

SPIKING
THE GIRL

SPIKING
GABRIELLE LORD
THE GIRL

HODDER

Hodder Headline Australia

First published in Australia and New Zealand in 2004
by Hodder Headline Australia Pty Limited
(A member of the Hodder Headline Group)
Level 17, 207 Kent Street, Sydney NSW 2000
Website: www.hha.com.au

This edition published in 2005

**National Library of Australia
Cataloguing-in-Publication data**

Lord, Gabrielle, 1946- .
  Spiking the girl.

  ISBN 0 7336 1980 0 (pbk.).

  I. Title.

A823.3

Text design and typesetting by Bookhouse, Sydney
Printed in Australia by Griffin Press, Adelaide

To Ken Bruen

Gra agus bheannacht

PROLOGUE

Tasmin jogged down the hill, long legs striding out in navy trackpants, blonde ponytail swinging, and adolescent breasts bouncing under a brief sports top, her school backpack jerking up and down in time. Headphones filled her ears with her favourite singers, but even that couldn't block out the memory of what she'd heard yesterday.

It couldn't be true, she insisted to herself. Eddie was just trying to frighten her. Or impress her. He did that sometimes when he'd had too much to drink. She hadn't really *meant* it when she'd said she'd go to the police. It was just the terrible shock of hearing what he'd said had happened to Ames. She didn't think Eddie would tell anyone about what she'd said. And what good would it do anyway if she did tell what had happened? It couldn't change anything. And it would mean the end of everything—everything they'd worked for.

Tasmin jogged on, her feet keeping time with *It's over, it's done, it's over, it's done.* Wasn't everyone telling her that? To put the past behind her and get on with it? And Amy would *want* her to keep her dreams, surely. *It's over, it's done and Amy is gone, it's over, it's done and Amy is gone* went her feet, but her mind kept wishing that Eddie hadn't told her.

Go away, she told the memory. These things happen. They're happening all the time.

She turned the corner, wishing she weren't going to school. She wanted to leave. What was the point of staying on any longer? How could the stuff she was supposed to be learning at school have anything to do with real life?

She tried to block out her concerns by dreaming of the promised new lifestyle. Sleeping in till really, really late, then coffee and a leisurely brunch at the beach. Afternoon shopping, parties every night. Three or four lucrative modelling assignments during the week. No more boring classes and rushed homework. No more heavy backpacks filled with boring textbooks. She would be sharing a flat with Cee at Bondi. Last year, she and Amy and Cee had talked about moving out together. Now there were only two. She hoped Cee would still be keen. She'd noticed Cee had become more distant, more disapproving, of late.

She took her mind off that by thinking of the exciting way things were shaping up, the approaches she'd had from working with the guys from the club. She wouldn't even need a stupid Higher School Certificate. But trying to talk to Mum about it would just mean another fight like last night's and she couldn't bear the thought of that. *I could get work* right now, she thought, high-paid work, too. Fun work. She'd already proved that. But she couldn't tell her mum about any of that.

She avoided a pile of dog shit without altering her rhythmic stride. The only good things about Netherleigh Park had been her friends and the secret. Tears pricked the back of her eyes. Even though it was a year, she still missed Amy. Tasmin blinked and sniffed, took a deep breath, trying to dismiss the memories. Eddie had just been trying to frighten her. Maybe he was even trying to put pressure on her, get her to work for *him*. Make her think she needed his protection or something. No way. She would definitely put what he'd told her about Amy right out of her mind. She shouldn't have threatened him with going to the police. It'd just spoil everything, ruin her whole future, if the police started looking into things. She thought of her mother's response and her resolve hardened further. No way. The future was where she wanted to be. Right now.

Tasmin took a deep breath before starting up the hill, then noticed Mrs McAdam's red Merc stopped at the lights at the top. *Shit!* She mustn't be seen by their neighbour running to Netherleigh Park. Since Amy's disappearance, her mum had practically made her swear on the Bible that she would get the bus each morning. But Tasmin needed the exercise. In the world she was moving towards, she needed to keep her perfect adolescent figure. Everything she ate went straight to her hips and the five-kilometre run to school each day was a good workout.

The traffic lights changed and Tasmin dived into the driveway of a large block of flats, taking cover behind a clump of yellow hibiscus bushes. Mrs McAdam's Merc sailed past as Tasmin peered through the dark green leaves. She hadn't been seen.

She bounced out again, taking the hill in long strides and thinking about the letter she was composing to Romeo. Very explicit. Very *hot*. That was the other saving grace of boring old school—torturing the teacher. She and Cee could giggle over it before she hid it.

Tasmin winced as she nearly went over on an ankle. Snapping her attention back to her stride, she glanced at her watch. If she kept up this good pace she would be there in less than fifteen minutes. She started panting as the hill made her calf muscles and quads burn; her ankle began to throb. To take her mind off how hard it was, she thought of racing into the school grounds, grabbing her spare uniform and shoes from the sports room, having a quick shower and then reporting, fresh and sweet, for her one-on-one History essay meeting.

But then a blue Ford slowed down beside her. Tasmin looked across, not recognising the car. Surely it wasn't her stepfather trying to put more pressure on her? Or some sleaze trying to pick her up? It took her a moment to see past the dark glasses. When she realised who was driving, her heart skipped a beat and she stopped jogging, pulling the earphones off.

He smiled at her. 'Want a lift, Tas?' Then his face became more serious. 'We need to talk.'

Tasmin thought fast. She could text Cee—that's if Cee had sneaked her mobile into school—and Cee could write a note for her. Maybe.

'Okay,' she said.

Until yesterday, she'd have smiled.

ONE

Gemma pulled up in front of the address Daria Reynolds had given her and sat there for a few moments, taking in the scene. Her fingers traced the gaping hole in the Celtic pendant round her neck as she tried to put last night out of her mind. Jimmy Barnes was singing that *'the last plane out of Sydney's almost gone'* and Gemma switched him off, thinking how she wished she could fly away with it. Wherever she went though, Gemma knew she'd take her grief and regret with her. Wearily she gathered up her briefcase and the empty folder she'd started with 'Daria Reynolds' and the case number written on the cover. If it hadn't been for last night's poisonous, terminal fight with Steve, Gemma would have delighted in the perfect summer morning awaiting her outside, the magpies carolling in the trees overhead, beautiful yellow roses in the small front garden beyond the footpath. Then she felt the shadow again and shivered. Condition orange was still prevailing, her every instinct flashing a warning. She couldn't shake the feeling that someone was on her tail. But why and who? Maybe it was just paranoia, projecting her own work onto some other agent.

She checked the Bondi Junction streetscape in the rear-vision mirror. Only a couple of parked cars on the road—all vacant. No one sitting inside them, pretending to be reading the papers or a road map. She waited in case someone was circling the block. But no one drove past. Settle down, she told herself. Her increasing sense of danger must be because of last night—the gaping injury caused by Steve's walk-out. There was a hole in her heart.

She gripped her briefcase and, giving the street one last sweep, got out and locked the car before walking up the short path to the house. Smoky glass panels on either side of the front door provided an ad hoc mirror, and she pushed a stray lock of tawny hair back behind her left ear. The ancient fragrance of frankincense caused her to wonder. It must be coming from inside the house.

The front door suddenly opened. Gemma's first impression of the slight woman was that Daria Reynolds appeared to be younger than she probably was. An Alice band held back her hair above a pale, round face.

'Miss Lincoln? Please come in.'

Gemma stepped inside, noting the four heavy-duty locks on the door. This woman took security seriously. She followed her hostess into a large living room. Daria Reynolds was too thin, but shapely, in her simple black dress cinched with a narrow red leather belt. The room was hot and

Gemma immediately saw why. Masses of candles flickered in front of crowding religious paraphernalia: icons, statues and pictures of saints. She was glad she hadn't sent Spinner on this particular job. He'd go crazy at all this Popish superstition.

'Please sit down,' Daria whispered, gold crosses swinging from her ears, pink pearl rosary beads around her neck. Gemma wondered why she was whispering until she realised that the feathery, sibilant voice was the woman's normal speaking tone. Gemma put her briefcase down and pulled out her notebook, pen ready.

'It's good of you to come to me,' Daria added. She would have been a pretty woman except for the anxious shadows around her eyes. 'I find it increasingly difficult to leave the house. Except for church.' She pulled up a venetian blind, allowing daylight into the stuffy room, and the candles paled.

Outside, a siren wailed and Gemma idly wondered if anyone she knew was driving past. After eight years out of the job, there weren't many faces she recognised anymore. Her best girlfriend, Detective Sergeant Angie McDonald, was one of her few remaining links to the service.

'Can I get you anything?' Daria hovered.

'A coffee would be nice. Milk and no sugar.'

The woman's absence gave Gemma a chance to take in more of the extraordinary display. It wasn't just Popish, she now realised. This was a very ecumenical gathering: the Buddha, a menorah with lighted candles, Jesus and the Chinese goddess of mercy were among the figures Gemma could identify. Displayed on a black lacquer stand, Michael Archangel plunged a heavenly lance through the body of a demonic dragon. Would a candle lit to this fellow, the patron saint of police, help her salvage the mess with Steve? No. It was too late now. *Go away!* she'd screamed at him out of the depth of her rage last night. *I never want to see you again! Just get the hell out of my life!*

And so he had.

Gemma felt tears burn and focused her attention on a peculiar carved angel that reminded her of the vicious winged monkeys from *The Wizard of Oz*. She didn't have any time for tears. After this interview, she'd go straight to Netherleigh Park Ladies' College. Keep busy, girl, she told herself. It was going to take her a long time to rebuild her business to how it had been before the crash of last year. Despite the good work of the risk management team called in by Mike, Gemma knew she'd lost contacts and goodwill that had taken her years to develop.

From the kitchen came the aroma and sounds of coffee-making. Daria Reynolds hadn't said much on the phone, just enough for Gemma to work out that she was having man trouble. One popular service Gemma's business offered was the very reasonably priced Mandate, a service available to women who had their doubts about the man in their life, or the man they were inviting into their life. For around five hundred dollars, Gemma could check out that the man was in fact who he said he was, that he worked and lived where he said he did, and, in some cases, that he had no major criminal record. Most of this information was legally available, but it might take an unpractised searcher weeks to discover it, whereas she could check it out in about twenty-four hours. Was Mr Reynolds up to mischief? She gritted her teeth, trying not to remember the way Steve had walked away without a backward glance, and Daria appeared carrying two cups on a small square tray.

'I'll need to know more than what you told me over the phone, Daria.' Gemma took a sip of coffee. 'You said you were having some sort of trouble with your husband?'

'Ex-husband,' Daria corrected, perched on the edge of her seat opposite. 'I divorced him eighteen months ago.' She raised her eyes to a statue of a bearded saint holding a staff and lily. 'Even though it hasn't made any difference. Even though divorce is against my religion.'

Outside, a second siren wailed louder and closer and Daria Reynolds automatically blessed herself. The woman seemed quite self-possessed, Gemma thought. Exhausted, but collected. She showed none of the agitation you'd expect from someone unbalanced. Nor did she seem to be under the influence of tranquillisers.

'What can I do for you?' Gemma asked, pen poised over her notebook.

The woman lowered her eyes. 'I'm at my wits' end,' she whispered. 'He just won't leave me alone. He keeps coming back.'

'His full name and date of birth?'

'Vincent John Reynolds. 19 September 1953.'

Gemma jotted the information down.

'I'm terrified of him,' Daria whispered, head lowered.

That was evident but Gemma noted it. The assembly of saints and celestial beings started to make sense. 'Is he violent? Has he threatened you? Assaulted you?'

There was a silence.

Gemma leaned forward, speaking gently. 'Mrs Reynolds, I need to know things like this. I understand this isn't easy for you but I have to ask these questions.'

Daria stood, moving suddenly like a woman twice her age, and went to a box on the mantelpiece. She took out a narrow stick of incense and lit it with a cigarette lighter, waved the flame out and stuck the smoking stalk in a crystal holder. Finally she sat down again.

'He doesn't touch me.' Again, a long pause, the pressure of silence building. 'He comes at night.' Her voice barely registered.

Like a vampire, Gemma thought, and the religious icons made even more sense. Almost as the thought came, a candle sputtered and died with a sharp crack. Daria jumped out of her seat again to attend to it and Gemma had to strain to pick up her words.

'I wake up and he's there, beside me.'

Daria returned to her seat and hunched in it. 'I wake up and I can smell him.'

Gemma felt the hairs on her neck and arms prickle.

'And I know he wants to have sex with me.' She looked at Gemma. 'Please,' she whispered, 'I don't know what to do.'

Even after divorce, Gemma thought, some men just don't get it. And some women don't get it either. Daria Reynolds just lies there. Why the hell doesn't she ring the police? Get the bastard thrown out of the house? She felt irritation rising.

'You're wondering why I don't take action, why I just let this sort of thing happen, aren't you?' said Daria before Gemma could speak.

'I've done everything I can,' she continued, 'and he's never touched me. I always feared his violence, he knew that. But that wasn't the reason I divorced him.' She put the lighter down, eyes watering either with tears or incense smoke. 'He was . . . unnatural. He wanted unnatural things from me—disgusting things. I had to get away.' She threw her head up in defiance. 'I refused. I told him what he wanted was sinful. Finally, I divorced him.'

'And you hoped that would be the end of it?' Gemma prompted.

'I prayed he would find some other woman. But even after he—' The defiance had been short-lived. Now her face was stricken.

'After he what?' Gemma asked.

Daria shook her head, and Gemma noticed for the first time how pale and sick she looked. It's unhealthy, she thought, to stay shut up in a place like this, with all these images and candles. Daria Reynolds needed fresh air. Not to mention a life.

'But it's no use,' Daria whispered. 'He won't leave me alone. I can't get away from him. Nothing I do makes any difference.'

Gemma considered. Even after a divorce, some couples just couldn't get untangled. 'You've been to the police?'

'I've done all that,' said Daria with a sigh. 'But the police are no use. They don't seem to take it seriously because he isn't violent.'

'But surely if he's trespassing . . .'

'They came round a couple of times but they couldn't find him. They think I'm making it up. They're very polite, but I can tell what they're thinking.'

In the corner, another candle flared up, then just as suddenly went out. Daria replaced it with a new one. All this holy stuff sure keeps her busy, Gemma thought.

'Did you take out a restraining order?' she asked. 'An Apprehended Violence Order? If he breaks an AVO, they have to arrest him.'

For the first time, the woman's eyes flashed with the anger of the good girl who's done everything she's supposed to do yet things still aren't going the way they should.

'Of course I took out an AVO!' she said. 'I did everything that the law advises—even before the divorce—and it didn't help me!'

'Who did you talk to?' Gemma waited, pen poised, ready to note down the name.

'The police at Waverley,' said Daria, 'and then the chamber magistrate.'

'Do you remember the police officer's name?' Gemma asked.

Daria reached up to the top of a saint-infested bookcase and took a card down, passing it to Gemma. Senior Constable Diane Hayworth. Gemma jotted the name down, making a mental note to drop in on Diane Hayworth at Waverley Police and make a few enquiries regarding Mr and Mrs Reynolds.

'Did you follow up on it?' she asked and handed the policewoman's card back. Too many women took out AVOs and then didn't have them enforced. So far, this wasn't sounding like a job Gemma wanted to take on, though right now she couldn't afford to be choosy.

'Of course I did,' said Daria. 'I keep telling them. But they don't believe me.'

'What about security, Daria? Are you sure your house is secure?' Gemma asked, though she remembered the multiple locks at the front door.

Daria stood up and went to the window to touch the wrought-iron grille. 'This house is a fortress,' she said. 'But it's no use. Nothing can keep him away.'

The woman's passivity irked Gemma. 'He must have keys if he's getting in,' she said. 'Have you changed the locks?'

'I also did that before the divorce!' Another flash of fire from the wispy woman as she moved away from the window. 'There's something I should tell you,' she said. 'Something you should know.'

As Daria stood with the light from the window behind her, Gemma became aware of a dark, menacing atmosphere building in the room. The glare of candles and heady incense made her feel sick.

'But if I tell you,' Daria continued, 'I know you'll refuse to work for me.'

The brooding heaviness was getting to Gemma. Was she just imagining that the room was closing in, like something from a Poe horror story? Daria seemed to be struggling to find her words as she stood staring at one of her saints. Come on, Gemma urged inwardly. Spit it out!

The silence continued.

'If there's anything that will help me in working for you,' Gemma prompted, 'you must tell me. I'd only refuse to work for someone if what they wanted was illegal. Is that what's concerning you?'

Daria shook her head. 'It's nothing illegal,' she said. 'But you've got to help me.' Her voice was despairing. 'Someone has to help me. You were suggested by a woman I know. You have the right background.'

Gemma, touched by the other woman's desperation and deciding to take on her case, didn't immediately note the odd remark. A breeze lifted the curtains at the window and all the candles bowed in the same direction.

'I'll do what I can, Daria. But you've got to do your share.' Gemma picked up her briefcase and another candle sputtered and hissed. She took out one of her brochures. 'This is the information about my charges. If it's acceptable to you, we can put the house under surveillance. That way, we've got him on video.'

Daria stared at the brochure while Gemma made some rapid calculations. She didn't have any bubble-packed spycams in the car just now.

'I usually take a deposit at this stage, Daria,' she said, remembering the shopping she needed to do. 'One thousand dollars would be fine.'

Daria nodded, unsurprised.

'If you can give me cash,' Gemma continued, 'I'll make it GST inclusive.'

Daria left the room and returned with twenty fifty-dollar bills which Gemma tucked in her wallet.

'We'll also put a covert camera in your bedroom, just to be—'

'But that's what he wanted to do!' Daria took a backwards step, nearly knocking her untouched coffee over in her distress. 'He expected me to behave like some whore, like some prostitute in a porn movie! He wanted to make videos of me and his disgusting filthy behaviour.'

She bent down and moved the coffee cup to a safer spot, then looked at Gemma and her breathing calmed a little as she gathered herself. 'I'm sorry,' she whispered, the dark hollows in her face deepening. 'I know that's not what you meant. I didn't mean to say all that.'

'Okay,' said Gemma, finally breaking an awkward silence. 'Before I go, I'd like to look around. Check the layout of the house, see the exits and entrances.'

She went outside, Daria following, and they walked right round the house as Gemma checked the windows. They were all screened and locked, except for the front ones, which were grilled. Gemma searched for any scrapes or tool marks on any of the frames but they were all quite dusty and untouched.

'He must have a key,' Gemma repeated, turning back to her companion.

Daria shook her head. 'He hasn't.'

'Perhaps he got in once and was able to get hold of one? Had it copied, got it back without you noticing?'

Daria Reynolds stared at her. Again, Gemma wondered about her new client's grasp on reality. Then Daria slowly turned her gaze towards the back garden, squinting against the bright sunlight. The spooky moment passed.

Gemma finished her examination of the outside of the house and they went back inside. She followed Daria down the narrow hall, away from the smoky front room. She went into the two bedrooms, both of them with locked windows; the first smelled like the spare room and needed a good airing. The second, the erstwhile marital bedroom, was similarly decked out with icons and statues, although the candles in here had all burned out.

Gemma glanced at the bedroom ceiling, thinking about where she or Spinner might put the spycam. 'Do you have smoke detectors?' she asked, unable to see any. Daria shook her head.

'Don't you think all these naked flames everywhere could be a bit dangerous?'

Daria stared hard at her again, then took a step forward. 'I know what's dangerous.' Her tiny voice contrasted with the way she'd closed in, invading Gemma's space.

Gemma stepped back, deliberately putting distance between them. Daria immediately closed up the gap. 'Now, Miss Lincoln, I have a question for *you*. Is it true that your mother was murdered?'

Gemma's shock must have showed on her face because Daria Reynolds's expression changed. 'I'm sorry if I've offended you. Believe me, I wouldn't be asking you this if it weren't important. You must understand that.'

'Important?' Gemma rallied. 'To whom?'

'It's important to me.' She paused. 'If it's true.'

'What can my personal circumstances possibly have to do with your situation?' said Gemma, suddenly angry.

'I don't mean to pry or distress you. It is important for me. That's all I can say at this stage. It is true, isn't it?'

Gemma remained silent but Daria Reynolds took her confusion for affirmation. 'So would you please light this candle and walk through the house with me?'

Gemma's initial reaction was to refuse. But the soft beseeching so obvious in Daria's huge eyes touched Gemma. The best thing to do was humour her, do the job she wanted and send her a large bill.

Gemma took the long white candle passed to her,

inclined it to be lit and followed her new client through the house, proceeding in and out of the remaining rooms. She'd worked in a lot of weird places, Gemma thought, but never in a million years did she think she'd be wandering round a stranger's house with a lit candle in her hand.

'Thank you,' Daria whispered when they'd finished. 'I also want someone to watch the place at night.'

'You want physical surveillance as well as cameras?'

'Yes.'

'That will be very expensive.'

Daria Reynolds handed Gemma a key from under a vase in the hallway. 'You can throw the key back through the window grille when you've finished. And as for expensive, I don't really care.'

'We'll get cameras installed in the back and front gardens,' said Gemma. 'And in the bedroom. When would be convenient?'

'How about now?'

Gemma watched while Daria Reynolds hurried to her small silver Honda and drove away. It's as if she suddenly doesn't care anymore, Gemma thought. As if my visit here today was all that's necessary to sort out a stalking ex-husband. If only, Gemma thought. I'd be a rich woman.

She went back to her car and picked up the radio, calling Spinner. 'Tracker Three. Copy, please.'

The sound of her number one operative's voice was calming. Spinner was a gem—her most treasured business asset. It was hard work being a surveillance operative, out on the road all day. His particular talent lay in his silent patience, his capacity to sit, hour after hour if necessary, waiting for a cheat to slip up, to forget to adopt the limp, just once, on the way to get the newspaper, or forget the bad back and start building a swimming pool. Spinner would be there with his zoom camera, shooting his damning footage, getting it all down for the insurance companies' assessors. His contemporaneous notes were clean, clear and concise, despite his truncated education—or maybe because of that. Gemma was blessed to have him on the payroll. Good road operatives were hard to find—and even harder to keep. Since last year's collapse of her business, Spinner was her only full-time employee, with Mike Moody, ex-Federal policeman and in-house IT manager, now just working part-time—as the need arose and her finances permitted.

Gemma told Spinner what she wanted.

'I'll meet you there,' he said after she'd filled him in and given him the address. 'And give you the files of the jobs I've finished. You can take them back with you to the office. Save me driving over later on.'

Gemma rehoused the radio then checked the street up and down. It looked innocuous, incapable of hiding evil or danger, just a pleasant suburban morning streetscape. So why this beating of her heart? This crawling of her scalp?

Gemma took a deep breath, before pulling her

laptop out and taking it back inside Daria's house. Balancing the computer on her knees, she transferred the scrawled notes she'd just written into her electronic file: the date, time, address, the weather, their conversation, everything necessary to ground her report as far as possible in reality.

When she'd saved her notes, she folded the laptop lid down and gazed sightlessly through the window. This time yesterday everything had been fine with Steve. She'd gradually been getting closer to letting go of her jealousy and pain around his infidelity. But when he talked about the possibility of them buying a bigger place together, those issues had suddenly loomed large again. The argument had flared. Now it didn't matter if she had all the time in the world.

Her mobile rang and she dived for it, eager for distraction from her sad thoughts.

'Miss Lincoln?' A frail, female voice. 'It's Rowena Wylde here. Do you remember me?'

It took Gemma a few seconds to cut through the shock. Remember her? Of course she recognised who her caller was—psychiatrist Dr Rowena Wylde, her late father's colleague and mistress, whom she'd briefly met some years ago.

'I haven't got much time,' the woman continued. 'In fact, Miss Lincoln, I'm dying.'

Gemma made some sort of murmuring noise, rallying as fast as she could. It's not often people say that straight out, she thought.

'There's something you should know,' Dr Wylde

continued. 'You and your sister. Something I must tell you. It concerns your father—your family.'

Gemma was surprised at the depth of the feelings this woman's words aroused in her; she wanted to protect, defend, her family, her mother—the mother she barely remembered.

'What could you possibly tell me about my family?'

'Something that you need to know. Something I should have told you a long time ago.'

'And what might that be?' Despite herself, Gemma was intrigued.

'Please,' Rowena Wylde's voice was already weaker now, 'please visit me. It's not the sort of information that should be delivered over the phone.'

Extremely curious now, Gemma agreed and, after reacquainting herself with the psychiatrist's address and telephone number, made a time for later in the week.

Once she'd rung off, she continued to sit, pen frozen in her hand. What could it be, she wondered? Was it something about their father? Their mother? Perhaps it was information relating to their father's imprisonment or their mother's murder.

Yesterday, she'd felt her world swerve off its axis, unbalanced by the absence of Steve. Now she had Daria Reynolds's ex-husband and Rowena Wylde's phone call to deal with. She noticed that one of the candles on the mantelpiece still guttered, sending up a column of black smoke. She went to pinch it out and saw that it stood in front of the image of an angel, all in black with huge dark wings. Gemma squashed the tiny flame, noticing the writing at the bottom of the picture. Asrael, Angel of Death, she read. She shivered.

TWO

Gemma hurried out to her car, calling Kit's number on the way. She wanted to talk to her about Rowena Wylde's call but her sister wasn't answering, replaced by the warm words of her voice mail inviting a message. Probably with a client, Gemma thought, glancing at her watch. Her sister ran a busy psychotherapy practice and was often difficult to catch on the phone. Gemma left a message and slid into her car, putting the mobile back in its travelling holder near the radio. She needed food, suddenly hungry. She decided to head off and find something to eat with Spinner when he arrived.

She switched on the ignition and pulled out, almost collecting an oncoming car. The blaring horn and screech of brakes shocked her into immobility and the driver of the car sped past, swearing.

When she'd calmed down, she drove to a nearby shop and bought some pastries and a drink, then returned to Daria Reynolds's place, letting herself in with the key Daria had given her. She left the white paper bag of pastries on the table, then walked right through the house again, eerier now with its owner absent. The place stank of stale incense and smoke and she hoped Spinner wouldn't be too much longer. This was the sort of empty time she didn't want right now.

She sat down with a fraud investigation magazine she kept in her briefcase for quiet moments, nibbling on a pastry, looking through an article on high-resolution micro cameras. One in particular took her fancy, so compact it fitted into the top of a functional pen.

She heard the distinctive sound of Spinner's white Rodeo ute pulling up outside, reminding her of the early days, when they were the only two workers in her business. Putting the magazine down on the table, she looked out the window. Today Spinner was 'Fletcher Bros Plumbing'. He had several magnetic signs that he could slap along the length of the utility, and hanging in the operatives' office were various tradesmen and courier outfits—Spinner's 'dress-up' clothes.

She watched him as he got out, knowing that if anyone rang Fletcher Bros Plumbing they'd get Spinner's friend Darren Fletcher, who was, Gemma knew from experience, a good plumber. Spinner did a quick check round the front of the house, then started up the path. She felt a surge of affection for her colleague, aka Bede MacNamara, the wiry little ex-jockey who'd got too heavy for the gallopers.

She opened the door for him and he walked in

looking tired and sad, his wizened face more furrowed. 'What's that smell?'

'Incense,' Gemma said. 'This client burns a lot of it.'

He peered closer. 'Is that thing around your neck supposed to be like that, or is something missing?'

Gemma looked down at the pendant. It had been a gift from Steve in happier days: plaited silver serpents encircling what was now an empty oval. She lifted the heavy dark silver chain from which it hung. 'There used to be a very handsome polished onyx in it,' she said. 'But I lost it up at Nelson Bay a couple of days ago.'

Spinner pulled a couple of folders out of his bag. 'This report is ready to go back to the insurers,' he said, handing her a file. 'I need to process the video and I can do that when I come over to the office next.'

Road operatives like Spinner were rarely in the office. Their workplaces were the roads, businesses and houses they did surveillance on. They dropped in only to collect more briefs or carry out the clerical work they needed to do.

Spinner found a place in the living room to put his kit and the remaining folders under his arm before looking up and seeing the collection of icons and statues. 'Stone the bloody crows.' Because he wouldn't swear, Spinner was forced to fall back on expressions from earlier, simpler times when he was riding gallopers round country training tracks. Gemma found it a disarming habit. But only when she was in a good mood. 'What the hell are all these?' he continued.

'I thought you'd know. You're the God-botherer in this turn-out,' she said.

He looked around the room, spotting the fraud investigation magazine. 'Anything interesting in that?'

She shrugged. 'Couple of good investigations from the US. And a feature on those cute little micro digital cameras,' she said, heading down the hallway.

Spinner snatched up his bag from the table, shaking his head as he followed her to the master bedroom. 'Those James Bond things,' he said, 'they're only bloody gimmicks. I don't know why anyone would buy them. They're bloody expensive, too.'

'I want one,' said Gemma. 'One of those tiny cameras is something we should have in our stock.'

'Hey,' said her ace agent, looking into her face when she turned to explain the job to him. 'What's up?'

Spinner's knockabout, good-bloke manner hid an extremely sharp mind. For a fleeting second, Gemma wondered if she could talk to Spinner about Rowena Wylde's phone call. No, she decided. This was family business—she'd speak to Kit first.

'Steve and me,' she said, deciding to tell him one of the reasons for her agitation. 'We've separated.' She tried to maintain a steady voice. 'And it's final.'

Spinner threw his carry bag onto the double

bed. 'That's sad,' he said. 'Me and Rose are in the same boat. Or not in the same boat. We're just not getting along anymore.'

'What are you two fighting about?' Gemma knew that arguments between couples could be about anything. It didn't seem to matter what the subject matter was—its only function to be a carrier of the hostility.

Spinner looked uncomfortable. 'Religion.'

Gemma heard something rustling outside and glanced through a gap in the curtains. A dust devil materialised, spun up the path a little way, then dissipated. She couldn't say 'I told you so', but the thought of charismatic fundamentalist Spinner and exotic Greek Orthodox Rose Georgiou trying to get it together over holy communion just didn't work.

'Rose is at me all the time to convert,' Spinner was saying. 'Become Greek Orthodox. She says if I can't do that for her, then I don't love her.'

'Can't you just go along with it? What's the difference between one lot of religious business and another?'

Spinner shuddered. 'Are you serious? Orthodox! They're even worse than Catholics!'

Nobody could be worse than Catholics, Gemma thought.

She crossed to the big window and wrenched the curtains right back, letting light into the room. Spinner looked around, avoiding the further clutter of saints and angels standing on the dressing table.

'What are we here for?' he asked.

'An ex who won't take no for an answer.'

Gemma pointed to the central light fitting in the bedroom. 'We could spike that light.'

'Boss, you've been off the road too long. Don't you want the potential of live feed all the time?'

Gemma was rattled. She had forgotten the need for constant current. If Spinner wired up the spycam in the light fitting, power would only be available when the light was switched on.

'I'll use that,' said Spinner, pointing to a small black clock radio on the right-hand bedside table. 'As well as the power being on all the time, the spycam can be easily integrated.'

Gemma filled Spinner in with more details about the Reynolds case while he squatted by his bag, sorting through cabling, pliers and other tools until he found the package containing the small camera, which, with all its fittings, was about the size of a bottle top. He held it up to her. 'We'll never need anything smaller than this.'

'Maybe,' she said.

'We'll install motion-activated hook-up for the outside. Back and front. Then we've got the place covered. And that way you can check in at any time with your GPRS mobile. It'll email stills to your laptop if you want that.'

Gemma had recently upgraded to a general packet radio service phone which meant she was always logged on to the network and internet connection.

'She wants physical surveillance, too,' said Gemma. 'Best if you pick it up on your laptop.

You'll be the one sitting out there.' She pointed to the street.

Spinner set about his business, installing the necessary equipment, hiding the tiny camera lenses near the eaves outside.

'I'm presuming,' he said, when he came inside again and squatted beside the bedside table, 'that there's no pressure here? That we haven't got a tight schedule?'

I have been off the road too long, Gemma thought. Vincent Reynolds could walk in any time and bust them doing this. 'Daria only mentioned nocturnal visits.' It sounded lame.

'What is he? Some sort of fruit bat?' Spinner said, removing the backing of the small clock radio unit and peering inside. 'That's good,' he added. 'I can connect the voltage regulator there and splice in the power wires. Pass me those little pliers.'

Gemma did so, then glanced out the window again, remembering how she'd nearly died a couple of years ago because someone had wired up a light fitting the wrong way. Past the rustling leaves of the ginger plant outside the window, all was quiet on the street. The few Indian mynahs picked at a plastic bag on the nature strip.

'Now, pass me the drill. No, the cordless one, please.'

He drilled a tiny hole in the plastic, fitted the spycam into position with the microphone, taping it securely inside the housing. 'There. How does that look?' he said, putting the clock radio back down on the bedside table.

Gemma stood back to look at it. 'Very good,' she said. 'I wouldn't know it was there if I hadn't seen you do it. It just looks like the button for some other function.'

'Yeah,' said Spinner. 'The perv function.'

Another hour and Spinner had checked that everything was working, turning the power back on while Gemma, inside, adjusted the green digits on the clock radio according to her watch. She checked to make sure the radio functioned, catching the end of the news: '. . . *alleging that Scott Brissett sexually assaulted her twenty years ago. Brissett has denied the allegations, saying they are a tissue of lies and that he will be taking legal advice on the matter.*'

Gemma switched it off and gave Spinner the thumbs-up at the window, then went outside, taking the white paper bag of pastries. She locked the house and threw the key back through the grille in the window. Back in her car, she gathered up the file for one of the new jobs that she wanted to discuss with Spinner. Then she joined him in the white Rodeo, putting the pastries on the console between the seats while Spinner opened his laptop. Sitting here with Spinner reminded her of her early days as a surveillance operative, living, breathing, eating, even peeing on the job in the back of a van.

'Let's check it one more time,' he said and started running through the program.

'Who's Scott Brissett?' Gemma asked. 'The name's vaguely familiar.'

'Vaguely familiar?' Spinner looked at her in disbelief. 'Boss, where have you been?'

Gemma shrugged apologetically.

'Scott Brissett,' Spinner continued, 'was a Wallaby and a Waratah legend. He's on television all the time. He's just become the corporate face of the Boofhead Cup.'

Gemma knew from overhearing previous discussions between Spinner and Mike that the Boyleford Cup was an international rugby play-off, second only to the World Rugby Cup. 'You know that sporting heroes aren't my strongest point,' she said. She recalled a recent television news item and a weathered sportsman speaking with a group of French players. 'Is he that good-looking guy in the ad with a scar through one eyebrow? Late forties?'

Spinner nodded. 'That's him. Some GPS kid split his face open in his school years in competition footie.'

Spinner adjusted his receiver and laptop and looked up with satisfaction. 'It's all working well,' he said. 'And that reminds me. You and Stevie-boy will be right as rain. You two are an institution.'

Gemma shook her head. 'Not this time.'

'How did the fight start?'

'Does that matter?'

'Sure it matters. It's where the conflict lies.'

She thought about the origins of the fight. 'Steve started talking about us getting a place together.'

'And?' Spinner prompted as the silence lengthened.

Gemma shrugged, feeling uneasy. 'It started me

thinking. About all sorts of things. Lorraine Litchfield for one.'

'The crim's widow? The blonde bombshell whose weapon of choice was a Colt M1911?' Spinner's words were tinged with respect.

Hot anger and shame arose as Gemma remembered a scene involving Steve, the widow Litchfield and the wrong end of that same Colt.

'She put me through hell,' said Gemma, recalling the overstuffed room, the looming gun and the other woman's overpowering scent. 'I can't forget that he slept with her,' she said.

Spinner made as if to speak.

'Don't even think about it!' said Gemma. 'I don't want to hear any bullshit about what an undercover cop might have to do. Don't give me that line of duty crap!'

Gemma thought she would never forget the one and only time she'd met stunningly beautiful Lorraine Litchfield, nor her terror and complete humiliation at the hands of the jealous woman who'd waved the heavy weapon around and forced Steve at gunpoint to choose between the two of them. '*Baby*,' Steve had said, indicating the mirror in which the three of them were reflected '*There's no contest. Look at you. Look at her.*' Slowly, Lorraine had lowered the Colt. And Gemma had wanted to die.

She tried to counter this memory with another: the sweet scene some days later at the hospital, where Steve had made it very clear to Lorraine that he loved Gemma, and Lorraine's enraged response had been, '*You're dead, bitch!*'. But that memory wasn't enough and it was too painful to stay in the past. Gemma forced herself back into the present.

'Steve said he's tired of being punished by me about something that meant nothing to him. He brought up how I'd endangered him last year. I let him have it about Lorraine Litchfield. Things went from bad to worse.'

She shrugged, trying to minimise the pain of their fight. It was painful, too, to acknowledge that the memory of Lorraine Litchfield still exerted such a grip. Even though she'd completely disappeared from their lives like the thirteenth fairy at Sleeping Beauty's christening.

Gemma bit into a pastry, still starving. 'Steve got angry,' she continued. 'I got furious. He walked.'

'Hey!' Spinner interrupted. 'We're on!'

On the laptop's small screen, Daria Reynolds's double bed and the dressing table beyond it could be seen. Then the screen changed as feed from the cameras at the front and back of the house rotated with the internal view. Anyone approaching the house from any direction would be captured on video. Anyone in the bedroom would be picked up by the camera in the clock radio.

Satisfied with the reception from Daria Reynolds's room, Spinner packed up his receiver, laptop and handycam while Gemma flicked through the completed cases.

'I've never seen you like this,' Spinner said. 'Your colour's lousy.'

Suddenly his radio crackled. 'Tracker Two here. Copy, please.'

'Copy, Mike,' Spinner responded. 'What's up?'

The static behind Mike's voice made him a little hard to hear. 'I'm trying to contact Gemma. She's off the air.'

'She's here with me. Stand by.' Spinner handed Gemma the radio.

'Mike?'

'I've just had a call from a Mr Bertram Dowling. Wants to make an appointment with you.'

'My diary's on my desk. Try and fit him in tomorrow morning.'

Spinner rehoused the radio.

Gemma's mobile rang and she switched it over to voice mail. Just a few moments, please, she thought, without being online to the whole world.

'I'm sad, Spinner,' she said. 'My heart hasn't accepted the news about Steve.' She felt like crying and covered her face with her hands. She felt Spinner gently take them away.

'Look,' he said to her, still holding her hands, 'I'm sure you could salvage things. Don't ever lose hope.'

'Don't you dare go religious on me!' she warned.

'I wasn't going to.' He sounded hurt. 'Remember I'm your friend as well as an employee. I know you. I know Steve.' He relinquished her hands. 'Have you ever thought,' he asked 'that maybe your attitude's pushed Steve away?'

'Me push him away? How do you work that out?' Now she felt irritated.

'Okay, okay,' said Spinner. 'I'm sorry. I was out of place.'

'I've got to get going,' she said, still unreasonably angry with him.

She climbed out of the Rodeo and headed for her own car. Spinner gunned his engine and did a U-turn. As she sat in her car the reality of the break-up with Steve hit her like a dumper at Maroubra. The anger left her and suddenly she felt like howling.

An hour later, red-eyed but with fresh lipstick, Gemma drove through the grand entrance to Netherleigh Park Ladies' College, past the letters carved in gold on the tall sandstone pillars of the wrought-iron gates. The main building was set back from the road and Gemma drove slowly past what had once been rolling lawns and playing fields but was now built up with modern additions. Behind her, the constant roar of the traffic dimmed to a distant hum, absorbed by greenery and dark, ancient Moreton Bay figs. The winding driveway ended at a magnificent Georgian mansion, the original building, now overshadowed by additional wings.

Gemma parked her car in a visitors' bay and got out. Groups of girls in the distinctive light blue, green and mauve tartan of the school uniform chatted in groups and, as she mounted the steps towards the main door with its 'Office' sign, she could hear someone practising piano scales very fast, up and down, the major scale followed by the minor and melodic minor. If only I could play like that, Gemma thought. She'd done no practice this week and Mrs Snellgrove would give that disappointed little smile and shake her de Beauvoir-scarfed head. Attending to more business started working its magic, her thoughts quickly switching from Steve and the curiosity arising from the phone call of a dying woman.

At the office, a woman with a pure white elf lock peered at the ID Gemma showed through the sliding window.

'Gemma Lincoln. Here to see Miss de Berigny. She's expecting me.'

The elf lock beckoned to a passing senior girl. 'Tiffany,' she said. 'Please take Ms Lincoln to Miss de Berigny's office.'

Tiffany didn't look thrilled at this, but she nodded and Gemma followed the willowy teenager up the grand staircase to the second floor.

'What's on the next floor?' Gemma asked, noticing the staircase rose to yet another level.

'Dormitories,' said Tiffany. 'For the country boarders.'

Gemma followed Tiffany along the hall, past other offices and rooms. The piano scales sounded much closer now.

'Someone's a good pianist,' said Gemma, as much to break the silence as anything else.

Tiffany flashed her a look. 'Claudia's good at everything,' she said in a voice edged with anger. 'Some people have all the luck.'

They turned a corner and her guide indicated a

door on Gemma's right. Before Gemma could thank her, the girl had darted back round the corner and vanished. Gemma knocked on the door.

'Come in,' said a high-pitched voice. 'Just push it.'

Gemma did so and found herself in a large, bright north-facing room where two tall French windows overlooked the driveway and the dark green masses of fig trees. The principal advanced, her hand outstretched in welcome, a wide red smile showing perfect white teeth, dark hair glossy in a French roll.

'Miss Lincoln. Beatrice de Berigny. Thank you so much for agreeing to come.'

The two women shook hands, and Gemma sat in the proffered leather chair. After the gothic, incense-filled Reynolds place, this room with its well-appointed academic furnishings seemed another universe. Yet something was stirring Gemma's instincts in a negative way.

Miss de Berigny smoothed her black skirt over her knees as she sat on the other side of the colonial cedar desk, laptop in front of her. With slightly too much ivory foundation, dark red lipstick and pencilled eyes, Madame de Berigny's face had more than a suggestion of a mask, thought Gemma.

'I've been told you're the right person for this job,' the principal was saying, shrewd eyes glittering under the almost invisible brows. In the gaps between her words, distant chromatic minor scales reached impossible velocity. 'Detective Sergeant

Angie McDonald recommended you,' Miss de Berigny continued. 'You know her?'

'For many years,' Gemma said. 'We worked together when I was in the police service.'

'You are no doubt aware of the dreadful incident that befell our school last year. The disappearance,' she could barely say the word, 'of one of our most promising students.' She hesitated. 'It is still unsolved. Although the police claim everything possible is being done.'

Gemma recalled reading about Netherleigh Park in the newspapers and nodded. She remembered it didn't seem likely the girl had run away. Her bank accounts had remained untouched.

'As you can imagine, it's had a very bad effect on the school,' Beatrice de Berigny was saying. 'Far worse, in fact, than I would have thought likely. Morale is low. Enrolments are down for next year and we've lost several students already. Other parents are talking of taking their daughters away.'

Gemma remained silent, her eyes flicking over the desk's polished surface.

'It's so unfair,' the principal said. 'And illogical. The school had nothing to do with the girl's disappearance.'

That remains to be seen, thought Gemma, and said, 'Please tell me what happened.'

'One of our Year 10 students, Amy Bernhard, disappeared one morning. One minute she was here with her friends in the school grounds, next minute . . . ' The principal made an expressive gesture with her hands. 'Vanished into thin air.'

Gemma noticed that when Beatrice de Berigny smiled, the upper part of her face, especially her eyes, remained unmoved.

'Miss Lincoln, if the parents knew that the school had initiated an investigation of its own, it would surely encourage them to recover their faith in us. It would indicate that we are prepared to go to any lengths towards solving this case. And preventing anything like this from ever happening again.'

Gemma wondered what she could do or find that the police wouldn't have covered already. 'Do you have any sense of what might have happened to Amy?'

Miss de Berigny looked across to the large French windows. 'I have a feeling that it wasn't family problems. Although I do know there were issues with her stepfather.' She raised an eyebrow. 'Two failed marriages,' she said. 'It must be hard for a young girl growing up with all that going on.' Again, she hesitated, then lowered her voice. 'But what troubles me are the rumours. Nothing of substance. But they don't go away.'

'Rumours about what?' Gemma was intrigued. 'And from where?'

'That's just the problem—no one knows. A couple of teachers told me that some of the girls told them that Amy and her friends had a secret. Something they alluded to—you know the way girls tease each other. "We know something you don't know" sort of thing.'

'But you have no idea what this secret might have been?' Gemma asked.

Miss de Berigny shook her gleaming head. 'When I asked Tasmin and Claudia, they said they'd only been teasing. That there was no secret.'

'And you believed them?'

Miss de Berigny looked hard at Gemma. 'I had to. I had nothing to go on. Nothing to support my questions. As I said, it was all rumour. You can't imagine how rumours develop and flourish in this sort of environment. Three hundred girls and their hormones.'

Gemma wrote the words 'rumours of a secret' and circled them with a big question mark.

'It's a year now and there's been no trace of Amy Bernhard. Her mother still hopes,' said Miss de Berigny. Gemma felt a sudden pang. 'But the police are overworked,' the principal continued, 'and new crimes tend to push old ones out of the picture. Sergeant McDonald felt you'd be the best person for this sort of investigation.'

Miss de Berigny folded her hands gracefully in front of her on the desk. 'The school committee also thinks that obtaining your services is a good idea. Would you be willing to undertake such an investigation on the school's behalf?'

Gemma hardly had to consider. 'I can do that,' she said.

Miss de Berigny smiled, her eyes joining the rest of her face. 'May I ask how one goes about this? I know nothing of these sorts of things.'

'I'd go over the police case notes,' said Gemma,

her mind racing ahead and wondering how in hell she'd get hold of those, given that she was dealing with an ongoing investigation. 'I'd check out witness statements, re-interview people where it looks interesting—'

'What do you mean "re-interview where it looks interesting"?' said Beatrice de Berigny, her interruption taking Gemma by surprise. 'Well, with witness statements, for instance, the police are so stretched that sometimes alibis aren't properly followed up. I'd want to check out that sort of thing,' said Gemma.

'Oh? Is that likely—that alibis might not have been checked properly?'

The principal's friendly smile had vanished and her mouth was now set in an anxious line.

Suddenly, Gemma recognised she was encountering resistance. 'If there's a problem with any of this, Miss de Berigny, we need to talk about it now, so we both understand what's required from the other. Otherwise we won't have a deal.'

The principal hesitated, putting a gold pen back into its jade holder and fiddling instead with the cover of her black diary. 'It's just that some of my staff might not like being re-interviewed or having their alibis and statements questioned. Being forced to go through it all again might make them very uncomfortable.'

Abduction and possible murder *is* uncomfortable, Gemma almost said. Instead, she tried reassurance. 'I would handle things as delicately as possible. I'm sure they'd understand.'

'What I'm trying to say,' said the principal, 'is that perhaps you wouldn't have to go to extremes. You could just do a little bit of work on the case here and there, fit it around your existing work. You must be very busy. So that you'd officially be on the case, but there wouldn't be the need for it to take up a great deal of your time. After all, it is in police hands.'

Gemma raised an eyebrow, deciding to tackle this head-on. 'Are you saying you want me to give the *impression* that I'm investigating Amy Bernhard's disappearance rather than actually doing so?'

Beatrice de Berigny looked shocked. 'Oh, no,' she said. 'That's not what I meant at all. I just meant that seeing as it's all been done before, there wouldn't be the same sort of need as in the first investigation.' Under the ivory foundation, Gemma noticed the woman's skin reddening. Bullseye, Gemma congratulated herself. You got it in one, girl. 'I'm sorry if I gave that impression, Miss Lincoln.'

'Gemma,' said Gemma, pulling out her brochure and placing it on the polished cedar surface. Despite the ambiguous manner of her client, this could be a good job, with good contacts. Certainly the income would be welcome. 'This is a list of my hourly rates,' she said. 'You should be aware that something like this is going to take a lot of time and it's going to cost real money.'

'We'll find the money, Gemma,' said the principal, taking out a gold credit card. 'Would a one-thousand-dollar deposit be acceptable?'

Gemma processed the payment, noting the

principal's signature, and passed back the credit card. With this and the money from Daria Reynolds, she could pay the phone bill and do some shopping. Even though she had no appetite just now, a fridge full of good things and a nice chilled bottle or two could only do her good. Maybe she'd buy a new lipstick.

Miss de Berigny opened a drawer in her desk and pulled out a business card. 'This is Amy's mother's address,' she said, writing an address on the back. 'I've spoken to Lauren Bernhard and she's happy to talk to you. She will have details that might be helpful.'

Gemma thanked her and took the card, noticing the intricate flourishes of gold and green illumination decorating the 'B's of the principal's name.

'I'd also like the names of Amy's closest friends,' Gemma said. 'And it would be good if you could mention to their families that I'll be having a chat with them. With their permission, of course.'

Beatrice de Berigny cocked her head to one side. 'I shall do that straightaway. I'll ring their mothers and do everything I can to clear your way.'

She keyed in a few commands on the laptop and Gemma heard the printer on the small desk under the window start to work. Miss de Berigny got up from her desk and walked over to the window, waiting while the page printed.

Gemma studied her: the tailored clothing, the low-heeled court shoes, the erect posture of a woman who knows people notice her.

'I love this school,' said Miss de Berigny. 'I've

given all my energy to it for fifteen years. Other women have children. I have Netherleigh Park.' Gemma was startled by the intensity of her expression, the passion in her eyes. Then it was gone and Miss de Berigny raised her eyebrows, smiling. 'I will do anything necessary to protect it and its reputation.' She took the page from the printer and handed it over to Gemma.

Gemma ran her eyes down the names and addresses of Amy's friends. 'I'll start as soon as I can,' she said, straightening up and slipping the paper into her briefcase. 'I'll look after this investigation myself.'

'That's exactly what I had hoped for,' said the headmistress, returning to her desk. 'Your personal touch.'

Again the smile, a brief woman-to-woman moment, and all at once the interview was over and they were walking towards the door which suddenly flew open. Gemma jumped back as a man barged in.

'Oh, I am sorry.' His face gleamed with sweat. 'I didn't realise you had company. I should take more care where I'm going.'

Gemma turned to the principal, wondering who this man was. Perhaps the art or music teacher?

'Did you want to see me, Mr Romero? You were late again this morning,' said Miss de Berigny, her expression changed. Her voice, angry in tone, was also tight and anxious. Gemma thought she saw fear, too, in the pencilled eyes.

'Tasmin Summers,' said Mr Romero, waving a

hand. 'She was supposed to be here early this morning to go through her term History essay outline with me. She wasn't in class just now. I thought she might be with you.' He paused. 'I can see she isn't. Sorry.'

As he backed out and headed off down the corridor, Gemma's eyes caught the diamond and gold tie pin holding his mauve and green cravat and she wondered if all the teachers wore the school colours.

'I can find my way from here,' said Gemma to the principal, extending her hand. But Miss de Berigny didn't move to take it. She was a thousand miles away.

Gemma dropped her hand and waited.

'Oh, Miss Lincoln. Goodbye. And thank you again.'

Gemma headed down the two flights of stairs, her mind turning over the curious interlude. You don't get to be principal of Netherleigh Park without being a skilled strategist and politician, she mused as she climbed back into her car. She went over the interview notes. Beatrice de Berigny wants to tell the board that she's doing everything possible, but it's pretty clear she doesn't really want me to turn up anything new. Or was that just a normal, protective response—a principal protecting her staff? And Mr Romero had walked straight into the principal's office without knocking. Only someone very close would be allowed to do something like that, Gemma knew. Often only members of a family were permitted that sort of familiarity.

Beatrice de Berigny, despite her maidenly title, was married to a well-known businessman. Are Beatrice and Romero lovers, Gemma wondered. The idea was intriguing. Then she recalled the principal's icy response. Maybe not, thought Gemma as she drove out of the school grounds. Then why did her voice sound so strained? And why did she look so scared?

Gemma was pleased to be back home again. Her apartment was one of four asymmetrical areas developed in the 1960s by an entrepreneur who'd divided up a grand old nineteenth-century mansion originally built by W.C. Wentworth. Her dream was to make enough money one day to be able to buy the apartment directly above hers and have a terrace by the sea. She surveyed the grounds, glancing upstairs at her space-in-waiting. The For Lease sign in the window of the first-floor apartment remained. Coastal views north and south could be seen from up there. It even had a view to the boatshed she'd rented last year as a studio for sculpting. Now, in the place of her boatshed, stood a smart café, with decks on three sides, opened seven days a week in summer and on the weekends during winter months. In a few more years, she thought, the eastern suburbs will be nothing but wall-to-wall cafés, hair salons and security firms' offices.

On her way to the front door, she patted one of the lions she'd sculpted that guarded her entrance.

Glossy, with a mottled iron glaze that gave them more of a leopard look, they strained forward, jaws wide open in their eternal silent roar, looking very fine against the tubs of glaring white petunias and native shrubs on the western wall. She let herself into her place, thinking how this time yesterday had been the last few hours of two perfect weeks at Nelson Bay, swimming and lovemaking, walking and talking, delicious fish meals, too much wine, and long warm evenings along the beaches, where curving dolphins split the turquoise mirror of the inland bay and delighted children splashed to get closer to them.

She tried calling Kit again, only to find that according to her sister's new voice message, she was out of town for a day or two. Gemma hung up the phone, frustrated that Kit hadn't yet got a mobile. She wondered again what Rowena Wylde might know about their family.

She spent the rest of the afternoon tidying up outstanding jobs and, despite Spinner's lack of interest, ordered one of the micro spycams. She carefully entered her notes from her visit to Netherleigh Park Ladies' College into her notebook. She remembered how Miss de Berigny had said she'd do anything to protect the school. In her report, Gemma highlighted the word in bold type. *Anything*.

THREE

Next morning, as soon as she'd showered and dressed, Gemma made herself a cup of tea and sliced an apple. She was eating it on the timber deck under the umbrella when she heard Mike's car pull up on the road at the front of the building. Very handy with technical know-how, Mike Moody worked fifteen to twenty hours a week for Gemma, and for other security businesses the rest of the time. She glanced at his figure on the CCTV monitor in the corner of her living room as she went to let him in. Though he and Spinner had keys, they only used them if Gemma wasn't at home.

'Hi. How's it going?' Gemma asked, opening the grille.

Mike nodded in answer and she followed him into the operatives' office, across the hallway from her own. 'How about you?' he asked. The pink shirt he was wearing emphasised his well-built upper body and the light tan on his powerful arms.

Gemma shrugged. 'Been better.' She was

pleased to see him. Mike's was a comforting presence, especially with the emptiness in her heart.

Gemma went into her own office, delicately furnished in soothing light greys and white with a huge recently re-covered club-style armchair under the window. Taped to the wall above her colour monitor was a double-page article from the newspaper's weekend magazine: 'Sex, Signs and Subterfuge' by Amanda Quirk, a journalist acquaintance. Gemma examined the picture of herself that accompanied the article mostly grey and half in shadow, apart from her dark red lipstick, suggesting she was mysterious and even a little forbidding. Published earlier in the year, the piece focused on Gemma's Mandate option, and had resulted in many enquiries and a steady building of work. After last year's catastrophic penetration of her sensitive files, the phones of her business had almost stopped ringing. But now, slowly at first, but lately with more regularity, they'd started again. Business was picking up.

She took the card Beatrice de Berigny had given her out of her briefcase and dialled Lauren Bernhard, mother of Amy, missing now for a year. She heard the desperate eagerness in the woman's voice when she answered. Does she hope it might be Amy every time the phone rings, Gemma thought. She explained who she was and asked if she could make an appointment time.

'You can come round any time,' said Lauren. 'I'm always here. Waiting.'

Waiting, Gemma thought. For a daughter to come home. Or a grave to be found.

She collected the new files together, intending to offer some of them to Mike. As well as the jobs she'd delegated to Spinner, she had a brand new contract with Australian Access Insurances, thanks to the efforts of a friend. She was hopeful of more. She was just heading towards his room when Mike suddenly appeared in the doorway. 'Do you know the rent of that upstairs flat?' he asked. 'Maybe I should enquire about it for me. It'd cut down on travel time. I'm already spread all over Sydney.'

Gemma hesitated. The thought of Mike in the upstairs flat made her feel uneasy, for some reason that she didn't quite understand. Some instinct was saying, 'Not a good idea. It's good to have a bit of distance between job and home. Are you sure you want to be so close?'

Mike pointed down the hallway towards her apartment. 'You've only got an interconnecting door.'

'Exactly,' said Gemma, 'and work dominates my life way too much.'

Mike leaned against the door frame, folding his arms. 'Maybe you have a problem with me being up there? Too close to your space?'

Gemma ran her fingers through her hair, pushing it back behind her ears. It really needed cutting. 'I'll give it some thought.' It was her stock reply when unsure.

'Keep me informed. If you really don't like it, I

won't do it.' He looked more closely at her. 'You okay?'

Gemma realised she was feeling wobbly and close to tears, but she nodded. 'Yeah. Just got a lot on.'

'Don't forget that appointment in your desk diary with Mr Dowling. I put him down for 10 a.m.'

Mike glanced past her to the cut-out magazine article taped to the wall. 'That photograph doesn't do you justice.'

Gemma felt her cheeks flush. 'Here,' she said, proffering several new files. 'See what's there that you can work in with your other jobs.'

He took them and she checked her diary. 'I'd better do a bit of housework if I've got a client coming,' she said, picking up her briefcase. Ducking past him, she was aware of his gaze following her down the hall.

She closed the door that sheltered her private life from the offices. There was definitely a charge between Mike and her. No use denying it. And with Steve gone, she'd have to be careful about entanglement. She picked up the small oval portrait of her mother on the table near the doorway and looked at the hint of a smile on the serious face, the eyes so like Kit's. You were years younger than I am now when you died, she thought, searching her mother's face for similarities to her own. And when this was taken, how could you know that you had only a short time to live? She put the portrait down.

Why had Daria Reynolds asked that strange question about her mother's death? Again, the shadow fell across Gemma and she re-experienced the unease she'd felt earlier. Then it had been because she'd felt someone on her tail. Now it felt more like an old sadness. To change her mood, she logged on and checked Vincent Reynolds with CrimeNet and her other sources. There were no results, but this didn't necessarily mean he was a cleanskin. Unable to settle, she sat at the rented piano and propped up the new piece that Mrs Snellgrove had given her. Much more pianissimo, her teacher had written. Gemma attempted to sight read. The result was so dispiriting that she put the music back on top of the piano and got up again. Keep busy, she scolded herself.

Back in her office, Gemma checked her email then turned her attention to her notes on Amy Bernhard. She recalled Beatrice de Berigny telling her that her friend Angie had recommended Gemma to follow up the police investigation into the girl's disappearance. Perhaps Angie still had some records of interviews on her laptop— although access to this information might be problematic.

While she considered how to proceed, she wrote the covering letters for several completed insurance jobs and made out the accounts. This made her feel a little better; she needed the several thousand dollars these would bring in to maintain cash flow and keep paying Spinner and Mike. Gemma was just clearing her desk when a glance out the office window revealed an elderly man approaching the entrance. She opened the security grille and shook his proffered hand. 'Mr Dowling.' She led him into her office where he removed his cap and balanced his walking stick against the desk.

'What can I do for you?' she said, after he'd made himself comfortable.

'I'm not sure where to start,' he said. 'It sounded like just the thing. But I don't know what to do, where to turn.'

'What do you need from me, Mr Dowling?' she asked, guessing from his faint smell of old leather and moth balls that he was well into his eighties.

In reply, the old man took a card out of his top pocket and passed it to her. 'This is the mob I want you to take a look at. It sounded like a good service.'

Gemma read the logo headed up by an embossed diamond in silver ink. *Forever Diamonds*, it said. *Now your love can be truly eternal.* There was an address in Trafalgar Street, Newtown, and Gemma wrote it down in the new file.

'I took Shirley over to them in her little box, like they told me to, and left her there.'

Gemma, puzzled by this information and about to ask if Shirley was a cat or dog, was saved from what would have been a terrible gaffe by Mr Dowling's next remark.

'Shirley is—was my wife. The best wife a man could ever have.' Tears filled his eyes. 'They have this process,' he continued, 'where they transform the ashes of your loved one into a diamond.'

Gemma recalled she'd read something about this process quite recently, claimed by both the USA and the USSR to be not only feasible, but capable of producing near gem-quality stones.

'It's expensive,' said Mr Dowling. 'Nearly nine thousand dollars all up by the time I'd had the diamond made into a little ring. I used the gold of her wedding ring.' He fumbled for a handkerchief and blew his nose. 'I picked it up last week. It looks good.'

He put his hand into the inside pocket of his sports jacket and pulled out a small jewellery box. 'Here.' He put it on the desk beside Gemma. 'You can take a look for yourself.'

Gemma opened the lid. A small bluish-grey stone winked from a band of gold. 'May I?' she asked. After he nodded, she took the ring out and looked at it.

'And you're concerned that it's not genuine?' she said, putting the ring back in its housing. 'You'd need to take it to a good jeweller for that sort of information.'

'It's not that,' said Mr Dowling. 'It's a genuine diamond all right. I took it to my old watchmaker up at the Junction.'

'Mr Dowling, I don't understand. What do you want me to do?'

Mr Dowling took the box back from her and turned the ring in his fingers. 'You see,' he said, 'I keep looking at it and putting it on. But then I take it off again. I just can't wear it. I did for a day or so, but then I got this terrible feeling.'

He put the ring into its slot in the black velvet and snapped the lid shut. He leaned closer. 'Miss Lincoln. It's just not Shirley, I know it isn't.' The sadness in his eyes was replaced with anger. 'I don't know who it is in this ring, but it's not my wife.' He put the box back in his pocket. 'That's why I want you to check out these people. There's been a mix-up, I'm sure of it, and now I've got nothing of her. I want you to find out what became of Shirley. I want her back. Someone else is wearing my wife. While I've got goodness knows who.'

His voice caught on the last few words and he looked as if he were about to cry. It wouldn't be the first time that had happened in this office, Gemma thought. Right now, she felt like crying herself.

'Mr Dowling,' Gemma warned him, 'without getting someone in there undercover, it could be impossible to find out how they really manage their business.'

'I hoped you could just ask the right questions,' he said, looking dejected.

'Sometimes, that's sufficient. I'll see what I can do myself,' she said, 'and, should it become necessary to put someone in there, I'll let you know before incurring any extra expenses.' She touched his arm. 'Now, how about a cup of tea?'

Gemma spent the rest of the morning compiling new files and writing up her notes on Mr Dowling. She reviewed the information he'd given her about Forever Diamonds and checked them on the net. She'd never had a case quite like this one before.

Then, she changed into her shorts and T-shirt

and went for a run along the cliffs, hoping that a good sweat would relieve some of her stored-up grief and frustration. She stretched out, passing the eroding angels and broken columns of the seaside cemetery which contained her murdered mother's grave. Fat skinks plopped off stone ledges and disappeared into the grass at her passing. No breeze came from the flat surface of the Pacific and she thought she must be mad to be running in the building heat.

Back home, she showered and changed and went to her office. She checked her mobile—there was a text message from Angie: *Call me.*

'I can't talk for long,' said Angie, sounding strung out. 'It's jumping round here. Another girl's gone missing. From the same school.'

'Netherleigh Park? I was only there yesterday. Thanks for the referral, by the way. The principal wants me to work on Amy Bernhard's disappearance.' Gemma paused.

'So you've met Madame Beatrice de B? She's really something, isn't she?' Angie lowered her voice. 'It's a madhouse here. Half are off on sick leave, half are at court and the other half are just plain mad.'

'That's three halves, Ange.'

'Smartypants! I'm supposed to be compiling a list of possible VMOs—violent major offenders—for the boss so he can send them on to ViCLAS at the Crime Commission. Plus I'm on call-out for hostage negotiation.'

'Well, Ange, you always say you like it hot.'

'Not this hot. G-for-Gross is supposed to be

assisting me as well, but ever since he got promoted to Inspector he's been impossible.'

'Promoted—Bruno Gross? How did that happen?' It was painful for Gemma to think of Bruno, with whom she'd had a brief, ill-judged affair nearly ten years earlier.

'God knows. He must have blackmailed someone. Or bribed them. His idea of policing these days is to lock the door of the station, take the phone off the hook and put the telly on.'

'What's ViCLAS?'

'Violent crime linkage analysis system. Supposed to identify and track serial offenders. They want to marry my VMOs with theirs. G-for weaselled out of it and dumped it on me. So here I am with a tower of files. Gotta go, hon.'

'The name of the latest missing girl—is it Tasmin Summers?'

'How'd you know that?'

'Someone was looking for her yesterday, when I was at Netherleigh Park,' explained Gemma, looking at her watch.

'You'd better come in and we'll have a chat,' Angie suggested.

As Gemma looked in the fridge, deciding on what to eat, she wondered where Taxi was. He should have appeared by now, nagging for food. Finally she made a couple of cheese crackers, brewed a pot of tea and, deciding to do things in style to cheer herself up, fetched a large crystal jug and a tray from the large sideboard near the dining table. The tray, its decanters and the matching crystal jug were almost the only family possessions she still had. The decanters, wide and heavy-bottomed, were specially designed for stability on the tray in heavy seas and even the tray had a little fence around it to keep articles from sliding off. They had come from long-widowed Aunt Merle's master mariner grandfather. Gemma filled the crystal jug with apple juice and carried the tray back out to the timber deck, remembering Aunt Merle who had raised Gemma and Kit after the loss of their parents.

Despite the still summer day and the hazy blue of sky and ocean, Gemma felt storm-tossed. She bit into a cracker and cheese and went looking for Taxi, checking all his secret hideouts. Sure enough, she spied a lump under the cream and blue damask cover of her light summer doona. 'There you are, you straight-tailed, orange-flavoured cat!' She dragged him out and hugged him, wondering if a cat was all she'd be hugging for quite some time. She carried him out to the deck and put him down, watched him arch his back then roll over and stretch front and back legs into star paws.

Gemma made herself get back to work. She printed out her notes and information on the manufacture of synthetic diamonds and was reading them when she heard something. She glanced up at the CCTV monitor to see Spinner arriving. She let him in and went back to her chair. 'I thought you weren't going to come in,' she said, swivelling round.

'I've got that video to process,' he said, patting the camera bag. 'And I want to print out a couple of reports. Then they're done.'

It was Gemma's policy to present the evidence and her account at the same time at her office. That way, there was a definite incentive for the client to pay up. No pay, no info. Normally, she'd be feeling pleased about these small successes. Today, however, her bruised heart could not rejoice.

'And I remembered this.' Spinner passed her a clipping. 'It was in last weekend's colour magazine.'

Gemma opened it out and read. 'Boyleford Brissett: the legend'. She glanced through it, then put it to one side and went back to finalising her notes and copying them onto the laptop. One day, she told herself, she'd practise doing everything straight onto it. But often a notebook was simpler and easier. She was aware of Spinner moving around in the office across the hall and the printer clicking and whirring. Later, he came to her door.

'Boss, I'm getting some takeaway for tea. Want me to get you something while I'm out?'

Gemma looked at her watch. The afternoon had flown in the end: it was after seven. She hadn't shopped for days. She knew exactly what was left in the fridge—a half bag of carrots, the carcass of a chicken that needed burial and a packet of drying prunes. Even the cheese and biscuits were running out.

•

When Spinner returned with some takeaway Thai, Gemma smiled and said, 'Come and eat with me if you like.'

He followed her into the flat and she put a couple of place mats on the table with plates and cutlery. They ate in companionable silence, enjoying the flavours of the food.

'Bloody hell!' she said halfway through the meal, jumping up from the table. 'I'm supposed to be at my music lesson!' She had completely forgotten.

She flew round getting ready, cleaning her teeth, grabbing her music book. 'Lock up behind you?' Spinner nodded.

Mrs Snellgrove, teacher of the pianoforte and president of the Paddington Historical Society, opened the door with a gentle scolding for Gemma's tardiness. 'You're a naughty girl, Gemma,' she said, ushering her in, the free-swinging diamond at the bottom of her fan brooch glittering as it moved. 'That's twice in a row you've been late now.'

Gemma murmured an apology and walked through to Mrs Snellgrove's living room, crowded with historic photographs from a hundred years ago, flat irons, kerosene lamps with delicate hand-painted shades and a collection of tin mechanical toys that had belonged to Mr Snellgrove when he was a boy.

Mrs Snellgrove opened the piano lid, diamond rings sparkling as she patted the piano stool, her late husband's watch swinging on her frail wrist. Gemma pulled out her music and set it up on the piano while her teacher made herself comfortable in her cane chair.

'That pendant,' said Mrs Snellgrove, 'it's very unusual. The empty centre, I mean.'

'It's supposed to have a stone there but I lost it when I was on holidays.'

Mrs Snellgrove patted her shoulder and looked at the piano. 'So I don't suppose you've had much time to practise "Jungle Drums" and "Gingerbread Cakewalk"?'

'Not really.' Gemma felt about eight years old as her music teacher sighed and shook her head.

'Well, then, let's just start them again, shall we? Now, right hand first. Nicely curved fingers. One, two, one, two.'

When the lesson was finished and Gemma gathered up her music, Mrs Snellgrove hovered. 'Gemma, my dear. I wonder if you could help me?' she asked.

'I'd be delighted.' Gemma had become very fond of Mrs Snellgrove and her eccentric, loving ways.

'My mother asked me, actually.'

Gemma recalled that Mrs Snellgrove's mother still 'did' for herself in her small apartment at Dover Heights.

'She's ninety-two, you know, and almost blind. But she's very active, knows her way round her flat, and we're all agreed that the best thing is to support her in her own little place as long as possible.' Mrs Snellgrove adjusted her pearls. 'She lost her old pussy cat recently and I think she's lonely and imagining things.'

'Like what?'

'She keeps insisting that there's some sort of animal in her apartment. Ethne and I go there once a week to visit and do a quick whip around, although Mother really is quite able. We've checked the place out thoroughly. There's simply nowhere for an animal to get inside. It's a second-floor apartment. But Mother is adamant about this animal! She says she can feel it touching her legs.'

'What do you think?'

Mrs Snellgrove's face became very still. 'I think it's the beginning of the end,' she said. 'The doctor wants her to go into a nursing home. She says that once old folk start seeing and hearing things, we just have to accept that the time has come.' Mrs Snellgrove's voice was sad. 'Anyway,' she added, brightening up, 'Mother read about you in the papers and she knows you're one of my students. She was very taken with the idea of one of those cameras you use. She told us that if you put a camera in her flat, she reckons it will prove there is an animal in there.'

'We could do that for her,' Gemma said, 'and keep an eye on her.'

The look of relief on Mrs Snellgrove's face as she nodded made Gemma smile. 'Mother said that if you could keep an eye on men who were playing up, you could certainly find out what animal it is that's bothering her.'

'Let me know when you're next visiting your mother,' said Gemma, 'and I'll come along and set up the camera myself.'

Gemma spent most of the weekend keeping busy, trying not to think about Steve. On Saturday, she checked out Netherleigh Park's website, searching the net for references to the disappearance of Amy Bernhard and making notes.

Sunday morning she went for a run around the cemetery, pausing at her mother's grave and picking a bunch of wild yellow daisies that flowered around the graves in early summer. She lay them next to the headstone and stood there for a few moments before resuming her pace.

Later in the afternoon, she took herself to the movies, recalling the last time she'd been at the Ritz only a few weeks ago, with Steve sitting beside her, his arm around her shoulder, his hand stroking her neck.

She did some piano practice and watched television before going to bed, wanting to be up fresh and early for the start of the new week.

After breakfast—toast and the last scraping of the honey jar—the next morning, Gemma introduced herself on the phone to the mother of Claudia Page, making a time to see Claudia, best friend of Amy Bernhard and Tasmin Summers, after school that afternoon.

Then, as Angie had requested, Gemma drove to the Strawberry Hills police station, waiting outside while Security buzzed upstairs. Within minutes Angie appeared, carrying her smart maroon briefcase. Her auburn hair was newly cut in a gamine style that suited her wide-boned face and she was even wearing tiny pink pearl earrings with her white blouse and trim grey suit.

The two women headed for a coffee shop. 'I can't stay long,' said Angie. 'There's a pile of files almost up to the ceiling that I'm supposed to be going through in my big joke spare time. To send to the Crime Commission for scanning the old ones into the system.' She suddenly frowned, looking hard at Gemma. 'You look awful. What is it?'

'Steve,' Gemma said. 'We've broken up.'

They walked into the Baccarole, ordered at the counter, then sat in the furthest corner where they could see who might come in. Gemma pulled out her notebook.

'Are you sure?' asked Angie.

'Sure as anything.' Though she felt like crying, Gemma slapped the notebook down on the table. 'I don't want to talk about it right now.'

'But Gemster, you have to. You can't just break up like this. What happened?'

Gemma swallowed hard. She knew how relentless Angie could be when pursuing a line of questioning. 'We went away for two weeks to the Bay. It was so nice. On the way back, Steve started talking about maybe buying something together— moving in together. So I had to think about whether or not I could trust him. The subject of Lorraine Litchfield came up and one thing led to another.' She fiddled with the notebook. 'I ended up screaming at him to get out. He reckons I've got commitment problems. Me—when he's the one who's out screwing other women!'

Angie started to say something then stopped.

'No, go on,' said Gemma. 'Say it.'

'I was going to say I think you're being too hard on Steve. No, don't blow up at me. He's not out screwing other women, Gemster.'

'I said I didn't want to talk about it,' Gemma repeated.

'Sometimes the boundaries get stretched,' said Angie, 'with undercover work.'

Gemma picked up the notebook and opened it, pen ready. 'Tell me about this other girl who's gone missing from Netherleigh Park,' she said, determined to change the subject. Then she noticed something as Angie searched through her own notebook.

'You're actually wearing make-up to work, Ange!' Gemma exclaimed. 'Eye shadow. And is that mascara I see?'

Angie blushed as she changed the subject. 'How did you know Tasmin Summers's name?'

'Answer the question, Angie!' Gemma started laughing. 'Ange! You're blushing! You're wearing make-up and you're blushing! Hey, you'd better tell your girlfriend what's going on. And I want to know everything.'

Angie looked up at the waitress arriving with their coffee and Angie's raisin toast. 'I'm starving,' she said, grabbing a piece and pushing the plate towards Gemma.

'What's his name, Angie?' Gemma insisted.

'His name's Trevor.' She dropped her voice to a tremulous whisper.

Gemma blinked. 'Please!' she said. 'Not Trevor.'

Angie's eyes flashed. 'What's the matter with Trevor? You're such a snob, Gemster. It's a loyal, devoted, down-to-earth man's name.'

'Okay, okay. Although imagining a gorgeous Trevor is straining my brain. So who is he?'

'Trevor Dawson. One of the tactical guys.'

'Oh, that Trevor.' She also remembered something else. 'You said never again, Angie. No more muscleheads, you said. You pleaded for me to remind you about it if you ever so much as looked in that direction again!'

Angie wasn't listening. 'He was my protection last week, when I was negotiating. Would you believe—a crazy Cypriot, a knife-wielding eighty-one-year-old grandmother and a 280-kilogram bloke who wouldn't take his medication.'

'All in the one house?'

'All in the one week. One after the other, smartarse.' Angie couldn't stop smiling. 'It kind of went from there.'

'I'm already worried about where it went! "Bloody mongrel bastard dickhead" were some of the kinder names you called the last guy.'

'Trevor's not like that. He's really sweet. He's sensitive. He writes poetry.' Angie grabbed another slice of raisin toast. 'Gemster, you've gotta love him.'

Gemma raised an eyebrow. 'Ange, I don't think loving a poetry-writing special weapons operative called Trevor is in my repertoire.'

'You just have to start learning,' said Angie and sipped her coffee, all misty-eyed. 'Gems,' she said, 'I'm hopelessly smitten.'

'Ange. It's only been one week. Can't you get unsmitten?'

Angie pulled out a folded piece of paper and passed it to Gemma. 'Take a look at this. This is the first poem he wrote to me.'

'Shall I compare thee to a summer's day? Thou art more lovely and more gorgeous. Rough winds shake the darling buds, but you are a bud, darling, that I want to shake, rattle and roll.'

Gemma looked up from her reading to see Angie's starry eyes. 'Isn't that just so sweet?'

'I'm sure I've heard something like it somewhere before.'

'Oh, you!' Angie snatched it back. 'Your problem is you're too cynical.'

Gemma was astounded. 'Me, too cynical? Compared with you, I'm bloody Mother Teresa!'

Angie's mobile rang. She picked it up, listened for a moment and hung up. 'I've gotta go. That was Eastern Beaches. Someone's just found some skeletal remains in a bushland reserve near Botany. They've secured the place and they're waiting for Merv. I'll go with him.'

'Who's he?' Gemma couldn't resist. 'Trevor's evil twin?'

'Major incident response vehicle.'

'Let me come. Sneak me in. This could be related to the Netherleigh Park case.'

'I can't. You know that.'

'I could be a SOCO from the bush. Getting city experience.'

For a second, Gemma could see her friend was considering it.

'You'd never pass the ID check,' Angie said. 'Someone would pick up your name somewhere along the line, there'd be questions asked and I'd be shot. *I'd* end up in the bush. It's not like the old days, girl. You know that.'

Angie put her briefcase on the table and waved away the money Gemma proffered. 'I'll get this,' she said. 'You mind the bag.'

Gemma couldn't resist peeking. Inside was a folder with the name of the missing girl, Amy Bernhard, printed down one side. She slid it out and teased out some of the contents. She started to read the printed-out statements.

My name is Claudia Zahra Page. I am a Year 10 student at Netherleigh Park in the same class as my friend Amy Bernhard. I last saw Amy on the morning of the second of December when I was on the bus going to school. Tasmin and I were down the back and I saw Amy at the front of the bus . . .

Claudia had been the name of the student playing those high-velocity scales during her visit to Beatrice de Berigny, Gemma remembered. She wondered if it was the same Claudia she'd organised to interview later today.

'Hey,' Angie said, coming back to the table. 'You shouldn't be reading that.'

'But, Ange, I can help. Now that there's a second girl missing, you're going to be stretched as buggery.'

'Too true, but I'm also brief officer at the moment. I'd be fried if any of this goes astray. Give it here.'

Gemma relinquished her hold on the statement from the Amy Bernhard folder and watched while Angie stashed it back in her briefcase. They stood up to go and Gemma lowered her voice. 'Angie, listen to me. I'm offering you the sort of corruption that can be really helpful. You need me. This overzealous squeaky-clean stuff is interfering with ordinary, decent law enforcement.'

'I know, I know, but you want to complain, you join the queue.' Angie's phone rang again. 'Bloody phone!' she said and grabbed it. 'Okay, okay!' she muttered into it then looked around for somewhere to put her briefcase. 'Hold this for me?'

Gemma obliged as Angie wrote down information and rang off. 'You can mind my bag while I'm gone,' she said, looking over the top of her sunglasses. 'I'll come by your place and pick it up when I get back.'

Gemma gave her a grateful nod.

'Just be discreet, honey. Not that the living dead I work with would notice.' As they stepped back onto the street, Angie added, 'If you get caught, I'll deny everything and say you nicked it. Okay?'

Before driving home, Gemma called in at a print shop and spent a small fortune copying the contents of Angie's briefcase. She worked quickly, and noticed that most of the papers were printed-out witness statements.

She made good headway through the traffic back to the flat, but couldn't shake the shadow that seemed to have penetrated her spirit. Angie's excitement over her new man served to highlight Steve's loss. The huge ache in her heart felt even worse than yesterday. Even the bright sunlight seemed only to make the dark shadows under trees and buildings more intense.

Maybe it would be nice to have Mike move in upstairs, she thought. But no, there was something in the way he looked at her, and it just wasn't a good idea to get involved with a colleague, not to mention an employee.

Her mobile rang and she prayed it was Kit, though it turned out to be one of the insurance companies. Could she take on another job? They'd fax the case notes. It involved a man who claimed he'd lost his sex life forever. Gemma pulled up outside her house wishing she could afford another roadie. Last year she'd had three employees and she'd been pretty well able to stay at home base. There'd been enough to do to keep her safe, dry and warm in her own office which she enjoyed. But one of the three had betrayed her, she remembered. Not so safe, after all.

Inside, Gemma tried to ring Kit but just got the same message. Sighing, she poured herself an orange drink and took it out to the deck. It was a perfect blue and gold Sydney coastal day, with a white-tipped sea and gulls celebrating in spirals over a distant fishing boat. Her restless mood made a run attractive so she went off, heading towards Phoenix Bay. On her return, she was drying herself after a shower when she heard a sound near the front door. Swearing because she was still half-naked, she was relieved to see it was only Taxi playing one of his favourite games: lying on the doormat outside and pushing his paw under the door, hoping to find something exciting on the other side.

Later, dressed, with the towel wrapped around her wet hair, she glanced up to see Mike walking towards the front door on the CCTV monitor.

'You smell good,' he said, going into his office and putting his bag down.

'Thanks,' said Gemma, wondering why she'd never really noticed just how good-looking Mike was. 'Want some coffee?' she called out.

'That would be great.'

She carried a mug in to him and he turned on his swivel chair and smiled up at her. 'Thanks heaps.'

For a moment, she felt awkward and self-conscious. 'No bother,' she replied, laughed and hurried away. She towelled her hair on the timber deck in the sun while Taxi pestered her about her sandwich. The phone rang as she got into a game with Taxi; it was Mrs Snellgrove, who was about to visit her mother.

Gemma and Mike picked up Mrs Snellgrove and drove to her aged mother's apartment. Despite her impressive age, Mrs Annie Dunlop proved to be as able as her daughter had described, insisting on making afternoon tea for everyone and offering slices of home-made date and walnut loaf. She made her way round her small apartment with great agility and, like her daughter, wore numerous rings and brooches.

After chatting for a while, they fitted the camera in a corner so that it could take in the whole room and the doorway through to Mrs Dunlop's bedroom.

'It's movement-activated,' Gemma explained. 'It has a little memory and can store pictures.'

'I don't want that animal here in my flat. I want my little cat back. Little Pusskin. I was used to little Pusskin,' Annie insisted.

'We'll check up in a week or so,' said Gemma, noticing the old lady feeling around for the plate of slices on the table and only then remembering that she was almost blind. She clearly knew this flat like the back of her hand.

When they left, Mrs Snellgrove gave Gemma a hug. 'Thank you so much. What do I owe you?'

'We'll talk about that later,' said Gemma. 'When we find out what's going on.'

She and Mike drove back to her place and she went down the hall, leaving Mike in the operatives' office while she attended to household chores. A little while later, over the spin cycle, she heard Mike call out.

She came out of the bathroom to see him hesitating on the hall side of the door dividing her apartment from the front office area.

'I thought you said you were going on another job,' she said. 'An hour ago. Don't stand there. Come in.'

He came into her living room and passed her the empty plate and mug. She took the things into the kitchen and dumped them in the sink.

'Gemma?'

She swung round.

'I'd better be on my way.'

She watched after him as he disappeared out the front door, wondering why she felt so disappointed. What had she expected him to say?

Turning, she checked her office to find a fax in the tray. She glanced over it. It was about the new job from the insurance company. Mr Gordon Pepper was seeking huge amounts in compensation after a work injury had left him completely impotent. He claimed he couldn't achieve an erection let alone climax; that his sex life was finished. Poor sod, Gemma thought. She felt for him. She took the fax across the hall and put it on the desk Spinner used.

Trying Kit again, she went straight through to voice mail once more. Maybe she'd gone down the coast for a couple of days. Come home soon, Kit, she prayed.

Household jobs done, invoices ready to send, Mr Dowling's file in her bag with the pile of copied witness statements to read whenever she had a spare moment, Gemma drove to Forever Diamonds. On the way, her mind kept wondering about Rowena Wylde's information concerning her family—Gemma definitely needed to speak to Kit before her appointment with Rowena Wylde the following day.

She stopped off at the post office, then drove to Trafalgar Street, Newtown, and parked opposite a white goods warehouse. She walked over, pretending interest in a marked-down freezer, chatting with the young salesman.

Forever Diamonds, she discovered, had started up eighteen months ago and, despite the locals' initial scepticism of such a business having any takers at all, seemed to be doing good trade. She said she'd think about the freezer, thanked the young man and left, hovering outside the Forever Diamonds shopfront. Taped to the glass of the door, on a piece of stationery with silver-embossed edges and the stylised diamond logo she'd already seen on the card Mr Dowling had shown her, was an advertisment: *Part-time Receptionist required. Experienced, reliable people-person. Sensitivity a must. Hours to suit. Must show good refs.* For a split second, Gemma considered the position herself.

She pressed the buzzer and the door clicked open, revealing a front office decorated with red velvet curtains and matching plush chairs. It reminded her of an undertaker's premises or the foyer of an old-fashioned theatre. A perfectly groomed young man in a dark suit behind a long polished counter looked up at her arrival. He stepped out and proffered his hand.

'Raymond Gardiner,' he said. 'I'll be with you in a moment. Please make yourself comfortable.

Perhaps you'd like to read a little about the wonderful work we do here?' He handed her a glossy brochure and indicated a red plush seat.

Gemma took the brochure and sat, while Mr Gardiner disappeared. She started reading.

Forever Diamonds™ understands that burials and cremations are usually very sad occasions. Our service provides a beautiful, irreplaceable reminder of the past, a keepsake to remember the love shared between yourself and your dearly departed one. As almost a quarter of the human body (by weight) is carbon, Forever Diamonds will take a portion of that carbon (perhaps the heart, in case of burial, or the ashes released after the crematorium process) and reduce these to their essential carbon. Then, using our unique and internationally acclaimed techniques, a genuine diamond is produced. This is then cut by our qualified tradesmen in traditional ways that best enhance the shape and quality of the resulting diamond. You can choose from a range of tasteful designs to have your beloved's diamond mounted as a ring, necklace or tie-pin. Now, love really is forever.

Gemma's reading was interrupted by the reappearance of Mr Gardiner. 'Please come through. I'm trying to do everything today.'

'Including compressing remains into diamonds?' Gemma smiled.

'Oh, no,' he said, then realised she was joking. 'Actually, we prefer to call them "cremains". It sounds more dignified somehow.' He ushered her through, without breaking his commentary. 'I was hoping you were here to enquire about the job?'

'I'm afraid not,' said Gemma as she followed him into his tiny office, a cubbyhole to the right of the counter. On its wall was a series of glossy framed photographs showing the sizes of diamonds available, from a quarter right up to a full carat, depending on the amount paid and the amount of carbon used. Tasteful italic printing explained the process she'd read about in the brochure.

She noticed a small diamond flashing on Mr Gardiner's little finger and pointed. 'A relative?'

He nodded. 'My dear mother, actually.' He stared at the jewel for a few moments. 'I was very pleased with the way she transformed. Although I had to have her remounted on a larger setting after nearly losing her down the plug hole.'

Mr Gardiner gave Gemma his full attention. 'So, you are wanting someone transformed? Please sit down.'

Trying desperately to keep a straight face, Gemma pulled out her business card and handed it to him before sitting opposite in the cramped space. 'I'm acting on behalf of a gentleman, Mr Bertram Dowling,' she said. 'Who had the remains—I mean, the cremains—of his wife Shirley . . .' she hesitated, 'transformed by your business.'

Raymond Gardiner hit a few keys on a laptop on a tiny cedar table beside his chair, then nodded. 'That's correct,' he said. 'Mrs Dowling. It was only a month or so ago. His wife came up really nicely we all thought.' He frowned. 'Is there a problem?'

'Mr Dowling feels very strongly that it isn't his wife. In the diamond.'

'What?' Raymond Gardiner's surprise was evident. His narrow eyebrows arched. 'Not his wife? Of course it's his wife!'

Gemma waited while he studied the computer screen. 'There she is. Lovely. Point 25 carats. Good colour too—lovely grey-white. We call that shade Twilight Mist.'

'Is it possible there could have been a mix-up somewhere in the process? Could someone else's cremains have been processed and wrongly attributed? Could he be wearing someone else's wife?' Gemma said, having to remind herself that she was a professional acting on the behalf of a client, and if the job was a bit out of the ordinary—well, so was a lot of life.

'That couldn't possibly happen.' Mr Gardiner was adamant. 'Every job is numbered and a strict receipting record kept of the sequence of the transformations. It's a process that requires great skill and very expensive equipment and energy. We have highly skilled technicians here.' He indicated a heavy steel door, like a fire door, in the wall behind him.

Gemma glanced in its direction. 'I'd like to see it, if I may.'

Raymond Gardiner actually wagged a finger at her. 'I'm afraid it's not possible to go into our industrial section,' he said. 'There's fierce competition in this field. I can't let our competitors know how we do this at such a manageable cost. It's a highly secret process, Miss Lincoln. And there are issues of privacy and decorum, as I'm sure you'll appreciate.'

'How often do you do the process?' she continued.

'We transform once or twice a week. You can imagine our energy bills are enormous. The presses consume huge quantities of power over a long period of time. We are, after all, trying to duplicate Mother Nature.' He gave a peculiar smile. 'But each job is very carefully monitored and numbered. It would be quite impossible for there to be a mix-up. We place the cremains in numbered platinum crucibles.'

'So you do it all here?' Gemma indicated the unseen factory behind the door.

'That's right,' he replied. 'Everything's done in the one place. On these premises. So there's no chance of any mix-up or loss during transfer from one place to another. It's a foolproof system.'

Gemma stood up. 'Thanks for your time, Mr Gardiner.'

If she wanted to get a look in there, she'd have to find another way.

'Please, call me Ray,' he said, turning to her as he opened the door. 'I'm sorry Mr Dowling is unhappy with the result. It's a very sensitive issue. Maybe the old gentleman is still in shock. Still grieving,' he said. 'It's some sort of denial. He can't believe that his wife is now reduced—or rather enhanced, as I like to think—into a precious stone. It's not uncommon. I'm sure he'll settle down.'

He hesitated. 'And if there comes a time when you want someone transformed,' he said, 'I hope you'll think of us.'

Gemma thanked him.

Before going back to her car, she walked around to the laneway behind Forever Diamonds. A tall wire fence topped with serious razor-wire coupled with a closed roller door and a small grilled window kept the premises very secure, backed up by a discreetly hooded security camera covering the rear yard. As Mr Gardiner had inferred, this firm was taking no chances with industrial sabotage.

Back in her car, Gemma looked up the number for Kevin, an acquaintance who'd worked in various governmental technical surveillance units and had now retired to make customised electronic knick-knacks for the deeper, darker end of the surveillance and espionage industry. She asked him about the process at Forever Diamonds.

'Sure,' he said, in answer to her questions, 'it's a growing business. Mother Nature uses her own energy sources to do this and it does take huge amounts of power. But the technology's been around for nearly half a century and it's getting better all the time. Both the US and the Russians have made synthetic diamonds. The diamonds were all yellow but in recent years there's been a lot of work done on mopping up the nitrogen particles while the crystals are forming. That's when the carbon is transformed. To do this, you need extremely high-pressure presses working together for long periods of time. If this firm is charging nine grand or so, my guess is that a lot of it would be recouping their power costs. They've got to build up pressure equal to one million kilos per square centimetre. Then run that over twenty-four hours or more. Plus the costs of running a furnace at 1480 degrees Celsius. And that's not counting the platinum cooking pot they need.'

'The manager mentioned the platinum crucibles,' Gemma said. 'When Mr Dowling showed me the ring, it looked like a pretty ordinary little diamond.'

'No doubt it was,' said Kevin. 'Probably lots of metal inclusions and poor colour. A manufacturer in the memorial business isn't after quality stones. He's just making a keepsake. Different priorities for the clients, too. If they wanted a top-class diamond, they'd have gone to a good jeweller.' He paused. 'So what's the problem?'

'Mr Dowling says it's not his wife.'

'He's a hundred per cent right on that! It's only her carbon.'

'But that's just it. He's saying it's not even her carbon.'

'How can he tell?' Kevin chuckled. 'All of us are made of recycled materials.'

'He's adamant and distressed and he wants me to find out if there could have been a mix-up with the resulting diamonds.'

'That might be tricky. People in that sort of business don't want to disclose their secrets.'

'I've noticed,' she said, then, noticing the beep of call waiting, said she'd ring back later.

'Guess what?' Angie's voice hissed through the earpiece. 'Those remains at Botany. No good for a visual, and it's not official. But the bets are that it's Amy Bernhard.'

Gemma thought sadly of Lauren Bernhard. 'So it's a murder inquiry now?' she asked.

'I'd say so. She was lying on a patch of waste-land. Her mother ID'd a gold chain.'

'I've already spoken to Amy's mother,' Gemma said, thinking this was the day Lauren Bernhard had been dreading for a year.

'In a way, she'll be relieved,' said Angie. 'They all say it's worse not knowing.'

Maybe it is, thought Gemma. But at least there's always some little hope until the final ID. 'Now Tasmin Summers is missing,' she said. 'Let's hope she's just run away.'

'Yes,' said Angie. 'Let's. I'll keep you posted, girlfriend. Meanwhile, I'd better swing by and pick up my briefcase. Call me when you get home?'

Relief flooding her that she'd already photo-copied everything, Gemma tried to change the sombre mood. 'I've just talked to a man who was wearing his mother on his little finger.'

'Love it,' said Angie, who had a fractious rela-tionship with hers. 'Can I get mine done too?'

FOUR

The house where Claudia Page lived was a huge grey mansion in Maroubra, built along faux Tuscan lines and surrounded by a garden of spiky bromeliads and cacti. Tinted glassed-in verandahs enclosed the front and sides of the house like huge wrap-around sunglasses.

Claudia answered the door, still wearing the distinctive tartan school uniform, and invited Gemma inside across a wide expanse of rug-strewn marble. Mrs Page looked up from speaking on the telephone and waved. Gemma perched on a black leather couch, taking in the opulence of her surroundings. Silk Persian rugs were scattered about, textured cream and green velvet curtains partly revealed a glass wall through which a palm-lined swimming pool was visible. Beyond that was the brilliance of the blue Pacific. You didn't get a place like this for less than five or six big ones, thought Gemma.

Claudia sat opposite her. She had a classical beauty that relied on perfectly proportioned features, refined eyes and brows, beautiful sculpted lips and a fine chiselled nose.

A mobile phone sang and Claudia dived into her pocket, pulling it out. Gemma noticed it was the latest model, as smart as her own, with a little screen and video capacity.

'Can't talk right now,' Claudia whispered to her caller. 'Later.'

'Please,' said Gemma, opening her hands. But Claudia had rung off and the mobile hung loosely in her slender fingers.

'Boyfriend?' asked Gemma.

Claudia's blush revealed the answer. She pressed her lips together, as if to make sure no information about him escaped. Or was it to stop herself from smiling with pleasure?

Gemma felt a pang of envy, then scolded herself for being jealous of a teenager. She glanced down at the small screen on the girl's mobile and craned to see the digital images she was reviewing. But Claudia, after stopping at the frozen image of a good-looking smiling youth, switched the memory function off then slipped the mobile back into her pocket.

'So, tell me about life, Claudia. How is it for you these days?' asked Gemma.

Claudia looked away, staring out to sea through the glass wall of the room. Now that the joy of the boyfriend's call had faded, she seemed infinitely sad.

'Is it hard,' Gemma asked, 'being where you are? At school? At home?'

Claudia nodded. 'I hate it here. And I hate school.'

'But I heard you playing the piano. I heard how brilliantly you were doing your scales—melodic minors. Things I only dream about. I only started learning last year.'

Claudia regarded her coolly. 'I'm good at most of the things I do. I wouldn't know how to be otherwise.'

'Claudia,' Gemma began, the name sounding so formal and proper, 'tell me about Amy.'

Claudia shrugged. 'What's to tell? She's gone. Life goes on.'

It sounded tough but Gemma could hear little cracks around the edges of the hard, young voice. She leaned forward, inviting confidence. 'Hey,' she said, aware of the need to escape the oppressive richness of their surroundings. 'If it's all right with your mum, let's get out of here and grab a coffee. I know a really cute place.'

Twenty minutes later, they were walking along the path that led down to the Boatshed Café at Phoenix Bay. Beyond the café, the sea rolled in, waves breaking on a big swell with a few surfers out the back.

The two of them passed a wedding group—a petite bride in clouds of white, clustering with her fuchsia-coloured bridesmaids for the photographer while the tuxedoed men of the party stood aside. Clouds of heavy perfumes followed Gemma and Claudia right down to the beach.

Every male eye lingered as they stepped onto

the deck that ran along the southern side of the café and took a seat; Claudia had changed into white jeans and a blue and white striped shirt tied in a knot, revealing her tanned belly. Gulls wheeled and squabbled on the beach or glided over the waves and a dog made futile dashes at them. A handsome waiter in a French apron took their coffee orders.

'That's better,' Claudia said. 'It's good to get out.'

'Things difficult at home?' said Gemma gently.

Claudia looked out to sea. 'It's coming up to the HSC year and all that. Dad's always away and Mum's . . . well, she's either away too, or she's on my back.'

Gemma let that one go for the moment. 'Claudia,' she said, 'I need your help. I need to know anything about Amy that could be helpful.'

She had decided not to mention that Amy was probably dead. Not until it was official. Claudia was still staring at the sea and Gemma could see the tiny reflections mirrored in her large eyes. 'Amy's father divorced her mother when she was little,' she prompted. 'That must have been hard for her.'

'I suppose so,' said Claudia. 'But she didn't know him. He'd left a long time before. It was her stepfather who was giving her a hard time.'

Gemma wrote that down and underlined it.

'What do *you* think happened to Amy? Do you have any idea why she might have disappeared?'

Claudia shifted in her chair, clearly uncomfortable. This girl knows something, thought Gemma, feeling sure Claudia was running stories through her mind, trying to decide how much to tell, how much to keep concealed. Gemma decided on an ambush. 'What is it, Claudia? What do you know that you're not telling me?'

'Stop pushing me! You're harassing me!' exclaimed Claudia, moving back in her chair, as far away from Gemma as possible. The body language spoke volumes.

'Claudia, it's my job to find out what happened to your friend. Part of that is asking questions that you might not like.'

'The police have asked all the same questions and they can't seem to find out what happened to Amy,' said Claudia. 'Why do you think you're going to do any better?'

There was something smug in her manner, almost a quiet triumph. You do know something, Gemma thought. Something big.

The handsome waiter presented the two cappuccinos they'd ordered with a flourish, placing them on the table as if he'd manifested them out of thin air. Gemma stirred her creamy coffee while Claudia emptied two sachets of sugar into hers; the atmosphere eased somewhat between them.

'I don't mean to harass you, Claudia,' soothed Gemma, though she wished she could lean harder. 'But I want to know anything that might help us discover what happened to Amy. She was your friend. You must care too.' She picked her cup up again. 'For instance, I want to know about the secret.'

About to take a sip from her cappuccino, Claudia stalled, mid-air, with the cup a few inches from her lips. Then she tilted it too quickly, spilling coffee down her front. 'Ouch!' she cried, awkwardly jumping away from it, flinching at the heat, dashing at the stained blue and white shirt with a paper napkin . . .

Gemma passed her more napkins. 'Get some water on it. Quick!'

The waiter ran to help, and once cold water had been dabbed over the stained area, Gemma continued. 'I was asking you,' she said, 'about the secret.'

'The secret?' Claudia said, now all blue-eyed innocence. 'What secret? There is no secret. That was just something we used to tease the others with.'

'I don't believe that, Claudia.' Gemma kept her eye contact steady. The earlier flash of fire she'd witnessed wasn't the spark of outraged innocence, but the clashing of defences. 'You see,' she went on, 'I think there is a secret. And I think that secret is the reason why Amy is—'

She almost forgot herself and said 'dead', then recovered just in time and changed the word to 'disappeared' but not without a little distortion to the first vowel sound. Claudia, now alert and sensitive to every nuance between them, pounced on it.

'You were going to say that Amy is dead! Weren't you? Weren't you!' Her voice had an unstable edge and she spoke so vehemently that tiny specks of spittle flew.

Gemma hesitated, mind working furiously to

find a way to smooth this over. Around Claudia's eyes, shadows gathered like storm clouds.

'Claudia,' Gemma spoke in a gentle tone, 'let's forget about questions. Let's just enjoy our coffees. Maybe you can tell me a little about school—what interests you have?'

'I don't have time for interests,' Claudia snapped. 'I haven't got a life, just study. And practice. Especially now.'

Gemma noted the remark. Why especially now? Now that Amy was gone?

Deciding she wasn't going to get much further, Gemma paid the bill, and they walked back up the path to the road. The bridal party was being stuffed into two cars, clouds of tulle and the trains of billowing frocks stowed inside safely.

'I wonder if they're going to be happy?' Gemma said, thinking aloud.

'Why should they be?' Claudia's voice was hard with contempt. 'What's "happy" anyway?'

They continued up the track in silence, the unspoken looming huge between them.

Gemma drove Claudia back to her house and parked outside. Claudia hesitated, not getting out, her hand on the car door handle. 'I'm scared.' She turned to face Gemma. 'Tasmin is missing now.'

'Can you throw any light on that?'

Claudia shook her head. 'I think she might have just run away.'

'But why now? And where would she run?'

Claudia gave a shrug.

'And if she had run,' Gemma added, 'wouldn't she have said something to you?'

'Tasmin was much closer to Ames than to me.'

Claudia threw the car door open and Gemma expected her to get out, but instead she closed it again and remained sitting, staring ahead. Gemma fished one of her cards out of her briefcase and Claudia hesitated, took it, studied it for a long moment, then slid it into a pocket.

'I know Miss de B said you were helping with the investigation—into Amy's disappearance,' she said. 'And that you're not the police. But how are you different? You sound the same as that red-headed policewoman who talked to me earlier.'

'Detective McDonald?'

Claudia nodded.

'I worked with Angie McDonald years ago. But now I'm a licensed investigator. Sort of free-range, freelance,' Gemma explained. 'I'm not tied up by procedures like the cops are. But on the other hand, I haven't got the sort of access to things they have.'

'But you're quite separate from them?'

'Quite separate.' Gemma saw tears welling and softened towards the girl.

'I'm the only one left now,' Claudia whispered.

'That's why,' Gemma said as gently as she could, placing a hand on the girl's arm, 'if there's anything you can think of, anything at all, please contact me. Or Angie McDonald.'

Gemma thought Claudia was about to speak, but the moment passed and instead she swung out of the car and hurried to the front door without looking back, pressing the buttons that caused the door to slide open and disappearing inside. Gemma sat looking after her.

Next morning, Dr Rowena Wylde showed Gemma into the large sitting room of her Pymble house. Gemma was shocked by the change in her appearance. Despite their fleeting acquaintance, she remembered a robust, elegantly suited woman with all the presence of a powerful middle age. Now, dwindled to a pale wraith, her face showing the grey transparency of the dying, she wore a tired dressing gown and a little cap, like a tea cosy. Gemma stood at the window, unsure how to proceed after the initial greetings, while Dr Wylde shuffled to a cabinet in which various trifles and treasures were displayed behind glass. She unlocked the door beneath the display section, and drew out a small framed photograph.

'God knows why I've kept this all these years.' Gemma could hear it was a struggle to speak. 'I thought perhaps you might like it, Miss Lincoln,' she breathed.

Gemma saw that it was a photo of her father, taken, she imagined, in the early years of his marriage, when he was a leading and respected psychiatrist developing his theories about mental illness. She looked at his handsome features, the thick, brushed-back hair, the hint of a smile, the way his head was cocked forward as if he were

about to say, 'Have I got something to tell you!'
She handed it back. 'I don't think I want it.'

The two women sat in silence for some time, the
framed picture on a small table between them.

'You said that you had something important to
tell me. Concerning my family.' Feeling extremely
tense, Gemma deliberately relaxed her neck and
shoulders, loosening the tightness, breathing deeply.

'You will remember,' said Dr Wylde, 'how I told
you there had been another woman involved with
your father at the same time I was.' She laughed.
'I was so jealous of her then.'

'Yes,' said Gemma.

Outside, lorikeets screeched and both of them
watched as a flock screamed and fought over the
red blossom fronds of a rainforest tree at the end
of the garden.

'I didn't tell you everything,' said Rowena Wylde.
'I mentioned the affair and that the woman had suicided.' She paused. 'I didn't mention the baby.'

Gemma stiffened with shock. 'There was a baby?'

'I can't even imagine what jealousy feels like now,'
said Dr Wylde. 'But back then I found out the
woman's name. Kingston. Beverley Kingston. The
family lived at Hargreaves Street, Paddington.' Her
drawn face lifted in a half smile. 'I know that because
I went through your father's pockets once when he
was visiting me here and found a letter from her.
That's how I found out about the affair and the baby.'

'And when was this?' said Gemma, her voice
trembling. She felt her world had changed yet again,
swung off orbit into a new and alien trajectory. 'I

mean,' she whispered, 'how old would Kit, my sister, and I have been?'

'You were only a little thing.'

'So the child would be younger than me?'

'You're thirty-seven? Thirty-eight now?'

Gemma nodded. 'Nearly thirty-nine.'

'So she'd be—'

'She?'

'Oh, yes. It was a girl.'

Gemma felt something move in her heart. Another sister. A woman who'd be thirty-three or four. She tried to imagine her. Would she have the Chisholm jaw and thick tawny hair like she had? Or would she favour the Lincolns' pale skin and fine dark hair?

'Let me get you a whisky,' said Dr Wylde. 'My physician told me not to drink and I said, "Why? Are you worried about my health?"' She laughed.

Gemma wanted to be out of there, fast, out of that house, away from the woman who had known her father in such a way. She wondered if her mother had known about this Beverley Kingston and her pregnancy. Perhaps the reason for the fight her parents had on the day of her mother's death was about her father being involved with two other women—the woman she was sitting with now and the suicided Beverley Kingston. She suddenly felt nauseous and stood up. 'I must go.'

Rowena Wylde remained seated as Gemma walked to the doorway. 'Are you sure you don't want that photograph of your father?' She called after her. 'If you ever find your half-sister, don't you think she might like to see what her father looked like?'

Gemma paused, irresolute. Finally, she came back into the room and took the photograph from Rowena Wylde, slipping it into her briefcase.

Dr Wylde returned to her chair and Gemma let herself out and into the brilliant, hot summer day. She stood a few seconds, blinking tears away.

She was hardly aware of driving and was halfway across the Harbour Bridge when her mobile rang. It was Kit.

'Thank goodness you're home at last,' said Gemma. 'I need to see you now. Can I come round?'

Kit was in her garden, dark hair tied back in a ribbon, cheeks flushed with the heat, cutting back a climbing rose that was threatening to take over the entire western wall. She kissed Gemma and glanced at her watch. 'I'm expecting a client in twenty minutes.'

Gemma tried to sit down under the umbrella, but she couldn't be still so she went to the pond and stood watching dragonflies hovering while Kit pulled her gardening gloves off and washed her sweaty face under the tap. 'I've just come from Rowena Wylde's place,' she said, turning to Kit.

At the sound of the name of their late father's mistress, Kit made a little exclamation of surprise and turned the tap off. 'And?' She straightened up, wiping her hands on a hankie.

Gemma took a deep breath. 'Do you remember me telling you ages ago about the other woman our father was involved with? The one who was threatening suicide if our father didn't leave our mother?'

Kit nodded. 'Yes. One of his patients.'

'Rowena Wylde told me that this woman had a baby girl. To our father.'

The two sisters stared at each other.

'I wonder what became of her?' Kit said eventually.

'I've been thinking about that,' said Gemma. 'Maybe a grandmother brought her up?'

Kit sat down at the table. 'Or she was adopted out?'

'We must find her,' said Gemma quietly, then dug around in her briefcase and pulled out the framed photograph of their father. 'Dr Wylde gave me this.'

Kit took it, studied it, handed it back. 'I'm not sure I've made my peace with him,' she said as her doorbell rang. Shielding her eyes from the sun, she kissed Gemma and watched as she let herself out, then started to go inside.

'I'm going to find her,' Gemma said emphatically.

'As long as she wants to be found,' Kit called after her.

Gemma climbed into her car and found the address of Amy Bernhard's mother. She needed to take her mind off her own family.

FIVE

Lauren Bernhard let Gemma in, barely glancing at her ID, and led her right through the house to an enclosed garden room surrounded by a verandah. 'Until the detectives came round yesterday with Amy's gold chain,' Lauren said, 'I could hope. There was always the chance that she'd turn up. Now the hope has gone. And I have a funeral to look forward to.' She turned to face Gemma, who saw that behind the woman's dark blue eyes lay an ocean of grief. 'When she's given back to me. They told me there wasn't much of her left. Just her bones and some hair. And the gold chain.'

'I'm so terribly sorry, Mrs Bernhard. I can't imagine what it must be like for you.'

'No,' said the other. 'You can't.'

The back verandah had a clothes horse with some washing drying on it and a couple of cane chairs on either side of a square table.

'Sit down,' said Lauren and Gemma did. 'Even though I know she's dead now, I keep thinking she's just going to run inside and slam the door behind her. I was always yelling at her not to slam the door.' She brushed something from the surface of the table. 'What did you want to ask me?'

'Her father,' Gemma said. 'What sort of terms was she on with him?'

Lauren raised her eyes to heaven. 'Him? Same terms as anyone was. Take a numbered ticket and wait your turn.' Gemma saw she was gripping the sides of the chair. 'Andrew's not a bad man, he's just a hopeless father,' she said. 'I divorced him years ago, when Amy was just a little thing. It's tough for him, sure, but less so.'

'So they didn't see each other much?' asked Gemma.

Lauren shook her head. 'His new wife didn't get on with Amy. She didn't encourage any visiting.'

'And your second husband? How did Amy get on with him?' Gemma asked, remembering what Claudia had said about Amy and her stepfather.

There was a long silence. 'At first,' Lauren said, 'they seemed to be okay together.'

'And then?' Gemma prompted.

'It's hard to explain. But, to cut a long story short, they ended up fighting about everything. Arguing all the time.'

Gemma remembered Miss de Berigny's remarks about two failed marriages.

'And then, after he left and disagreed with the Family Court, he joined a lobby group,' Lauren continued.

'Can you tell me more about that?'

'It's a mob called Fathers for Family and

Marriage,' Lauren snapped. 'They wear black and mask the lower half of their faces, just like the bad guys in the old cowboy films.'

'I've seen them,' Gemma recalled. 'They lobby the Family Court and hang around the homes of their exes.'

'That's them,' Lauren nodded. 'They call it "vigiling for family and marriage". I call it stalking. Eric really found himself when he joined them. Suddenly—and for the first bloody time, I can tell you—marriage was sacred. Now, it's like he's got religion.' She appealed to Gemma. 'Can you imagine what it feels like to have a dozen or so masked men dressed all in black standing outside your house?'

'I can't. But I know I wouldn't like it one bit,' said Gemma, the image disturbing. 'I'd like his contact details, please.'

Lauren got them and Gemma copied the phone number and address into her notebook.

'Anything else that might be helpful?' she asked.

'Only that there was a funny incident in October last year. Alistair from next door told me he'd seen a man in the bushes outside Amy's room. I'll bet it was one of those blackshirts. Could even have been bloody Eric. Although I think Alistair would have recognised him if that had been the case.' She gave a wan smile. 'Amy used to say the initials FFM stood for Fathers who've Fucked their Marriages. She could be quite outspoken at times.'

Gemma recalled the statistics regarding the prominence of stepfathers and de facto male partners in sexual and other abuse. 'Did you report the peeping incident to the police?'

'Yes, I did,' Lauren said. 'I spoke to the detective in charge of the case—he thought it might have been kids. He said they'd look into it.'

In light of the girl's disappearance only a month or so later, Gemma hoped there'd been more action than the old 'look into it' routine. She'd definitely check it out. 'What's your next-door neighbour like?' she asked.

'Alistair? Oh, he's harmless. Funny old chap. He's lived alone since his mother died a few years back.'

Gemma made a note to call on him then returned her attention to her companion. 'Lauren,' she said, 'help me. I need to find out what sort of girl Amy was.'

Lauren Bernhard closed her eyes for a long moment before speaking. 'How can I tell you that? How can I tell anyone how she was?' Lauren stood up. 'Amy was my daughter.'

Gemma rose, too. Lauren briefly touched her arm. 'Come with me.'

Gemma followed her upstairs until they came to a closed door with a folksy painted shingle: *Amy's Room*. Lauren opened the door and Gemma followed her in.

Lauren sat on the bed. 'Amy was this sort of girl,' she said, indicating the room.

Gemma looked around. It was full of bright colours: a red and blue bedspread and, on top, four dramatic red and black velvet cushions decorated with the suits of cards—hearts, diamonds, spades and clubs. School banners and pennants, along with American and Australian heart-throbs of screen and television, adorned the bright yellow walls. Various pots of nail polish, lipsticks and lotions clustered on a small dressing table next to the window and a large portrait of Amy wearing an off-the-shoulder white evening dress hung over the bed.

Opposite the bed, a large teddy bear wearing an exotic feathered mask and draped with the Eureka stockade flag sat on a desk which also held pens, pencils and a large computer and keyboard. Below it was a box piled high with clothes. Lauren noticed her looking at it.

'The police searched all that. And checked her emails and everything. But they didn't find anything.'

'This is a very well-equipped study room,' Gemma said.

'Yes,' Lauren agreed. 'I even got broadband on especially for her. She liked to be up with the latest. Andrew started helping financially last year. I had to ask him, but, to his credit, he came to the party.'

On the shelf next to the teddy bear stood a photo of Amy with a friend on each side, the girls' arms around each other's shoulders, laughing in the Australian sunlight, healthy beautiful girls with gleaming hair and perfect teeth. Gemma picked it up.

'Claudia and Tasmin,' Lauren said. 'Thick as thieves they were. They did everything together. You know how girls of that age are.'

Gemma studied Tasmin Summers, now missing

too. She was slighter, less developed than the other two, a sylph with glossy dark hair and strong brows.

'Did Amy take anything with her that day? Apart from the usual school things, I mean,' Gemma asked.

'No, just the usual, although I noticed she'd taken her make-up purse. But that wasn't really unusual. She sometimes took that.'

'Nothing else? No extra clothing or anything like that?'

Lauren shook her head.

Gemma stood in silence, looking around the bedroom, taking it in. She was getting something of Amy's flavour, her interests. Slowly she put the photograph down, glancing again at the exotic mask worn by the teddy. She reached over and touched it. 'May I?' Lauren nodded.

With its silver and black feathers spraying sideways in a starburst, the mask was designed to hide all the upper face and hair. Gemma held it up to her face in front of the mirror and an exotic birdwoman stared back at her, beautiful and a little sinister.

A silence seemed to spread like a ripple through the room until Lauren stood up, breaking the spell.

Back home, Gemma put the photograph of her father in the drawer in the hall table and closed it firmly. The portrait of her mother stood above it on the polished surface.

Later, after Angie had picked up her briefcase,

Gemma sat in the last of the evening light, on the timber deck with her laptop, the purloined photocopied case notes in a pile on the wooden table, trying to bring her straying thoughts home.

She paused from typing up her notes from the edgy conversation with Claudia and the interview with Lauren Bernhard. Now she had the contact details of both Amy's father and stepfather. She wondered how thoroughly either of these men had been investigated in the initial enquiry after Amy's disappearance. Might a man who had a serious grudge against his ex-wife have something to do with the disappearance of her daughter? Statistically speaking, stepfathers and de factos were the most dangerous men in a young girl's world. Such men accounted for a high percentage of sexual and other abuse—up to and including murder.

Gemma made a sketch of Amy Bernhard's room, as well as she could remember it. She looked up from her notes. Normally honeyeaters flitted in the bushes near the edge of the cliff but they were finding their roosts for the night. Waves of anger and grief about Steve assailed her. She tried to black them out by thinking about her long-lost half-sister. What sort of friends did she have? Was she happy? Were there photographs of her with her arms linked around her mates? Maybe she was still living in this city. How had she dealt with the suicide of her mother? Did she even know about it?

Turning her focus back to the case of the two schoolgirls, Gemma considered the similarities linking them. They were best friends and both students of Netherleigh Park. In victimology, Gemma knew, every tiny thing was important.

She read over her notes again and reflected on the interview with Claudia. The girl was rattled. She definitely knew more than she was letting on—of that, Gemma was certain. A few more shakes and maybe she'd drop off the branch.

She settled down to read more of the photocopies of the 'borrowed' witness statements. As she read, she started to get an even clearer picture of the relationship between Amy, Tasmin and Claudia. According to all the witness statements, the trio were inseparable. *They go everywhere together*, Gemma read.

> *I catch the same bus. They always sat together on the bus and if anyone tried to sit up the back in their places, they just weren't allowed. Last time I saw Amy was when we were going home on the first of December and she was huddled up at the back of the bus with Tasmin and Claudia as usual, giggling together like they always do. Next day, I heard she'd left the school grounds some time during the morning of the second of December. I don't know any reason she might have gone missing.*

Gemma put the witness statement at the back of the folder. I must talk to Tasmin's family, she thought, pulling out the next one, another student.

> *My name is Tiffany Louise Brown and the last time I saw Amy Bernhard was the morning of December*

second when we were at the bus stop. The bus was quite crowded that morning. Amy is in the same class as me, but we do different level Maths. Someone told me she'd gone missing from the school grounds that morning. I can't think of any reason why she might run away.

Gemma remembered that Tiffany was the name of the girl who'd showed her the way upstairs at the school, and who'd said somewhat resentfully that Claudia did everything extremely well. She made a note of Tiffany Brown's address then read the next statement.

My name is Sandra Margaret McCauley and I teach History and English at Netherleigh Park. On the morning of the second December I was on playground duty during morning break. Usually, there are two of us, one to cover the back playground area and one for the side nearest Koolah Avenue, but I was covering both areas as Miss Handley had called in sick. I didn't see Amy Bernhard leaving the school grounds, but it would be quite easy for any student to slip out during the morning unnoticed. People are often coming and going from both entrances during the day.

Gemma put this face down on the table then pulled out the next photocopied sheet out. It was Claudia's own witness statement, the one she'd partly glimpsed while in the café with Angie.

My name is Claudia Zahra Page. I am a Year 10 student at Netherleigh Park in the same class as my friend Amy Bernhard. I saw Amy on the morning of the second of December when I was on the bus going to school. Tasmin and I were down the back and I saw Amy at the front of the bus. I knew she had to race to a meeting with Mr Romero before our History class but she did not turn up to the class. At lunchtime, Mr Romero asked me where Amy was and I said I hadn't seen her since that morning. I went home after our Art class finished. Later that night, I heard Amy had gone missing and that the police had been informed. I don't know any reason she might have run away or any other reason for her to be missing.

Gemma read the statement again. Amy had a meeting with Mr Romero before History and then she didn't ever come to class. Had anyone checked that out? She recalled the way Mr Romero had interrupted her initial meeting with Miss de Berigny, looking for Tasmin Summers. She made a note to herself then found Lauren Bernhard's witness statement directly under Claudia's.

My name is Lauren Grace Bernhard and on Friday second December I said goodbye to my daughter Amy who was running late for school. Her father was in Hong Kong at the time. Amy didn't have any breakfast that morning and left in a hurry. She was wearing school uniform as normal and carried her school bag. When she didn't come home after school as expected I rang her friends Tasmin Summers and Claudia Page, but they said they hadn't seen her. Later, I rang the police and reported that she was missing. It was the police who told me later that Amy had gone missing from school that day. She has never done anything like this before.

That you know about, Gemma couldn't help thinking.

Then she found the statement from the now missing Tasmin Summers.

My name is Tasmin Anne Summers and the last time I saw my friend Amy was on the bus on the morning of the second of December. There were a lot of people waiting at the stop because the earlier bus hadn't stopped. I was sitting up the back with my friend Claudia Page. When we got to school, I went straight to the toilets because I was wearing make-up and Miss de Berigny puts anyone wearing make-up on detention. I had to go to a meeting before school and did not notice that Amy was missing until Miss de Berigny asked me if I had seen her. I told her that I hadn't. I don't know of any reason why Amy would run away.

Gemma stretched her neck and shoulders. The light had faded and she switched the deck light on and sprayed herself with citronella to keep the mozzies at bay.

The next piece of paper was not a witness statement, but a memo.

Intranet Memorandum
From: Supt JS Buisman
To: D/S Bruno Gross
Re: Missing Person: Amy Bernhard. CN #039–4303
Bruno,
After our discussion of yesterday and the situation that you described to me I think it would be best from the legal angle that you step aside. I have decided to take you off this case and will allocate someone else to take over. Please be ready to hand over all relevant paperwork, case notes, etc, when directed.
Yours
Jim

Gemma read it again. Bruno Gross had been the detective in charge of the earlier investigation and he'd been relieved of this position and someone else put on. Why? What was 'the situation' they'd discussed? She made a note to track down Jim Buisman and underlined it. She recalled how it was often messy when a job changed hands, with more than the usual chance of procedures not being followed up and information slipping between cracks during the handover. This would be multiplied if the original investigator had been someone like G-for-Gross.

The last adult to have spoken to Amy appeared to have been Mr Romero. Surely he should have been interviewed? She made a mental note to ask Angie if he had ever been properly followed up; she knew that it took only one incompetent or lazy member on an investigating team for all the work

done by the others to be undermined. She shuffled through and found the witness statement she
was very keen to see—that of Mannix John
Romero.

> I have been teaching Art and History at Netherleigh
> Park for six years and I teach Amy Bernhard Art
> and History. On the morning of the second of
> December I was delayed in traffic and arrived late
> for my teaching duties. I first noticed that Amy was
> not in class that morning, but it wasn't until the
> end of the day that I heard she had gone missing.
> She is a good student and I don't know of any
> reason that she would go missing.

Had Bruno picked up the hole in Mr Romero's
statement that the teacher hadn't mentioned that
a pre-school-hours meeting had been arranged
with Amy? She needed to talk to Mr Romero as
soon as possible . . .

Gemma sorted the statements into two piles:
those she'd read and noted, those yet to be examined. From the second pile, she picked up the
statement from Mr Alistair Forde—the harmless,
funny old bachelor who lived next door, Gemma
remembered.

> I live next door to the Bernhard house and on the
> night of the thirty-first of October I was changing
> the light bulb when I happened to look outside and
> saw a person crouching in the bushes outside one
> of the rooms of the Bernhard house. I could see him

even though the person was keeping down because of the outside automatic light on the side passage of my house. I went downstairs and as I was walking up the side to challenge this person, he turned around and I got a good look at his face before he took off, running in a northerly direction and disappearing over the back fence. The person was not familiar to me. I rang Lauren Bernhard and told her what I'd seen.

Gemma stood up and went over the railing, leaning against it. The sky and sea were now the same luminous steel colour as the last of the reflected light from the west bounced back from the surface of the ocean. Despite the citronella, she realised she was being targeted so she gathered up the piles of papers and took them back inside. She hunted through the unread statements but couldn't find any other reference to the incident reported by Alistair Forde. It was probably just an entry on the local police station's running sheet with NFA—no further action—beside it.

The next statement was from Amy's father.

My name is Andrew Bernhard and I am divorced from Amy's mother and have been living at the above address in Brisbane for the last eleven years. I was attending a business meeting when my ex-wife contacted me and told me that our daughter Amy had not been to school on the second of December and that she'd called Amy's friends and was worried . . . Amy is a good girl and has never done anything like this before.

How would you know? Gemma thought. She quickly skipped through the rest of the statements. There should be one from Eric Stokes, Amy's step-father, president of the FFM—but there wasn't. Had he been overlooked too? All the more reason for her to visit Eric Stokes.

Next Gemma turned her attention to her copies of the running sheets including the names and addresses of the people the police had contacted in the first days of Amy's disappearance. Could Amy have headed north to see her father and met with foul play? She thought of the Ratbag—the kid who'd lived next door to her in the adjoining unit until he and his mother had moved to Melbourne. He'd run away, back to Sydney, and camped out on the cliffs near his old apartment until Gemma had stumbled on him and taken him in for a few days.

Gemma stood up and stretched. There was something right in front of her, something important. Something she wasn't getting, something she wasn't seeing. Something that didn't add up. She needed a break. But first she needed to organise an interview with Mr Romero. Both Amy and Tasmin had been expected at pre-school meetings with him on the mornings they'd disappeared. Her mobile rang and she snatched it up.

'It's me,' said Angie, her voice sounding tired. 'I knew you'd want to know straightaway. I've just come from the morgue and the initial examination of Amy Bernhard. She's been officially identified.

'The body was rolled up in a piece of vinyl and the doc's only got skeletal remains to work with. But the vinyl might have protected some evidence. There was no clothing found on or near her—nothing except a piece of nylon cord. Samples have gone to the Division of Analytic Laboratories in case there's anything on them. The doc's saying it's going to be one of those tricky ones. Still, it's pretty amazing what he can get from a pile of bones.'

'Did you notice,' Gemma began, 'that both Amy and Tasmin were supposed to have a meeting with their History teacher—'

'I did,' said Angie. 'I tried to contact him today but he's off sick. I'm going to talk to the school body on Friday night—I'll catch up with him then. Or track him down. By then, we might have something helpful from the pathology report.'

'How's the investigation going?' Gemma asked.

'The strike force is being put together right now. We're going to check out all the teachers—their backgrounds, employment histories.'

'As long as Bruno doesn't get that job,' Gemma said. 'Make sure it's given to someone who'll do it.' She paused. 'That reminds me—did you see that memo from a super taking Bruno off the earlier investigation? Someone called Jim Buisman?'

'Vaguely. I didn't take much notice. I was concentrating on the witness statements.'

'Where can I find Buisman?'

'Last I heard he was HOD. I'll ask around.'

'Hurt on duty' was often used as a door out of the police service, Gemma knew. Angie sighed. 'Now I've had to go and cancel a date with Trevor. Why don't these kids just stay home and behave?'

'Did you?'

Angie laughed. 'Trevor's got to go away on a job.' She lowered her voice. 'He sent me this huge box of red roses and a box of chocolates. And in the chocolates was another poem. Listen . . .' Angie started reading. '*How do I love thee? Let me count the ways . . .* Isn't that just gorgeous?'

'Lovely.'

Gemma was sure she'd heard it before. Even so, she couldn't help a pang of envy. Angie was happy and in love. Not like me, she thought. Home alone with witness statements and mozzies. There was a pause during which she focused back on the subject.

'Who've you got on the strike force?' she asked, wondering if she'd know any of the names.

'Would you believe, Sean Wright?'

'You poor thing,' said Gemma. 'G-for-Gross and Mr Right in one task force. You should get danger money.'

'Hey, cheer up, honeybun. You sound edgy or something. What's up?' Angie asked.

'We've just discovered—Kit and I, I mean—that we've got a sister. A half-sister.' Gemma filled her friend in.

'Would your father's name be on the birth certificate?'

Gemma considered. 'She was in love with him.

She said she was going to kill herself if he didn't leave our mother.'

'Then I'd say most definitely your father's name will appear on the birth certificate. Why would she be coy about it? She'd *want* to name him as the father of her child if she was in love with the man. She'd want to get him on paper. Then it's almost official,' said Angie.

Gemma's mind went through some fast calculations. 'So I should be looking for a female child, father's name Chisholm, born . . .' She hesitated. 'That's where it gets really tricky. We haven't got a birth date. Only the year.' The online individual search facility she used would probably require her half-sister's full name. And their records might not go back far enough anyway.

'You're not going to be able to get into Births, Deaths and Marriages,' said Angie. 'Not unless you bribe someone, blackmail them, seduce them or know a good hacker.'

It certainly wasn't going to be easy, Gemma conceded. Identity theft was the crime of the season and, apart from the person in question, only parents could now access birth certificates. Even then, three forms of ID were required. For a wicked moment, she wondered if Mike could hack into government records. It had certainly been done before. But she dismissed the idea as crazy. It would be the end of her professional life. And his. Serving time at Mulawa women's prison was not an attractive proposition. Green had never been her colour.

'So where are you going to start?' said Angie.

'You might have to door-knock every house in Hargreaves Street.'

'I'll start at the usual place: electoral rolls. Although without a first name that would hardly help.' Gemma had a sudden inspiration. 'Angie, you said it! Of course she'd want to get him on paper! She may even have wanted to get him *in* the paper! Announcing the happy event. Perhaps she put "Kingston–Chisholm. A daughter".'

'Do you reckon?' said Angie. 'And then go off and top herself?'

'It's a start,' said Gemma.

'You'll have many happy days in the State Library, peering at microfilmed newspapers. Three hundred and sixty plus, not counting public holidays,' said Angie, ringing off.

Gemma brought her attention back to the two girls from Netherleigh Park. The status of the investigation into the case of Amy Bernhard had changed from missing person to murder and this immediately made Tasmin Summers's sudden disappearance more ominous. Gemma also wanted to speak to Mr Mannix Romero as soon as possible, sick or not. Her phone rang again.

'Sorry to ring so late,' said Beatrice de Berigny, 'but I need to ask you something.'

'As a matter of fact,' said Gemma, 'I was going to ring you. I need to talk to Mr Romero. Check a couple of things with him.'

There was a silence before Miss de Berigny spoke. 'I want you to come and talk to the school body on Friday night. Dectective Sergeant Angie

McDonald is going to address the girls and the staff and I've invited their families as well. If you could come too, I'm sure it would make much more of an impression—cover all bases. I've sent notes home with all the students about it and considerable interest is being shown.'

That would be a perfect opportunity, Gemma thought, knowing that she didn't need to check her diary. Her nights were all free now. Too free.

'I'll mention to Mr Romero that you want to talk to him,' Miss de Berigny went on. 'He's not well just now.'

'With your permission,' Gemma added, 'I'd like to have a look around the school too, especially the classrooms.'

'You're very welcome to do that,' said the principal. 'I'll arrange it myself. One of the senior students could show you around.'

'One more thing,' said Gemma. 'Tasmin Summers.' She noticed the principal's sharp intake of breath at the name. 'What do you know about her family situation?'

'Her father is in the military,' said Miss de Berigny. 'The youngest general in the army.' She paused. 'He's away in the Gulf at the moment.'

'And Mrs Summers?' Gemma asked.

'She runs her own film production company. Brilliant woman.'

After ringing off, Gemma headed back into the kitchen and opened the fridge. She needed to talk to the brilliant producer, Mrs Summers. She stood there, staring into the fridge, deep in thought. Still the same miserable items—the drying chicken carcass blighting the interior. She pulled it out and put it in the rubbish, scolding herself. Gemma Lincoln, your fridge is a disgrace.

She started making a list. Sometimes, ordinary routine chores—like shopping for herself—could be very soothing.

SIX

Gemma drove to Kings Cross, the shopping list in her briefcase. The big 24-hour supermarket in the Kingsgate Centre was convenient and well stocked. Mechanical Christmas carols sounded behind the clash of trolleys and the too-loud announcements about pricing.

Despite the recent attempts to clean up the Cross, the spruikers were already out, trying to drum up business nevertheless. Two of the worst clubs, operating as unlicensed brothels, had not been able to renew their leases and were now boarded up, plastered with advertisements for rock bands, moving-house sales and singles clubs. Maybe I should take note of that last number, Gemma thought bitterly.

Lugging grocery packages back to her car in the underground parking station, some atavistic sense stirred in her. Badly lit, with dark corners and stains on the ground, the car park revived a memory of the frequently replayed, jerky security footage of a woman who had been the subject of an intense murder investigation caught leaving a car park. She had never been seen again.

Gemma swung around but there was no one in sight except a young mother battling with the shopping, a tired toddler and a baby, clearly not knowing which one to attend to first. But still the signal from some ancient part of Gemma's brain persisted: someone is watching you.

She stowed the shopping bags in the boot and got back into the car, wanting to be out of there fast. Reversing quickly, she swung the car towards the exit sign, using the mirror to keep an eye on her rear. Two other cars swung out straight after her—a red Volkswagen and a white Ford. All traffic had to turn left at the exit and she watched the progress of the other two vehicles. The red VW peeled off near Bayswater Road, but the white Ford stayed behind, two cars back—the classic 'two for cover' of physical surveillance. She wondered why they'd bother. It was clear she was heading home with her shopping, and there was no secrecy about where she lived—her business was listed in the phone book.

She drove in a wide circle around the Cross, returning finally via Woolloomooloo and into the parking station again, the white Ford staying with her. She indicated left but suddenly swung into a just-vacated spot, braking sharply. The white Ford went past, fast now because he knew he'd been pinged, the driver just a colourful blur with dark hair. She jotted down the part of the rego she'd managed to get, abandoned her own car and hurried on foot up to street level, keeping an eye out for the Ford.

The nightclub, Indigo Ice, was shut and she had to lean on the bell for a while before the door was yanked open. The stench of alcohol and cigarette smoke spiked with the sharp stink of vomit hit her.

'Who's making all that racket?' A man's angry face appeared. 'Gemma! It's you! Come in, come in! Sorry about the mess. The cleaner packed it in last night. Good to see you.'

Kosta Theodorakis, her late friend Shelly's boyfriend, led her through the dark, deserted club. With the chairs piled up in groups and a mop and bucket in the middle of the floor, the space looked like the set for a cabaret act.

'Someone's on my tail, Kosta,' she said, bypassing the usual pleasantries. 'Someone in a white Ford. Multi-coloured shirt. Dark hair. Rego with a three, six and seven in it.'

Kosta shrugged. 'No one I know. You'll need a drink.' In Kosta's world, most people were being tracked, one way or the other.

'Not right now,' said Gemma. 'I just want to know who it is and why. I've had this feeling for a few days now. And today I spotted him. Ask around for me—see what you can find out about who might be tailing me? And why?'

'But Gemma, babes. You're the investigator.'

'I don't want to draw attention to myself,' she said. 'I go asking around and everyone and everything pulls back. You know how toey people get. You can go where I can't go.'

'Anything I can do for you, I will. You know that. Friends for life, we are.'

He took a swig on his beer and walked over to a wide scissored broom which he started pushing around the floor, gathering butts, ring-pulls and other assorted debris. Gemma wished she'd brought her camera with her: a Greek man sweeping an interior floor, the assistant manager of the club no less.

'Give me that,' she said. She pushed it along in a wide square. There was something very satisfying about seeing the dust and dirt and bits of paper all being collected in the vee-shaped arms of the broom.

'I still miss her heaps,' Kosta said, swigging more beer. 'Whenever I see you, I think of the Shell. What a good woman she was.'

Gemma gave him a hug.

'So watcha doing these days?' he asked. 'Apart from getting yourself into strife. Haven't seen you for ages.'

'This and that,' she said. 'Busy looking into the disappearance of that girl from the flash ladies' college last year.'

'Everyone knows what happened to her!' said Kosta with a pitying look. He pulled out his cigarettes. 'That's old hat. You wanna know?'

Gemma pulled out her notebook. This was too easy.

'She ran away to Brisbane, to live with her dad.'

'And?'

'And that's where she is. She's no more disappeared than I am when the licensing demons come round.'

'So how come her body turns up wrapped in vinyl near Port Botany?'

'Shit! Is that what's happened?'

'That's what's happened.' She put her notebook away. 'Where did you get the Brisbane story?'

Kosta went all vague. 'Oh, everyone was saying so a while back. Her father was involved in a modelling agency when he was in Sydney. Used to have an office round here. Few doors up.'

Lauren Bernhard hadn't mentioned anything about that, thought Gemma. But then why would she? Could that have been the secret? She made a mental note to follow the lead. 'So how's your business?'

Kosta shrugged. 'I don't know whether it's this terrorism business or whether that new club in Darlinghurst is taking people away from me.' He picked up a business card and threw it to Gemma who caught it as it spun past.

'Deliverance,' she read. 'The very best in cool. Day or night. We deliver.' The 'D' of the club's name was a cleverly stylised razor blade cutting a line of powder.

'That's pretty bloody blatant,' she said. 'What are the cops doing about that?'

Kosta did his best Greek grimace, shrugging, mouth turned down. 'What do you think? Fuck all.'

Gemma frowned. 'I know how cops think. They might be turning a blind eye, or even getting a piece of it, but they wouldn't tolerate this being shoved right in their faces. They're practically advertising that they're dealing.'

'They did a few busts and got nowhere. The owners are pillars of the community. Rotarians, that sort of thing.'

'Who are they?' Gemma wanted to know.

'You'd know the names if I could remember them. Some bloody foreign name.' Kosta wasn't being ironic. 'Believe me, if I had any dirt on them, I'd be dishing it. They're the bloody competition. They're hurting me.'

Gemma glanced down at the provocative logo.

'But I reckon it's more than just a new club on the scene,' Kosta continued. 'You ask any of the girls. They'll tell you business is slow.'

Gemma handed him back the broom and picked up her briefcase, preparing to leave. 'You tell me anything you hear, right? About those schoolgirls.'

'Right.' He started sweeping. 'Know any good cleaners?'

Gemma walked back to her car second time around, checking every white Ford she passed. None of them contained the driver in the colourful shirt. She unhoused the radio and called Spinner. 'Where are you?' she asked.

'I was on my way home.'

'When you're not busy with Daria Reynolds, could you do some counter-surveillance for me from time to time over the next few days? If you see a white Ford sticking to me, I want to know.' She gave him the partial rego she'd noted down.

'I'll keep an eye on you, Boss,' said Spinner and called off.

•

Long experienced in making use of the girls' breathtaking network of information, Gemma drove to Baroque Occasions, the licensed brothel in Darlinghurst that her dead friend Shelly had paid off over many years, 'lying on her back'. Too many sex workers accumulated addictions and bad relationships rather than property. But Shelly, smart and educated, had left her daughter, Naomi, a two-storey terrace, nicely restored, with a couple of large rooms downstairs, a small kitchen and extra bathroom beyond, and two bedrooms and a luxurious spa bathroom upstairs.

'Come in, come in.' Naomi smiled, delighted to see her mother's old friend. 'What can I do for you?' In her shorts, T-shirt and bare feet, she looked fit, healthy and about fourteen. She wasn't that many years older but looking after her mother had caused Naomi to grow up fast and she was as savvy and sophisticated as many women twice her age. Like her mother, she wore no make-up when she wasn't working; her hair was in two streaming tails on either side of her head.

'I wondered if you'd heard anything on the street,' said Gemma. 'About the missing schoolgirls.'

Naomi shook her head.

'You look like you've just stepped out of an advertisement for Danish ice-cream,' Gemma continued. 'All scrubbed and wholesome.'

Naomi laughed. 'Want a cuppa?'

'Sure,' said Gemma. 'How's tricks?'

Naomi put two yellow cups on the table, pushing textbooks and an exercise book out of the way, turning down the radio. 'Not as many as I'd like. Business is slow. We had the Americans here for a few days and that was fantastic. I worked my arse off. In a manner of speaking. I thought you might be here because of Hugo.'

'Hugo?' Gemma was astonished at this mention of the Ratbag. She'd only recently been thinking of the boy. 'Don't tell me you've seen him!'

'Seen him? I had to hide him last night. He was on the run.'

'Tell me what happened,' said Gemma.

'He lobbed in here when I was doing my homework—about midnight, I guess. Don't laugh. I'm doing my HSC at tech. If it's a bit quiet of an evening, I duck out here and work on my assignments.' She indicated the pile of textbooks. 'He was tired and hungry. Hadn't eaten for a day or so. Said he'd had a fight with his mother and pissed off a couple of days ago. He'd been crashing at some guy's house but the guy wanted sex and it freaked him out. I was going to ring you about him but he'd gone by the time I got up. Which was late, nearly midday.'

'That's the second time he's done this,' said Gemma. 'Things must be tough at home.'

Naomi rolled her eyes as she poured Gemma's tea. 'Tell me when it's not.' She opened a cupboard. 'I've got some nice little bickies somewhere. Want one?'

Gemma nodded to the biscuits. 'If you see him again, Naomi, let me know fast, will you?'

'He's a great kid,' said Naomi. 'You'd think his parents would be proud of him.'

'Yeah.' Gemma picked up one of the books on the table. 'What's this like?' she said, holding up *The Big Sleep*.

'Haven't read it yet,' said Naomi. 'We're studying "Noir" fiction.'

'That won't be hard for you,' Gemma laughed. 'You live noir!'

Naomi tipped some Tiny Teddies onto a plate. 'I don't want to be selling my arse for too much longer. I'd like to get into managing places,' she said, nipping a teddy in half. 'I'd like to build up to a few houses. Good, safe, legitimate businesses. Classy service. That's what I'm aiming for. That was always Mum's dream. She never quite made it, but I could. I've got a couple of girls who'll work for me at very short notice if we need more staff. They're smart as tacks. Between us, we've got every sort of woman the mugs could want—mumsy, nursie, schoolgirl, dominatrix, water sports, SM. We offer every possible humiliation that money can buy!'

She laughed and pushed a long tail of blonde hair back over her shoulder. 'You wouldn't believe how weird some mugs are.' News on the hour started and Naomi turned the radio up a little.

Gemma went to the kettle and topped up her strong tea. 'Try me.'

'There's this guy who comes every week and prays over me.'

Gemma dunked a Tiny Teddy and lost it.

'He is truly weird. First he prays over me, then he gets me to undress and, while I'm doing that, he starts wanking. He wants me to do the same. So I do the Meg Ryan thing—very convincing.' She smiled. 'You can't imagine how weird a guy sounds when he's praying and wanking at the same time!'

'And that's it?'

Naomi nodded. 'He doesn't touch me. Then he prays over me again while I get dressed and off he goes.' She bit the head off a Tiny Teddy. 'I wish they were all as easy as that. Mum had her toe-sucker for years.'

'I should get out more,' said Gemma. 'I always learn something when I visit you.'

'I used to do these regular well-paid outcalls—sometimes with Robyn or sometimes just alone—for this mug who always had a friend with him. Fantastic house at Watsons Bay. Really classy. They were loaded, I reckon.' She finished the last of her tea. 'Lots of photographs of a big boat—a yacht or something—which the active one said belonged to him. The quiet one would pin me down while the other mug acted out his rape fantasy. I'd have to struggle and scream. They wanted to tie me up but that's something I've never allowed. As it was, I always got Kosta or someone to drive me there and wait outside. No way I'd do an outcall without security. I'd always offer the inactive one something.' Naomi grinned. 'Anything he wanted. Always looking for that extra buck for that extra fuck.' Her face grew serious again. 'But he never took me up on it.'

She stood up, carrying her empty cup to the sink. 'They were a strange pair. The inactive one was always waiting for me on this big leather lounge or the floor. He wasn't anything to look at, but the other one was a well-built, good-looking guy. Bit knocked around but a good body.'

'Maybe they were bi or something?'

'Who knows? It was always in the study—the office—and there were heaps of sporting trophies along a shelf. I never got the chance to see what they were for, but some of them had initials on them, like GPS or something. I asked them if they'd gone to private schools. For some reason, they found that very funny.' Naomi shrugged.

'Private schoolboys can be very up themselves,' said Gemma, feeling angry on Naomi's behalf.

'Wonder what happened to them? I lost two good-paying mugs.'

'Maybe the watcher found that Viagra works for him so he can do it himself,' Gemma suggested. She took her cup over to the sink and dropped it into the sudsy water, rinsing it and stacking it next to Naomi's.

Naomi's mobile rang and her normal voice vanished, replaced by her working voice: a breathy siren's, docile and accommodating.

Gemma signalled goodbye and drove home via Double Bay, thinking of families—of Shelly and her daughter Naomi; of her father and Kit and herself. And of her unknown sister. She had just pulled up outside her place when the radio crackled again.

'Tracker Three, copy, please.'

'Spinner? What is it?'

'I just followed you home. Picked you up at Baroque Occasions.'

Spinner, she thought. What a pro. She looked around. 'Where are you?'

She heard him laugh. 'On my way back to work. I left you at McPherson Street.'

Inside, her thoughts tumbling round, Gemma made coffee and a smoked salmon sandwich while Taxi smooched around her legs, purring like a V8. But when she finally gave him a piece of expensive salmon, he sniffed it and walked away. That's cats for you, she thought.

Up early the next day, Gemma determined to do as much work as possible in the morning and take a few hours in the afternoon to check through newspaper archives in the State Library, looking for her half-sister.

After breakfast, she set about rereading the witness statements. Looking up from time to time to let things sink in, this time she pinned down the something that had teased her yesterday. With her red pen, she drew a circle around it, isolating it from the rest of the print. She read through the other statements again and kept coming back to Claudia's.

It might be just an oversight on the part of the

witnesses, or things might have been different that morning because the bus was so crowded, but there it was—the discrepancy, or at least the possibility of one she'd been hoping for. There was absolutely nothing else that supported Claudia's claim that Amy had been sitting towards the front of the bus on the morning of the second of December. They always sat together. Why on that morning, of all mornings, had Amy not been with her two friends? And now that it wasn't possible to re-interview Tasmin Summers, there was only Claudia's word for how things had been that morning.

Gemma looked up in triumph to see pure white jet trails spiking the sky above her. A break, at last. Only a tiny one, but somewhere to start. She jumped up and hurried back inside to her office.

There were so many things she wanted to get onto, but she knew she needed to do an hour of paperwork before she got back to young Claudia and leaned on her a bit.

Her mobile rang. It was Angie, ringing from a public phone. 'Want to talk to you about something. Can I detour your way?'

'I'll be here,' Gemma said.

It seemed only a few minutes before Gemma glanced out the window to see Angie arriving, loaded with shopping bags.

'You've been busy,' said Gemma, taking some of the bags from her and following her down to the living room. On the radio, she heard Scott Brissett announcing his decision to sue the woman who'd made false allegations about him.

'I want a quick shower,' Angie said. 'And the use of your shampoo and blow-dryer.' She lifted up a shopping bag. 'I've got a new outfit and the shoes I bought last week.'

'I'll get you some clean towels.'

Angie dropped her briefcase on the table together with the shopping bags. 'Trevor's in town for a day and a night—sudden change of plans— and we want to make the most of it.' She started digging through her briefcase. 'There's a really nice photo of him in the *Police News*.' She pulled out a copy and opened it at a page with the corner bent down, passing it to Gemma.

There was Trevor, all tooled up, waving his baton around and firing off a blast from his capsicum spray, all the time with one eye on the photographer. Gemma looked closer at the regular features and smiling face. 'Hey!' she said. 'I remember him! I even worked with him once.'

'When? What job?' said Angie, suddenly alert.

'Give me a break, Ange. It must be ten years ago! I can hardly remember the details. But I remember him. He talked about that bad shooting at Bexley.'

'That's right. His partner shot a guy who was shooting at them. That's when Trevor decided to apply for the Terribly Rough Gentlemen,' Angie said, referring to the now disbanded Tactical Response Group. She took the magazine back, gazing fondly at her beloved, then pulled out a large envelope.

'Look,' she said, 'I could lose my job over this, but I want you to have a squizz at this.'

Gemma took the envelope and drew out a path report, frowning as she started to read it. 'It's the doc's findings on Amy Bernhard,' she said.

'That's right,' said Angie. 'I'm supposed to be passing it back to Bruno as soon as I've signed it.'

'Bruno?'

'He's supervising the investigation.'

'But he was taken off the case,' said Gemma, looking up from the document and remembering the memo she'd read. 'He was in charge of the first investigation and then removed from it. Remember that memo from Jim Buisman mixed up with the witness statements?'

'He's back with bloody bells on now,' said Angie.

'No wonder you're worried,' said Gemma. 'With Bruno G-for-Gross supervising and Sean Wright as a team member.'

'Exactly,' said Angie. 'I need all the help I can get. Most days, we've got a third of our people away. Sick leave, court attendances.'

'I've noticed something in the witness statements that I want you to see,' Gemma said. 'Go have your shower and I'll dig it out.'

While Angie showered, Gemma brought out the relevant statements and the phrases she'd underlined and placed them in a pile for Angie to look at. Then she read the autopsy report Angie had brought with her. Positive ID had been obtained via the gold chain recognised by Amy's mother and further confirmed by the dead girl's dentist.

Gemma flicked through the detailed weights and measurements until she came to the summing up. From the skeletonisation of the body, the post-mortem doctor believed that Amy had died very shortly after she'd disappeared. Some of the smallest bones were missing, probably through the action of scavenging animals. There were no visible signs of violence on the bones, the report stated, the only injuries being post-mortem. Rats had chewed through the blade of the left scapular, the tiny crescent-shaped bite marks were clear in the photographs. No obvious signs of violence, Gemma reflected, meant no ante-mortem breaks and none of the linear marks on bones that would indicate penetrating knife wounds. She recalled something one of the scientists had said to her years ago: 'Absence of evidence doesn't mean that evidence is absent', meaning it could just be harder to discern. The green and white nylon cord told an ominous story. Amy had been restrained. Gemma looked closer at the photos of the small length of cord that had been attached to the girl's right wrist. She spent some time with the tight close-up of the knot but it looked like a common reef knot. Nothing interesting there. She studied the pictures of the patterned vinyl—quarry-tile-type squares in soft terracotta.

Gemma was putting the report back into its envelope when Angie suddenly appeared, enveloped in a mist of steam, perfume and excitement and looking superb in her glamorous underwear. She slipped a clingy, slinky top over her head before pulling up her skirt and twisting to zip it up.

'What do you think, girlfriend?' she said, giving Gemma a flirtatious look.

Gemma smiled. 'Trevor is a lucky man.'

Angie plugged in the hair-dryer and dried her new haircut into a glossy curtain.

'We're meeting for lunch and staying at Graingers at the Rocks. Trev has to leave early in the morning. I'm on call tomorrow but I'm hoping to get some more shopping done. There's a gorgeous jewellery place down there, not far from the cop shop. Lovely gemstones.'

'Amy's body just lay there, under a pile of vinyl only a few metres away from a busy highway, for a year.'

'There's no pedestrian access,' Angie explained, straightening up and switching the dryer off at the mains. 'Okay. How does that look?'

'See for yourself,' said Gemma, indicating the mirror on the wall opposite the dining table. 'Very, very gorgeous.'

Angie stood in front of it, patting and fluffing her hair, turning her head from side to side. 'The piece of land she was found on is part of a Water Board easement. There's no reason for anyone to ever go there. Unless, of course, they wanted to dump a body. The grass and weeds were almost up to my waist when we went out there.'

Gemma tapped the envelope containing the post-mortem report. 'Thanks for this. Any joy with that vinyl or the nylon cord?'

'We've sent photos off to all the manufacturers. Should hear back from the makers soon, I hope.'

'And the knot?'

'That's gone to our knot man,' Angie said then started laughing.

'What?'

'His name. You'll never believe it. Mr Colin Roper.'

'Remember Sergeant Basham?'

Angie laughed again. 'He bashed 'em all right.'

'Talking of mean bastards,' Gemma said, 'I'd really like to know why G-for-Gross was taken off the investigation when Amy first disappeared last year.'

Angie turned from the mirror. 'You think he'd say something.'

'You were involved in it at the same time. I thought you'd have noticed his unique presence.'

'That was only after Amy had been missing for months. I got the feeling the case had been neglected because of understaffing. Bruno definitely wasn't involved by the time I was on it.'

Angie put the envelope with the post-mortem report back into her briefcase. 'You said you'd spotted something in the witness statements?' she said.

'Yes,' said Gemma. 'Take another look at this.' She pushed the copies of the witness statements across the table. She'd marked the relevant bits with bright pink highlighter.

Angie read through them a couple of times. 'That's interesting.' She pushed them back. 'I'll let you follow that up. And then you can brief me. I'm flat-strap at the moment trying to push for more resources. We've got one lousy computer between the five of us. Julie Cooper and Sean are supposed to be assisting us—when they've got the time away from their stuff at Child Protection. We've got the use of one car. And Bruno's supervising. Which means not doing a goddamn thing if he can avoid it. But you can bet he'll be there as soon as a press conference is called, preening his bloody tail feathers.' She shot Gemma a cheeky look. 'I hope he was better in the cot than he is in the job.'

Gemma grabbed the dryer, switched it on and chased Angie round the room.

After sending her friend off prepared for an afternoon and night of love, Gemma spent far too much time doing her BAS statement—already overdue—and cursing John Howard and all those who'd believed his claims of 'simpler tax-paying'.

Next, she called the number Lauren Bernhard had given her for her first ex-husband. But Amy's father wasn't answering so she left a message with her number. Then she called Eric Stokes, Amy Bernhard's stepfather, who answered straightaway.

'Fathers for Family and Marriage. How can I help you?'

'Eric Stokes?'

'And you are?'

'Gemma Lincoln. I'm an investigator working on behalf of Netherleigh Park for Beatrice de

Berigny. I'd like to make an appointment to speak to you about your stepdaughter, Amy.'

He'd know by now, she thought. But just in case, she hadn't said 'late stepdaughter'.

There was a short silence. 'I can make time for you tomorrow,' he said.

Gemma arranged a time and put the mobile down. It was telling, she thought, that he'd said nothing about his stepdaughter. Nothing at all.

She took her car into the city, found a spot in a parking station and started the search for her half-sister at the State Library, viewing microfilm. It was a slow, painful business finding the Births, Deaths and Marriages section, then slowly scrolling through them. She found a couple of Chisholms but the mother's name wasn't the Kingston she was searching for. And the babies were male. After what felt like hours, she looked up, her neck stiff. She stretched, wishing she had enough money to delegate this boring job to someone else. But she needed Spinner and Mike out on the road if she was going to rebuild her business. She'd have to do a lot more of the boring jobs herself until things picked up.

She was up to March of the *Daily Telegraph*'s listings when she looked at her watch again. Around her, people searched or scribbled, heads down, absorbed in their own quests. Maybe this is a wild goose chase, she thought. Maybe Beverley Kingston never advertised the birth. After all, the baby wasn't 'legitimate'.

She walked out onto the steps. It was a glorious

late afternoon—a cloudless, pearly sky and the trees of the Botanical Gardens an intense dark green on black across the road. A couple of very early bats flapped overhead and a sudden wave of fear took her breath away. She took some deep breaths and remembered her trainer's words about SA, situational awareness. She took stock of the people striding or driving past. None seemed to have the slightest interest in her. Her mobile buzzed and she dug it out, grateful for the distraction. It was Andrew Bernhard, Amy's father, returning her message.

'I'm in Sydney and free right now,' he said. They agreed to meet in half an hour in a café near the hotel where Bernhard was staying in the Cross.

Gemma returned to the Domain parking station, the haunted feeling hastening her steps. As she pulled out in her car, she checked her rear-vision mirror. No white Ford appeared. She drove up to the Cross and found a parking spot near Darlinghurst police station.

She quickly spotted a man in the café talking on his mobile in the corner seat as Andrew Bernhard. She dawdled outside for a few moments, pretending to examine the cakes in the window while she checked him out. He was a handsome, heavy-built man in his late forties, well-dressed and completely focused on his telephone conversation. Gemma watched a little longer then went inside, heading straight for his table.

Andrew Bernhard looked up as she approached and almost immediately rang off, half stood and put his hand out. They shook and Gemma sat down, putting her briefcase at her feet. As soon as she'd neared him, his demeanour had changed. Now he was the grieving father. You're a con man, she thought.

After offering her condolences, Gemma cut to the chase. 'Someone told me that Amy ran away to Brisbane. Before she disappeared. What can you tell me about that?'

He shook his head. 'That's not so,' he said. 'Amy didn't ever come to Brisbane.'

'But maybe she contacted you? Told you she was coming? Wanted to show you her modelling portfolio?'

'I've already told you,' he said. 'She didn't come to Brisbane. She didn't contact me. I know nothing about a modelling portfolio.' He gathered up his mobile. 'I told my ex-wife I'd talk to you about what Amy was like, that sort of thing. I'm not here to be interrogated by you.' He rose from his seat. 'Now, if you'll excuse me, I must go. We have a funeral to organise.'

Gemma stood with him. 'Are you saying you weren't involved in a modelling agency? That there was—is no such agency?'

'You have no authority to ask me anything.'

'Mr Bernhard,' Gemma said, 'why do I get the feeling that you're not committed to any investigation into what happened to your daughter.'

'I don't have to talk to you,' he said.

She passed her card to him. 'If you think of

anything that might cast some light on Amy or her state of mind when she went missing, please ring me.'

Andrew Bernhard left, leaving her card on the table.

On her homeward drive in the golden evening light, Gemma took a diversion and found the Belle-vue Hill address that Beatrice de Berigny had given her for the family of Tasmin Summers. Behind a four-wheel-drive tank in the driveway, she noticed an unmarked car. So, she thought, detectives were inside.

She sat in the car for a while, taking in the large white house with timber verandahs facing north-east over Rose Bay and thence out to sea. A formal garden curved down to the stone wall. Proserpine Avenue was definitely a multimillion-dollar address. Was this another family home where huge amounts of money, a father away on military exer-cises and a mother preoccupied with her work, provided the background for a disappearing daughter? Gemma called Mrs Summers on the number provided by Miss de Berigny, but could only leave a message on voice mail.

Gemma found herself thinking of Claudia Page and the grand mausoleum in which she and her mother lived. Claudia must be feeling very vulner-able right now. Time to lean on her.

She rang the Page household. Claudia answered. 'I'm sitting outside your friend Tasmin's house,' Gemma said. 'It made me think of you. Are you okay?'

'I think so.' The girl's voice was strained, tremulous.

'It might be a good idea to stay home for a while. I'm sure Miss de Berigny could ask your class teachers to send home whatever work is required.'

'Mum's already got me staying home. She reckons I'll be safer here, too. But I'm going crazy stuck here all day. And Mum's on my back all the time about practising. It's all she thinks of.' A pause. 'Does anyone know what's happened to Tasmin yet?'

'Claudia, I've seen the witness statement you gave the police. And Tasmin's. Do you want to change anything you wrote in that?'

She heard the sharp catch in the girl's breath. 'Change what? I don't know what you mean!'

'Why wasn't Amy sitting with you and Tasmin that morning?'

'She was. We always sat together.'

It's hard to remember a lie told a year ago, Gemma thought, because it's not located in your recall of past events. Truth, on the other hand, stays available, as part of the sequence in memory.

'In your statement,' Gemma reminded her, 'you said you saw Amy sitting at the front of the bus.'

'Did I? Then she must have been.' The answer was too quick, defensive.

'I'm surprised you forgot that. Seeing it was the last time you were ever to see your friend again.'

There was silence on the line.

'You all caught the bus at the turnaround stop,'

said Gemma quietly. 'You always sat together in the seat across the back window. But that morning Amy didn't sit with you. I want to know why. I want to know why, on the morning of her disappearance, Amy did something different.'

Again, the long silence, then, 'Mum's home. I've got to go.'

Gemma pressed on. 'I'm going to keep working on those witness statements, Claudia. And the witnesses. I'm determined to get to the truth.'

There was a click as Claudia rang off. Gemma cursed, angry with herself. She hadn't handled that very sensitively. Maybe, she thought, if she hadn't lost her mother so early, she'd be better at this sort of thing. Whatever the case, she needed to find a way to break through the girl's evasiveness.

Gemma drove home and went immediately into her office where she checked the spare laptop for the images being transmitted from Mrs Annie Dunlop's living room. But the program wouldn't run. She'd done a test run as soon as she got back after Mike had installed the camera and it had been working perfectly. She scribbled a note for Mike to organise a visit to check the installation and the program as soon as possible.

She flung herself on the lounge and Taxi pounced on her, making bread on her stomach. Briefly, she wished she was a nice normal housewife, doing whatever they did at this time of day. Making school lunches for the next day, watching television. Feeling wilful and guilty, she dialled Steve's number but went straight through to voice mail. She hung up again. She had no right of appeal. Even if he picked up the phone when she rang, what could she say to him that would change what had happened? *Look at yourself, Gemma*, he'd said. As if the fight and resulting separation had been somehow all her doing.

She felt restless and unhappy and couldn't settle in for the evening, she had no appetite. Somewhere, Angie and Trevor were feeding each other oysters and champagne. Somewhere, Steve was getting on without her. Somewhere, the slender bones of a young girl, her shoulder blade chewed by rats, awaited burial. And somewhere, a young woman of thirty-three or four—with half her genes the same as Gemma's—was going about her business. She lay back on the lounge. What about her own life? Did she fill it up with other people's dramas because she didn't feel enough on her own? Was that what Steve had meant? He'd been offering her himself, wanting to buy a place with her, where they could build a life together.

Gemma put Taxi gently down on the ground. Her first job was to find out what happened to Amy Bernhard. Now get on with it, she scolded.

But she couldn't get on with it. Memories of happy times with Steve would not let her go. She had a bath but that didn't settle her either. She felt edgy and restless and the crack in her heart, instead of healing over, seemed to be widening. Wrapped in two towels, she went into her bedroom and, flinging open the wardrobe, looked through her clothes, finding herself drawn to a cheeky black skirt and a white scoop-neck spandex singlet edged with black diamantés. She inspected her shoes and decided on black high-heeled sandals with diamanté ankle strap. If she fell off those, she'd need to be medivaced home. She practised walking in them until she found her equilibrium, grabbed her briefcase, pulled out her purse and stashed the credit card in her bedside drawer so that she couldn't get into too much trouble. She stashed two fifties and her mobile in her little square evening bag. Just about the right size to stow a man's heart in, she'd joked when she'd bought it.

Locking up, she went up to the road to her car, admiring the way her legs looked in the diamanté ankle-strapped heels. Damn it, she thought, swinging them into the car and slamming the door, she'd check out Deliverance as well as the talent. Ask a few questions. She was a free woman. A cutting-edge nightclub might be just the thing to mend a single Sydney woman's broken heart. And she hadn't forgotten how to party.

Gemma parked a few streets behind the main drag, wishing she'd brought some flat shoes for the walk up. Most of the businesses around here had closed down, apart from those servicing tourists. She cut through one of the smaller streets swaying gracefully, she hoped, on the impossible heels, passing by the rear entrances of the takeaway places and tourist shops. Finally, she turned into Macleay Street. The doorman outside Deliverance gave her an appraising look and greeted her. It had been ages since Gemma had done anything like this and for a second she regretted it, wishing herself safely and boringly at home with Taxi on her lap. But once inside, the driving rhythm of the DJ's selections blotted out anything cerebral and she fronted the bar, checking the list of drinks on the wall. The place was packed and she understood what Kosta had been grizzling about.

Gemma ordered something called Liquid Cocaine and watched while the barman poured double vodka, topping it up with white wine and Red Bull. He swirled it all together and put it in front of her, announcing the price as if he was proud of it. When he came back, Gemma surveyed her change from one of the fifties. At this rate, she wouldn't be drinking too much.

'This is a great club,' she gushed. 'Who owns it?'

The barman shrugged. 'I just work here,' he said.

She went to a table in a corner, away from the throng near the bar. Around her, fragments of words and even whole phrases kicked in between the surges of the music. Looking around, she noticed a number of Sydney celebrities—a glamorous newsreader, a famous soap actor and a criminal lawyer among other vaguely familiar faces. She also noticed small packets being pushed across table tops and knew the people involved weren't playing Pass the Parcel. A tall girl, her sparkling dress looking as if it had been glued onto her, staggered past Gemma's table, brushing something from under her nose. Gemma felt sure that one or two of the bulky men who were moving round the tables were off-duty cops and wished Angie were with her—she might even know their names.

She finished her drink too quickly. Liquid Cocaine, she discovered, tended to make the drinker feel reckless, especially when taken on an empty stomach. So she went back to the bar and ordered Sex on the Beach. It might be the closest she was going to get to doing the wild thing for some time. The barman mixed an alarming mêlée of peach schnapps, vodka and various fruit juices topped up with champagne. A young man made a half-hearted attempt to pick her up, but very quickly changed the focus of his attention when the girl in the glued-on dress collapsed herself onto his lap.

Later, common sense warned her against the Pink Pussy—vodka, pink champagne and pink lemonade—but by then she was halfway through it. With something like half a bottle of vodka alone, not to mention the other forms of alcohol starting to compromise her system, Gemma knew it was time to leave. She managed to walk quite normally into the night air—warm and gently putrid after the icy air conditioning inside Deliverance. She knew she shouldn't drive, so rang for a cab. The first available car would be sent, but there was a delay. Gemma waited for what seemed a long time, plenty of cabs driving by, but all engaged. From time to time she had to fend off men who tried it on. She removed her high heels, wishing she could ring Steve to come and pick her up. Then she thought of Mike. He'd bailed her out once before. Feeling a little self-conscious, she called him.

'Sure,' he said. 'I've just put my target to bed. Where are you?'

He arrived so quickly that Gemma, thinking an attempt was being made on her honour, stepped back in alarm when a car pulled up at the kerb. Then she saw Mike leaning across the front seat, holding the door open.

'Am I glad to see you,' she said and scrambled in, holding the diamanté sandals, her legs feeling far less reliable than the pair she'd been using when she left her place. 'These damn things were killing me.' She sank back gratefully. 'My cab hasn't showed and it's been ages.' She realised she was quite affected by alcohol and regretted not eating earlier.

He looked her up and down. 'What are you doing here?'

'I thought it was a good idea to check this place out. It's a dealer's paradise in there.'

Gemma settled back and watched Kings Cross going about its business before they headed down the hill to Rushcutters Bay. She was intensely aware of Mike's presence, even his scent, which was a comforting mixture of clean male and some other spice. Thinking dreamily how nice it was to be driven home safely like this, it was a jolt when the car stopped and she realised Mike was pulling up outside her place. The evening was still warm and as he switched the ignition off, the tune on the radio, inaudible till then, suddenly came into focus.

'Oh, I love this song,' she said, leaning forward to turn it up. Mike moved to do the same and they collided, then apologised together. This made her laugh. *'I know, it's only rock 'n' roll,'* screamed the singer. 'But I like it,' Gemma and Mike sang together. Gemma grinned. Bugger the neighbours. She felt about seventeen as they belted out the song together. And when Mike leaned over and gently kissed her, she experienced only a second of indecision before kissing him back, hard and hot, winding her arms around him, dislodging herself from her seat, moving over against him, trying to negotiate the gear stick. Everything went hot, hard and fast. Mike scooped her up and started pushing her dress away from her knees, running his hand along her thigh. Gemma was dimly aware of 'Wild Horses' as she lost herself in the kiss. Finally she broke away, panting. 'I'd better go.'

But despite her intentions, she remained, staring at him, as if seeing him for the very first time, unsure of this exciting stranger she'd discovered wearing the body of a colleague. She couldn't leave the car, she couldn't do anything except kiss him again, this time more desperately. Her blood crashed loud and hot in her ears. Through the heat and the vodka, Gemma heard a tiny voice say, 'Stop this now and say goodnight. You can put it down to the Liquid Cocaine and Pink Pussies. All you'll have to do is apologise in the morning.' But another, more urgent voice was saying, 'Do it, do it now! In the car, like kids! It will be so good!'

She couldn't remember feeling this degree of

desire for ages. She pressed against Mike's strong body, yearning to get closer, her hand closed over his crotch, cupping his penis. Heat haze and Mike's mouth close to her ear.

'Come on, Gemma. Not here,' he said.

But she wilfully struggled for his belt. 'I want to liberate you.' She thought that was very funny. 'But I can't find your buckle.'

She tried swinging herself over to get on top of him. But she bumped her knee into the steering wheel, the other grazing painfully against the clasp of her evening bag, forcing it open, spilling the mobile and coins over the passenger seat.

He indicated the flat but she was too fired up. 'No, let's do it here,' she breathed into his ear. Again, she swivelled on her right knee, struggling to get her left leg over to straddle him. But there was something unyielding under her right knee as she moved. Damn it, she thought. If it was the evening bag, she'd break the bloody thing, although right now she hardly cared. She moved her knee off it and stopped worrying about whether or not she might be breaking anything because now she was in position, kneeling over Mike, with only the fabric of her knickers and his jeans between them. Finally, she unzipped him and his cock sprang out to meet her.

'I can't wait!' she said. 'I want you inside me.' She pulled her knickers out of the way and started to lower herself onto him. At the same time, Mike began to press himself home. Words formed in her head of how good this felt but she was past speaking them. The softness of his kiss contrasted with the hardness of his erection. Gemma gasped, thinking she might die of pleasure. Through her rising excitement came another sound. A voice. A very familiar voice.

'Gemma? Gemma?' Gemma froze. It was Steve.

'Shit!' Mike hissed. 'He's on the bloody phone!'

Gemma's desire and Mike's cock fell away.

'What the hell's going on?' Steve's disembodied voice. 'Did you call me just so I could hear you screwing another man?'

She scrambled off Mike, almost kneeing him in the face, adjusting her clothing, struggling to find the mobile.

'Steve? I didn't mean to ring. I must have pressed your number by accident.'

The effects of the drinks evaporated. Now Gemma's mind was horribly focused. Steve was on the phone and he'd heard everything since she'd knelt on her mobile. Beside her, Mike zipped himself up, rebuckled his belt.

'It's not like that,' she said, feeling honest because now it certainly wasn't like that. 'It's just Mike here with me. We're back from a job. We were having a chat and I must have pressed your number by mistake.'

She heard him click off before she'd finished and she switched the mobile off. Clutching it, she swore, leaning forward. She felt the biggest fool in the world. She'd practically tried to ravish Mike, and meanwhile God knows how long Steve had been on the line. This was the worst thing to have happened. Beside her, Mike stared straight ahead. She'd insulted him as well, belittled him with her dishonesty. He'd heard her make him part of a pathetic, cowardly lie.

'I'd better go,' she said, wishing she'd done so about six minutes ago.

'Yes.' He still didn't look at her. 'I think that's the best idea.'

Gemma got out of the car on legs that would barely hold her up, clutching her evening bag and the sandals. She felt nauseous. All the vodka sloshed together in the pit of her stomach and drained down into her shaky legs. Suddenly the diamanté sandals seemed pitiful and ridiculous.

Managing to get down the steps and through the front garden, Gemma grabbed at the mail on autopilot. She heard Mike's car pull away as the outside light came on and she fumbled her door open. Staggering in, she dumped the letters and the sandals on the hall table.

'God,' she said out loud, falling on the blue leather lounge. 'That was so pathetic!' How could she make what had just happened somehow unhappen? She didn't know what part of it was worse: her attempt on Mike or the fact that Steve had heard her practically having sex with another man.

Taxi clicked across the floorboards and jumped on her stomach, settling down in a ball. His warm weight was a comfort once the nausea eased. She stayed there for a while, nursing her misery. Despite the amount of alcohol in her system, sleep was out of the question. Soon, probably tomorrow or the next day, she would have to face Mike again. How could she have hurt both him and Steve in one fell swoop?

Gemma bowed over and hung her head between her knees before rallying and making some Milo, then sat staring sightlessly at an English comedy. Eventually, she took half a Mogadon and went to bed.

SEVEN

The ringing of her mobile dragged Gemma out of bottomless sleep. She made a few lunges for it, pushing Taxi out of the way.

'Hullo?' She struggled to wake up through the storm of a splitting headache and the full awfulness of last night's memories. The front seat of Mike's car. Steve on her mobile. She flinched again and not only because the woman on the line was screaming in her ear.

'You were supposed to help me! He's just been here! Where were you? You went through the house with me! I paid you! You were supposed to stop him!'

Gemma sat up in bed. It was actually a relief to have an angry client to deal with. It kept her mind off the cringing embarrassment that welled up and spilled over whenever she thought of last night. 'Mrs Reynolds, Daria. Please calm down.' She glanced at her watch. It wasn't yet five in the morning and the east was lightening in a streak above the sea. 'I'll contact my operative and see what he's got on video.'

'I don't need video! I need you to be there! You were supposed to stop this from ever happening again!'

'Daria, listen to me. Our brief was to get evidence of your ex-husband getting into your house. My operative wasn't instructed to act against him. He can't do that. We have to be very careful about that sort of thing. The police—'

'The police! They're useless and so are you! I thought you were the right person, but you failed me!'

This was going nowhere. As decently as she could, Gemma said goodbye and rang off. The phone immediately rang again and she switched it over to voice mail. She threw herself back on the bed. What was the woman going on about? The right person indeed. The right idiot, thought Gemma, reliving last night's atrocious embarrassment. How different it all looked in the clean white light of early morning without a belly full of booze. There was no way back to sleep—her mind was racing with regret and frustration. It was only 5 a.m. and she couldn't deal with this without strong coffee and a shower. Her head throbbing, she made up a cocktail of vitamins and aspirin, swallowing it down with water and fighting a gag reflex for a few seconds after.

By the time she'd come out from the shower with clean hair, a glowing body and coffee aroma filling the air, the sun was shining radiant gold light over a brilliant blue ocean. She poured herself a coffee and went down the hall to her office. She was going to have to contact Mike, she knew. Apologise. But there was nothing she could do about Steve. The pain in her heart wasn't the sort that analgesics could touch.

Once she had some of her brain cells firing, she radioed Spinner. 'Base here, Tracker Three. Copy, please.'

Spinner's radio crackled into life. 'Copy, Boss.'

'I've just fielded a hysterical phone call from Daria Reynolds,' Gemma said. 'I'm surprised you couldn't hear it from where you are. Which is?'

'Across the road from her place. I saw the lights go on half an hour ago.'

'That's about when she was abusing me! Yelling at me that her ex got in again.'

There was silence on the radio, just the occasional crackling of the frequency and the distant distortions of other voices as an aircraft flew in, breaking the curfew.

'What? No one came near the place,' said Spinner. 'I've been here since about nine last night. I can tell you everything that moved in this street since.'

'That's not what she's saying. You should've heard her.'

'The woman's a nutter. Probably got the horrors. All those idols in the house. Think about it—how the hell could anyone get in? She's got technical surveillance everywhere and me sitting out here wasting my life as well. She's got more money than sense.'

'You sure you didn't doze? It's easy enough to do.' Any surveillance operative knew that a moment's inattention could be the moment the target moves. And usually was. Even an ace worker like Spinner might have had a lapse from pristine vigilance. There's a first time for everything, Gemma thought.

'I did not doze.' Spinner's voice sounded hurt. 'And even if I did, which I bloody didn't, those external cameras are movement-activated. They automatically film anything that moves and I'm alerted via the laptop. And all the cameras are live.'

'Okay, okay,' said Gemma.

'Look,' he said, 'if it'll relieve your mind, I'll review everything captured on the memory and ring back. Okay?'

'Okay.'

She called off and went back to the living room, sprawling on the blue leather armchair. Taxi had clawed holes all up one side, so that it looked like a sieve. He didn't care that she'd paid over three thousand dollars for it and the matching lounge. To him, it was just a top scratching post. She checked the message on her voice mail. It was more of the same from Daria Reynolds. The way she phrased her complaints made the event sound like Gemma's fault. As if she didn't feel bad enough already. It was definitely past time to talk to Diane Hayworth at Waverley police, Gemma decided, the officer whose card she'd seen at Daria's place.

Gemma did a couple of hours in her office, clearing email, sorting and finalising several accounts. She neatly bound the surveillance reports that she or Mike or Spinner had done together with any video evidence ready to be given to the clients, along with the bill. She totalled up what she could expect in the next few weeks and it wasn't as much as she'd hoped. The thought of approaching the bank again made her heart sink. She reviewed her job sheet. There was plenty to be getting on with and no time to waste, she told herself sternly. She cleared her desk, cleared her throat and rang Waverley police station, asking to speak to Diane Hayworth. She wanted to gather as much intelligence as she could on Daria Reynolds and her ex.

'She'll be in later. Can I take a message?' came the reply.

Gemma said who she was, and asked if Diane Hayworth could ring her as soon as convenient and glanced at her watch. Heading down the hall to see whether any of the mail she'd dumped on the table last night contained cheques, she picked up the diamanté sandals as well, stopping when she heard a sound. Someone was moving around in the top apartment. Gemma went outside and looked up. The For Lease sign was no longer there. Please don't let it be Mike, she thought, clutching the sandals and feeling sick. She couldn't bear that. But surely he'd have mentioned it again if he were about to move in?

Back inside, Gemma glanced at her desk diary and realised she had a couple of hours to fill before her meeting with Eric Stokes, president of Fathers for Family and Marriage. She retrieved her car, reparked it closer to the city then caught the bus into the State Library, continuing her search through the microfilm stocks of old newspapers.

After an hour of useless searching, her mobile rang and, aware of the disapproving glances around her, she hastily gathered up her belongings and took the call out to the foyer.

'We've got to talk about last night, Gemma,' said Mike, taking the initiative. She should have rung first, Gemma realised. Now she'd have to cop this one sweet.

'Mike,' she started, 'I was completely out of order. I'd had three cocktails in a very short time. I'm not making excuses, just letting you know the reason for my behaviour. I'm really sorry that I made such a fool of myself. And that I did it with you, of all people. A valued workmate.' Feeling the blood burning in her cheeks and her heart pounding in her ears, she glanced around the foyer, sure that everyone was listening to her.

'It wasn't all you,' he said. 'I made the first move. And I was a willing party from there. I should have escorted you to the door and said goodnight. Not sat in the car with you, singing old songs.'

'It's not the singing old songs that worries me.'

There was a long silence during which she remembered, with excruciating clarity, the moves she'd made. 'We need to talk about this face to face,' she said eventually. 'Meanwhile, can I ask a work-related question?' She'd just remembered her scribbled note about Mrs Dunlop's webcam.

'Try me,' he said, sounding miserable.

'Can you check the connection at Mrs Dunlop's? I tried to view her place last night and got zilch.' She paused. 'You remember her and her animal?'

'I'll have a look. It was working fine last time I checked.'

She said goodbye and rang off. A lot of things were working fine before, she thought as she started the walk back to her car.

Eric Stokes lived in a dark-brick block of flats in Potts Point. Gemma found the flat number she was looking for and brought all her attention to the job ahead of her, putting aside as much as she could of the previous night's embarrassing memories. She went down some steps and along a crazy-tiled path littered with junk mail and the occasional unclaimed bill until she came to the front door and pressed his flat number. He buzzed her in and she walked through a foyer carpeted in faded red. A large container of dusty plastic flowers stood on a table in front of a segmented mirror from the fifties.

Gemma·took a deep breath and knocked on Eric Stokes's door. She heard his heavy tread and the door opened.

Stokes wasn't much taller than Gemma. He was wearing black jeans and a checked shirt. With a thick moustache, longish hair and a furrowed face, he reminded her of a hard-drinking, hard-living country and western singer.

'Come in, Miss Lincoln,' he said, shaking her hand with a grip that was unforgiving. 'Excuse the mess.'

Gemma followed him into a room that stank of ashtrays and where bookshelves along all available wall space overflowed with untidy files and binders. A large desk at the end of the room was also piled high. 'I'm president of the FFM association as you probably know. At the moment, we haven't got a secretary or a treasurer and I'm doing everything.'

'I'm here to talk about Amy,' said Gemma, watching him closely. 'I won't take any more of your time than is necessary.'

He removed a pile of folders from an old armchair. 'Take a seat,' he said.

Gemma perched on the edge of the chair, not wanting to sink into it—it was far too low to be comfortable. Around her, photographs of her host in family groups or posing with his rifle over various dead animals caught her attention. Looking more closely, she saw that the photographs showed Stokes with two different family groups. It seemed Eric Stokes had been on a second marriage too.

'Fire away,' he said.

Gemma looked back at him from the photographs. 'Could you describe your relationship with Amy Bernhard?'

He perched on a stool near the desk, pulling out a packet of cigarettes and offering her one. 'Do you mind?' he asked with a smile that wasn't very convincing. Gemma shook her head. He lit up and cocked one leg horizontally across the other. Now she could see he was wearing riding boots. You are a cowboy, Eric Stokes, she thought. A rootin', shootin' cowboy with two marriages, a lot of dead animals and a smoking habit.

'Amy wasn't an easy kid to get along with,' he finally said. 'She never really accepted me.'

'It must be hard for a young girl when her father's place is taken by a stranger.'

He didn't like that. 'I was a better father to her than her real father. At least I was there.'

Gemma realised she'd have to tread very carefully. This was a man, she reminded herself, who'd been dismissed as unsatisfactory by two women already. 'Did Amy appreciate the fact that you were there?'

He didn't answer straightaway but inhaled on the cigarette and looked away.

'I don't think she ever saw the real me,' he said eventually. 'She was just pissed off all the time. That I'd taken the place of her father. Nothing I did was good enough.' He paused. 'It was hard. I tried to be there for her.'

'How did you do that?'

Again, the long pause. Was he reflecting so as to answer truthfully, or spending time creating answers that he thought she'd like to hear?

'I talked with her about things. Tried to get the right values into her. But it was no use. Her mother had no control. No discipline. See, the trouble with the kids of today is that they don't have any discipline. In my day, you didn't dare speak to adults the way kids do today. We were taught respect. We got a boot up the arse if we didn't.'

Gemma tried to imagine Eric Stokes being of any use whatever to a young girl and failed in the attempt.

'I hear you still go there to the house? That you and your friends spend time—' She caught herself just in time from saying 'hanging round' and finished, 'outside your ex-wife's house.'

'We vigil,' he said. 'We hold our vigils to bring attention to the destruction of the sanctity of marriage in this society. We're men who've been cut out of the lives of our women and children.' The way he said the last phrase made Gemma think of covered wagons and the Wild West. Was that how Eric Stokes saw marriage and family?

'Mr Stokes, I'm here because you are a person who was connected to Amy at one stage. Do you have any idea who or what might have caused her disappearance?'

Stokes picked up a framed photograph that had been lying face down on his crowded desk. He passed it to her. 'Look at this. This picture says it all. We were all getting along fine,' he said.

I don't think so, Gemma thought, as she studied the picture. Lauren and Eric had their arms around each other, but Amy was standing apart from both of them, a lost little girl, glaring at the photographer. Gemma studied her. Had her own face worn that look as a teenager, she wondered.

She passed the photograph back. 'I'm surprised the police didn't take a statement from you.'

'They wanted one. I was away pig-shooting near Bourke when Amy disappeared and when I got back they expected me to go down to the police station and make a statement. As if I'd had something to do with it.' He paused. 'I told them I had better things to do with my time than waste it hanging round police stations and if they wanted a statement from me, they could damn well come to my place and get it.' He almost spat with contempt. 'Naturally, no one ever came round to pick it up.'

'So you've done a statement?' said Gemma. Angie would be interested to hear that.

'Of course I have. I don't have anything to hide. I wrote it out myself. But no one bothered to get it from me.'

'I think the police prefer it if you go to a police station and do it there.'

'I'm sure they do,' he said. 'They've got fancier ways of verballing people.'

'Did you go away for long?'

He leaned back on the stool, sizing her up, she thought. 'I was with a couple of mates.'

'Other members of FFM?'

'That's none of your business.'

Gemma decided to lean on him. 'You probably know, Mr Stokes, that statistics show stepfathers are the most dangerous men in the lives of adolescent girls?'

Eric Stokes's whole physical presence became larger, more menacing, and the skin of his face reddened behind the moustache. Gemma was pleased she was perched on the edge of the chair, ready to bolt. Pleased, too, that he wasn't between her and the doorway.

'Now that sort of remark,' he said, 'is exactly the kind of filth that the lesbian so-called psychologists try to foist on people! It's the sort of shit I'd expect from all those weirdos who want homosexual marriages and all that garbage. I'm a person who's trying to bring back normality—to uphold the sanctity of marriage, not destroy it! That's just crap!'

'Unfortunately,' Gemma kept her voice mild, 'it's not crap. And it's not meant as a personal insult to you. It's a fact of criminal statistics.'

'I've told you—she never accepted me. Stuck-up little girl with all her fancy girlfriends from that fancy college.' Eric Stokes's chip was revealing itself to be bigger with every word he spoke. He wagged his cigarette at her. 'I did everything I could to win her over. She was just a stubborn, difficult girl. She needed to be taught a lesson about respect.'

Here we go again, Gemma thought. How was it, she wondered, that people who were so contemptuous of others somehow expected 'respect' in return? She kept her voice very low. 'And were you the person who thought he should teach her that lesson?'

Gemma was suddenly aware of a silence. The poky flat with its piles of folders and files was now still. Nor was there a sound from the foyer beyond the front door. Even the street outside was oddly quiet. It was as if Stokes's fury had frozen everything into immobility. Suddenly he crushed his cigarette and stood up. 'I think you'd better go.'

Gemma didn't like the idea of having to get up in front of him, and hated the idea of him walking behind her. She was spooked, every instinct warning danger. She stood up and took a diagonal side-step, always keeping him in her line of sight, ready to bolt at the first sign of overt aggression. Then she was at the door and he loomed in front of her to open it. She stepped outside, nodded to him and heard him slam the door behind her. It wasn't until she unlocked the door of her car that she realised her legs were shaking.

She left a message for Angie that Eric Stokes had made a statement and that it would need to be collected from his flat. Was this yet another of Bruno Gross's omissions?

Gemma needed to get rid of some excess nervous energy so she drove to the Maroubra Seals gym. She parked and grabbed her gym clothes from the boot of the car, slinging the bag over her shoulder. Overhead, an international jet made its approach, landing gear lowered, heading into the south-westerly.

The gym had been refurbished some time ago and was filled with gleaming new machines. Gemma missed the old days before the gym upgrade. Gone were the club ladies with their perfectly set hair and white plastic earrings who'd pedal the exercise bike for a few minutes between fags, then go back downstairs to the pokies. Now, serious young people in lycra sweated into designer headbands. Gemma worked her way through several of the machines, until her legs ached and sweat ran down her forehead. She wanted to look as good as Angie had in her underwear. Not that there was anyone round to notice, she thought, as she finished on the stepper. She had a quick sauna, a shower and hurried outside, glowing with virtue.

As she headed for home past the rolling blue and white breakers of the Pacific, she realised that the shadow that had been hovering over her the last couple of days had suddenly lifted. It felt like the removal of a curse. She breathed deeply.

Before she could even sit down in her office, Spinner called.

'Hi. Have you got to the bottom of what's going on over at Daria Reynolds's place?' Gemma asked.

'Absolutely bloody nothing's going on that I could see,' he said. 'But I've got something to show you.'

A little while later, she buzzed Spinner in; he was waving a manilla envelope. He prepared the video and called her over to the operatives' office when it was ready to watch. From the doorway, Gemma saw the front garden and footpath outside the Reynolds's place frozen on the screen of the monitor.

'Watch this,' said Spinner.

It was very boring viewing. A few passers-by had been caught in the earlier hours of the night: figures walking past, left to right, right to left. But as the tape went on and the night went on, the only times the camera activated was when a cat walked one way, then returned in the same direction, as cats do, and repeated this activity on and off throughout the night.

'What about inside?' Gemma asked after they'd fast-forwarded through the external tape.

'You'll see that in a tick,' Spinner said.

The grainy security footage showed Daria's bedroom. Suddenly the sleeping figure stirred in jerky time lapse and the bedside light came on. Gemma leaned forward. She could see Daria Reynolds's lips moving. She was talking to someone. Then her mouth dropped open in a silent scream.

Gemma came further into the room. 'What's she going on about?'

Daria Reynolds was sitting up in bed, clutching the sheet around herself, screaming at someone.

'I can't see anyone,' said Gemma.

Spinner stopped the replay so that Daria Reynolds suddenly froze, mouth open.

'Follow her eye line,' he said, directing Gemma to a place on the monitor screen. 'She's staring straight to that point there. Just off screen. He's just out of camera range.' Spinner sounded frustrated. 'I was sure I had the room covered.'

'But that still doesn't explain how he got in in the first place.'

'There's no way he could have got in. And yet there it is.'

Gemma picked up the remote and pressed play. Daria Reynolds continued her silent scream, shrinking from something they couldn't see, while the front of the house showed no movement except for the changing positions of shadows as the earth turned and the moon set.

Disconsolate, Spinner started packing his camera and laptop back into the carry bag. 'I'll have to go back,' he said. 'Do the job again. Put another camera in. He must have dug a tunnel, that's all I can say. Or dropped through the roof.'

'That just might be possible,' Gemma considered. 'There've been some robberies recently where the thieves removed tiles from the roof and did exactly that—came in through the ceiling.'

'Boss,' Spinner said, as if he were talking to a child, 'if that's how he was getting in, I think she would have mentioned it. Don't you?'

Gemma shrugged and walked with him to the front door, worried about the intensity of his mood. As he stepped outside Spinner turned. 'I'll go round and talk to her,' he said. 'Organise another time to redo the cameras.'

'It isn't just this, is it?' she asked.

Spinner was silent a moment. Then, 'Rose doesn't want to see me anymore. Reckons she can't be with a man who doesn't share her religion.'

Spinner's words tapped into Gemma's own loss and tears pricked her eyes. Humans are just so perverse, she thought. We'll think of anything, even God, to destroy a relationship.

'I'm sorry, Spinner. I know how you felt about her.'

'Feel,' came Spinner's sad voice, barely audible; then he collected himself so that when he next spoke he sounded more like the old Spinner. 'I was thinking of having a little break. Going bush to see Mr Pepper.'

'Who's lost his pecker,' Gemma said, trying to cheer him up, pleased he'd already gone through the insurance company's faxed case notes.

'He's moved to Bathurst to live with a relative,' Spinner said. 'I was thinking of taking a few days up there—if Mike and you can cover Daria Reynolds's place. Fresh air. Wide open spaces. Do the business and have a bit of time to myself.'

'Sure,' Gemma said. 'Just let me know what days you won't be around.'

After grabbing herself a coffee, Gemma found that Senior Constable Diane Hayworth had left a message for her on her office phone. She immediately rang back, but Diane wasn't in the office, so she continued working through the afternoon, sorting through the jobs-in-progress files. She needed to eat, she realised; she could carry on working over dinner, outside.

Things were looking better in the fridge since she'd shopped. She put two cutlets under the griller and made a salad, poured herself a glass of wine. Sitting in the humid, warm evening, with the deck's spotlight shining onto her work, she reviewed the current cases.

She started with the Amy Bernhard investigation, rereading the notes she'd made after the uneasy meetings with Andrew Bernhard and his successor, the hunting cowboy, Stokes. Gemma opened a fresh Tasmin Summers file and made a note to act on the contacts given her by Beatrice de Berigny as soon as possible.

Daria Reynolds's folder she moved to one side; she felt sure they'd have a result on that very soon, despite their client's anger and her unseen intruder. Hesitating over Mr Dowling's file, feeling overwhelmed, Gemma leaned back and listened to the sea surge, soft and low, against the rocks. No wonder she was tired. Even when she was a police officer, her workload hadn't been so heavy. And she'd been a member of a much bigger team. If Mike decided to leave in the middle of all this work, it would be disastrous. And if he stayed, she'd somehow have to find a way to live with her feelings of shame.

She carried the folders back inside, locked the sliding doors and pulled the curtains. Her apartment was cooler now. Jumping at a sudden noise, she realised how the fear that she thought had lifted, was still there, running just under the surface of her consciousness. But the sound hadn't come from her place; it had come from the flat upstairs. She remembered the time she'd flatted beneath a fireman and how the sound of him walking around in his great big boots when he was called out used to wake her up at night. Please, no more firemen, she prayed. A nice, single, professional woman was what she'd like up there. Someone who read and stared out to sea like the French Lieutenant's woman. Someone quiet.

Then her mobile rang. It was Angie, her voice thick. Had she been crying?

'What's up, Ange?'

'Trevor's gone. I feel really miz. And he couldn't say how long he'd be away this time. Some special training thing he's doing with the Academy. Terrorist games. I don't know when I'll see him again.'

'You wanna come over?' Gemma glanced at her watch. 'I can make up the sofa bed for you.'

Angie sounded a little brighter. 'I'll bring the report from the knots man. That's just arrived back.'

Gemma remembered Mr Roper and the green and white nylon cord found around Amy Bernhard's fine wrist bones. Maybe the knot expert could throw some light on this investigation.

Gemma was spooning ground coffee into the percolator when she heard Angie arriving. Her girlfriend's eyes were red-rimmed and she sniffed as she came inside.

'Angelface! You've been crying!'

Angie flashed her a look. 'Crying! No way. They were having Officer Survival training and I got roped in. I crept into the office to grab some things and got caught as a volunteer for capsicum-spray training.'

'You didn't!'

'Some of the guys stepped forward. I had to. The honour of my sex was at stake.'

'Bugger that. You're supposed to be put in the lifeboats first.'

'Not in the New South Wales cops, believe me. I copped a spray. I couldn't see for ages and there I was, trying to do baton strikes in braille.'

The two friends sat under the stars on Gemma's deck, a piece of chocolate mud cake and a peanut toffee slice glistening under the spotlighting, fresh coffee steaming in two mugs. Gemma fetched the folders of purloined witness statements and plonked them down on the table.

Angie pulled out an envelope. 'It's such a nice thing, to breathe,' she said, blowing her nose again.

'I thought you were going shopping, not capsicum training. So what's happening?'

'Trev didn't wake me when he left earlier. But he wrote this beautiful poem.' She passed it to Gemma. 'I found it on the bedside table when I woke up. With a single rose across it.' She blew her nose loudly.

'*Farewell*,' Gemma started reading. '*Thou art too dear for my possessing, but I will gladly give top dollars for you. You are so gorgeous, too good to be true. I can't bear the thought of losing you. I'm so lucky for choosing you.*'

Gemma passed it back, frowning. To her, it seemed to contain a lot of conflicting ideas. Not to mention sounding plain silly.

'Well?' Angie demanded. 'What do you think of that?'

Gemma shrugged. 'Poetry isn't my thing.'

Angie looked at her more closely. 'You still brooding over Steve?'

'It's not just that.' She told Angie about the incident in the front of Mike's car.

'Hell, Gemster girl. We all do silly things from

time to time. You remember me and that beast of a weapons instructor?'

Gemma tapped the folder of papers. 'Remember that Mr Romero, the History teacher, was late for class the morning Amy went missing? I want to know why. Not only that, but he also had a meeting with Tasmin Summers the morning she disappeared.'

'I've got Julie chasing up the employment histories of Netherleigh Park's male teachers, with Romero top of the list.'

'Good,' said Gemma. 'I hope he's back on deck tomorrow night. I want to check up on his alibi for the morning of December second in person—the morning Amy went missing.'

Angie frowned. 'Surely that would have been checked out when she first disappeared?'

Like kids playing a game of Snap, their eyes met and both spoke at the same time. 'Bruno!'

'How he's got himself promoted to inspector is a bloody miracle. That's why I need all the help I can get. Here, skip through this. As long as you promise discretion.' Angie delved into her briefcase and fished out a large manilla envelope. 'Here's Mr Roper's report on the cord and the knot found on Amy Bernhard's body.'

Gemma took the contents out of the envelope, pulling the photographs away from the paper clip so she could read the report, skipping a lot of the technical language. She looked at Angie. 'What's this S-laid and Z-laid business mean?'

Angie grabbed the report back, frowned. Then

passed it over again. 'He explained it to me over the phone,' she said, doing a quick scribble on the margin. 'See how the letter Z starts on the left-hand side . . .'

'And S starts on the right. Right?'

'Right. Z-laid means the rope strands twist from the left and S-laid means they twist from the right.'

The cord that tied Amy wasn't nylon as Gemma had assumed from the photograph, but one of the new generation of fibres, lighter and stronger than the old natural fibres or the nylons and polymers. And expensive.

'He says it's an uncommon rope,' Angie summarised. 'They call them exotics. This particular one, Vectran, is imported by a mob called Tektanika.' She glanced at the report again. 'Most commonly used in quality fishing lines. And kite lines.'

'So we're looking for some guy who abducts girls to go fishing and fly kites?' Gemma poured herself another coffee. 'Still, it's something to get started on. I'll find out where the importers have sold it, which retailers carry it.'

Angie sipped her coffee and put it down. 'Oh, by the way, I checked out that fellow for you— Alistair Forde.'

'The Bernhard family's next-door neighbour?' Gemma had all but forgotten him.

'He seems to be a clean-skin,' said Angie, turning her attention back to the forensic knot man's report. She picked up one of the photos of the knot in the cord. 'Mr Roper says the knot is an odd one.' She turned the photograph around to show Gemma.

'That's just an ordinary old reef knot,' said Gemma. 'What's funny about that?'

'It looks like an ordinary old reef knot. But it isn't. It's like a mirror image of one. Mr Roper says it's what ships' chandlers and provisions merchants used in the old days to trap pilferers. They'd tie this special knot, and the thief, not noticing the subtle difference, would retie using a reef knot.'

'So what is it?' asked Gemma.

'We should be looking for someone who can tie a thief knot.'

EIGHT

Friday morning Gemma spent at Netherleigh Park, first talking to the girls in Tasmin and Amy's classes, with private interview time allocated to their closest friends, then interviewing the teaching staff, as she'd requested. Except for Mr Romero, who was ill, they were all happy to discuss the two girls with her. None of them were able to add anything to their original statements. Apart from a few more girls who claimed they'd heard about the secret, no one had been able to shed any light on what it might have involved.

She also talked with Amy and Tasmin's friends and relatives, following up suggestions made by schoolfriends. None had any further information to offer.

In the afternoon, Gemma hurried off to her piano lesson, which Mrs Snellgrove had kindly agreed to bring forward a couple of hours. She scolded Gemma for not practising and Gemma promised to mend her ways.

Friday evening arrived with Gemma not looking

forward to having to go back to Netherleigh Park. Dressing with one eye on the time and another on the television news, she took in the car bombs, people screaming, paramedics running. Business as usual in the world, she thought. She was zipping her skirt when the sports segment began, showing file tape of Scott Brissett—identified by the name under his handsome face—laughing with a couple of huge Spaniards, contenders for the Boyleford Cup. As Brissett dealt with the interviewer, the deep scar running through his eyebrow and across the bridge of his nose somehow appeared more interesting embellishment than blemish. He looked triumphant. The newsreader announced that the woman who had named Brissett as a rapist had publicly withdrawn her accusation and file footage showed the ex-footballer and his wife holding hands and fending off reporters as they hurried to a car. Brissett seemed to have some difficulty stepping down to get into the car, Gemma thought, noticing him wince. He was going to sue the woman for damages, the newsreader concluded.

She arrived at Netherleigh Park a bit before eight o'clock, thinking of the unknown killer who had tied a thief knot and dumped a girl's body near an industrial area. '*Hollywood nights, those Hollywood nights!*' Bob Seger mourned on her car radio. This would be no Hollywood night, Gemma thought, parking on the street some distance from the school's grand gates. Walking up the driveway, the sun bright and low in the western sky, Gemma picked her way through the fermenting meal of squashed figs, their yeasty scent mingling with that of star jasmine. In another hour or so, the bats would be busy in the huge Moreton Bay figs overhead.

Already, people were heading towards the main entrance—where Gemma noticed a police car parked—in family groups or as singles. Prefects wearing their badges practised their meet-and-greet skills, ushering Gemma and the rest of the arrivals along a hallway decorated with sporting shields and portraits of past principals wearing academic robes and bad haircuts.

The school hall was huge. Its wide foyer area was already crowded with parents, students, friends and teachers streaming through the tall folding doors into the main body of the hall. Gemma followed them in. She saw Angie near the wide steps to the curtained stage, her briefcase beside her, deep in conversation with Miss de Berigny who was elegant in a navy sheath dress and large pearls. The hall filled rapidly.

Gemma turned to a tall girl standing near the doorway—every inch the prefect except for one fluorescent orange lock of hair pinned back behind her ear. Things have changed, Gemma thought. 'Is Mr Romero here yet?' she asked.

The girl shook her head. 'He's been away the last couple of days.'

'Is he a popular teacher?' Gemma asked.

The girl gave a small shrug. 'He's okay, I suppose. I wouldn't call him popular.'

Gemma recalled the man and his eccentric cravat and diamond pin. She supposed he'd be more a figure of fun than a heart-throb. She made her way over to Miss de Berigny who was now heading up the stage steps.

'Miss de Berigny?' Gemma called.

The principal turned, brows raised in two perfect arcs.

'After I've spoken,' Gemma continued, 'I'd like to have a look around the school as we discussed on the phone. Perhaps while Sergeant McDonald is speaking? That would save time.'

Miss de Berigny hesitated. For a second, Gemma thought she might change her mind, but then she nodded, beckoning the tall prefect over. 'Katie, will you please show Miss Lincoln around the school? The classrooms and staffrooms? Here are the keys.' She handed them to Gemma. 'Return them to me when you've finished.'

The chatter in the hall died down as Beatrice de Berigny took the stage and began her introductions, smiling at her audience.

'Thank you so much for coming tonight. I want to reassure you all that everything that can be done regarding the disappearances of two of our students is being done. Tonight, Detective Sergeant Angie McDonald will talk to you about how the investigation is going and in what way the public might be of assistance. You can ask any questions you might have. I've also asked Miss Gemma Lincoln, who is helping with a private investigation on behalf of Netherleigh Park, to speak to you all.' Miss de Berigny looked around. 'Miss Lincoln?'

Gemma stepped up onto the stage next to Miss

de Berigny, aware of the silence, the attention of everyone on her.

'Thank you,' she said, looking around at the hundreds of faces. 'What I have to say won't take long. I'm here to ask every one of you to go over what you recall, what you've heard, or what you might know about Amy Bernhard and Tasmin Summers. Anything about their lives and interests. And I want to make a point. If anyone comes to me with information that they've so far been withholding—perhaps because they didn't want to be seen as betraying a secret, or feared that any police interest might expose certain things they didn't want exposed—I want to reassure them. You would be protected.' She paused and looked around, searching the faces. 'Information can be given to me anonymously. Either by phone or at my email address. Okay?'

She took out a solid wedge of her business cards. 'Cards are going to be passed around the hall. These have all my contact details, so please, everyone, feel free to take one. You can ring me, visit me or email me at any time.' Gemma passed the cards to Miss de Berigny who started distributing them along the rows of seated people.

'I'm quite separate from the police and I can guarantee privacy,' continued Gemma. 'Please help. One of your friends is already dead. The police hold grave fears about the safety of the other. Let's work together to put a stop to whatever's happening to the students of this school. I'm asking you all to help me. To help them.'

As Gemma stepped down and made her way to the back of the hall, buzz and chatter started again. Miss de Berigny climbed back onto the stage. 'Thank you, Miss Lincoln.' Polite applause died down and Miss de Berigny introduced Angie to the assembly. Gemma hurried from the hall, beckoning to Katie, the tall prefect, to accompany her. Once they were outside the hall, Gemma looked back through the double doors to see Angie on the stage, beginning her talk.

'Do you want to see the classrooms first?' Katie asked.

'I think I'd like to start with the History classroom,' said Gemma. 'Where Mr Romero teaches.'

Katie led her along the downstairs corridors until they came to a closed door. 'This is the History room that Mr Romero uses,' she said.

Gemma opened the door and switched the light on, immediately assailed by the smell of school room—that unmistakable mix of young humans, school furniture, grubby books, the ghosts of packed lunches, chalk, and government-issue polishes and other cleaning materials. Under the flickering fluorescent tubes were twenty-five plastic chairs and wooden tables maps, posters pinned to the walls and, out the front, a large blond wood desk with an overhead projector on it. She paused, looking round, imagining the room filled with lively girls and their teacher. In more than ninety per cent of murders, Gemma recalled, the killer and the victim knew each other. This was the room where Amy Bernhard, according to Mr Romero, had failed to arrive for her pre-school meeting. But even if she had turned up, Mr Romero wouldn't have been here to meet with her, Gemma remembered from his statement, because he'd been 'late'. There was another, more ominous explanation of why Amy had failed to appear and Mr Romero's lateness.

Gemma noticed a drawer in the teacher's desk and tried to open it. Then she saw it was locked. Mr Romero must have the key.

'Okay,' said Gemma, switching off the light and closing the door. She didn't want to betray too much to Katie. 'What about the staffrooms? And the teachers' offices?'

'Only the head teachers have those,' said Katie. 'You want to see the History office?' She was catching on.

'I do,' said Gemma.

Katie headed for a flight of stairs at the end of the corridor and Gemma hurried after her, walking past many classrooms until they came to a door at the end with Mr Romero's nameplate and discipline displayed.

'You'll need the keys for this one,' said Katie. Gemma sorted through the bunch until she found the relevant one. Opening the door, she felt around for a light switch and went in, while Katie stood deferentially by the door. Gemma looked around. It was a small, windowless room, much of it taken up by the large desk and typist's chair, crowded bookshelves lining the walls and a couple of plastic stacking chairs sitting on top of each other.

Above the desk, pigeonholes and shelving held exercise books, the occasional clay artefact and a closed laptop. Gemma reached over and took down Suetonius's *The Twelve Caesars*. A postcard fell out of the paperback and onto the desk—a Pre-Raphaelite painting of Ophelia drifting down the river to a muddy death, clothes transparent and suggestive, her gleaming young body boldly revealed, hair streaming in graceful arabesques against the dark flow of the river and the clutching willows.

Gemma studied the disturbing image a moment, then poked it back into the book. She quickly checked the contents of the two desk drawers; stationery supplies, a letter addressed to Mr Romero at the school and a couple of novels. She kept the letter and closed the drawers. Footsteps approaching heralded the arrival of Angie and Miss de Berigny. Katie had gone back into the corridor and Gemma slipped the letter into her briefcase. From outside came the sound of voices, car doors slamming and engines revving. The formalities of the information evening were finishing.

Beatrice de Berigny said with her brightest smile, 'Thank you, Katie. You may go now, dear. Your mother is waiting.' She turned to Gemma. 'Have you seen everything you wanted to see?'

'Not quite.' Gemma smiled back. 'There's a drawer in Mr Romero's desk in the History room,' she said, 'but it's locked.'

The principal shrugged. 'Then you'll have to wait till he comes back. I don't have a key for that.'

'I'm sure someone could drop by his place and pick it up if we need it,' Angie said, alerted by Gemma's interest. 'Let's take a look.'

Back in the classroom, Gemma and Angie went to the table while Beatrice de Berigny, pale and drawn underneath the ivory make-up, stood watching from the doorway.

'What are you doing?' she called, alarmed at the way Angie was now tugging at the drawer with all her considerable strength.

'Sometimes,' said Angie, grunting with the effort, 'these old drawers get stuck.' She gave a final tug and the drawer flew open, splinters flying. 'See? The wood warps.'

Gemma drew closer to look over her friend's shoulder as Angie pulled on a pair of rubber gloves and rifled through the pens, pencils and bits of chalk and paper—just teacher's junk, Gemma thought.

Miss de Berigny took a step into the room, frowning. 'I think you've just broken that lock,' she said sternly.

Angie, ignoring Miss de Berigny's remark, pulled the whole drawer right out, carefully examining its contents. Under a packet of whiteboard pens at the back of the drawer lay a stiff white envelope. Angie's gloved fingers opened and unfolded it, smoothing it flat.

Inkjet print, Gemma noted, although she couldn't quite make out the words. Angie quickly read it and shot a look across at the principal who had come closer. She carefully refolded the paper and dropped it and its envelope into a self-sealing plastic bag. 'I think I'd better take this, Miss de Berigny.'

Beatrice de Berigny's desperate eyes followed the movements of Angie's gloved hands. 'Why?' she whispered. 'What is it?'

'It appears to be a love letter, Miss de Berigny. From a pupil of this school to Mr Romero.'

Beatrice de Berigny looked as if she'd been king-hit. She opened her mouth, about to speak, then closed it again. Her eyes seemed huge now in their pencilled frames. 'Who wrote it?' she managed to say. Under the harsh fluorescent light, her face looked like a death's-head. 'Who is it from?'

Angie stuck a label on the plastic bag and scribbled the date and location of the find on it, together with her signature, and placed it in her briefcase. Only Gemma, standing a little to one side of Angie, had been able to see the initials at the bottom of the letter.

'Who is it from?' The principal repeated her question.

'It's only signed with initials,' said Angie. 'But I'm sure we'll discover in due course.'

'But if you told me the initials, I might be able to help you,' said Miss de Berigny, rallying.

Angie flashed her high-voltage smile. 'Maybe later, ma'am,' she said.

Beatrice de Berigny looked ill. 'It's a nightmare,' she said. 'Just when I thought things were settling down. Returning to normal. Then Tasmin vanishes.' She briefly closed her eyes, desperation in her voice, the tone of a woman trapped. Or, thought Gemma, is it a woman betrayed?

'What are the initials?' Beatrice de Berigny asked in a whisper. 'Please tell me that much.'

Angie, no longer smiling, deliberately snapped her briefcase shut. Only then did she raise her eyes to the principal. 'Miss de Berigny,' she said, 'maybe you already know?' She started walking towards the door. 'I noticed a laptop in Mr Romero's office. Would that be his?'

'Yes,' said Miss de Berigny, hesitant, anticipating Angie's next move. 'But I can't let you take it,' she added. 'Not without Mr Romero's consent.'

'Where is he?' Angie asked.

'At home. He's been away sick for the last few days.'

Angie expertly shot her gloves into the rubbish bin on the way out of the classroom. 'Okay, so Mr Romero isn't here,' she said. 'It'll take me an hour or two to get a warrant from a magistrate. With what I've got in here,' she indicated the envelope in her briefcase, 'and the fact that Mr Romero had meetings scheduled with both victims, we've got reasonable cause to search Mr Romero's possessions. We can do this quietly or we can make a big fuss about it. Which do you think would look better to the parents?'

Gemma could see the struggle reflected in Miss de Berigny's face—the fearful eyes and trembling mouth as the woman looked from Gemma to Angie. She's really stuck, Gemma thought. If she insists on a warrant, it'll look as if there's something to hide. But if she doesn't, she can't know what Angie might find.

Finally, the principal capitulated. 'It seems I have no choice, do I?'

Angie took the laptop and Gemma noticed that as the principal relocked the History office door, her hands were shaking. She accompanied them in silence to the main entrance, remaining at the top of the entrance steps to watch as they left.

Outside, in the darkness of the fig trees' canopy, leathery wings flickered and swooped in total silence just on the edge of the lights in the grounds. The fruit bats were moving in.

'Do you think something's going on between Romero and the principal?' Angie asked as soon as they were out of earshot.

'I've always thought that,' said Gemma. 'Or at least allowed for the possibility. I told you how Romero barged into Miss de Berigny's office the day I was there and said, "I thought Tasmin might be here with you".'

Angie looked askance. 'Oh, boy,' she said. 'You mean you think that's the secret—Miss de B having an affair with one of the students?'

Gemma shrugged. 'I hadn't actually thought of that. But of all the places Tasmin could've been in that huge school, he thinks to go to the principal's room?'

'Maybe the kid was always in strife. Or maybe he was creating a diversion, planting an alibi.'

'Maybe, maybe, maybe,' said Gemma as they approached the police car. 'At this stage, we don't have anything except a whole lot of maybes. But put yourself in Tasmin's shoes—her best friend's just vanished into thin air. Maybe something happened to cause her to bolt.'

Around them, the last of the parents' cars were pulling out of the school grounds.

'Did you see Miss de Berigny's face,' Gemma asked, 'when you said that about her guessing the initials at the end of that letter?'

Angie nodded, opening the passenger door of the police car. 'Hop in,' she said. 'I'll run you to your car.'

'Hell, I almost forgot,' said Gemma. 'I've got a letter too.' She pulled it out. 'I grabbed it from Mr Romero's office. I'm suspicious now about anything addressed to that man.'

'Read it,' said Angie, switching the car light on.

'*Dear Mr Romero,*' Gemma read, '*this is the third time I've had to ask you. Will you please tidy up your things? It's a disgrace and the neighbours say they saw rats. If you don't do this within seven days, I'm going to get a man in and get it all tipped. Sincerely, Mavis Ponzi.*'

'Not exactly a love letter,' said Angie.

'Sounds like someone from the body corporate,' said Gemma, restowing the letter.

A few short moments later, Angie pulled up beside Gemma's white Honda. 'I want to talk to Romero too,' Gemma said, opening the passenger door.

Angie shrugged. 'You can't come with me. But I can't stop you turning up at the same time I'm there. I'm going to drop this laptop over to the technical people—they're up all night anyway. Then I'll go to Romero's place.'

Gemma smiled, grabbing her notebook from her bag. 'Have you got the address on hand?'

Gemma, tired and hungry, stopped for a cappuccino and focaccia from Café Hernandez before driving to Mr Romero's address, a block of units in Paddington, not far from Centennial Park's northern gates. She pulled up behind Angie's car and hurried to join her friend who was pressing the security doorbell.

Mr Romero, in a grey tracksuit and old pink T-shirt, opened the door. With his glasses and tousled hair sticking up at the front, he reminded Gemma of a sad old cockatoo. Angie identified herself and walked in, as Romero backed away. Gemma followed, looking around, expecting to see a mess after Mrs Ponzi's complaint, but the place wasn't particularly untidy.

'Hello, Mr Romero,' she said to the surprised man, extending her hand. 'We've met before, at the school, but we weren't introduced. I'm Gemma Lincoln, employed by Netherleigh Park as a private investigator.'

He frowned, taking her hand in an automatic way, not recognising her.

His apartment, decorated in muted tones of grey, apricot and white, reflected his interests: framed photographs of ancient ruins hung on the walls and the French doors to the balcony were framed by half-size marble nude statues. Interspersed between the ruins were Pre-Raphaelite-style prints, similar to the postcard Gemma had found in his office at the school; they showed nymphs caught in various poses, pastel, sentimental, their draped clothes revealing more than concealing their nubile bodies. On the polished dining table, a dainty art deco maiden wound herself nakedly around a bronze centrepiece.

'What the hell do the police want with me?' Mr Romero remonstrated. 'I'm not at all well and you come banging on my door at this hour.' He turned on Gemma. 'What's going on? What's a private investigator doing at my place? I haven't done any-thing wrong!'

'Couple of reasons for this visit, sir,' said Angie. 'But first, you live here alone?'

'I do,' he said.

While Angie determined Mr Romero's marital status—divorced—and date of birth, Gemma looked more closely at the framed group of nymphs hanging on the wall near her. She noticed two things: first, that these weren't prints but watercolours signed 'Mannix Romero' in a flowing hand; and second, the faces and bodies of the nymphs were those of pubescent girls.

'I need to give you a receipt for the laptop I removed from your office,' Angie was saying. Gemma studied Romero's face carefully but discerned no change of expression. 'I'll get it back to you as soon as possible.'

'Why did you take my laptop?' Romero asked,

puzzled, Gemma thought, rather than scared. She continued checking the watercolours and found them to be all very similar—young girls, artfully and suggestively draped.

'The second thing is,' Angie continued, fishing the letter out of her briefcase, 'this letter we found in your classroom desk drawer. Obviously written by one of your students, declaring her love for you and wanting a private meeting.'

If Romero had seemed shocked at their arrival, this hit him like a body blow. 'A letter?' he repeated, faintly.

'If I tell you it's signed with the initials AB,' Angie pressed on, 'perhaps you might remember it better?'

Romero's mouth dropped open.

'Amy Bernhard has those initials,' Angie continued, waving it at him.

Romero tried to rally. 'That damn letter!' he cried. 'I'd completely forgotten it! Someone put it in my desk—I don't know who! I swear I have no idea. I should have thrown it away the minute I noticed it.'

'Amy had a meeting with you,' Gemma reminded him 'on the morning she disappeared. So did Tasmin Summers—both girls, before your class. And you arrived late to school on both days. Tasmin is missing and Amy is dead. And her initials are on a letter to you suggesting a meeting that morning.'

'But I didn't see her! There was no meeting! Either before school or at school. I missed her!'

Angie tapped the letter. 'Did you have a meeting with her somewhere else?' she said. 'At the beach—like this letter suggests?'

'Jesus,' he whispered, all the fight gone out of him. He sagged against the long white lounge, slowly sinking into it. 'Of course I didn't.'

'You admitted you were late to school that morning,' Gemma said. 'Why? What kept you?'

'For God's sake, I'm often late! It's just coincidence. Ask the principal. She'll tell you.'

'Mr Romero,' said Angie, pulling on another pair of disposable gloves and opening the letter. 'Let me read this to you. It might refresh your memory.' She was about to start when a voice calling from outside in the hall interrupted her.

'Mannix? It's me. Open the door, please!'

'That's her now,' said Mr Romero. 'She'll tell you. That I'm often late.' He hurried to the door and opened it to reveal Beatrice de Berigny. She stopped mid-step when she saw Angie and Gemma.

'Oh,' she said. 'I didn't expect to see you here.' No one spoke for a long moment. 'Something was found in your desk, Mannix,' she said finally. 'Some love letter from one of the students! Why didn't you tell me?'

'I've just been trying to tell them—'

'You know it's school policy. Anything like that must be brought to my attention immediately. If you'd done that, none of this would be happening.'

Not quite true, thought Gemma, but the letter did make things worse for the History teacher.

'You should hear this too,' Angie said, turning to

Beatrice de Berigny. 'You said earlier you might be able to throw some light onto the matter. Here it is.

'*Dear Mr Romero,*' Angie read, '*I am totally in love with you. You are the most sexy man I have ever seen. I just sit staring at you, wishing I could kiss you and put my arms around you. Whenever you walk around the classroom and come near me, I just melt. I so totally want to touch you. Please meet me before school on Wednesday. I will wait for you at the beach at eight o'clock. I dream of being alone with you. Heaps of love and kisses, AB.*'

All the colour had drained from Mr Romero's face. He was as pale as the marble nudes flanking the French doors.

'I'd completely forgotten it,' he whispered. 'I stuck it in the drawer and never gave it another thought.' He looked around his flat, throwing out an arm. 'I don't believe this is happening. Everything I say gets twisted around. Beatrice, you must believe me!'

Why was he appealing to her? Gemma wondered.

'Mannix,' said Miss de Berigny, 'you must get a lawyer. Don't say another word until you get legal advice.'

'Before you do that,' said Angie, 'may we search your apartment? We can do it quietly in the morning with your permission, or I can get a warrant.'

'Do it!' he cried, throwing up his arms in helpless protest. 'Do it whichever way you like. You won't find anything here!'

His words rang out dramatically and Gemma's deception detector flashed a red light. Something's going on, she thought. His words kept ringing through her head.

'We'll be back in the morning,' said Angie. 'You can stay or sit with a neighbour while we do the search.'

She was about to step outside when she turned to him again. 'Do you like fishing?' she asked. 'Or kite-flying?'

Romero stared blankly at her. 'What?'

'Do you?' Angie persisted.

'I've never done either in my life,' he said, distressed. 'What on earth are you asking me that sort of foolish question for?'

Angie smiled. 'Have a good night, sir.'

Angie and Gemma let themselves out, leaving Romero and the principal staring after them.

They retraced their steps, stopping in the foyer long enough to read the names of the occupants picked out in white plastic letters in a glassed-in box near the lift.

'No Ponzis,' said Gemma. 'I was going to ask him about Mrs Ponzi,' she said, 'but I want to keep that up my sleeve for a bit.'

'I can't see why anyone would be complaining about mess,' said Angie. 'Certainly not rats. His place was perfectly clean.'

They left the building, heading towards their respective cars. 'I'd love to be a fly on the wall,' said Gemma, 'and hear the conversation going on up there. Mr Romero looked so pathetic towards the end.'

'So did Saddam Hussein,' said Angie. She

indicated the plastic bag housing the envelope and letter she'd found in Romero's desk. 'Do you think it's Amy Bernhard?'

'It's only circumstantial,' said Gemma. 'Anyone with access to a computer could have written this. And put it in Romero's desk.'

'If that's the case,' said Angie, unlocking her door, 'we might find traces of them on the paper.'

'Someone could have set him up. Planted that letter in his desk.'

'Who?'

Gemma considered. 'The killer, for one. Someone on the staff who hates his guts? Take your pick. Anyone with a computer and an inkjet printer could have written it. Or a student with a grudge to get him into strife.'

'I'll pass it over to the physical evidence people,' said Angie. 'See if they can get a match from Amy Bernhard.' She got into her car and wound down the window.

'Don't you think,' Gemma said, 'it's weird that he should still have it? Why the hell would he keep something so obviously compromising him? It's a year since Amy disappeared. Now she's found dead. Wouldn't you think he'd get rid of it?'

'Did you notice all those half-naked young girls hanging on his walls?' she added.

Angie nodded, fitting her keys into the ignition.

'He painted those,' said Gemma. 'I saw his signature on them.'

'It's not looking too good for the old History teacher,' said Angie.

'But if he'd done away with Amy,' Gemma persisted, 'he'd hardly keep that incriminating letter.'

'Overweight, middle-aged school teacher,' Angie said, starting her car, 'finds gorgeous schoolgirl in love with him. Of course he's going to keep such a flattering letter. He can read it over and over and feel like he's really got it. What about all the married dickheads who keep text messages from their lovers? They can't bear to get rid of them either.'

Angie pulled her seatbelt across. 'God, I'm tired. I haven't had much sleep lately.'

'Stop boasting.'

'It's been a while. I'm allowed to boast.'

'Romero seemed genuinely puzzled by your references to fishing and kite-flying,' said Gemma, getting back to the subject.

'A person could still buy the cord and use if for other purposes,' said Angie. 'Sean's already checked with Tektanika, the people who make it. They supply a dozen or so retail outlets in New South Wales with that stuff. And a few more interstate. Doesn't exactly narrow things down.'

Gemma walked round Angie's car and knocked on the passenger door. 'Let me in. I feel like a goose standing here talking down to you.' Angie unlocked the passenger door and Gemma slid in. 'Both the girls had meetings with Romero,' Gemma continued, 'but Amy arrived at school that morning, whereas Tasmin went missing on the way to school. We need to keep those little differences in mind.' She tried to remember the witness statements. 'Amy's seen at school early but then goes missing.'

'Surely the killer wouldn't try something on at the school?' Angie said. 'Anyone could walk in any time.'

'Maybe that's what happened. Someone did walk in. Maybe Romero was getting hot and heavy with AB after the declaration of love in the letter and the principal walks in.'

'Or maybe they meet at the beach and go somewhere else. He tries something on, she panics, says she'll tell—bang goes his career—and he kills her. We'd better have a really good look at his place,' said Angie.

'And check out Beatrice de Berigny. Maybe she goes crazy with jealousy, kills Amy, tells Romero, and he colludes with her and the two of them dispose of her body,' said Gemma.

'Maybe she kills her and disposes of Amy all by herself,' Angie suggested.

'It's hard work, lifting and hiding a body,' Gemma reminded her.

'There's definitely something going on between him and Madame de Berigny,' Gemma continued. 'But why wouldn't she just dob on him, get him arrested and clean up the school? Or sack him on the spot if he's misbehaving with a student? That's better than leaving an ongoing situation like this. I can't believe she'd turn a blind eye to suspected seduction, with the possibility of abduction and murder, going on in her classrooms!'

Angie stretched her arms on the steering wheel, leaning back. 'But if they're both involved in some way, all that makes sense. It wouldn't be the first time a couple have got together for murder.'

'True. But why would she have employed me then?' said Gemma. 'The last thing she'd want would be closer scrutiny of Amy's disappearance. The whole thing was quietly dying. Bruno had been taken off the case, although she wouldn't have known that. But it had pretty well come to a standstill. Amy was fading into one of those missing girl posters you see peeling off walls in police stations. Why would Miss de Berigny want to stir it all up again?'

'But didn't you tell me you thought she was only employing you so she could impress the parents and the school board?'

Gemma nodded. 'Yes, that's what I first thought. But that was before Amy's remains turned up, when it was still only a missing person's investigation. It's asking for trouble, getting someone like me to sniff around.'

Angie hugged her shoulders to her ears, moving her neck around. 'God, I'm getting stiff. I'll have to get back into training with the muscleheads. My back's aching.'

'Too much sex,' said Gemma. 'But, Angie, why *would* she do that? What possible motive could she have, especially if she was involved in some way?'

Angie stared back at her, raising an eyebrow.

'You've got your smart cop expression on,' said Gemma. 'What are you thinking?'

'I'm thinking there'd be no danger in stirring things up again if you believed you were right

across the situation, in an unassailable position.'
Angie wound her window down and leaned an
elbow on the sill. 'Try this on, Gemfish. Beatrice
de B and Romero are lovers, like you suspect. Miss
Amy gets a crush on Mr Romero. Mr Romero—
like an idiot—responds. It wouldn't be the first
time a middle-aged man has fallen for a teenager.
Or a jealous older woman has got rid of her young
rival, for that matter. Just say Beatrice does away
with Amy, then writes an incriminating 'love' letter,
using the initials AB and stashes this in Romero's
papers in the classroom. That way, in one move,
she gets rid of the rival and punishes the faithless
lover.'

'It's a pretty big move. How often do the principals of exclusive girls' schools feature as
murderers?'

'Ask the lady friend of the Scarsdale Diet
doctor,' Angie said. 'Miss Jean Harris was the principal of a very ritzy ladies' college. Beautiful
manners. But that didn't stop her firing four
rounds into her cheating doctor boyfriend.'

Gemma swung the passenger door open. 'It's
late. I'd better get going,' she said, then thought
of something. 'That love letter in Romero's desk,'
she began.

'Yes?' Angie waited.

'Killers keep trophies.' Gemma hesitated, one
foot on the ground. 'And I can't stop thinking of
what Romero said when you told him you wanted
to search his place.'

'Remind me.'

'He didn't say, "You won't find anything", like you'd expect. He said, "You won't find anything *here*".'

They looked at each other. 'Meaning,' said Angie, 'that you might find something somewhere else?'

'The school?'

Angie shook her head. 'I doubt it.'

Gemma got out of the car. 'I can't think straight right now.' She patted the roof. 'I'll think about that when I've got more working brain cells. Nighty-night.'

NINE

It was after eleven by the time Gemma got home but she didn't feel like sleep. She was overwrought. Too many investigations. Too many questions. Mr Romero hadn't been alarmed at the thought of a search of his premises. And he hadn't been worried about his laptop being taken into custody. Yet all her instincts, not to mention the sentimental, suggestive watercolours he painted of young girls, told her he was 'off' in some way.

She caught sight of herself in the mirror of the hallstand and, for a second, didn't recognise her own reflection, seeing instead only someone who looked like her. Does my half-sister look like that, she wondered. She wished for a moment that she'd never heard Rowena Wylde's information. Right now, it felt like just another chore she had to do in a life that was already seriously overstretched.

As she went out of the sliding glass doors onto the timber deck, Taxi appeared from a secret location and started figure-of-eighting round her ankles. She bent to stroke him. What, she wondered, did she think she was going to do if and when she found her sister? And how would she approach her? Maybe she should just leave the whole thing alone. After all, they'd survived quite well until now without knowing about each other.

She went back inside, Taxi trotting behind, claws clicking on the polished floor. 'Okay,' she said. 'How about Sardine Supreme for supper? Sorry it's so late.'

The smell nearly knocked her off her feet when she opened the tin, but Taxi purred and applied himself to it smartly. The cat attended to, Gemma poured herself a weak scotch as a nightcap and took it into her office to sort through the mail. The micro camera had arrived and she checked all the components were there. The tiny lens was barely the size of a pinhead, and the fine cabling ran into a battery not much larger than a matchbox. She put the camera safely in her desk then turned to a letter that had caught her attention with its hand-written address. As she opened it, a small piece of paper fell out and fluttered to the ground. Gemma picked it up.

There is a contract out on your life, the carefully printed pencil words read. *Watch your back*.

Gemma's heart rate increased. All thoughts about Romero and the Pre-Raphaelite nymphs were swept aside at this threat. She tried to calm herself by thinking it was just someone's bad idea of a joke. But Gemma wasn't laughing. Hadn't every instinct been warning her lately that some-thing was wrong? She felt vindicated in a frightening way. She'd felt that shadow shifting over the last couple of days, but now it was right back in place.

Automatically she went to ring Steve, to talk with him, get his take on it. But with all that had gone on, and the latest embarrassing incident, Steve wasn't there for her anymore. She couldn't seek his help on this. Gemma felt very alone as she slipped the note and its envelope into another larger one, sealing it. She half considered calling Angie, but dropped the idea. She'd handled worse than this before. The scientists at the analytical lab might find something helpful on it. And if it wasn't a bad joke, if it was real . . . ? She tried to think who might want to scare her. Who might even want her dead. And why? Whom had she offended so grievously? Had the man following her in the white Ford been waiting for the perfect moment in a desolate car park, where the sound of a couple of pistol shots might go unnoticed, mistaken for a car backfiring?

Gemma hurried through her apartment, checking her boundaries, making sure the grilles were intact and the sliding doors onto the deck were well and truly locked. She checked the front garden on the CCTV. The only things moving out there were the petunias nodding gently in a night wind. But she didn't like the look of some of the shadows, hollow and black, where dark things could hide. She peered out through the glass of the locked sliding doors. Despite knowing she was well protected, that ill-written note had shocked her right down to the cellular level and she realised she was shaking. She snatched the curtains together, blocking out the night. No one was going to get her in her own place. And during the day, she'd get Mike—that's if Mike was still happy to work for her—to keep on her in traffic whenever he was free. Just when business was starting to pick up, she thought, along comes this.

A sound at the front door caused her to freeze. She dropped to the floor. Maybe it was Taxi pushing his paw under the front door to scrabble at the doormat. But no, her cat was safely curled up in one of the forbidden spots on top of the cedar sideboard, next to the ship's decanters, digesting Sardine Supreme. Again, she heard the sound. She strained to listen in the silence of the night. Creeping forward on hands and knees, she peered at the CCTV screen in the corner of the hall.

Someone was outside. Framed by the CCTV was a hooded figure.

She crept further along the hallway. The Glock 27 was uselessly locked away in the gun safe in her office and it would take her some time to assemble it. Her heart thudding, she studied the hunched figure on the screen. Someone wearing a hooded parka in the middle of summer. Was this a killer coming boldly to her front door to shoot her between the eyes and in the neck the moment she opened it? Slowly, sliding her feet along the floorboards, she glided down the hallway, keeping her eyes on the figure on the screen, feeling her way to the front door. She wouldn't stand in the doorway of the front hall; instead, she stepped sideways into the doorway to her office. That way, she was protected if the killer decided to blast through the fabric of her front door with a shotgun.

Once in position, she took a deep breath. 'Who's there?' The figure jumped at the sound of her voice, clearly nervous. She made her voice harder. 'What the hell do you want and what are you doing here at this hour?'

'Gemma?' A voice she didn't recognise. A male voice.

'Who are you? What do you want? Piss off before I call the cops!'

Still with her eyes glued to the monitor, she took another deep breath. 'I'm calling the cops right now!'

'No! Please don't! It's me, Hugo.'

Hugo. The Ratbag.

She saw the hooded image spread its hands in demonstration. 'It's me. Honest.'

'Step back,' she ordered. He did so and in the light she saw that it was indeed the Ratbag, taller, skinnier, with the bones of his face just starting to jut into manhood. He must be thirteen or so by now.

'Please let me come in.'

Now that she was feeling calmer, she realised he had the reedy tenor of the just-breaking male voice. Cautiously, she opened the door and he slipped in. She closed the door behind him, making him go ahead of her down the hall. Once they'd reached the door to her living room, he turned, eyes huge and shadowed in his pale, worried face. 'I'm in real shit,' he said.

Just what she needed. Someone else in strife. Gemma considered frog-marching him back down the hall again. He wasn't her problem. Let his parents deal with him. Let anyone deal with him, as long as she didn't have to. But despite the anonymous warning looming in her mind, she found herself patting him on the head. 'Join the club, kid,' she said.

Once he'd showered and was dressed in a white towelling robe with his hair slicked back into a ponytail, Gemma realised she was pleased to have Hugo's company. It took some of the sting out of the anonymous warning. Remembering, she glanced up at the security monitor and its coverage of the front garden. No one around.

Looking back at Hugo, Gemma saw that his face had changed subtly. She recalled the deep frown of puzzlement on his young brow. As if he'd endlessly tried—and failed—to understand the adults in his life and the world hurtling around him. He polished off her cutlets and a pile of pasta with tomato sauce—the best she could do without notice.

'You've run away again,' she said, as he bolted the food. 'Naomi told me.'

Hugo paused in his swallowing, but didn't answer.

'Tell me why.'

He was reluctant. 'Me and Mum had a fight,' he said finally. 'As usual. And Dad still hasn't got room for me at his place. It's been like over a year now. He reckons the builders are real slow.'

And I reckon he's a real jerk, Gemma thought, recalling her impression of Hugo's father, a well-dressed, ambitious man who'd left Hugo's mother and married a younger associate. The three of them had shared a pizza a year or more ago. He'd never shown a scrap of interest in his son.

'So how is your dad?'

Hugo shrugged. 'He took me out for a feed. Explained that I'd have to go home to Mum. But you know, Mum's got a new boyfriend. He tries to boss me round all the time.' Hugo put the fork down. 'I don't think Dad likes me. He never writes or contacts me.'

'I can hardly remember my father,' Gemma said. 'I mean, from when I was young.'

'Why?'

She told him a very abridged and cleaned-up version. 'He had to go away when I was about five. I didn't see him again until a few years ago. And then he died.' She didn't say how or in what circumstances. That scene was still too painful for revisiting.

Hugo put his knife and fork down because there was nothing left on his plate. 'Got any ice-cream or anything?' He looked around hopefully.

Gemma did a search in the freezer and, behind a small glacier, found half a tub of ice crystals that proved to have some chocolate ice-cream buried underneath. Hugo ate that and then several slices of toast, finishing off a month's supply of strawberry jam in one go.

Gemma sat on a chair and watched, wondering

what on earth she was going to do with him. 'I'd forgotten how you can eat,' she said.

Immediately, he put his hand in his pocket and pulled out a handful of large bills. 'Here,' he said. 'I can pay my way.'

Gemma stared. 'Where did you get all that?' There must have been hundreds of dollars in the pile.

'It's okay. It's legit.'

Gemma frowned, picking up the bills and giving them back to him. They were the real thing.

'Hugo. Where does a kid get this sort of money?'

'I'm trying to tell you. It's okay. It's my job. I get paid for doing deliveries. But I got busted delivering a package to someone. I had to run.'

'Delivering what?'

He shrugged. 'Not my business. I don't ask.'

'Who were you working for?'

'Eddie the Man. He works for this nightclub.' He looked sideways at her.

'Do you know what his real name is?'

The Ratbag shrugged.

'Which nightclub?' Gemma thought she knew the answer already.

'Maybe I shouldn't be telling you this. You're sort of like the law.'

Gemma remembered the business cards: *We deliver*, and the smart sketch of a razor cutting powder. 'You're talking about Deliverance,' she said and tried again. 'Eddie who?'

'Dunno. That's what everyone calls him.'

'You'll be in trouble big time if you hang round

people like him. Delivering substances, for God's sake!'

The Ratbag looked perplexed. 'I thought it was drugs.'

Gemma saw he wasn't joking. 'You knew you were working as part of a drug dealer's network and it didn't worry you?'

'I'm not doing anything wrong. I'm just like the postie. Eddie said to just make sure I keep out of sight during school hours.'

'Nice that he's so concerned for your welfare.'

He continued as if she hadn't spoken. 'After three o'clock, I'm just a kid on his way home from school. With my backpack. I wave at the cops on the pushbikes. No one takes any notice of me.'

'Oh Hugo, Hugo.' Despite all the mess she was in right now, Gemma's heart was touched. She knew what it felt like to be the kid nobody wanted. She remembered his courage on a terrifying night last year and felt a surge of affection for him. 'So what do you do during the day?'

'I hang out. I've got a friend at the Cross—Gerda. She's nice. Got some friends in the city at the games places in George Street. We bolt if we see a cop.' He paused. 'I can always pick them. There's a cop that hangs out at the club too. Hangs around with kids—girls, I mean. He wears a diamond stud to be real cool, but I just know he's a cop. I can tell them even if they're not in uniform.'

'I know what you mean,' said Gemma. 'So what's the shit you're in?'

The Ratbag shook his head slowly. 'Today, a

coupla rips bashed me up. Took my backpack before I'd finished my deliveries.'

'Rips?' Gemma hadn't heard the term.

'Rip-offs. You know, scavengers who steal other people's gear. They just cruise, watching and waiting.' He looked away. 'I told Eddie what had happened.'

'And?'

'Bastard thought I was lying to him. That *I* pinched the stuff from him.'

'Did you?'

Hugo looked hurt. 'Now you're doing it.'

'I've got to be sure,' she said.

He looked around the flat. 'Can I have a drink?'

'I've only got milk or water.'

'What's that over there?' he said, pointing to the decanters.

'That's hard tack!'

'That's what I meant.'

'No way! It's against the law. You're a minor.'

The Ratbag threw himself back on the lounge. 'All these bullshit rules to protect kids.'

Gemma knew what he meant. If adults really cared about children, she thought, this world would be a very different place.

'Have you still got your Glock 27?'

'Never you mind about that,' she said. 'Tell me about what happened with Eddie.'

'He went ballistic. I bolted. The dude with the diamond stud was pissed off heaps too.'

'Tell me about the rips,' Gemma coaxed.

'I can't. I didn't see them.'

Gemma glared at him. 'Hugo, I'm not sure I believe you.'

'True! They jumped me and they grabbed my backpack. By the time I got up off the ground they'd gone. But I had the money inside my trousers.'

Gemma finally stood up, went over to the decanters and poured herself another weak scotch, her mind going over what he'd told her. She could see the potential dangers ahead for Hugo—welfare interventions, DOCS trying to do their best despite the lack of staff and resources, then police, juvenile detention centres. The descent into the underworld. She came back to him. 'We've got to work out a plan, Hugo. This running away business of yours. This must be—what? The third time? I'll bet your parents have had enough of this.'

'But—'

'No buts. And I don't want you getting beaten up by irate drug dealers.' She didn't say, 'Kids have been murdered for less than this.'

'I could work for you,' he said in his reasonable way, and for a second she almost forgot he was barely thirteen. 'I'd be real good at that. Following people, sussing them out, bounty hunting.'

'Bounty hunting! I don't do that!'

'I would.'

'Get some sleep,' she said. 'It's late. We can talk about all this in the morning.'

She bunked him down on the lounge with sheets and a pillow and, because it was such a mild evening, a cotton throw over his feet. When she went past a few minutes later he was asleep in that way the young have when they have shelter, a full belly and a reasonably benevolent adult nearby.

Gemma's head ached and she realised she was exhausted. But before going to bed, she unlocked her safe and lifted out the gun case. Working quickly, she assembled the weapon, chambered the nine cartridges and pushed the magazine home. She took the Glock with her into her bedroom and put it under her pillow. She'd heard about colleagues deep in the world of undercover double-crosses doing this. She'd never imagined that one day it'd be necessary for her. Something in her felt defeated.

The Ratbag breathed gently on her sofa bed and she envied him the relative simplicity of his life. She put his washed clothes out to dry on the deck and went back to her bedroom, where she remade the bed, trying to settle down. Despite her physical exhaustion, she lay listening to how the soft surging of the sea smoothed over every other sound, softening and hiding them. She wished for clean, clear silence so that she could hear the slightest footfall. It was an ugly feeling that someone hated her enough to make such a threat.

To take her mind off the anonymous letter, she started wondering about Romero and his ambiguous language. She thought again about Mrs Ponzi and the rat problem. Eventually, after pulling the pillow around, she finally got it to feel acceptable. She was just dozing off when, from the living room, the Ratbag yelled something incomprehensible.

Gemma bolted upright. But as the silence closed around her again, she relaxed her vigilance a little. Taxi came in and settled on her legs, becoming impossibly hot and heavy. She pushed him to the side and finally went to sleep.

A sound awoke her at dawn and she was immediately fully awake, feeling for the Glock. She lay there, senses alert, but heard nothing; eventually she relaxed, pulling her hand away from the weapon, and lay back again, wishing she could recontact the dream she'd been in before being startled. She caught the tail end of it. It had been about Mrs Ponzi and the rats. She got up to find the purloined letter and read it again, standing next to her bedroom window.

> *Dear Mr Romero, this is the third time I've had to ask you. Will you please tidy up your things? It's a disgrace and the neighbours say they saw rats. If you don't do this within seven days, I'm going to get a man in and get it all tipped. Sincerely, Mavis Ponzi.*

The tone reminded Gemma of what a mother might say to an untidy child who refused to clean up his room. She thought about this while she disassembled the Glock and locked it back in its safe in her bedroom. She had a shower and dressed in a skirt and T-shirt and made breakfast, tiptoeing round the Ratbag who was still crashed out on the sofa bed. She made a mental note to ring Kit later.

She wanted to talk over what was best to do about the Ratbag.

Her mobile rang: Angie.

'The techies were up all night with Romero's laptop,' she said. Gemma could hear the disappointment in her voice. 'Squeaky clean. Nothing in the history that shouldn't be there.'

'I'm following up that letter,' said Gemma. 'From Mrs Ponzi.'

She went into her CD-Rom program and checked the name. There were three Ponzis—two out Parramatta way and one at Queens Park. Mr Romero lived at Paddington, Gemma recalled, which adjoined Queens Park.

She called the number and a woman answered.

'I'm ringing on behalf of Mr Romero,' said Gemma, after giving her name.

'You tell that man I'm going to throw all his stuff on the tip and send him the bill!' said Mrs Ponzi. 'I've warned him!'

Bingo! thought Gemma, this new development eclipsing her concern about the death threat. 'I'll come round,' said Gemma. 'See what needs to be done.'

'You'd better get on to your friend!' Mrs Ponzi warned. 'Otherwise, it all goes in twenty-four hours!'

After the initial introductions, Mrs Ponzi, a square-bodied woman of indeterminate age, took Gemma down the side of her neat Federation house to a fibro garage standing against the back fence. The old-fashioned double doors were bulging outwards against a padlocked chain, timber splitting around their hinges.

'See what I mean?' said Mrs Ponzi. 'The place is going to fall over if he doesn't come and clear it out. Joan next door has seen rats running along the eaves!'

They approached the garage's side door and Mrs Ponzi pulled out a tagged key and unlocked it. Spider webs festooned the nearby window.

'How long has he rented this place?' Gemma asked.

'Must be nearly ten years now,' said Mrs Ponzi, opening the door to reveal a densely packed room, crowded shelving around the walls lined with numbered and coded boxes, piles of history journals and magazines towering from floor to ceiling along the walls and more stuffed into overflowing boxes and cartons. Some of the journals had been chewed at one stage and shreds of paper strewed any available floor space.

'Look at this! How he can find anything in this mess is beyond me,' Mrs Ponzi clucked and scolded under her breath, looking around at the bundles of magazines tied up and piled into stalagmites.

Gemma made her way through them, thinking that Romero must be the sort of man who couldn't throw out anything. She checked the magazines—history, lifestyle, art and antiques seemed to be the most popular, as well as a huge collection of cuttings and old newspapers. Six grey metal filing cabinets piled almost to the roof with bundled paper, stood against the inside of the garage doors, the pressure from the stacked papers on top of them threatening to break open the double doors. In front of the dusty window, an easel and a table covered with brushes and dried paint held several sketches. Gemma threaded her way through the maze of paper to see them better. Coy nymphs in revealing robes posed artfully in sentimental, pastoral vistas. Some of the luminous figures had been completed with faint washes of colour, others were still only at outline stage.

'Since my husband died,' Mrs Ponzi was saying, 'it was good having the extra dollars for the garage. But look at the mess now.' She wiped her hands on the duster she was holding. 'I draw the line at rats.'

Gemma murmured something, barely paying attention. This was a treasure trove—Mr Romero's storage space. Gemma's attention was drawn to a shrouded shape on the other side of the easel, near the window.

'I'll leave you to it then,' said Mrs Ponzi. 'Do you know anyone else who might want to rent this? The phone line's connected and there's a toilet and shower in the laundry over there.'

Gemma thanked her. 'I'll think about it,' she said.

After the woman left, Gemma went over to the paint-marked shrouding and pulled it off to reveal a tripod supporting a high-powered telescope. Without touching it, she squinted through. It was already focused and she could see a young girl walking across a distant verandah, her hair wrapped in a towel, to disappear briefly behind a blurry obstruction before reappearing. Gemma followed her actions until the girl vanished through a doorway.

Gemma drew back, moving the angle of the telescope slightly so as to discover what building supported the verandah. She squinted through the eyepiece again and realised it was familiar. She was looking straight through the window of one of the glassed-in balconies that formed part of the dormitories of Netherleigh Park Ladies' College. Gemma realised she'd been holding her breath. Mr Romero, she thought, you are in deep shit.

Like a hurricane, Gemma went through the drawers in the filing cabinets, pulling them out, checking all their contents. They were filled with more bundled art magazines and more of the familiar watercolours, all in the same coy pastoral style.

In the lowest drawer of the fifth filing cabinet, she lifted out a sheaf of clippings and under these she saw a black fabric bag. As she lifted it out, excitement surged—she could tell what it was from the shape and the weight.

'Ahh,' she said out loud. 'There you are.'

Gemma unzipped the bag. No wonder Mr Romero hadn't cared two hoots about the computer from his school office being taken for examination, she thought. Carefully, she lifted out the black laptop and its cables and took it over to the art table, clearing a space for it among the unfinished watercolours. Mrs Ponzi had told her about the phone line being put on out here. Although she was longing to know what Romero might have stored on this secret laptop, Gemma knew she must leave it alone until the police technicians examined it. Just by switching it on and logging on, valuable data could be irretrievably lost.

She rang Angie. 'There's enough here to arrest Mr Romero,' she said, telling her about the laptop and the telescope trained on the schoolgirls' dormitory.

'Get the hell out of there,' said Angie. 'Lock the place up and I'll get the cavalry straight over.'

'You'll be arresting Romero once you've seen this, I swear!' said Gemma.

'Great work, honeybun, but someone else will have to have that pleasure—I'm already in the car on the way to a job. Coming down Oxford Street.'

'But I really need to talk to you about something. Woman to woman,' Gemma said, her mind returning to the warning note in the envelope in her office. 'I need to see you.'

'I can't put this off, Gems. G-for-Gross called in sick again.'

Sick *again*, Gemma thought. It might be worth running a quiet surveillance operation on Bruno. Catch him moonlighting. Have something to hold over the bastard. Something to deal with.

'Reckons he's got some ear infection,' Angie was saying. 'So I have to go out to Richmond now.'

'But it's urgent,' Gemma insisted. 'Couldn't you detour, just for a few minutes?'

'No,' said Angie. 'Some kids camping out there found something really weird. Looks like multiple human remains. We've got to make sure Tasmin Summers isn't part of it. Lots of human teeth.'

'Please, Ange. I *must* see you. This is serious.'

There was a silence. 'Okay. Feel like a spin in the country?'

'What, now?'

'Yes, now. I'll radio Sean with the address so he can get the troops organised to visit Mrs Ponzi. Then I'll pick you up in ten minutes. You can talk to me on the way. Okay?'

Gemma said goodbye to Mrs Ponzi. She felt mean not telling her that in a little while her house and grounds would be crawling with searching police.

She drove home, her mind jumping between the new information she'd uncovered about Netherleigh Park's senior History teacher and the pencilled death threat that she wanted to talk about with Angie. Mr Romero was definitely prime suspect now. She briefly thought of Beatrice de Berigny and what this would do to her beloved college. And what if, she thought, Miss de Berigny was also implicated?

Once at home, she quickly put on some lipstick, changed into pants and sturdy R M Williams boots, grabbed an apple and left a note for Hugo telling him she'd be away for a few hours.

She put a twenty-dollar bill next to the note, then took it back again, remembering the wad of cash he'd had in his pockets. She stopped in her tracks. Something was wrong. Hugo had told her his backpack had been taken by heavies. That might be so, but how come he had all that money? No one ever has the drugs and the money together. Hugo was lying to her. Eddie whoever might be capable of exploiting a kid as a courier, but there was no way he'd break the first and last commandment of dealing. If Hugo was delivering coke and other prohibited substances to people, there was no way he'd be handling the money as well. Deliverance's customers must work on a credit system.

Gemma went over to where Hugo lay sleeping on his back, hair tousled, eyelashes surprisingly long against his cheeks, just a little boy. Her hand that had been about to shake him awake dropped back to her side. She'd deal with it later. She went into her office and picked up the warning note in its envelope, slipping it in her briefcase. Then she heard Angie's car outside.

Traffic was light on the Anzac Bridge. The huge bronze soldier, head bowed in eternal grief, stood frozen over his Lee Enfield rifle. White sails shone in the morning sun and a light breeze belied the rising summer heat. Angie turned the police radio down so that it was no more than a murmuring presence punctuated with soft static.

'Good on you, girl,' said Angie, after Gemma had told her the whole story of what she'd found in Mrs Ponzi's garage. 'No wonder he wasn't worried about us taking his school computer. Can't wait to have a chat with him.'

'Guess who turned up on my doorstep last night?' said Gemma.

'Stevie boy? I told you—'

Gemma shook her head. 'The Ratbag.'

Angie frowned. 'The Ratbag?'

'Young Hugo,' Gemma reminded her. Used to live in the flat beside mine.'

'He's always turning up on your doorstep,' said Angie. 'What does he think he is? A homing pigeon?'

They drove in silence for a while, passing outlying suburbs leafy with trees and small-acre holdings, where horses grazed and project builders had delivered too many massive houses, badly proportioned, shoddily constructed. As they headed further west, the heat started rising and Gemma turned the air vent louvres in her direction.

'Tell me more about these teeth,' she said.

'A detective rang from Parramatta. Some kids had camped out Richmond way and, to cut a long story short, they're talking multiple human remains.' Angie slowed for a red light. 'So even though it's a long shot, one of us has to go out there and take a look.'

She squinted in the bright sunlight and gestured to the glove box. 'Fish around in there, will you? You'll find some sort of visitor's badge.'

Gemma opened the compartment and found a plastic card on a safety pin.

'Are my sunglasses in there too?' asked Angie.

Gemma shook her head. 'There's only the street directory.'

'Damn. I was sure they were in there. I'm blind these days without them.'

Gemma frowned, reading the lettering on the

badge under the clear plastic. 'The Western Australian Police Academy?'

'Stick it on. And grab the directory. I've marked the page. We're looking for a property half a click past the Warners Creek turn-off.'

As they approached their destination, Gemma spotted the cars. A marked police sedan was parked near the entrance to a run-down paddock. Next to a derelict fence, now not much more than trailing barbed wire between hand-adzed fenceposts, stood a smart blue Saab.

Angie pulled over and the two of them walked through old iron gates that had stood open for years, Angie muttering, 'Just stick close to me and try to look intelligent.'

It felt fifteen degrees hotter out here and sticky little bushflies homed in on their eyes, lips and nostrils. A tall young woman in linen slacks stood near some stringy eucalypts. When she turned round her face was familiar to Gemma. She tried to place it as she and Angie hurried over.

'Melissa Grey,' said the young woman, waving flies away and putting her hand out. 'I'm with Photographic at Parramatta.'

'Angie McDonald,' said Angie, extending her hand. 'From Sydney.' The two of them shook hands and Angie turned to introduce Gemma. 'And this is—'

'I know who this is.' Melissa smiled.

'We know each other.' Gemma shook Melissa's hand. 'We met in circumstances somewhat similar to these. Standing around in the bush.'

'That's right. You were with Nick Yabsley at that fire site last year.' Melissa glanced at the Visitor badge, then turned and indicated a house across the road. 'My partner's gone over there to try to find out who owns this piece of land.'

'So who belongs to the Saab?' Gemma jerked her head back in the direction of the road.

'The forensic anthropologist,' said Melissa. 'She was out here before we arrived.' Gemma noticed a space-suited figure bending over near a burnt-out eucalypt at the edge of the scrub.

'We haven't taped off yet,' said Melissa. 'We don't know how far it extends. I'm taking what photos I can while I'm waiting for the rest of Crime Scene.' She glanced at her watch. 'They shouldn't be much longer.'

The forensic anthropologist approached them, her gloved fingers bagging what looked like greyish stones.

'Francie Suskievicz,' she said, introducing herself, her blue eyes soft but shrewd at the same time behind her glasses.

Angie noted it down, checking the spelling. 'What've you got?' she asked.

'A lot of teeth.' Francie waved another plastic bag towards them. 'And this looks like part of a female pelvis. The rest is too fragmented and charred.' She shook the bagged teeth. 'At first, I thought it might have been an ancient burial ground. But several of the teeth had amalgam fillings, so it's definitely more recent. Seems to extend from that ridge over there,' she said, pointing, 'to where those trees start.'

That was a big crime scene, Gemma thought. A roughly cleared area about the size of a football field, rising to a ridge at one end, straggly eucalypts along one side, the road on the other.

Angie took the bagged piece of bone and shook it, looking at it from another angle. 'How many involved?'

Francie pulled a face. 'Can't really say. Not at this stage. I've already got enough teeth to indicate several people. Depending on how many more I find, it's quite possibly a lot more.'

Gemma peered more closely at the bone fragment Angie was holding. It was astounding that Francie could tell what part of the body it was from, let alone the gender.

Angie passed it back to Francie and shielded her squinting eyes with a hand. 'So what do you think?' she asked.

Francie shrugged. Now that her face was relaxed, Gemma could see she was a pretty woman, younger than she'd thought. 'I don't know what to think. Looks like someone's burned several, possibly five or six, bodies somewhere then buried the remains here.' She looked at her watch. 'I'm going to be here for some time. This whole area is going to have to be sieved.'

Angie pulled two business cards from her briefcase and gave one each to Melissa and Francie. 'Okay,' she said, 'Parramatta Homicide called me and I came out here, but there's not much I can do right now. Once this place is marked out and you know what you've got, let me know and I'll take it from there.'

She gestured to Gemma and the two of them walked back to the car.

'No way I'm spending days sieving dirt,' said Angie. 'I could just see Francie going to her car and passing a few around. I leave that to the youngsters these days.'

She opened the car and switched on the air conditioning, leaning over the top of the door while the interior cooled down.

Gemma opened her door and climbed in. 'It's a long time since I've been in the crime scene field. I'd forgotten all the fun of the heat and the flies. And the stink.'

'This lot is way past stink,' said Angie, also climbing in and slamming the door. She swung the car around. 'Let's get back to town. They'd have picked up Romero by now.'

They drove in silence a while and Gemma took the liberty of finding a nostalgia station on the radio. '*This is the end, my friend*,' Jim Morrison warned. Gemma looked out the window to distract herself from thinking of Steve.

They were just on the outskirts of the city when Angie's mobile rang. She fumbled for the earpiece, listening intently. 'Great work, Tracey,' she said finally, ringing off and Gemma waited expectantly.

'Okay,' said Angie, turning to her. 'Tracey Lee and her lot are going through the laptop you found in the garage. There's a whole lot of images of Amy in her bedroom.'

'Romero was the peeper?' Gemma said, surprised.

Angie shook her head. 'He didn't have to go out peeping. Amy was a webcam girl. And so was her friend Tasmin Summers. We found evidence of an archived website. Those girls were sending their bedrooms all around cyberspace. Tracey's copying all the details for me. She's got Tasmin's laptop too. Dangerous stuff for schoolkids.'

'You remember how naive we were at sixteen?' Gemma said.

'I was doing a man's work on the farm at sixteen, running a family,' said Angie, 'and studying. Dad had long gone and Mum was doing her best. I didn't do naive.'

'What I'm saying,' said Gemma, 'is the whole world had access to Amy and Tasmin.'

'You said it. School banners on the walls, uniforms. You wouldn't have to be supercop to work out who and where those girls were. They were practically handing out their addresses.'

'So Romero got those images quite legitimately?' Gemma said. 'Damn. I thought we had him cold. This makes everything far more complicated.' She thought of something. 'How come that webcam was never found in Amy's bedroom when the first investigation was on?'

Angie turned to her. 'Did you see it when you looked through her room the other day?'

Gemma shook her head. 'There was only a big old computer there. But I wasn't doing a search.

I was there to get a sense of the girl. Getting to know her.'

'How could the original investigation have missed that Amy and her bedroom were online?'

They both turned to each other, speaking in unison. 'Bloody Bruno!'

'Bruno missed finding an old lady in her flat when I was still in the job,' Gemma recalled, winding the window down because Angie had switched off the air conditioning. 'Mind you, the place was a bit of a mess. And she'd been dead for a while.'

'Somewhere in Amy Bernhard's room there's a laptop and a camera,' said Angie. Gemma recalled the big velvet cushions decorated with the suits of playing cards, the patriotic teddy bear wearing his flag.

'Soon as I get back in town,' said Angie, 'I'm turning that girl's room upside down until I find it.' She paused. 'And talking to the boss about widening the search for Tasmin Summers.'

'Count me in,' said Gemma. 'You know you'll need a hand.'

The city loomed ahead, and an aeroplane disappeared behind the buildings towards the south.

'Bruno's got to be moonlighting,' Angie finally said.

'Yeah. I was thinking the same. Or maybe he's having an affair.'

Angie threw her head back in mock horror. 'A woman would have sex with him?'

Gemma was stung.

Angie flashed her a wicked grin. 'He sure hasn't

got approval for a second job, because I've already asked.'

'That wouldn't stop Bruno. He could be doing VIP protection.'

Angie considered. 'God help the VIPs.'

'I toyed with the idea of tailing him,' admitted Gemma. 'Seeing what he does, where he goes. Then, when I've got some dirt on him, maybe he could be helpful.'

'Helpful? Bruno?' Angie gave Gemma a look then leaned back in her seat, stretching her arms on the steering wheel. 'I asked him about that memo—the one from Jim Buisman taking him off the earlier investigation.'

'And?' Gemma prompted.

'And he hit the roof. Accused me of trying to dig up dirt on him. I told him to stop being so paranoid, that he'd given me the memo himself accidentally mixed up in the case notes. That shut him up.'

'But did he say why he'd been removed?'

'Reckoned it was a personal thing. They didn't see eye to eye over certain things is how he put it. I told him I thought him and old Jim Boozeman saw eye to eye over everything. Including a schooner or ten down at the Kensington Club.'

'If I had the time,' said Gemma, 'I'd keep an eye on him. Maybe there is some dirt to dig.'

She took the warning note out of her briefcase and waved it. 'Speaking of dirt—I got this in the mail. I've sealed it up and I don't want to open it again.'

'What is it?'

'Something I want you to pass on to the analytic lab. See what they can get off it. I'd get Lance at Paradigm to do it except I know they're up to their eyeballs in work.'

'Why? What is it? Death threat or something?' Angie said, grinning. The grin faded as Gemma spoke.

'That's exactly what it is. Anonymous tip-off. There's a contract out on me.'

'On you? You're not the type!' exclaimed Angie.

Gemma reached over and slid the sealed envelope into Angie's slim bag on the back seat.

'So what exactly did it say?'

'There is a contract out on your life,' Gemma quoted. 'Watch your back.'

'Who do you suspect?'

Gemma shrugged. 'There's no one I can think of.'

'What about last year? The way your files were outed? And you had some trouble with that one fellow,' said Angie, making a fast right-hand turn.

'Some trouble? Ange, the bastard tried to kill me!'

'That's what I mean. Maybe you've offended someone else?'

Gemma thought of the confidential jobs made public last year. It was quite possible that she'd mortally offended more than one vengeful person.

'I'll see what the scientific fellows make of it,' said Angie, settling down in the right-hand lane. 'So are you taking it seriously? You should.'

'Of course I am,' said Gemma 'I'm watching my back.'

'You should probably make it official.'

'What? Tell the police?' said Gemma.

'You're hurting my feelings,' Angie retorted.

'What the hell could "official" do that I can't?'

'Then we've got a record of it—'

'When I'm dead that'll be a great comfort!'

Gemma stared sightlessly at the houses, the traffic, the glare off the enamel and chrome of the cars ahead. Above, she heard a jet whining closer.

'Okay,' she said. 'Make it official.'

TEN

Angie phoned ahead as they neared Lauren Bernhard's house to warn of their arrival, treating her gently. Then, with Lauren standing in the doorway, Gemma and Angie made a thorough and systematic search of Amy Bernhard's bedroom, starting at floor level and moving slowly higher. Barely had they begun on the lower middle grid of the room when, well hidden at the bottom of the big box of clothes and old toys, Angie found a small black laptop wrapped in a shawl and the webcam hidden in a teddy bear.

Lauren Bernhard's dismay was obvious as she moved closer to inspect what Angie had discovered. 'I didn't know she had one of those. How could she afford something like that?' Lauren looked from Gemma to Angie. 'How could she have been running that from my house and me not know anything about it?'

'The cost of running the webcam wouldn't show up on your accounts,' Angie explained, 'because you're on broadband.'

'I thought access to the net would be helpful to her studies.' Lauren's voice was a whisper. 'Instead she was broadcasting her life, her bedroom, to the whole wide world!' Her voice rose in anger and distress. 'I can't believe this! I knew nothing about it!'

'We'll need to take the laptop.' Angie's voice was gentle. 'We'll get it back to you as soon as the technical people have checked it out.'

'Is there someone you can ring?' Gemma suggested, not liking to leave Amy's mother so clearly distraught. 'Someone who could come over and be with you for a while? It might be better for you not to be alone.'

Lauren Bernhard's face clenched. 'What good would that do? They'd have to go again.' She picked up the teddy bear, which had hidden the webcam and its cable and put it back on the shelf again, redraping the Eureka flag. 'Anyway,' she said, 'alone is how I am.'

The two of them climbed back into Angie's car, Gemma carefully stowing Amy Bernhard's laptop onto the floor behind her seat. 'The day of the laptops,' she said. As she spoke, Angie's mobile rang.

'Bruno?' Angie turned to Gemma and winked. 'What a surprise! We were just talking about you.' Gemma saw the smile on her face fade. 'Leave the copy on my desk, please.'

Finally she rang off and started the car. 'Two things,' she said. 'He's still off work—just dropped in to leave his medical certificate. The call was to tell me the full PM report is in on Amy Bernhard.'

'And?'

'It gives us nothing that we didn't already know from the prelim report.' She paused. 'But the best bit is,' she grinned at Gemma, 'that Bruno's just discovered that both Amy and Tasmin seem to have had websites. And webcams! He's going to look into it.'

Angie stopped outside Gemma's place. 'Keep the visitor's badge,' she said. 'You never know when it might come in handy.' Gemma started to get out of the car. 'And get Spinner to keep an eye on your cute arse,' Angie added, leaning over.

'I've done that already.' But, Gemma realised, he couldn't be there all the time.

She hurried down the steps to her front garden, letting herself in as Angie sped away. She found the Ratbag still tangled up in sheets on her lounge, watching television. She walked over and switched it off. Hugo threw the sheet over his head and lay back, a shrouded mummy, but Gemma dragged it off him.

'Hugo. We're going to have to do some serious talking. About your future.' She sniffed the air. 'You've been smoking dope!'

'So?' he said, careless.

'So not in my house, sport. Okay?'

'Okay.'

'I'm serious, Hugo. This is a business I'm running here. And if I'm ever going to employ you, I'll need you to have a clear mind. I don't want some brainfucked dopehead on my staff.'

He nodded, impressed by her language. 'Okay. What's to eat?'

She sent him up to the shops to buy a barbe-cued chicken for a late lunch, and rang Kit. After bringing her up to date with everything except the warning note about the contract, she told her sister about Hugo.

'He seems to always end up at your place,' Kit said. 'He must really like you.'

For the first time, the idea pleased Gemma. Maybe the kid could stay for a few days. It would be a distraction from her heartache about Steve and her fear concerning the threatened contract. And it was nice to have some company. 'His parents won't be too impressed,' she said.

'Have you found out any more about our half-sister?'

Gemma thought a moment. 'I wanted to talk to you about that.'

'Because,' Kit continued, 'I was thinking that your music teacher of the Paddington Historical Walks Society might be just the right person to ask about the Kingston family of Hargreaves Street.'

'Kit, I'm not so sure about it now. That's what I wanted to talk about.' She heard the Ratbag arriving back. 'I have to go. I'll call you later.'

They both wolfed down chicken with fresh rolls and salad at the dining table—it was too hot out-side on the deck. Taxi nagged around, jumping up on the table and generally being annoying, until Gemma had to lock him in her bedroom so they could eat in peace.

Outside, a flock of rock pigeons flew past, disappearing beneath the level of the cliffs. Gemma remembered the Ratbag's earlier devotion to a small injured falcon. She recalled his intensity, his perpetual frown and expression of bewilderment, still evident in his face now.

'Hugo,' she said. 'I've decided that you can stay here for a couple of days.'

The worried frown lifted. Not a smile exactly, but a brightening of his features.

'But you must try to sort things out with your parents,' she continued. 'You can't just keep arriving on my doorstep every year. You're not a migrating bird.'

'I like it here. I liked living here when me and Mum lived next door. You're cool.'

'That's not the point.'

The Ratbag was demolishing the rest of the chicken so she salvaged a bit for Taxi's dinner. Then she cleared the table and he helped stack the dishes in the dishwasher, trying to be as good as good can be.

'How much money have you got with you, Hugo?'

He pulled fistfuls out of his pockets. 'I had about three hundred. But I spent some.'

'I hope Eddie No Name decides not to come after you for that amount.' She watched while he stashed the money back in his pockets. 'First thing, I want you to ring your mother and tell her that you're safe. You can tell her you're quite welcome here for a couple of days, but that something has to be sorted out,' she said, handing him the phone.

'Would you talk to her?'

Gemma shook her head. His faith in her was touching and she wished she had Kit's wisdom.

Reluctantly, he picked up the phone. It rang for a while and she saw his whole face change when someone answered. 'Hi, Mum. It's me,' he said, then listened for what seemed like minutes to the heated response from his distant mother, looking pained but resigned. His deep frown was back along with the puzzlement.

Gemma had the feeling he'd heard it all before. Finally, he passed the phone to her. 'She wants to talk to you.'

Gemma took it.

'Is it true?' Hugo's mother asked. 'He can stay there for a few days?'

'Yes. I'm happy to have him,' Gemma replied.

'I don't know what I'm going to do with him. He's a very difficult child. We have to sort something out,' Hugo's mother continued. 'Something that Hugo is happy about.' There was a pause. 'I'll ring his father and we'll work something out. And thank you for offering Hugo hospitality,' she added.

That sounds rather grand, Gemma thought, ringing off. Is that what she'd done? But there wasn't time to feel pleased with herself. She had to deal with one of her clients. She turned to the Ratbag. 'I have to go out for a couple of hours, Hugo.'

'Get some decent food, will you?' he said, waving a twenty-dollar bill at her.

'Pizza?' she said, taking it. He nodded.

Gemma rang Beatrice de Berigny and drove to Netherleigh Park.

Beatrice de Berigny let her into the small sandstone residence, once the gatekeeper's house, now an elegant home to the presiding school principal of the college. Inside, the stone walls were hung with tasteful art and distant glimpses of the harbour to the north-west and the bays and marinas of the harbourside beaches to the east could be seen through the gauzy curtains. A framed photograph of Miss de Berigny's merchant banker husband stood on a table. Somewhere, Gemma had read that he preferred living in the marital home in Woollahra.

The principal of Netherleigh Park had been crying, Gemma was sure. She looked older, plainer, without her usual make-up. 'It's all been a most dreadful shock,' she said as Gemma followed her in. 'I just don't know what I'm going to do. The phone hasn't stopped ringing in the office. I've even had some calls on my private line although it's supposed to be a silent number.'

She wiped her eyes with a tiny handkerchief and seemed to recover. 'You must excuse me, Miss Lincoln.' Her voice was icy now. 'We've never had a staff member arrested before. I've just come back from taking him some personal items.'

'What's Mr Romero saying?' Gemma asked.

'That he's completely innocent. That all he did was use that telescope as an aid to anatomical accuracy in his paintings.'

'I've heard about the images he had on his

laptop,' Gemma said. 'They might have been anatomically accurate, but that's not all they are.'

The principal averted her face. 'I am so absolutely shocked and stunned by all this.'

Gemma wished she could see Beatrice de Berigny's face as she spoke. There was some other quality underlying her words. Was it rage? Humiliation?

'But,' the principal continued, 'he's an adult and there's no law against downloading the sorts of things he did. It's all a matter of personal taste.' The bitterness in her voice as she uttered these words could have corroded steel, Gemma thought. 'He's screaming that he's completely innocent,' Miss de Berigny continued.

'I need Mr Romero's employment details,' said Gemma.

'What relevance would they have?'

Is the woman stupid, Gemma thought. Or is this just stalling?

'I need to have a look at where else he's worked,' she said patiently. 'I'm surprised the police haven't yet contacted you about that.'

'He'll never work in teaching again,' said Miss de Berigny after a pause. 'Besides, that sort of thing is confidential.'

'Miss de Berigny,' Gemma was getting irritated, 'I'm investigating a murder case. "Confidential" doesn't really apply when two of your students were displaying themselves and their bedrooms to the world and the dead body of one of them is found dumped on a vacant lot. Especially when images of both girls have shown up on Mr Romero's laptop.'

Those words had a sobering effect. Beatrice de Berigny sank onto a pink linen lounge and blew her nose on the tiny hankie.

'Just let me do my job, please.' Gemma's voice was hard. 'Both the girls had an early appointment with Mr Romero the day of their disappearances. According to him,' Gemma continued, 'neither girl showed up for those meetings. And he was late arriving at school on the day of Amy's disappearance and also Tasmin's disappearance.'

Gemma let that sink in.

'I don't understand what's been going on.' Then Beatrice de Berigny straightened herself up and, right in front of Gemma's eyes, transformed into her professional self. She picked up a set of keys from the table. 'Follow me, please,' she said. 'We need to go over to the office.'

Twenty minutes later, Gemma was driving home, copies of Mr Romero's CV safe in her briefcase, thinking over the way Beatrice de Berigny had transformed from genteel obstruction to cooperation. What had happened to make her change that way? Had the awful possibility of one of her employees being a murderer finally penetrated her consciousness?

She drove back to Lauren Bernhard's and parked her car opposite. The house summered in the deep shade of the trees around it and the leafy hedges that separated it from its neighbours. On the left stood the two-storey house in which Mr

Alistair Forde lived. Gemma got out and crossed the road, enjoying the slight breeze that moved the trees. Languid roses dropped petals as she stepped up to his front door. *How many doors have I knocked on,* she suddenly wondered, *with my questions? And who have I offended to the point of wanting me killed?*

She turned her attention back to the man Lauren Bernhard had called a harmless old bachelor.

When Alistair Forde answered the door, Gemma noticed how he shrank back. 'Yes?' he asked, the lines in his face deepening. Was it suspicion or just puzzlement? In his hand, he gripped a model battleship. 'I'm gluing this,' he said. 'Have to keep it firmly pressed for a minute or two.'

Gemma flashed a smile and her ID and briefly explained the reason for her visit.

'You'd better come in then,' he said, stepping back as she did.

The house seemed very dark after the brilliant afternoon and she was happy to follow him out to a less dim place, a large room with windows onto the back garden, but partly covered with dusty venetian blinds that looked permanently fixed at half-mast. She waited as her eyes adjusted, but because the house was aligned east–west it was still rather dark inside. Then she took in her surroundings. All the surfaces were covered with models: aeroplanes, battleships and tanks.

'You'll be wanting to know more about that dreadful business next door. Young Amy Bernhard.' The whites of his knuckles showed as he pressed the topside of the small plastic ship onto its hull. 'I don't know what the world's coming to.'

Gemma hurried on. 'Can you tell me about the person you saw in the garden? The one you mention in your statement.'

'Just over there he was.' Mr Forde pointed through the venetians with the plastic destroyer.

Gemma went to the window. Dead flies lay along the sill and small patches of cobweb filled the lower corners of the pane.

'I'm particularly interested in what you saw that night, Mr Forde,' she said. 'Can you point out exactly where the person was?' She strained but could see no bushes. 'You said the person was crouched in bushes. I can't see anything like bushes from here.'

She straightened up again. Forde was looking distinctly uneasy. He put the plastic battleship down, then picked it up again, fiddling with it.

'You won't see from there.'

'Where did you see from?'

Did he make the whole thing up, Gemma wondered. Some people would do anything to feel part of something, even an investigation into a missing person. Made them feel important. 'Are you sure you saw someone that night?'

His face shifted, irritation. 'Of course I did.'

Gemma waited, letting the silence build the tension.

'I saw it from upstairs.'

'I'd like you to show me.'

'What? Go upstairs?'

For a moment, Gemma was spooked. Did he have his mummified old mother up there? Would he come after her with the carving knife like Norman Bates in *Psycho*?

'Yes,' she said. 'I want to go upstairs and have a look.'

'But why? What good will that do? There's nothing to see now.'

Don't be too sure of that, sport, Gemma thought, sure now that Forde was hiding something. He shrugged and put the model destroyer down on a table near the window and, in silence, Gemma followed him up a flight of stairs and along a corridor until they came to a half-open door.

'This is my bedroom,' said Forde. His tone was plaintive but she walked in and looked around. A dark, cramped space—a single bed, a wardrobe and a chest of drawers surmounted by a cedar mirror on a small stand. A large table pressed against the flowery curtains hanging on each side of the window. Strange place to put a table, Gemma thought, as she tried to lean across it to look outside. 'You saw the prowler out of this window?' Her disbelief was evident.

Forde nodded.

'Not with this table here.' She made it sound more of a statement than a question. Forde seemed to have shrunk further since coming upstairs; she was reminded of a snail pulling back into itself.

'It wasn't there that night.' Now he sounded sulky.

'Can you help me move it then, because you

couldn't have seen anything out of the window with that standing in the way.'

Silently, the two of them lifted the table away and Gemma noticed the deep impressions left in the carpet by the table legs. Even now, standing close to the window, she could barely see any of the hedge and bushes that separated the properties. She stood on tiptoe. That gave her a slightly better vantage point. Gemma did a few rough spatial calculations. She worked out that the window towards the back of the house next door belonged to Amy Bernhard's bedroom. But unless she was able to get higher up—stand on a table, for instance—she wasn't able to see over the fence between the properties.

She turned back to Mr Forde, who stood in the doorway, his hands in his pockets. 'In your statement, Mr Forde, you said you were changing a light bulb. Can you please show me which one you meant?'

Forde looked around the room as if the shaded light fitting had the habit of moving around and appearing in unexpected positions. Finally he pointed to the shaded light hanging in the middle of the room.

'That one?' Gemma moved to stand under it, then looked towards the window. 'But you can't see out the window from here! What did you mean?'

'I pulled the table over to reach it. And I could see from up there.' Forde fidgeted with a button on his shirt, twisting it. 'You can see from up there,' he indicated the light fitting, 'if you're standing on the table.'

'And which room was the intruder outside?' Gemma peered out again, trying to see the hedge near Amy's room.

'He was crouched down there. In the bushes outside her bedroom.'

'Are you sure it was this window you looked from? I don't mean to badger you, Mr Forde, but I want to get it clear in my head. If you were standing on the table in the middle of the room, I don't see how it would be possible to see out the window at all. Let alone be able to see someone down there in those bushes over the fence.'

'I'm taller than you. So I can see down there better than you.' He was rattled. 'I want to go back downstairs now. I'm in the middle of making something, you know.' His voice had become querulous. 'I don't like being interrupted.'

'Thank you,' said Gemma, stepping back from the window. 'That's very helpful. Let me give you a hand putting the table back. Where does it normally stand?'

'No need for that,' he said. 'I just pushed it over when I was doing the carpets earlier. Like I said, it's not usually there at all.'

This must be the only room that Mr Forde does any housework in, Gemma thought, following him downstairs again, the information she'd just absorbed going round in her mind. This time, instead of leading her back through the house, he headed her off near the front door. 'You've seen what you came for. You must excuse me,' he said. 'I'm rather busy just now.'

'Of course. You've been most helpful.' More than you know, pal, she thought.

She walked outside and heard the front door close behind her. In this job, it's a shame but we always assume the worst of everyone, she thought. Not a nice character trait. But niceness doesn't get them arrested and put away. She wondered just how many neighbours knew which bedroom was which in the house next door. Not only did Mr Forde know where Amy slept, but he was lying through his teeth about that table. And Gemma knew why. She thought of Angie's workload; her own wasn't any lighter. She needed to talk to Kosta.

Scrolling down to his number, she rang him, leaving a message asking him for any information about an Eddie who worked at Deliverance. She was also curious to discover if he knew anything about the man with the diamond stud.

She turned off William Street into Macleay, taking a detour on her way home, her senses stimulated by the biscuity odour of cooking. She suddenly longed for ice-cream in a cone. She found a parking spot on Macleay Street; the late afternoon sun still hot and making rainbows in the fine spray from the El Alamein fountain.

Across the road at the ice-cream shop, a family group were walking out, licking their cones, the kids' ones piled high and sprinkled with hundreds and thousands. The mother and father, arms around each other, swapped ice-creams. Then the father noticed ice-cream dripping from the chin of the smallest of the children and quickly wiped it off before it could fall on his clothes. The adults laughed together and then kissed in that easy well-oiled way that long-time couples have. Gemma felt a pang of jealousy. Why didn't she have a nice husband like that and a couple of happy kids? She looked again at the family group. Then she looked closer and, in that moment, the man swung round and made eye contact. Too late Gemma turned away. Oh my God, she thought. It can't be. It's not possible. It mustn't be.

But it was.

Back home, she tried to take her mind off what she'd just seen at Kings Cross by making a detailed study of Mannix Romero's CV. He'd been educated at Bathurst, she read, worked in one of the local banks as a clerk for five years before going back to college and training as a teacher. Then he'd taught History and English at Bathurst High School before resigning after seven years and apparently leaving the public system. He'd spent twenty years working in two private schools before joining the staff at Netherleigh Park some years previously. She made a note of the two private schools—St Angelica's in Bowral and Boronia House in the lower Blue Mountains—jotting down the office phone numbers.

There was nothing immediate or obvious in the pattern of his employment history to excite her suspicion. But she'd definitely check up; find out why he'd left his last jobs. If there was a breath of scandal surrounding Mannix Romero, Gemma was determined she'd sniff it out.

After another night with the Glock under the pillow, Gemma rose early to hear the Ratbag still snoring gently. After she'd showered and dressed, she and Taxi had breakfast under the big sun umbrella, watching the nor'easter wrinkle the sea. She barely tasted her toast and marmalade, haunted by what she'd seen yesterday evening out-side the ice-cream shop and what she was going to do about it, her mind compulsively going over and over it, until it almost pushed aside the notice of a murder contract. She went into her office and waited while her email messages downloaded. Her email program sounded and she opened her inbox. Most of it was junk about penis enlargement, cheap Viagra and Zanax or offers of pornography. She went through, deleting them. She wasn't fast enough for one though and it started opening on her screen. *If you want to know what happened to Amy and Tasmin, check this website*, said the sum-mary. There was no name in the sender field. Gemma's heart beat hard as she clicked on the link www.xxxtremelycuteschoolgirls.com and waited for the website to unfold. She was disappointed. *This page cannot be displayed*, said her browser. Gemma tried again, using variations of the web-site's name. Her search engines came up with similar material—over twelve thousand references. Checking each of those just wasn't possible; she'd get Mike to see if he could trace the sender instead. Meanwhile, she sent the email onto Angie. It could be a crank, but someone had taken the trouble to find Gemma's email address. And she wanted to know who that someone was.

The Ratbag shuffled out, still half asleep heading straight to the fridge, until she sent him to have a shower, promising to make him scrambled eggs. After he'd showered, he ate them and then another three slices of toast spread thickly with peanut butter as well as two more with honey before helping her with some pruning, chopping away at the scrubby bushes below the timber deck and cutting back an old lemon tree that Gemma had never known to bear fruit. As she piled the offcuts into bundles and tied them up, she found herself thinking again of what she'd seen outside the ice-cream shop.

She woke the next morning with the scene still in her mind. What a way to start the week, she thought.

The doorbell sounded later and she looked up to see Mike's burly figure taking up a lot of room on the CCTV monitor. She went to the door to let him in and stood back as he entered, noticed that he was avoiding eye contact. 'Mike,' she said before he could start unpacking his camera, 'can you please come into my office and have a look at something that came in last night?'

'Sure,' he said, briefly meeting her eyes.

She pulled up the email that contained the

schoolgirls' website address. He leaned over, frowning at the message on her screen. 'Open it and let's have a look,' he said.

'That's just it,' she said. 'The website's been taken down. There is no website.'

'Do you think it's a genuine tip-off?'

Gemma shrugged. 'Can't say. But I sure want to check it out.'

Mike peered closer. 'The email's from anonymous at Hotmail,' he said. 'It'll be hard to trace. We can only try.' He paused. 'There are a couple of reports hanging over from last week that I need to write up. That real estate job—the one Spinner was doing, checking out the neighbours for the interested buyers?' He pulled out a diskette. 'These are Spinner's notes. Looks like they'll be buying next to the neighbours from hell if they go ahead.'

He indicated her laptop and held out the diskette. Gemma didn't take it. 'Mike. We have to talk.'

'Yes,' he said.

She finally took the diskette from him and put it on the desk. Mike picked it up again, fiddling with it, glancing at her. 'I'm getting plenty of other work. I can hand in my notice. I think that's the best thing to do.'

Gemma felt shocked. Though she'd foreseen this as a possibility, now that it was actually happening it felt terrible. And she'd occasioned it herself with her intoxicated, wilful lust. 'Mike. Please. Don't say that.' She hesitated. 'Unless it's really what you want to do.'

'It's not what I want to do. It's what I think I

have to do.' He threw her another long look then busied himself with his video camera, his broad back turned against her.

'I have to accept responsibility for what happened,' she said. 'But can't we find a way that doesn't mean you have to go?'

He turned round at this and she saw the sadness in his face and the concern. 'Look,' he said. 'You can't go because you're the boss. I can't stay because I overstepped a mark the other night. And a certain situation occurred.'

'God, you sound like an incident report! And you didn't "overstep" anything!' Gemma's voice rose sharply. 'I pulled you over whatever "mark" you're talking about. I made the first move.'

'No. I kissed you.' He was looking at her intently and she wondered what was going through his mind.

'But I took it further,' she persisted, unable to look into his eyes any longer. 'It's not fair that you should lose your job because of my behaviour.'

'We don't live in a fair world. You must have noticed. And like I said, there's plenty of work for me.'

A sound came from Gemma's apartment and Mike frowned. 'Who's in there?' Then, shaking his head, 'Sorry. That's none of my business.'

'It's the Ratbag. He's staying over for a couple of days.'

'That kid?'

She nodded.

'I thought it might've been Steve.' Again, he spoke without looking at her.

She was incredulous. 'After what he must have overheard the other night?' Immediately Gemma regretted bringing the subject up again. She continued, talking too fast, awkward and off-balance, 'I don't know quite how to say this, but if you and I—I mean, if we could somehow just put the other night behind us. What I'm trying to say is, I'd like us to get back on a professional footing. Forget those few minutes. Forget they ever happened. Maybe you're—*we're* making more of this than is warranted.'

A long silence. Then, 'Maybe.'

They stood together in more silence a moment.

'I'm really sorry for my part in it. And now, I'm going back to work,' Gemma said. 'I'll call you later, after I've spoken to the cop at Waverley about Daria Reynolds's husband. What's a good time? I don't want to disturb you.'

'I don't mind if you wake me up,' he said with the hint of a smile. 'I'll get cracking on tracing that Hotmail email before I crash.'

Gemma turned to go back to her office.

'And I'll consider what you've suggested,' he added. 'Maybe the situation can be salvaged.'

God, she thought. He made her sound like a shipwreck.

'I've checked the Annie Dunlop program,' he continued, and Gemma recalled her music teacher's old mother. 'It seems to be working okay now.'

She thanked him and settled down to check her email—slow today, with several virus alerts—then she rang to check that Diane Hayworth was at work, toted up the account so far for Daria Reynolds, adding ten per cent GST and another ten per cent for nuisance tax and put the account and the records of their surveillance work in her briefcase, leaving them by the front door. Down the hall she went to tell Hugo she was heading out for a while, do her hair and apply some lipstick and mascara. That done, she went back to the operatives' office. She hadn't forgotten her intention to gather more intelligence about Bruno Gross—maybe Diane Hayworth might be helpful. And after the incident at the Cross, it was imperative that she contact Trevor Dawson. *Hi, Trevor,* she planned on saying. *Haven't seen you for ages, then I bump into you at the ice-cream shop at Kings Cross. Nice family you've got. So when do you intend to tell my best friend Angie about them?*

'Mike,' she said, 'I'm going out for a while. Can you lock up when you've finished here?'

He nodded but didn't turn round.

Waverley police station adjoined the busy local court and it was hard to find parking. Gemma had to walk a short distance, passing small groups of people outside the courtroom doors. Hairy young men dressed in unaccustomed suits accompanied by well-dressed lawyers. A gaunt woman with hair pulled back harshly and long black earrings puffed desperately at a cigarette before going through the doorway.

At the police station counter, Gemma asked for

Diane Hayworth. Diane, an attractive woman in her thirties, hair in a smart French roll, came out to meet her and took her through to her shared office space.

'Do you want a tea or coffee?' Diane asked, handing Gemma back her card.

'No, thanks,' said Gemma. 'Just a seat.' She sat on the chair Diane had pulled up near her desk.

'You used to be in the job, didn't you? I used to work with a girl who worked with you,' Diane said. 'She told me a bit about what happened to you. Why you left the job.'

'Yeah. It's a long story,' said Gemma, not wanting to revisit it. 'That was eight years ago.' She glanced around. It all smelled and looked much the same to her.

'You were shafted is what I heard,' said Diane.

'You can believe that.'

'And I heard that the men involved were promoted.'

'That too, is true.'

Diane gave her a hard look. 'Some things stay the same.'

'They do,' said Gemma. 'Does the name Jim Buisman mean anything to you?'

'Not much. He's off on indefinite sick leave. I hear he still reports for duty at the Kensington Club every day. He's one of the old pisspots.'

Gemma took a deep breath, thinking of what she'd accidentally seen outside the ice-cream shop. 'Do you know where I can get hold of Trevor Dawson?'

Diane took a brief phone call, then turned her

attention back to Gemma. 'Dawson? He used to go out with a girlfriend of mine. He's in the State Protection Group now,' she said. 'Used to be with the old TRG.'

'I need to contact him urgently. Have you got a number?'

'I used to have their number here somewhere.' She hunted round on her desk, lifting files and pads. 'So what's Daria Reynolds saying? No, don't tell me,' Diane paused in her search, 'I think I can guess.'

'She engaged me to run a surveillance operation,' said Gemma. 'Her ex-husband keeps breaking into the house and harassing her.'

'That's exactly what she told us,' said Diane.

'She's not very happy with the police. She says you're useless. That you're not doing anything about her husband stalking her. And trespassing.'

Diane sighed and took down a small address book that had been hidden behind an official book of by-laws. 'That woman is hard work. We went and talked to her and explained what she could do about it. When he was stalking her.'

'She reckons he still is,' Gemma said. 'I checked him out. He's a cleanskin. But maybe you know what he's like?'

Diane frowned, intent on something. 'Here it is. I knew I had it somewhere.' She glanced up. 'The number for the state protection guys.' She scribbled it on a card.

Gemma took it and slid it into her wallet, her mind preoccupied with Daria Reynolds and her stalking ex-husband. 'She says he's still stalking her,' she went on. 'Breaking into the house at night and, according to her, you haven't responded.'

Diane Hayworth stared. 'How could we respond—under the circumstances?'

Now it was Gemma's turn to stare. 'What do you mean? What circumstances?'

'She hasn't told you then?'

'Told me what?' Gemma was starting to get impatient. Why was Diane Hayworth stalling like this?

Diane lifted down a folder from the shelf near her computer screen. 'I printed this off for you— seeing as you were a colleague once—so you could read a copy of the case notes.' She passed the folder to Gemma. 'You can keep those.'

Gemma took them, curious. Diane leaned back in her chair, as if the whole thing was now out of her hands. 'I don't know who's been getting into Daria Reynolds's place,' she said. 'But it sure as hell isn't her ex-husband.'

Gemma opened the folder, leafing through photocopied incident reports.

'He isn't in a position to be stalking anyone,' Diane continued.

It took Gemma a moment or two to take it in. She stared at the print-out in disbelief.

'Vincent Reynolds has been dead for over a year,' Diane was saying. 'He's buried in Waverley Cemetery.'

ELEVEN

Gemma was hardly conscious of driving to Daria Reynolds's place. She swung the car against the kerb, jumped out and, clutching the print-out Diane Hayworth had given her, hurried up to the door. Again, the sickening smell of incense filled the air, reminding her of the weird candle procession. She rapped on the door.

After waiting a few seconds, she knocked again, harder this time. She listened intently for any sounds from the interior. What on earth was the woman on about? She stepped back and then made her way round the back of the house, calling out as she went, but there was no answering reply. The place seemed empty.

Gemma went back to the front, where she shoved one of her cards under the door with 'Ring me asap!' scribbled on it and underlined.

Daria Reynolds, you've got a helluva lot of explaining to do, she thought, as she drove away.

On her way to the Kensington Club, Gemma tried calling the State Protection Group number Diane Hayworth had given her. She left her name and a message asking Trevor Dawson to ring her urgently.

She rang several other contacts, who all promised they'd do what they could to get in touch with him.

Gemma parked a little way from the club, an ugly 1960s building of glass and concrete with a huge bronze fountain shaped like a box jellyfish in the foyer. The stench of stale tobacco and old beer hit her as she stepped inside its icy, overcooled interior. Beyond the box jellyfish, she could see through to a huge barn-like area where banks of flashing, whirring or spitting poker machines stood in long lines. She signed the visitors' book and looked around. She vaguely remembered Jim Buisman as a fair, bristly man, with the sort of reddish skin that deepens in colour over the years, either through weathering or alcohol. The club made her feel claustrophobic with its absence of windows and its ceiling hung with tiny lights that made it forever midnight. Through the noise and clatter of hundreds of people, she could smell the bistro and the fish cooking. She made her way between tables and chairs, people arguing, laughing too loudly or staring out at nothing. Over against a wall, with a schooner glass in front of him and reading a folded-down paper, she recognised the man she was seeking.

She walked up to him and put her hand out. 'Jim Buisman?'

'Who wants to know?' Buisman looked up at her, his shaved head a little to one side, squinting over his bifocal reading glasses. He was not pleased to be interrupted.

'I'm Gemma Lincoln,' she said with what she hoped was a disarming smile, hastily sitting before he could respond. 'Licensed investigator.' She flashed her ID. 'I'm hoping you can help me with a couple of questions.'

'Doubt it,' he said, looking down his nose at her ID and picking up the schooner glass.

'Let me buy you one,' she said chirpily.

'I remember you,' he said, leaning back in his chair and showing his large beer belly. 'You used to hang around with that smart little redheaded number. Annie McDonald.'

'Angie McDonald.'

He gave no sign he'd heard. 'I'm out of the job. HOD.'

'Shoot-out?'

'Milkshake.'

'They can be bloody dangerous.' Gemma couldn't resist. 'Specially the double malted.'

'When you slip on them in the meal room,' he said through his teeth, 'they can break a foot bone.'

Gemma regretted her flippant response and tried to make peace. 'What are you drinking?' He told her and she went over the long bar. By the time she got back with his new beer, he was deep in the sports section again and the glass in front of him was empty.

'So,' he said, folding the paper away as she sat down. 'What do you want from me?' It seemed he'd forgiven her now that the schooner had arrived.

As he drank the beer, she brought him up to date with what had happened since Amy Bernhard had disappeared, explaining her place in the investigation and asking him about his supervision of the original investigation when Amy was listed as missing.

'It's a homicide case now,' he responded. 'I heard she'd turned up on a bit of scrub near Port Botany. What have the scientific boys found?'

'Very little. All they've got is some fancy cord tied round a wrist. And an unusual knot.'

'Colin Roper can get a lot from knots,' said Buisman, turning his attention to a huge colour television in the corner of the room where a horse race was in progress.

'This one was called a thief knot,' said Gemma. 'Apparently it looks almost identical to a reef knot.'

Buisman grunted, not taking his eyes off the screen as the horses thundered down the straight.

'And you'll no doubt remember,' Gemma pressed on, 'that Bruno Gross was senior investigator in the initial strikeforce after Amy went missing.'

'So?' The winner flashed past the post and Buisman threw his newspaper down in disgust.

'I've sighted a memo sent by you,' Gemma persisted, 'taking Bruno Gross off the whole investigation. You mentioned a "situation".'

The energy between them suddenly changed. No longer was he the bored ex-cop, barely tolerating questions about something he couldn't care less about. Buisman's ruddy brow wrinkled and, although he affected a frowning forgetfulness, his eyes, when he took the bifocals off and placed them on the table, were hard and clear, wary and full of vigilance. 'You expect me to remember some piece of paper from a year ago?'

'If there was a situation warranting you taking someone off a case, I don't think you would have forgotten.' Gemma leaned in closer, working hard to pick up the subtext in his demeanour. 'I'd remember making a decision like that—taking someone off a case. And sending them the memo about it.'

'You women are pretty smart like that. You never forget anything.' He picked up his paper again. 'You should've seen the letter my ex-missus left me when she walked out.' He unfolded the newspaper and put the bifocals back on, turning his attention to another race, another horse's name with a red biro circle around it. 'Thanks for the beer. But I can't really help you.'

Gemma sat staring at him. He was lying, of that she was certain. Slowly she stood up.

Buisman glanced up. He leaned forward, as if he were about to confide in her. 'I'll give you a tip, just to show you that I can still appreciate a pretty girl.'

Gemma held her peace and waited.

'You mentioned a thief knot,' Buisman continued. 'I remember a violent offender who used a thief knot. A rapist. Colin Roper pointed it out to me. It was about twenty years ago. Used the girl's own scarf in one case. It's probably filed away somewhere in an old exhibit bag.' He attempted a smile but it went nowhere near his eyes. 'We never got that bastard.'

As she stepped outside, Gemma glanced back. Buisman, no longer involved with his sports newspaper or the races on the big monitor, was huddled in conversation on his mobile. Gemma would have taken bets about who was on the other end of the line.

'Your sister rang and the new tenant from upstairs knocked on the door,' said Hugo when Gemma arrived home.

'What?' She'd been miles away, wondering what Buisman was hiding under the booze and the horses.

'The new tenant upstairs,' the Ratbag reiterated patiently, the expression on his face saying: *See? I can be helpful to you.* 'He said to tell you that the gas man's coming in the morning to do some work for him and do you want any repairs done or anything?' He passed her a business card.

'When was this?' she said, looking at the gas man's card.

'About an hour after you left. He's offering a fifty per cent discount on bayonet fittings. Summer rates for winter jobs, he said.'

'Who said?'

'The new tenant said. About the gas man. What's the matter with you? You're not listening.'

Gemma focused her attention. 'What does the new tenant look like?'

'He's just an ordinary-looking bloke. Real cool shirt. Bit of a beer belly.'

'Come on, Hugo. If you want to work as a PI you're going to have to do better than that.'

Hugo beamed. 'Okay!' He took a deep breath. 'I'd say he was about one and a half metres tall, with dark hair—I mean, what you could see of it. He was going bald at the front. He had a tatt on one arm, but I couldn't—'

'Good work,' she said, cutting him short, relieved. It wasn't Mike.

'Have you got a bayonet?' He looked so impressed it was hard for her to disappoint him.

She explained what they were and put the gas man's card on the dining table, thinking she'd ring him later. Another bayonet fitting in her office would be ideal, especially at a discount. It got cold in there in winter.

'And Mike said be sure and let you know about the courier delivery.'

'What delivery?'

The Ratbag pointed towards her office. 'On your desk.'

A note in Mike's writing sat on top of a security courier package. Gemma picked it up. *This came and I signed for it*, Mike had written. *I opened it because it wasn't addressed personally to you. Who got this? I hope it wasn't you.*

Gemma pulled out the contents. It was the pencilled words of warning about the contract. She could see traces of the various techniques it had been subjected to: dusted and sprayed with glue. With it, on official letterhead, was the analyst's report. Gemma scanned it. Ruled paper from a small spiral notebook, the report stated, with partial prints that were unmatchable. A photocopy of the ESDA impressions—those slight indentations from the writing on earlier pages—showed a series of names of what were possibly racehorses or racing dogs and ticks or crosses beside them, as well as the words 'Ring beautician'. The report further suggested that the use of pencil possibly indicated someone who didn't usually write letters. Unfortunately, none of this fancy information would help to find the writer; although it suggested a woman, Gemma thought, or possibly a man who shared a notebook with a woman.

She put the note back in the package and rang Kit, telling her about Daria Reynolds and her husband, the walking dead. She heard the silence of Kit absorbing the strange story.

'Could be a number of things,' Kit finally said. 'Maybe she's so guilty about the relief she feels to have him dead, that she's punishing herself by hallucinating him back.'

'I wondered about that too. But why those questions about me? About our mother's murder? And me being "the right one". She's wasted my time and then has the cheek to wake me up and abuse me!'

They speculated a bit longer and then Kit said, 'Tell me, what's put you off trying to locate our sister? You were so keen before.'

'A number of things. Second thoughts, I guess. She's got all the sad things that make for a very difficult life.'

'Like us?' Kit asked.

'Worse,' said Gemma. 'Absent father, mother who suicided, then maybe fostering. Or adoption. What if she's already dead? Suicided? Or on the streets? Or a hopeless junkie?'

Kit was silent for a while. 'We had a difficult time of it too, but we've both made good lives for ourselves, Gems. And—'

'Sometimes I wonder if I've made such a good fist of it,' Gemma cut in. 'You've often said I work in a dangerous world—a world in which I sometimes expose myself needlessly. We've had fights about it in the past.'

Thinking of these made her decide not to tell Kit about the warning of a contract to kill her.

'Anyway,' she continued, 'I haven't had time to do anything much to find her apart from checking newspapers on microfiche. I've been flat out. I'm beginning to think that the arrival of the baby was never announced in the press. I've searched through almost all the birth announcements for that year. I haven't got round to asking Mrs Snellgrove—'

'You sound stressed out, Gems. Come around and have lunch with me tomorrow,' Kit said. 'We'll have a sisterly chat.'

'Here's something that can't wait till tomorrow,' Gemma said. 'Did I tell you Angie's in love with one of the State Protection guys?'

'You didn't.'

'Well, sister, she is. I've never seen her like this.'

'That's great.'

'No, it isn't.' Gemma hesitated. 'I was up at Kings Cross and I nearly bumped into him. He was eating ice-creams with his wife and kids.'

'Are you sure about that?'

'About as sure as I can be. From what I saw. I'm trying to find him—get his side of it before I talk to Ange.' She hesitated. 'Any good ideas about how to approach Angie if I have to?'

'It's his job to tell her,' said Kit. 'When was he going to do it—or did he think he could just go on like that, living two lives?'

'A lot of guys in the job do that,' said Gemma thinking of Steve. 'And get paid for it what's more.' The sudden sadness she felt made her blink. 'I've got calls out for Trevor Dawson. I'm going to say to him that if he doesn't tell Angie the truth in the next twenty-four hours, I'll have to. And I'll have to keep out of her way till then. I couldn't pretend everything's normal with this on my mind.'

'She'll hate you if you tell her,' said Kit, 'and she'll hate you if you don't.'

Gemma considered the options. 'She'll hate me more if I don't.'

Gemma rang off and walked out to the deck, past the Ratbag who was watching television. She leaned against the railing but pulled back, a tenderness in her breasts reminding her that she was due to bleed any moment. She'd ask Mrs Snellgrove if she had any knowledge of the Kingston family, she decided. But no more active searching on her part. Not just now, at any rate. There was already too much going on.

She went into the operatives' office and switched on the laptop Mike used, finding her way to the surveillance program on her music teacher's mother. Annie Dunlop's flat came into view. Gemma watched the flickering coverage for a minute or two even though the old lady was not in her lounge room. All was still so she closed the program and went back to her own office where she rang Lauren Bernhard.

'Just thinking of you,' she said. 'Wondering how you're getting along.'

'I'm getting along,' said Lauren. 'Day after day. Night after night. Each one takes me a little bit further away from my Amy.' There was a silence. 'But the police have been kind. A couple of them came round to have a cup of tea with me, and talk about what they've found on that laptop. That website business.'

The technical people, Gemma thought. 'I'm pleased to hear they're keeping you in the loop,' she said.

'They found a lot of email from the website's message board.'

Gemma waited.

'She had a lot of fans,' Lauren added. 'She and her friend Tasmin.'

'I'm not surprised. She was a beautiful girl.'

There was a silence while Lauren composed herself. 'They ran a competition called Dickhead of the Week where they'd post some of the messages they got from fans who'd offended them. They got the rest of the fan club to vote which one was the stupidest.'

Another long silence. Gemma knew it was her role to listen.

'My daughter,' Lauren finally said, 'had this whole other life, her own fan club, and I knew nothing about it.'

'The police who checked her computer,' Gemma began. 'Have you got their details?'

Lauren read from the two business cards they'd left with her. One of the names was familiar to Gemma from training days at Goulburn Academy—Tracey Lee, one of the rare Asian women brave enough to join the New South Wales police. Gemma suddenly remembered that it was a Tracey Angie had spoken with in the car on the way back from Richmond to check out the multiple human remains. There was no answer when she called Tracey Lee, so she left a message on her voice mail. Then she called her music teacher.

'Yes?' Mrs Snellgrove's pleasant voice. Gemma imagined the diamond at the base of the fan brooch wobbling as she spoke. 'It's Gemma, Mrs Snellgrove.'

'Mother's been going on about that animal again,' said Mrs Snellgrove. 'Have you seen anything that could account for it on the camera?'

'We've had a bit of trouble with the program the camera runs on,' said Gemma. 'But it all seems to be working well now. So far, there's been nothing untoward.' She paused. 'Actually, I'm not ringing about that. Or about music. I'm trying to trace someone who lived in Paddington a long time ago. You might have heard of the Kingston family? A woman called Beverley Kingston?'

'Everyone knew the Kingstons,' said Mrs Snellgrove. 'They were a very well-known family. Beverley's father was a highly regarded businessman. And Mrs Kingston was very active in the Black and White committee.' She lowered her voice then, as if she were speaking about something indecent. 'Sadly, Beverley took her own life.'

'I heard about that.' Gemma realised her heart was beating hard. 'I also heard she had a baby.'

'Then you know as much as I do. It was a very sad story. The poor soul was under psychiatric care, I believe. Much good it did her. Then she had the baby.'

Gemma lowered her own voice, trying not to hate the memory of her father. 'Do you have any idea what happened to that baby?' she asked.

Please, please, she prayed. Please say you do. Please say she was raised by so and so and now she's happily married with children and living on the Gold Coast. And then I can just leave the whole thing alone.

'No,' said Mrs Snellgrove. 'I don't. The family moved quite soon after the suicide and that was that. It was over thirty years ago, my dear.' There was a pause. 'Why do you want to know about the Kingstons?'

'Do you know what she called the baby?'

'I'm afraid I can't help you on that, either. It was

a big disgrace in those days, to have a baby without a father.'

But that baby did have a father, thought Gemma. My father.

'Are you acquainted with the family?' Mrs Snellgrove was asking.

Gemma felt sadness welling up. 'Yes,' she said. 'In a way.'

The moment she put the phone down, it rang and the caller introduced herself.

'Tracey Lee!' said Gemma. 'Thanks for getting back to me so quickly. I think you've already spoken to Angie about the Amy Bernhard case?'

Gemma explained how she'd been contracted by Netherleigh Park Ladies' College. 'I was sent an anonymous email,' said Gemma, 'suggesting I check out a website, but when I tried to visit, the website had gone.'

'I shouldn't be telling you this, but I know Angie rates you very high,' Tracey said. That might all change very quickly, Gemma thought, mindful of what she might have to tell her friend quite soon. 'We found a couple of other links connected to the girls' website. Really ugly ones. What was the name of the site you were emailed?'

'Extremely cute schoolgirls,' said Gemma, 'spelt with three or four Xs.'

'That's one of them,' said Tracey.

'Involving Amy and Tasmin?'

'It's hard to identify the girls in the videos. But we think Amy and Tasmin feature in some of them. I've run off copies for Angie.'

Good, thought Gemma, thinking she'd get to see it. 'There was also something called Dickhead of the Week,' Gemma continued.

'That's right,' said Tracey.

'Could an aggrieved dickhead of the week go homicidal and trace the webcam site?' asked Gemma.

'We're checking that out,' Tracey said. 'But it's a slow slog and we haven't got the resources. I don't expect the electronic stuff to get us very far in this investigation. These kids spend hours blogging and jumping around from site to site. Even if there was a way to trace them all, which there isn't, we simply don't have the necessary people. Or the time. Or the money.'

'You don't happen to know where I can get hold of Trevor Dawson?' It was a long shot, Gemma knew, but sometimes you got lucky.

'Didn't he go mad?'

Gemma heard Tracey call out to someone at the other end of the line, then she was back. 'I'll ask around for you. Ring me in a day or two.'

She was gone before Gemma could thank her. A day or two could be too late, she thought.

She sat down at the piano and lifted the lid back. She couldn't face Mrs Snellgrove without practising another week. She started with the newest piece, *Greensleeves*—right hand first, then the left hand. Haltingly, she put them together. It actually sounded a bit like it was supposed to. She repeated the first page, heeding the notes about dynamics, swelling from pianissimo to forte, and nearly jumped out of her skin when Taxi suddenly crash-landed on the base notes, sounding like a thunder clap.

'Get off!' she yelled, scooping him up and dumping him on the floor. He stalked away, tail lashing, jet ears swept back, his sure sign of displeasure. She felt a twinge in her lower belly and went to the bathroom to check her tampon supply. Only a few left. She made a note to buy some more and stuck it to the fridge under John Howard's terrorism magnet.

The Ratbag came in, hungry as usual, and she sent him for some Thai takeaway. He grizzled about the walk involved, but she bribed him by saying she wouldn't object to him watching a Terminator movie. After they'd eaten, Gemma went to her office while Hugo watched Schwarzenegger deal with baddies.

Her mobile woke her just before sunrise. Gemma groped for it. Angie. Gemma's heart sank. She didn't want to have to talk to her best friend until she'd dealt with Trevor Dawson. Gemma prayed that Angie wouldn't mention him this phone call.

'We've found Tasmin Summers,' Angie said. 'She's at the morgue. The water police brought her in.'

There was a silence while Gemma took this in. She thought of the radiant teenager, smiling with her friends in the photograph in Amy's room. 'Where?'

'Floating off North Bondi. Couple of clicks off the beach.'

'Any cause of death yet?'

'We'll have to wait for that. Maybe later this afternoon. You can come in and have a look at the video. Later on, when everyone's gone home.'

Gemma thought of Jim Buisman's remarks about a thief knot. She needed to get access to the violent major offender files Angie was sorting. 'Those VMOs you're going through—'

'Was going through. Until this murder investigation.'

'I need to see them, Ange.'

'Not possible. You can't come in here and do that, and there are too many of them for me to lug out in a briefcase.'

'I have to. This is a pattern. We've got two similar homicides: two young girls from the same school, same age, best friends. Both with websites.'

She could hear Angie listening. She hurried on, pressing her case. 'You know you need all the help you can get. G-for-Gross isn't going to give you what I can.'

'I step out of line with records like these and someone finds out, I'm gone!' Gemma recognised the finality in her friend's voice.

'No one will ever know,' she pleaded.

'This place has a thousand ears and eyes. I don't have to remind you.'

'But Jim Buisman told me something,' Gemma said. 'Something important.'

'What?'

'Let me look through the VMOs and I'll tell you.'

'No! Subject closed. Now tell me what Buisman said.'

'He remembers someone who used a thief knot,' said Gemma. 'Connected to a series of unsolved rapes in the 1980s. A girl tied with her own scarf. Let me go through those VMOs. Please, Ange. There could be something there.'

'You've already been given access to things you shouldn't have. I plan to retire with full entitlements. I don't want to be prosecuted under the Crimes Act.'

'Okay,' said Gemma. 'But when you go through the VMOs, remember to look out for the thief knot.'

'What did Buisman say about his reasons for taking Bruno off the original investigation?'

'Nothing. He pretended he couldn't recall.'

There was a silence.

'Gemster? Are you okay?'

'Of course I am. I'm just pissed off that you won't let me at those VMOs. And you were pissed off first.'

'Sorry.' Angie's voice softened. 'It's just the pressure round here.'

All Gemma could think of right this moment was Trevor Dawson sharing ice-creams with his wife and kids and how Angie was going to feel a lot more pressure when she found out about it.

'Look, come in later on,' said Angie, placating her. 'Buy me a coffee. We'll have a chat.'

That was about as good as it was going to get, Gemma thought as she put the mobile down and padded out to the kitchen. Bloody Trevor Dawson. How dare he put her in such an awkward spot.

The sun was already out of the water, blindingly golden across the vast expanse. She drew the blinds against it and put the kettle on. From her living room came gentle snoring. She looked in and saw the Ratbag and Taxi curled around each other in a tangle of fur and legs, the doona kicked to the floor. 'You tart,' she whispered, dragging Taxi from his spot, needing his warmth despite the rising heat of the early morning.

With the cat sleepily draped in her arms, Gemma unlocked the sliding door and went outside. It was a beautiful morning with the promise of a perfect day. Yet her heart was so heavy with what she knew about Angie's lover that she wished she could rewind the events of the last twenty-four hours. If she couldn't contact Trevor Dawson by the end of the day, she'd have to tell Angie what she'd seen. God almighty, she thought. Why is it all so difficult?

Now that Romero had been arrested, there was no need for her to chase up his employment history. The police would do that. She made a note of the schools he'd been employed in for her own records, noticing that he'd left his first job, a state school in Bathurst, because of the workload.

Gemma settled down to reading through several of the witness statements again, especially Tiffany Brown's. She picked up a pen and circled the bits of the girl's statement that she wanted to check. She rang Tiffany Brown's number, introduced herself to Mrs Brown and made a time to visit later that evening, explaining she just needed to ask Tiffany a couple of simple questions.

The gas man came and they decided to put a new bayonet on the southern wall of her living room as well as another one in her office. It seemed odd to be talking heaters when it was building towards a high of 29 degrees outside. The gas man had run out of fittings, due to the popularity of his special rates, but he would come back in the next couple of days, he said, to finish the job.

'Make sure you ring me first,' Gemma insisted. Tradesmen had an unerring instinct, she knew, to arrive when a woman is in the shower. He promised he'd call.

She checked her voice mail. No message from Trevor Dawson.

Late afternoon, she drove to Strawberry Hills police station and asked for Angie at the security desk. She was reading a poster about clandestine laboratories when she heard someone approaching. But it wasn't Angie. Bruno Gross, who seemed to spend *more* time on the job now that he was off sick, had walked out of the lift and was heading for the exit. Gemma could see how his good looks were already being subsumed by extra flesh around his jaw line.

'I want to talk to you, Bruno,' she said, catching him up. He looked at her as if she was something he'd found floating under a wharf. 'I've been talking to Jim Buisman, about why he took you off the original investigation into Amy Bernhard's disappearance.'

Bruno barely paused in his stride. 'I have nothing to say to you,' he said.

'Jim Buisman mentioned a situation,' she said. 'What situation would that have been?'

That stopped him and he swung around on her; she felt the old anger, the old hurt.

'That you're a bloody lazy incompetent officer,' she continued, 'who gets other people to do all the work and then takes all the credit?'

'Get off the premises!' he snarled. 'You have no business here.'

She looked past him to see Angie approaching. 'I'm here to see my friend,' said Gemma. 'I have every right.'

But straightaway she saw that something was wrong. Angie's face, usually alive with her ironic smile, was stern. Bruno gave them both a look and pushed his way outside.

Gemma turned to her friend. 'Angie!' she said. 'What is it?'

Angie turned in silence, called back the lift, which opened its doors immediately, and stepped inside. Gemma followed. Once they were inside, her face white with anger, Angie hissed, 'What's going on, Gemma? What are you up to?'

'What are you talking about?' Gemma had been on the receiving end of Angie's infamous temper once or twice before and had never forgotten it. 'Calm down and tell me what you mean.'

'You've got calls out to people. Diane Hayworth. Lots of others. Urgently wanting Trevor Dawson. And just now Tracey Lee rang and mentioned it.'

Gemma's heart sank.

'Why?'

Gemma tried desperately to decide what to say. 'Angie, I—'

'What the hell's going on?'

'I've been trying to contact him because I didn't want it to be like this.'

'Like what? I don't give a fuck how you wanted it to be. I want you to tell me what's going on!'

The lift doors opened but neither of them moved. Angie stood glaring at her and Gemma, not sure how best to proceed, stood mute. The doors closed and the lift descended, taking them back to the ground floor again. A smiling junior stepped in, then, picking up the atmosphere, looked away, the three of them standing in stony silence. When the lift doors opened and the junior stepped out, Gemma decided to meet Angie head on.

'Okay,' she said as the doors closed again. 'I hate to have to tell you like this. But I saw your friend Trevor on Saturday. Bumped into him at Kings Cross.'

Angie frowned, the anger mixing with bewilderment. 'Trevor? He's not even in Sydney,' she started to say. 'He's down in Goulburn at the Academy. Training course. You couldn't have seen him.'

'I saw him with a woman and three kids. At the Cross. Sharing ice-creams. A family group.'

'No!' Angie cried. 'That's not possible! There's some mistake.'

Gemma felt like Judas and put a hand on her friend's arm. 'I'm so sorry, Ange.'

Angie pulled her arm away. 'But he's at the Academy. He rang me just a while ago.'

Gemma didn't press it.

'Those calls you had out for him,' Angie started.

'He should face up to you and tell you himself. I was going to give him twenty-four hours. I asked a couple of people where he might be.'

A long silence followed; in it the gathering force of a tsunami, or the pre-quake rumblings of the earth before eruption. 'You said he was with a woman and three kids?'

Gemma nodded. She felt terrible.

'The bastard!' Angie's eyes blazed in a face pale with shock.

'I hate being the one to tell you,' said Gemma.

'The dirty low-down sleazy mongrel bastard!' Angie whispered. 'And you knew! You knew this morning! When we were talking on the phone!'

Gemma said nothing. What could she say?

'How could you do that? Know about this and not say anything? It makes me feel like an idiot!'

'I wanted to hear his side. See if I'd made some terrible mistake. Maybe he was just having an access visit with his kids. Maybe the woman was his sister. But I knew really—once I saw him kissing her.'

Angie looked stricken. 'And you're sure it was him?'

Gemma nodded. 'It was Trevor Dawson. He

kissed the woman and wiped the face of the little kid. Everything screamed "highly married" to me.'

Angie slumped against the side of the lift and her eyes filled. 'I can't believe it,' she said. 'I've done it again!'

'You haven't done anything. He's the one who's behaved like a shit.'

'Why didn't I see it? I'm supposed to be able to read people.'

'When the writing's too close, you can't read it.' As Gemma spoke, she sensed a deep warning, right through her cells, that these words also applied to her. Something, someone was too close. Who? What? Gently, she patted Angie's arm again. 'Come on. Let's get out of here. You need some fresh air.'

In the bar on the corner, Gemma watched while Angie had a fast scotch on the rocks. 'Why?' Angie's voice was shaky. 'How come I always end up like this? Why are the men I get involved with always bastards?'

Gemma took a swig from her brandy. 'You're asking me? I'm hardly a shining example of sensible relating with the opposite sex.' Memories of her misbehaviour with Mike and Steve's shocked voice on her mobile caused her to wince afresh. 'Maybe you didn't gather enough intelligence first?'

Angie looked at her, eyes wide. 'Did you? When you got involved with Steve?'

Gemma thought about that. 'I don't think so.'

'Steve isn't a bastard. He loves you,' said Angie.

'Maybe he did once. But he's sure got over that now.'

Maybe he did have other women, she thought. All over the state. All those years of jobs that took him away. All that undercover work. No questions allowed. Perfect cover for the worst infidelity. These were thoughts Gemma almost never permitted herself. Maybe Steve was just like Trevor Dawson. In fact, maybe he was just a younger, wilder version of her own father. Maybe there were children out there in New South Wales who had Steve as the absent father. Her dismal thoughts were interrupted by Angie banging her head on the bar like a crazy woman. The barman looked over briefly. Nothing broken and he was used to such sights, so he speedily went back to polishing and stacking clean glasses in shiny metal trays.

'It's okay,' Gemma called out to him. 'It's yoga.'

Angie lifted her head to stare gloomily at her drink, tapping her forehead. 'Have I got a sign in lights on my head that says "I am an idiot—have a go"?'

'Of course not. Stop blaming yourself.' Gemma ordered Angie another scotch.

Angie picked up the new drink and rattled the ice. She flashed a look at Gemma, tears in her eyes. 'I'm sorry about—you know—jumping down your neck just then. I suspected something was going on. And when I get frightened I go for the jugular.'

'I know. What else are friends for?'

Angie finished her drink and blew her nose. 'I feel like getting completely wasted.'

'Don't. We've got work to do.'

'I want revenge. I want to kill him. I want to knock over a bottle of scotch and get totalled.'

'I advise two out of three. Let's go back and make plans.'

'I want his wife to know as well. What sort of prick he is.'

'She will. Come on, let's go.'

'But what about his kids?' Angie was concerned. 'He's got little kids.'

'They know everything already. Kids might not know the details of it, but they know somewhere that their father is dishonest.'

'But if I out him, I'll be a marriage wrecker!'

'You're not married, remember? He is. Now come on.'

Angie put her head down on the bar again. 'I feel like howling. I thought he really cared about me.' She knocked a nearby stool over and it crashed to the floor. 'No one's ever written poetry to me before.'

'He probably does care for you,' said Gemma. 'It's just that he's got a wife.'

'I believed him. I thought he was going down to the Academy to fight terrorism.'

'He probably was. Some of the time.'

'All the time he's running home to his wife!' She bashed the bar. 'I feel so humiliated!'

'Maybe you should take the rest of the day off. Maybe I shouldn't be pushing you back to work.'

'No, you're right. I should go back. Because if

I did go home, I'd get drunk and God knows what I might do then.'

'Come home with me. Stay over tonight. You'll feel better in the morning,' said Gemma.

'Everyone must have known,' Angie wailed. 'People are probably laughing at me.'

'Don't be so paranoid. No one's laughing at you.'

Angie pulled herself up. 'I want to kill him.'

'So you said. I'll bet he's been getting away with this for years.'

Angie stared at her. 'You're suggesting I'm not the first?'

Gemma didn't have to answer.

'Of course I'm not.' Angie clutched the bar stool. 'We know about serial offenders. Whatever works for them they keep using. Of course there'd be other girlfriends!' She paused. 'And he probably photocopies his poems.'

'Those poems,' Gemma began.

'What about them?'

'I feel sure he copied them from other poets. The good lines, I mean. The rest was crap.'

'Second-hand poetry!' Angie wailed. 'Second-hand girlfriend. He's got a wife! Give me a good VMO any day. They seem quite straightforward compared to the likes of Trevor Dawson. At least you know what you're getting.'

Gemma gathered up her belongings.

'I'll bet he used the same poems on his wife.' Angie slumped over again, resting her head on her arms like a tired child. 'I can't believe I've been so bloody stupid.'

'Stop dumping on yourself. You know how charming psychopaths can be. It's their job to con!'

'Next time, I swear I'll employ you to do a probity check. From now on, if I ever so much as mention another man's name, you're to remind me that I've pre-ordered a probity check on him.' She paused. 'Not that it's very bloody likely I'll ever be interested in another man!' She sat up straight again. 'How am I supposed to focus on work now?'

'You will because you're a pro,' said Gemma.

Angie groaned.

'Those multiple remains?' Gemma said. 'Those teeth? Any more on those?'

'Francie called to say it's going to take a while. Reckons it's a charnel house. She's got half the Academy out there doing a fingertip search. They've found a whole lot of really tiny grave sites—very small sizes.'

Gemma felt sick at heart. 'God. Is it kids?'

'Francie couldn't say for sure. She says she's never seen anything like this.' Angie paused. 'But it could be some parent's idea of family planning.'

Finally, she stood up, grabbing her mobile and ordering a bottle of scotch from the barman. 'Wait here,' she said to Gemma. 'I'm going back to my office to pick up some gear. Where's your car?'

'Why?'

'I'm going to get some of those VMO files for you. You can take the fucking things! Why am I the only one who worries about the rules? Take them and read them and brief me if there's anything there. I've got enough work to keep me going for fifty years without reading through all those!'

They left the pub and parted company, Gemma to wait for what seemed a long time in her car before Angie reappeared carrying two large kit bags. Gemma unlocked the back door and Angie heaved them into the back seat.

Gemma studied her friend, seeing how hurt she was, how she was fighting tears. 'I wish there was something I could do or say to make things better for you.'

'For goodness sake, don't be kind to me,' said Angie, her voice wavering. 'I need to stay pissed off and furious.'

There was nothing anyone could do, Gemma knew. The only thing that helped this sort of thing was the passage of a certain amount of time. Angie climbed into the front seat, a sheaf of printed out emails in her hand. 'Listen to this,' she said. 'This is from the message board on the girls' website. Tracey Lee sent them across.'

She started reading. '*Hi Aymée and Tasmée, i really like your webpage. you are funny and cute. i love the way you put down all those jerks who email you and put their emails up as "dickhead of the week". i really love girls like you who put men down all the time. It is sooo creative . . . you can put me down any time and call me anything you like . . . so thanks for everything you've done for me tonight . . . if you don't know what that means, there's a whole pile of used tissues beside my bed that weren't there until I saw you in your bedroom. ps you're both real hot.*'

Angie looked up. The colour had come back to her face, although her eyes were still full of unshed tears. 'Is that what young girls want? Boys wanking over them?'

'How did Amy answer?' Gemma waited while Angie flicked through the emails, scanning them briefly.

'She just got nastier. *Maybe if you just stopped wanking all over your keyboard you might get a real girlfriend and stop bothering me. Or better still, the keyboard might blow up and electrocute you.*

'And this is the first writer three emails later: *You poor little fat shit, here's me trying to be nice to you but you can't recognise niceness when you meet it and your fake tan and your fake life and fake ideas just piss me off you and your phoney girlfriend should get a life. you haven't got a clue about anything. grow up you are so stupid i will show you how to really jam a site with like 50 web masters with cable modems STOP PLAYING WITH YOUR OWN SHIT or I might come round and fix you up real good.*'

Angie looked at Gemma again. 'I should learn some of these lines,' she said. 'Use them on Trevor. I'd like to jam his site all right.'

'What happened to funny and cute?' Gemma asked. Angie handed her some pages and she looked through them.

'All the replies start off being pleasant and interested in finding the girls' website,' Gemma observed. 'But then they start getting sexual and suggestive, the girls respond with insults, and the boys come back with abuse. And so it goes on until the end.'

Angie leaned back in the seat. 'Sounds like most relationships I know.'

Gemma considered. 'I'm remembering something Kit said to me. About relationships.'

'Don't. I don't want to hear it.'

'Okay, okay.'

'Do you think the girls might have angered someone so much that this person decided to track them down?' Angie said. 'First Amy then Tasmin? And sort them out?'

'That's what Tracey Lee was suggesting. And it's as good a theory as any we've got so far. It would be dead easy—what with the school banner spelling it out over the bed. He could just hang around at pick-up time, watching the kids at the bus stops, working out where they live.'

'That doesn't let Romero off the hook, though. Or the elegant Beatrice de B.'

'Or the old perv next door.' Gemma told Angie about her visit to Alistair Forde's house; her suspicions about what he'd been doing with that table against the window.

'I'll check the system for him again,' Angie said. 'He sounds like the sort of guy who has to have form.' She indicated the kit bags on the back seat. 'You've got a nice batch of violent major offenders to take home with you. When you've finished with these, I'll bring more over.'

Already, Gemma thought, her friend was

recovering from the worst of the shock and she admired her resilience.

Angie caught Gemma checking her out and made a face, waving the sheaf of print-outs. 'I don't know if Tracey will be able to get anything much from these email addresses. The servers might have something traceable. But hell, it could be any one of these guys. Or none of them.'

These schoolgirls had much bigger lives than anyone imagined, Gemma thought. Bigger, darker and more dangerous. 'Any point in checking it out with any of your integrated corporate resources?'

Any other time, Angie would have smiled. Some years ago, a police trainer had used the phrase when referring to police informants and Gemma and Angie had enjoyed using it ever since.

'I've already taken it to the streets,' Angie said. 'But the offender who carries out this sort of crime is usually a very isolated individual.' She started to get out of the car when her mobile rang. 'Trevor!' she said.

Gemma sat up straight. Angie's voice was smooth as satin. 'How nice. And how is it down there in Goulburn?'

There was a pause. 'I'll bet it's hot,' she said, agreeing with something he'd said and giving Gemma her deadliest narrowed-eyed look.

Gemma found herself almost feeling sorry for the guy.

'Sure,' said her friend, keeping her voice sweet. 'I can do that. Gotta fly. See you then. Graingers? Baby, I can't wait.' Gemma stared as Angie slowly put her mobile back on her belt. 'And it's going to get a whole lot hotter, you arsehole.'

Angie twisted round to the back seat again and pulled a small package out from under the files in one of the kit bags. She tore it open, took out a video cassette and glanced at the label. 'It's Tasmin Summers. From the SOCO video guys.' She looked up and down the street. 'Take it with you and have a look.' She put the cassette in the glove box. 'What's Trevor's wife like?'

'Huh?' Gemma was taken by surprise. 'Where did that come from? I hardly saw her.'

'Come on, you know. Pretend you're giving an eyewitness account.'

Gemma took a deep breath. 'Five foot four. Brown hair, fair skin, slim to medium build, about fifty-three kilos. She was wearing a blue patterned shirt with white jeans.'

Angie grunted. 'And the kids?'

'They looked like kids! Ange, give me a break. It was only a few seconds. I was shocked. I didn't take it all in.'

Angie gave her a look then glanced at her watch. 'I'd better get back. You look after those files now.'

At home Gemma found the Ratbag watching television.

'You need to get your Sky channels fixed,' he said. 'You should be able to pick up two more and they're just not working. I can't fix them.' He showed her the ones he meant. 'That should be the sport channel,' he said. 'And this one, I'm not sure.' The screen jumped in horizontal jagged striations. 'It's just a mess.'

'Okay, I'll call the technician,' she said. 'But now I need to watch a video,' she said. After some serious grizzling, he eventually obliged and switched the remote for her.

'What is it?' he asked.

Gemma wasn't at all sure that the Ratbag should view what she was sliding into the housing of her VCR. 'It's a tape of Spinner's church choir,' she said 'singing old-time favourites. "Tea for Two", "Doggie in the Window"—that sort of fun thing. I think you'd really enjoy it.'

He stared at her then rolled himself up into a standing position. 'I am so out of here!' he said.

'You don't want to sing along?'

'See ya,' he called as he went out the door and she settled down to watch.

After the official introduction, the footage showed blue water and, floating like a piece of driftwood, a partly submerged body. Gemma fast-forwarded, past the pale corpse on the deck of the water-police launch, hurrying the action forward until the body lay on the stainless steel table. The crime scene video's remorseless shots slowly panned over and around Tasmin Summers's slender body, her pale hands graceful in death, the ghostly pallor of the skin as if the sea had drained her of all trace of colour, the tiny diamond stud still shining at her navel, ending in a close-up on her sweet face, white and waxy. Her image shimmered frozen on the screen. Gemma felt a sense of loss; the world was the poorer for this girl's death.

She studied the close-up of the narrow wrist showing the green and white cord still attached, the deep abrasion to the skin beneath. Gemma peered more closely. Had the rope done that skin damage or had it been inflicted by a weapon? Had Tasmin tried to pull away and the cord had cut into her? The pathologist might be able to throw some light on it. She stopped the tape, took it out of the VCR and rehoused it, snapping the cover together.

Sitting at the dining table, she started to read her way through the VMO folders in the bags, flicking through the ones that didn't conform to what she sought. She traced the criminal records of violent offenders, following their development from brutal childhoods to brutalising juvenile institutions and from thence to further escalating and predictable attacks on other human beings. These were only halted with increasingly growing terms of imprisonment. There were also some victim statements, occasionally with certificates of analysis from the Division of Analytic Laboratories attached. Some were accompanied by packeted crime scene samples of physical evidence.

Gemma continued turning over pages of statements and reports. Glancing at her watch, she was surprised to find she'd been almost an hour going through the first kit bag. She put the files back and then unloaded half the contents of the other, larger bag. She flicked through, discarding the male on male outrages, eyes tuned to violent sexual assaults. She went through numerous of these, nothing sparking a connection until she came to a plastic sleeve, dated and labelled in faded type which didn't seem to be attached to any of the offenders' files. She looked closer and saw why. It was a victim statement, containing photographs and what looked like a packet of old physical evidence in a crime scene envelope. She peered into it and decided not to get too close—she could see what looked like the remnants of an article of clothing, a floral fabric streaked almost black with old blood. Gemma left it well alone, slipping the envelope back into the sleeve. From the looks of things, this case had never been solved. She flicked through the photographic images of the shocking injuries occasioned by violent rape then backtracked to the date of the case: November 1983. Was this one of the violent rapes Jim Buisman had mentioned? Gemma started reading from the attached witness statement, skimming through the beginning, becoming more involved as the horrifying scenes played themselves out in her imagination.

My name is Sandra Maree Samuels and my date of birth is 26 March 1968. I live with my mother and little brother at 10 Yarramalong Avenue, Campbelltown. I am in Year 10 at Hillsdale High. I met John at a party given by my girlfriend's brother and I went out with him on two occasions. On the second occasion, I had sex with him. I thought of him as my boyfriend so that when he suggested we meet some of his friends at a party next time we went out, I felt real happy that he wanted to introduce me to his mates. On 18 November, we went to the Picton show, then we drove to a house where he picked up four of his friends. I don't know where the house was. I had to sit on the knee of the man in the front seat because there wasn't enough room in the back. I wasn't too happy about this. I don't think John was his real name because one of the others called him by another name a couple of times and he got very annoyed at this and told him to shut up. We drove to some place out near the railway station and parked a bit off the road where John ordered me to have sex with all his friends. I said no I wouldn't and weren't we supposed to be going to a party and he said this was the party. I started crying and John yelled at me to shut up and called me a stupid fucking slut. He said that I knew what was going on and I should stop pretending I didn't. Then the one whose knee I'd been sitting on dragged me out of the car and started pulling my clothes off. I screamed and struggled and he bashed me in the face and I fell over. I couldn't stop crying so John turned the car radio up real loud. Then the first one pulled my knickers down and raped me and so did the others. I was begging John to help me and asking him why was he doing this to me but he just kept calling me a stupid slut who knew what she had coming to her. He told the others to hurry up. They were all screaming and yelling at me, calling me names, saying I was a filthy bitch and that if I hadn't wanted sex why was I here?

They kept telling me I'd agreed to be here with them and to shut up and just do what they wanted.

After they'd finished I hoped John would take me home, but he tried to rape me too. He couldn't get hard and shouted at me that I was a frigid bitch and it was my fault that he couldn't have sex with me. I tried to get up but the first one kicked me down again and then I heard a car pull up and three more men got out. I realised they were going to rape me too and I tried to get away but they caught me and two of them started bashing me. I think this was when my jaw and the fingers on my right hand got broken. The other three men then raped me. They all started drinking and I was able to crawl back to the car. I tried to find my clothes but I couldn't see properly and all I could find was my scarf on the back seat. I was bleeding from the rapes. I cleaned myself up as much as I could with the scarf. Then the one whose lap I'd had to sit on in the car saw me moving around and yelled at me. Then John came over and tied my wrists with the scarf so that I couldn't do anything. I just stayed there and sat in the car.

I don't know how long I sat there. I knew I should be trying to get away but I didn't have any strength left and I was in such pain. I was scared I'd bleed to death. Even though the car radio was on I could still hear them talking about getting rid of me. They were planning to kill me. This made me so frightened that I managed to start the car even though I don't know how to drive very well and my wrists were tied together and the fingers on my right *hand were swollen and didn't work properly. The men tried to run after me but I put my foot down and was able to drive back onto the road. I hit one of the men with the side of the car and ran over him. I got back on the highway and that's when I was involved in the accident with the other car and the police found me and took me to the hospital. At first they thought I'd been injured in the accident but then I was able to tell them what had happened to me.*

Gemma found she'd been holding her breath while she read. She looked at the photograph of the girl's blackened face, swollen like some grotesque rubber monster mask.

She took a break to collect herself and made a coffee. She felt she was floundering in an ocean of possibilities. Instead of this investigation narrowing down into clear focus, as it had seemed when she'd discovered Mr Romero's hidden telescope, Gemma felt that now it had expanded like the galaxy. It was just too big and she desperately needed some good hard physical evidence. So far, all she had was a fancy piece of exotic rope tied in a thief knot.

Maybe she was making her life even more difficult by reading all these VMO files. She leaned back in her seat, looking at the piled-up folders covering the surface of her dining table. She'd just have to keep slogging away, hoping like hell that something connected.

She turned her attention back to the rape from

twenty years ago and the old-fashioned typed case notes of the detective in charge. There was an addendum stapled to the girl's statement: NFA. No further action. There had been no follow-up. No more to the investigation than the initial statement and photographic records. 'Unable to follow up,' Gemma read. 'Victim left the hospital suddenly—no forwarding address.' Beneath this information someone else had added, 'Hospital staff say girl left when a man was admitted to the hospital.'

Gemma was about to pull the rest of the files out of the second bag, when a familiar name signing off an opinion at the bottom of a certificate made her look again. It was Colin Roper's signature. This must have been one of his earliest cases. She read the forensic knot man's findings. As she read, she jumped up out of her seat, feeling the elation of the hunter at the first sight of the prey. This was the reason she'd been reading through these files. Two events, separated by over twenty years, suddenly fused together.

She grabbed her mobile. 'Angie!' she said. 'Ring me. I've found something.'

She paced, waiting till her friend left the building and called from a public phone.

The second her mobile rang, she pounced on it. 'Angie! Listen to this! It's one of the cases Jim Buisman was talking about!' She started reading aloud from Colin Roper's report. '*The knot is similar in shape and form to the reef knot except that the working ends come out on opposite sides of the knot. The difference between this and the reef knot is not at all obvious to an observer.'*

'What are you reading from?'

'A victim statement that was in among the VMO files.'

'Yeah,' Angie's voice was impatient. 'But who? Which VMO should I go out and drag in?'

'Sorry,' said Gemma. 'That's the problem. Looks like charges were never laid. This is from a 1983 rape case. Colin Roper's talking about the knot that was tied around this girl's wrists. This is one of the thief-knot cases! At last, a definite connection.'

'What's the name of the girl?' Angie asked.

'Sandra Maree Samuels,' said Gemma, who'd noted it down. 'Date of birth: 26 March, 1968.'

'I think we should trace her,' said Angie.

'You bet,' said Gemma. 'Colin Roper will be interested to hear about this.'

'But you know what the experts are like,' Angie reminded her. 'Even if we get the offender, he's never going to say in court "these knots were tied by the same hands". He'll only say something like "this knot is indistinguishable from that knot".'

'Works for me,' said Gemma.

'Let's hope it works for a jury,' said Angie. 'But I'm jumping the gun.' She paused. 'Why the long delay between knots? If it's the same rapist-killer, or bunch of them, why the long period of time between crimes?'

'Ivan Milat didn't murder during the years he was in a stable relationship with a woman,' Gemma reminded her.

'And our thief-knot rapist might have been inside for the last twenty years for other violent crimes. Men like that tend to spend a fair amount of time as guests of Her Majesty.' There was a silence on the line. 'Now suddenly he shows up again. I'll check with COPS to see if any of our more recent VMOs were released just prior to Amy's disappearance. And I'll ring Colin Roper,' said Angie. 'And get back to you.'

'Don't forget!'

'And your old perv—you were right about Alistair Forde. He's done time. He's in the system all right, but with his surname spelled differently.'

'What sort of form?'

'Three convictions for indecent behaviour.'

'I knew it,' Gemma said. 'No way could he see out the window and down into the area outside Amy Bernhard's house from where he said he was. Reckoned he was standing on a table to change a light globe. He was standing on a table all right, but at the window, so he could get a good eyeful into Amy's bedroom. And that table was a fixture by the window although he said he'd just shifted it there.'

'But he still could've seen someone in the bushes outside Amy's room. Even if he was standing on a table having a wank.'

'I'm not saying there wasn't a prowler that night,' said Gemma. 'Forde reckons he chased him over the back fence. But his prior convictions put him in the picture.'

'Let's go visit him.'

TWELVE

Opening his front door, Alistair Forde cringed when Angie flashed her ID. He gave Gemma a filthy look. 'What are you doing back here? I answered all your questions. I reported that prowler to help the police! Now you're treating me like I'm the intruder. Why are you hounding me like this?'

'This is just a polite invitation,' said Angie. 'For a quiet chat.'

'What about?'

'About perving on girls through their bedroom windows. Standing on tables to get a better look. That sort of thing.'

Forde's face reddened. 'But I explained about the table! It was only by the window so I could vacuum the carpet.'

'Don't give me that crap,' said Gemma. 'You climbed on that table all the time to see into Amy Bernhard's bedroom. I could see the deep indentations the table legs had left on the carpet.'

His face suffused more darkly. 'It's the bloody

last time I'll do anything to help the police. If this is how it's going to be used against me!'

'We just want to be sure of a couple of things,' said Angie, smiling.

'I didn't do anything wrong!'

He was still saying much the same twenty minutes later. 'I only looked. Why are you making such a fuss about it?' He looked desperately first at Gemma, leaning against the wall in the corner, then at Angie opposite him.

To rattle you, sport, thought Gemma, to take you out of your comfort zone. To impress upon you that you could be in serious trouble. That way, you might be more inclined to tell us if you know anything.

'There's no harm in looking, and anyway,' he said, 'there hasn't been anything to look at for a year.'

'So you've been peeping on other young girls, have you?' Angie asked. 'Like Tasmin Summers? Did you go round to her place too?'

'I don't know what you're talking about!'

This time his perplexity seemed genuine. Recalling the mansion in Rose Bay—the steep formal gardens, the well-protected grounds—Gemma had to concede it would be hard for someone like Alistair Forde to do his number in such a place.

'I'm just wondering,' Angie said calmly, 'about your bid to be helpful. The way you reported a prowler outside Amy's window last year.'

'I won't bother again,' he muttered. 'Last time I'll ever try and be helpful.'

Angie ignored him, continuing, 'Because what

we've found in the past is that the person who reports something concerning a murder is often the real offender.'

'That's where you're wrong,' said Alistair with self-righteous smugness. 'It was well before that girl got herself into any sort of trouble.'

'I think you saw through Amy's window.' Gemma moved in closer, menacing him. 'You decided to get her all for yourself, didn't you.'

Alistair's eyes widened in shock and the blood fled from his face. With his hunched shoulders and the dry scaly skin around his eyes, he reminded Gemma of some old reptile checking its environment from under a ledge.

'You think I'm making it up?' Alistair cried. 'I tell you—I saw that man! He was crouched down in the bushes on Halloween night. And when I went down to see what he was up to, off he went, over my back fence! And that's the truth. I'll swear on my mother's grave!'

Gemma continued as if he hadn't spoken. 'Amy would've trusted you. You could easily pull up and offer her a lift and she'd hop in with you.'

'Me?' Alistair Forde shook his head. 'What would I be offering a lift to a young girl for? She'd just laugh at me.'

Gemma pounced. 'Is that what happened? Did she laugh at you?' she dropped her voice. 'And you decided to put an end to her laughing?'

Forde was actually backing away, till he hit the edge of a chair and almost stumbled. 'It's not true! You're just making this up as you go along!

Everything I say you twist! You're making every-thing I say into something ugly!' Sweat beaded his forehead and his breath came in shocked bursts.

Gemma closed in on him. 'What you do is some-thing ugly. Perving on young girls while they think they're safe and sound in their own bedrooms.'

Alistair Forde backed sideways around the chair behind him but Gemma followed him, step for step. He sat down suddenly, in another chair. God, thought Gemma, hearing his ragged breathing. She hoped he wasn't having a heart attack.

'Okay,' he said. 'I might have had a bit of a look from time to time. But I swear I never touched that girl. Never. On my mother's grave.'

Angie's mobile rang and she took the call. This gave Forde sufficient time to gather himself. He got up out of the chair, pointing a shaking finger towards the front door. 'I want you to leave my house now,' he said. 'I try to be helpful and this is what I get.'

Angie rang off. 'If you let us have a look round your backyard, we'll go,' she said. Gemma realised Angie didn't want the hassle of having to organise a warrant.

Forde hesitated, weighing up the situation. 'I've got nothing to hide,' he mumbled eventually and showed them out into the small fenced yard. 'But you're not coming back in here after today with-out a proper warrant,' he said, slamming the door behind them.

Alistair Forde watched from the window while they checked around his boundary line. The bushes in which he'd alleged he'd seen a prowler proved to be an overgrown ginger plant and a couple of hydrangeas that grew almost to the sill.

'Amy's window,' Angie remarked as they stood looking across at it.

'And then he's supposed to have taken off down the back and over the rear fence,' said Gemma.

The fence, covered in the glossy green leaves of star jasmine, stood on a slight inclination of the land. Angie hauled herself up on it, peering over into the adjoining backyard. 'It's all quite possible, what he's told us,' she said, jumping back down again, brushing bits of jasmine off her hands.

Back in Angie's car, Gemma put a hand on her abdomen, feeling bloated and uncomfortable. She would be very pleased when her period arrived.

'Let's head to the morgue,' said Angie. 'I phoned earlier today.'

'What about Forde?' Gemma replied, giving her friend an enquiring glance.

'I think he's telling the truth,' Angie said.

'Got your visitor's badge?' said Angie as they walked around to the back door and were buzzed in by the same morgue attendant Gemma recalled from eight years ago.

'I called Dr Annette Chang earlier,' said Angie, flashing her ID. 'The pathologist who did the PM on Tasmin Summers?'

'She's just finishing up now,' said the attendant. 'I'll take you down to her.'

Gemma followed him and her friend down corridors she remembered from her days in the job until they arrived at an open door. At the sound of their approach, Dr Chang, who'd been working at her desk, turned round. Perfect creamy skin was enhanced by the tiny pearls in her ear lobes; the refinement of her silk blouse and tailored jacket set off by her sleek black hair.

Gemma recalled the times she'd stood on the blue lino near the pathologist, patiently taking photographs at each stage of the examination and documentation. She'd spent many an hour watching the weighing and recording of the dead organs, the placing of tissue samples in little plastic cages, the brain in its bucket to harden for the neuropathologist.

'I'm here on behalf of Bruno Gross,' Angie said. 'I had a message that you'd finished your physical examination of Tasmin Summers?'

'My part is almost done,' said Dr Chang. 'But it could be a week or two before all the tests come back.'

'Anything you can tell me while we're waiting for the analysts' results?' asked Angie.

Dr Chang reviewed her screen, scrolling through a document. 'I do have the results of the diatom concentrations. I requested those ASAP.'

Gemma remembered this word. Microscopic algae, their filigree silica shapes as varied as snowflakes, diatoms occur in teeming numbers in waterways.

'At first glance,' the doctor was saying, 'it looked

like the cause of death was drowning. We found concentrations of diatoms in the lungs.' Angie and Gemma looked at each other as the doctor continued. 'But none in the other organ samples—brain, marrow, liver or kidneys.'

'So she didn't drown?' Gemma asked.

Doctor Chang shook her head. 'I found initial indications of opiates in her system, but again, we'll have to wait for the toxicology reports on the tissue samples before we can say for certain what she'd taken. I did notice a very strong smell of alcohol in the stomach contents.' She looked over the top of her screen at them. 'Very high concentration in the bloodstream too.'

'That deep laceration on one side of the wrist,' Gemma said, remembering the gash she'd seen on the crime scene video, 'where the cord was tied. What made that? Do you think Tasmin cut herself trying to get free?'

Dr Chang again shook her glossy head. 'By the time that cut was made,' she said, 'Tasmin was long past trying anything. It was a post-mortem wound. There were no vital reactions around it.'

Gemma took that in while the doctor stood, gathering up papers from the desk. 'Maybe someone lifted her body by the cord and the skin tore?' the doctor went on. 'Or possibly the cord became entangled with something underwater? Whatever it was, it exerted sufficient pressure and tension to cause that injury.'

Dr Chang packed papers and notebooks into a fawn and green crocodile briefcase and rose to feet enclosed in perfectly matching low-heeled shoes. 'If you'll excuse me,' she smiled. 'It's late and I have children to pick up.'

'Of course,' said Angie, stepping back to allow the doctor to switch her office light off and step out into the corridor. They walked towards the exit in silence until the foyer area.

'So if she didn't drown . . . ?' Angie began.

'I believe she died from the combined effects of various opiate depressants and alcohol, together with a physical obstruction to her breathing.' The doctor paused, just about to push open the heavy glass doors onto Parramatta Road. 'I found large amounts of semen at the back of her throat. And blood in her mouth.'

'Her blood?' The picture that was forming in Gemma's mind was not pretty. It seemed Tasmin had been exploited sexually in every possible way, and fatally.

'At this stage, I don't know. But I had positive reactions for semen in both vaginal and anal swabs as well.'

Gemma felt a sudden rage. 'You're suggesting she choked during oral sex?'

Dr Chang pushed the door open. 'That theory would not conflict with my findings,' she said. 'We'll know more when the DNA samples are profiled.' She made a graceful inclination with her head.

Gemma and Angie got the message and hurried outside.

'That's what might have happened to Amy,' Gemma said as they got into Angie's car.

The Ratbag wasn't in when Gemma finally arrived home again. Unable to shake the feelings of anger and sorrow aroused in her by Dr Chang's findings and the rape case she'd read about in the VMO files, she went out to the deck. The evening seemed heavy with unavenged, seething energies. Looking down, she saw that the neglected garden was wilting and decided to water it in the hot night air. She glanced up to the windows of the apartment on top of hers as she watered plants and saw that whoever had moved in still hadn't organised curtains.

She heard the radio crackle into life in her office. She turned the hose off and hurried inside.

'Tracker Three here, Base. Copy?'

'Spinner!' she said, snatching up the radio. 'Where are you?'

'I wanted to check with you about Daria Reynolds.'

'Don't waste another second on that woman!' said Gemma. 'Work out your hours and give them to me. Can you do that Bathurst job?'

'Yep.'

'And there's something else you can do while you're there.' Gemma's free hand scrabbled around on the desk until it located Mannix Romero's employment details. 'It's over twenty-five years ago, but someone who works or worked at Bathurst High might remember something. That was his first posting after teachers' college.'

She gave him a brief outline of the case and

Romero's name and date of birth, then told him about her first meeting with Romero, how he'd barged into the principal's office without knocking, the breathless love letter inviting a rendezvous hidden in his desk and her discovery of his second laptop and the telescope trained on the girls' dormitories.

'Why do you want to know, Boss? Wasn't he arrested?'

'Yes,' said Gemma. 'But I'm curious. And Angie is overworked.'

'I'll ask around. See what I can dig up.'

If anyone could unearth an old secret, it was Spinner, Gemma thought as she wished him a safe trip. She rehoused the radio and went back outside to finish the watering. A quiet evening on the lounge beckoned invitingly but she glanced at her watch. No rest for the wicked, she thought.

Gemma was almost at Tiffany Brown's place when her mobile rang. She picked it up and saw that Angie had sent her a text message—a website address followed by *Take a look at this! The techies found this archived on Mr Romero's laptop.* Gemma saved it as she pulled up.

Tiffany herself opened the front door when Gemma knocked. 'You're the lady on the staircase,' she said with surprise, 'who talked to us that night.'

'The lady on the staircase! That makes me sound like a ghost,' said Gemma and immediately regretted her comment. She'd forgotten how embarrassed adolescents can be by the remarks of adults. And worse, the words caused a shiver to run down her spine. *Someone's walking over my grave*, Aunt Merle used to say. I'm not ready to be a ghost, Gemma thought as Tiffany led her into an open-plan house. Half an acre away, a granite kitchen gleamed and in another corner a lounge was arranged. Tiffany plonked herself down on a damask sofa, sinking into the luxurious cushions like a spoonful of sugar into a cappuccino.

'I'll sit here, shall I?' Gemma asked.

'Oh, yes. Sorry.'

Gemma perched on a small upright chair as Tiffany waited expectantly, eyes bright in her softly freckled face.

'Tiffany, I need to ask you about your witness statement,' said Gemma.

Tiffany looked scared. 'Why?'

'Nothing for you to worry about,' Gemma reassured her. 'I just want to make sure I've got everything right. Just checking a few finer points. Okay?'

Tiffany still looked wary so Gemma hurried on. 'Let me just read it to you.' She pulled out the copy. '*My name is Tiffany Louise Brown and the last time I saw Amy Bernhard was the morning of December second when we were at the bus stop. The bus was quite crowded that morning. Amy is in the same class as me, but we do different level Maths. Someone told me she'd gone missing from the school grounds that morning. I can't think of any reason why she might run away.*'

Tiffany nodded. 'That's right. That's all true.'

Tiffany's mother appeared, crossing the kitchen. 'Everything all right?' she asked brightly, after the initial greetings.

Gemma assured her it was and Tiffany nodded. They heard Mrs Brown's footsteps fading as she carried a coffee upstairs.

'Tell me a bit more about where Amy was that morning,' said Gemma. 'Who she was talking to at the bus stop?'

Tiffany made a face. 'Who do you think? Tasmin Summers and Claudia Page, who else?'

'And was there anything about her that caught your attention? Anything different from usual?'

Tiffany shook her head.

Gemma considered something else. 'Have you any idea why Amy might have left the school grounds later?'

Tiffany shrugged. 'Who knows? Amy did pretty well whatever she liked.'

'And can you remember who it was who told you that Amy had left the school grounds that morning?'

Tiffany looked sheepish. 'I left that bit out,' she admitted. 'I didn't want to get her into trouble.'

'Who?'

'It won't get back to the school, will it? If I tell you something I left out of that?' She pointed to the copy of the witness statement.

'No,' said Gemma. 'This is just between you and me. Who was it you didn't want to get in trouble?'

'Claudia. She was the one who told me. But if

I'd put that in my statement, I thought it might get her into trouble—you know, because she didn't dob to the teachers that Amy had shot through when it all got serious later.'

Claudia telling Tiffany that Amy had left the school grounds in the morning. Gemma's suspicion was hardening . . .

'Let me get this clear,' Gemma said. 'You're saying that the person you call "someone" in your statement was actually Claudia Page?'

Tiffany nodded. 'Is it all right? You said when you spoke at the school that anything we told you would be kept in confidence.' Her young face contracted with anxiety. 'You won't say anything to the school?'

Gemma shook her head. 'I promise I won't say a word at the school.'

Tiffany relaxed a little.

'And you saw Amy talking to Claudia and Tasmin at the bus stop?' Gemma continued.

'Yes.'

'Did you see Amy get on the bus?'

Tiffany shook her head.

'Did you see her get off the bus?'

'No. But I was one of the first people off. She could have been behind me.'

'And did you see Amy at school that morning?'

'Uh-uh.' Tiffany shook her head.

Gemma stood up. 'Thanks, Tiffany.'

Tiffany uncurled herself, apparently disappointed that the interview was over. 'Is that all?'

Not entirely, Gemma was thinking. In fact, it's

just beginning. She was starting to suspect Amy Bernhard never actually made it onto the school bus.

Gemma pulled up outside her place and switched her radio off. She climbed out of her car, looking around fast; partly habit, this quick catlike surveillance of her territory was now even more essential. Underneath everything else going on in her life right now, the memory of that pencilled warning lay like an open grave, cold and dark, at the bottom of her mind. Even here, in her safe street, with her secure apartment close at hand, the warning stirred. But when she saw Mike's car parked on the street, her mood changed. She hurried down the steps to the front garden and went inside.

Mike turned on the swivel chair in front of his desk as she came into the operatives' room. Gemma hesitated, waiting for him to start first in a silence filled with crowding regrets and shame.

'Gemma,' he said, standing up and coming over. 'I was checking the current jobs. Looks like we're way behind on some of them.'

'We are. I've been caught up in the Netherleigh Park business. It's a double murder investigation now. And Spinner's off in the bush for a day or two.'

'So what would you like me to do?'

The nicest words a man can say to a woman, Gemma thought. She was tempted to invite him into the murder investigation, but drew back from that. Best they stay on separate jobs for a while.

'You could take over the Forever Diamonds investigation. I've neglected that brief. I really need someone to get into their factory. Report back on how they receipt and make sure the correct diamond goes to the right home. I know they're desperate for a receptionist.'

She considered. There were several good women in the security business who could work undercover. But could she afford one of them right now? Maybe she could do a contra deal with another female PI?

Mike checked Annie Dunlop's place on his laptop while Gemma filled him in on the details of Mr Dowling's complaint. She leaned over his shoulder to see the images, aware of Mike's pleasing male scents, determined to keep things businesslike between them.

'I think she must be seeing things,' said Mike as he checked Mrs Dunlop's lounge room on the screen. 'There's nothing moving in there except the old girl herself.' In the jerky time-lapse surveillance coverage, Gemma saw Annie Dunlop settling down into her big armchair, a cup of something on the table beside her.

Then they went through the outstanding insurance jobs and Mike selected several that Spinner needed to put to one side. Gemma left Mike organising his work on the new jobs and went into her own office, logging on to the website Angie had messaged her, the one found archived on Mannix Romero's second laptop. A banner came up.

Cute students by day; horny sluts by night at the Black Diamond Room! They can't get enough of the gang-bang squad. Cum see what they get up to!!

Gemma waited. The first image was an almost naked Amy Bernhard. Another hyperlink flashed under Amy's body: a black diamond icon slowly turning on its axis. Gemma clicked on it and a scene from pornoland unfolded—a glittering black chandelier lighting black satin sheets and cushions, with a bed in the foreground, a girl on it wearing nothing except a diamond garter, and a group of men.

Gemma clicked on 'foreplay', a ten-second tease to encourage viewers to cough up the details of their credit cards. The action started, the old in-and-out at every orifice, tight male buttocks, straining cocks, splayed female legs, eyes closed shut and mouth open wide in simulated ecstasy. Or anguish, Gemma thought. It's not possible to distinguish between those two emotional states from facial expressions. The jerky sound of the faulty streaming, the usual endearments—slut, bitch, cunt, whore . . . The footage fell short of any climax scene. Presumably the close-ups of the cum shots, the money shots, would have to be paid for. Gemma played it again. This time she knew there was no doubt as to who the girl in the video was. It was Amy Bernhard.

On the way back to her car, Gemma called Angie but got only her voice mail. She passed on to Julie Cooper the suspicion she was forming that Amy Bernhard had been at the bus stop the day she disappeared, but it seemed that she'd had other plans for that day and had probably never caught the bus at all.

Gemma rang off, wondering. Amy had her make-up bag with here. Where was she planning to go?

Gemma banged on Claudia Page's door, stood back, waiting to hear footsteps. Finally the door opened. When Claudia saw who it was, her eyes flickered with anxiety.

'I know about the secret, Claudia!' said Gemma quietly as she barged in. 'I know what Amy and Tasmin were up to. And you did too!'

She looked around 'Your mother in?'

Claudia shook her head. 'She should be home soon. She's having dinner with friends.'

Gemma continued: 'And I know why you didn't sit with her that day on the bus, you and Tasmin.'

Claudia hunched against the wall. There was a silence and Gemma felt the triumph of knowing she was right.

'Amy didn't ever get on the bus! She told you at the bus stop that she wasn't going to school and you spread rumours to cover her. You told Tiffany Brown that she'd left the school grounds. Why, Claudia? Why all these lies?'

Claudia's eyes were huge. Fear dilated her pupils so that she looked like some hunted nocturnal creature. 'I had to. I couldn't tell on her. I pretended she'd come to school like any other day. But then, when she disappeared—'

'She'd asked you to cover for her?'

Claudia nodded. 'We write our own notes. We can all forge our mothers' signatures. Amy was going to give me one, but in all the excitement that morning, she'd forgotten.' She faltered. 'And then, when it seemed that something bad had happened to her, it was too late. I was really scared that I'd be blamed. I know that sounds awful and selfish.'

'At least it's honest,' said Gemma.

'And Tasmin made me swear never to tell anyone about Amy. Because then it would spoil it for her. Just because Ames had run away. Or whatever.'

The two of them stood in silence. Gemma noticed a hall table where tall exotic lilies in a huge bronze urn spiked the air, filling the house with the smell of the tropics.

'It's the "whatever" that worries me, Claudia,' said Gemma. 'It was the "whatever" that killed her.' She'd almost said 'them' but she wasn't sure if Tasmin's death had been made public yet. She hardened her voice. 'You must tell me everything you know.'

Claudia seemed distracted. 'I thought she'd run away at first. She said she was going away with someone. The man who'd helped them set up the website.'

'Who is he?'

Claudia shook her head. 'Some guy. Old enough to be her father. He had a crush on her, she said. Told me he was stalking her.'

A long pause while Gemma noted this down and considered it. A stalker. Despite the letter and his telescope, that didn't sound like Mr Romero. He didn't need to stalk. A teacher had the right to be present in a student's life for hours a day.

'A letter was found in Mr Romero's possession,' she said, 'a sort of love letter signed by someone using the initials AB.' As she spoke, she sensed the tension building in Claudia. 'Do you know anything about that?'

Claudia looked down at her mauve-painted nails.

'That was Amy,' she said finally. 'She thought Mr Romero had the hots for her. She thought it would be fun to tease him. Her idea was to invite him to a meeting at the beach and then hide and watch to see if he came.'

'And if he did?'

Claudia shrugged. 'I guess she would know she was right.'

Fatherless girls, Gemma thought. Without knowing what they're doing, they put themselves in risky situations. She should know.

'But once Amy was found dead! Surely you could have spoken up then—about what you knew? It was a murder investigation!' Gemma wanted to shake her.

Claudia slumped against the wall. Her long hair hid her face like a curtain and when she pushed it back, Gemma saw the tears spilling from her lashes. Gemma collected herself. It was too easy, she thought, to dump it all on this frightened adolescent. Amy was not her responsibility. None of the adults in these girls' lives had taken enough real notice of what the girls had been up to.

'Let's go and sit down,' Gemma said. 'I'm sorry I said that. It was out of order. It was you who sent me that anonymous email with the address of that website, wasn't it?'

Claudia nodded.

'You were trying to help. But you wanted to stay hidden at the same time,' said Gemma softly.

Again the girl nodded, brushing the tears from her eyes. Poor kid, Gemma thought. In over her head with nowhere to turn and no one to talk to.

'I'll leave if you want me to,' she said.

'No,' the girl whispered. 'It's okay. I want to talk to someone about it. I feel relieved that someone knows. I didn't know what to do.'

They walked through to the huge conservatory area where the palms conspired to make odd shadows against the walls. Several mysteries had been resolved quite simply, Gemma thought. Romero had been telling the truth. Amy Bernhard hadn't shown up for the meeting with him for the simple reason that she hadn't been at school that day. Although she still had severe misgivings regarding Romero's use of the telescope for 'anatomical accuracy', his story of being held up in traffic was quite possibly true.

'When you feel okay,' Gemma said, 'tell me everything you know.' She sat herself on a chair while Claudia slid down onto the rug-covered floor, leaning against an oversized sofa. Gemma took out her notebook. 'It's time for you to share the burden of everything you know about the secret.'

Claudia dragged a little sequined bag over

towards her and pulled out a packet of cigarettes. She offered one to Gemma who shook her head, waiting while the girl lit it and inhaled deeply.

'Everything was okay at the beginning,' she said, as smoke curled around her beautiful face. 'It was just fun. At first, I even considered joining them on the first website. Getting a webcam and linking up. I took some of the pictures that are on it. Then Amy and Tasmin really got into the webcam thing. They set up a fan club so that people who found the website when they were online could email their responses. Some of the responses were so freaky they decided to start a Dickhead of the Week thing. I didn't want to be involved in that. I thought it was silly.' Claudia looked away, miserable. 'That's when it started to go out of control.' She put her head in her hands. 'It's all my fault.'

'I don't think so,' said Gemma, gently taking the cigarette from between her fingers and putting it safely down on the ashtray.

'The guy who'd given them the money for the website offered them modelling work,' continued Claudia. 'He claimed he was a friend of Amy's father. Just a few photo shoots. Amy got very excited. And so did Tasmin.'

Gemma scribbled a note to check Andrew Bernhard again. 'Who is this guy?' she asked.

Claudia picked up the cigarette from where Gemma had placed it. 'I guessed it was the man from the club. The one who used to let them in free.'

'Which club was that?' said Gemma, wondering if she knew the name already.

'A place called Deliverance. They told me they'd started to put video streaming on a link to their website. But they wouldn't tell me what it was showing. They'd changed the name too, so that I couldn't find them straightaway even if I'd been looking. Around then, they started having money to splash around. New clothes, new make-up. They kept putting pressure on me to come in on it too.'

'But you didn't want to?'

'I thought about it. I wanted money. I even went to an interview with the boss.'

'And?'

'That made up my mind for me. He was a total sleaze.'

'Name?'

'Vernon. Vernon something.'

'Can you tell me what he looked like?'

Claudia shrugged. 'Sort of old. Big fat thing. Purple face.'

'Colouring?' Gemma asked.

'Not much hair left. Big eyebrows.'

Gemma noted these details down with the name while Claudia continued. 'I tried to tell Ames and Taz to get out. But they wouldn't.' She inhaled on her cigarette and it caught in her throat, causing a fit of coughing. After the coughing subsided, she stubbed the cigarette out in the square marble ashtray. 'They didn't seem to mind that he was a sleazebag. I think by then they were smoking too much dope—maybe doing other drugs. And they loved having money. They spent heaps on clothes. Designer things. In the past, we used to get together to do our homework. All that stopped. They just weren't interested in school anymore.'

Claudia pulled a gold chain out from under her light sleeveless top. At the end of it was a caged black pearl. 'Ames bought me this. It's Versace. She bought herself a Versace watch. Told her mother it was a Taiwanese clone.' She fiddled with the pearl, rattling it softly in its filigree cage. 'Guess how much this cost?

'Didn't anyone notice?' Gemma asked. 'Jewellery? All those new clothes?'

Claudia shrugged. 'Amy's mother was too busy fighting with the cowboy.'

'Eric Stokes?'

Claudia nodded. 'And Taz got away with it by telling her mum that her father gave her the money.'

All the lies necessary, thought Gemma, to protect the dangerous lifestyle the girls were starting to embrace. And still nobody really noticed.

'You know nothing at all about this man who helped with the website?'

'No.' Claudia frowned. 'Only that he used to work as a bodyguard to Vernon a long time ago.'

'What about Vernon? Where did you meet him?'

'In a café. At the Cross. That big one on the corner. He even tried to paw me then.' Claudia made a face. 'He was disgusting. Yuk.' She shuddered. 'He had this big gorilla of a bodyguard with him that day too.'

Gemma wrote down, *Vernon and Gorilla bodyguard*. 'Did you get the bodyguard's name?'

'He called him Eddie.'

Gemma recalled that the Ratbag had offended an Eddie associated with Deliverance. Could it be one and the same person?

'Go on,' she said. 'You were talking about the money the girls were making. And the website.'

'Yes. I tracked down the website—even though they'd changed the name—and saw the Black Diamond hyperlink to the second site. It was credit card entry but they had a few seconds of video as a teaser. That's all I needed to see to know what was going on.'

'I've seen it too,' said Gemma.

Claudia looked up. 'So you know what it's like.' She paused. 'We had a huge fight about it. I told them they were just being used by a bunch of pornographers. I reminded them that they were both under-age. And then she went missing.' Claudia sniffed back tears. 'She'd always said one day she'd just run away to Queensland and live with her father. I thought maybe that's where she'd gone. Or gone off somewhere with this guy who had the hots for her. But when we didn't hear anything from her, we started getting scared. Tasmin made me swear not to say anything about it. She was really scared of Amy's stepfather too.'

Gemma thought of Eric Stokes and his dark self-righteousness. Fathers kill daughters in some cultures, she was thinking, if they break the rules.

'What was she scared of?'

'She knew he wanted to make trouble for Amy's mother after they split up. And that he'd use her,

Tasmin, too if he could. Taz was getting more unreliable and moody.' Claudia looked away, as if seeing it all somewhere else, in a parallel world that only she knew about. 'Plus she had stars in her eyes about some bloke. He was promising her the world. She wasn't seeing straight. He was in his *forties*!'

'God,' said Gemma, trying to keep her face straight. 'That's practically geriatric.'

'She was totally in love with him. Wanted to leave school. Said he'd said she could live with him and get heaps of modelling work.' She paused, raising her beautiful eyes to Gemma. 'It wasn't modelling work he was thinking about.'

She pulled out another cigarette. 'I couldn't tell anyone. I would have been in too much trouble. I know it sounds selfish but I couldn't afford to be expelled from school. Not coming up to the HSC year. I had to think of my mother and how she'd go ballistic. Then it all got worse and I got really scared. I thought the best thing to do would be to stay silent and send you the website details. Then I felt better about it. Like I'd taken action. Done the right thing.'

Gemma patted her knee. 'It was the right thing, Claudia,' she said.

'Now I'm really, really scared. Amy's dead. And Taz's gone missing.'

'But you weren't involved in the website,' said Gemma. 'You weren't involved in making those pornographic videos.'

'I know. But I'm part of the group.' Her eyes

brimmed. 'Whoever killed Amy might come after me.'

'That's not very realistic.' Gemma tried to comfort the girl.

'Taz said something that frightens me—that they wanted me. That I had the look they wanted.'

She certainly had the look, Gemma thought. An outstanding beauty, cool and classical. Debasing that, for them, would be twice the fun.

'Taz gave me something to mind,' Claudia went on. 'And the guy she had a crush on, he knows she gave it to me.'

Gemma was about to ask what it was when Claudia's mobile rang. This time, after a couple of whispered words, she hurried from the room. Gemma tried to overhear what was said but couldn't make out the low murmur. Was it the good-looking youth with the flashing smile who Gemma had seen upside down on the screen of the mobile the first time she'd interviewed Claudia? Gemma waited. If it was him, he seemed to have a lot to say. She wanted Claudia to hurry back, tell her about whatever it was that Tasmin had given her. If the killer knew that Claudia had something that might incriminate him, the girl was definitely in grave danger.

Minutes passed and Gemma started to feel uneasy. She walked over to where the marble paddock ended and looked through the door into the room Claudia had walked through. Gently, she pushed the door further open.

There was no one there.

'Claudia?' Gemma called, her voice echoing through the mansion, bouncing off marble and glass. She hurried through the unfamiliar rooms, checking downstairs. Then she quickened her pace, almost running upstairs. She knocked and entered door after door. She retraced her footsteps and ran downstairs again. This time she noticed what she'd failed to see before. The front door stood wide open.

'Shit!'

She ran outside onto the street. Nothing. She ran a little distance one way, then the other. There was no one around, just the occasional car passing. A man walking a large black dog turned the corner and she almost collided with him as she ran to check the next street. 'Did you see anyone?' she asked. 'A young girl? Tall, dark-haired?'

'No,' he said, shaking his head, pulling the dog to heel.

Gemma thanked him and crossed to the other side of the street. But it was empty. She hurried back to the Page house, calling Angie on the way. 'Claudia Page got a phone call while we were talking,' she said to Angie as she searched through the house one more time, making sure Claudia wasn't hiding away somewhere, flinging doors open again, rechecking bathrooms. 'Then she left the house. Went from right under my nose. I didn't even know she'd gone until too late.'

'What do you mean, gone?'

'One minute she was here talking to me, next minute she'd vanished. I checked out on the street.

Only saw a man and his dog and he hadn't seen anything.'

'You think there was a connection between the phone call and her shooting through?'

'It looks like it.' Gemma passed on the information Claudia had given her. 'She's got a boyfriend, name unknown. I'll ask around after him. And I've got a name for you—the man who interviewed her for modelling work. Vernon.'

'Great. Is that the best you can do?'

'He's fat, old and disgusting, according to Claudia. Balding. And,' she continued, 'Amy Bernhard did write that love letter you found in Romero's desk. Except it was a joke.'

'Did Romero know that?'

'How could he?'

'I'll check it out.' Angie paused. 'Any more on Vernon?'

'He has a gorilla bodyguard, called Eddie.'

'By the way, our techies are trying to trace the server of that Black Diamond website.'

'It was pretty explicit,' said Gemma.

'Not the usual sort of activities on the syllabus at Netherleigh Park Ladies' College,' Angie agreed. 'The techies are going overtime trying to get addresses from the girls' own websites. Some of the email responses were pretty off. Oh,' she added, 'I've traced Sandra Samuels.'

For a second, Gemma was puzzled. Then she remembered the victim statement and the thief knot from the terrible gang rape.

'Where is she?'

'She works as receptionist-housemother at a church-run youth refuge in the Cross,' said Angie. 'I spoke to her on the phone and she said no way was she going to talk to any cops about her past.'

'Maybe she'll talk to me,' said Gemma. 'Give me the details.' She noted them, but couldn't keep her fear down. 'Ange,' she continued, 'I'm scared for Claudia. She's got something that Tasmin gave her. And it might be that the killer knows she's got it.'

'We'd better find that girl fast.' Angie rang off.

Gemma made a thorough search through the streets near Claudia's house, asking neighbours if they'd seen or heard anything. Finally, feeling guilty and anxious, she headed home.

The Ratbag still hadn't shown up. He was missing too. She'd told Mrs Ratbag that her son could stay with her; she was in loco parentis and she was a failure. She'd been with Claudia and Claudia had simply sneaked out. I should have been more suspicious after that phone call, Gemma scolded herself.

A phone call to Tiffany established that Claudia did have a boyfriend.

'Damien someone. I only met him once. He used to walk her home from her music lessons before her mother banned him.'

'Claudia told me that Tasmin gave her something recently. Something that might be very dangerous for her to have. Do you know what that could be?'

Tiffany didn't.

Gemma headed out again. A short time later she

was knocking on Mrs Snellgrove's door and in a few moments it was opened by her teacher, clutching a dressing gown over her clothes.

'Gemma! This is a surprise! Is everything all right?'

'I'm sorry about the lateness of the hour, Mrs Snellgrove. But I need to ask you about someone you might teach.'

'Is everything all right with Mother?'

'As far as we can see,' said Gemma, 'there's nothing in your mother's apartment that shouldn't be there.'

'She was complaining again last night,' said Mrs Snellgrove, ushering her inside. 'Said she felt it against her legs.'

Mrs Snellgrove closed the front door. 'Now that you're here, I've got some news for you,' she said. 'About that Kingston girl.'

Gemma followed her down the hall into the living room. Her stomach was suddenly in turmoil. The subject of her half-sister had been driven right out of her mind by recent events and now here it was, all coming up again.

Mrs Snellgrove went to an envelope on top of the piano. 'I wrote the information down. My memory's not what it used to be,' she said, opening the envelope.

'No,' said Gemma, putting her hand out to stop Mrs Snellgrove. She wasn't ready for this.

'But,' said Mrs Snellgrove, hand frozen halfway into the envelope, 'I thought you wanted details about—'

'I did. I do,' Gemma said, gently taking the envelope from her teacher. 'Thank you.' She slipped it into her pocket. Now wasn't the right time. 'I'll take it with me,' she said and gave Mrs Snellgrove a reassuring smile.

'Do you teach piano to a girl called Claudia Page?' It was a long shot.

Mrs Snellgrove shook her head. 'No, dear.'

She peered closer. 'Is everything all right? You look very pale.'

Gemma realised the little diamond drop at the bottom of Mrs Snellgrove's fan brooch was missing. She put her hand out. 'You've lost a diamond,' she said. 'From the bottom of your fan.'

'Never mind. There are plenty more. I'm sorry I can't be more helpful.'

Gemma went straight home again, ringing the Page house on the way and getting Mrs Page who had just arrived back from dinner and was concerned not to find Claudia home. Gemma explained what had happened.

'Might Claudia be with her boyfriend?' she asked.

'No,' said Mrs Page. 'I've just phoned. They're both missing.'

'His name?' Gemma asked.

'Damien. Damien Wilcox.'

Gemma thanked her, taking the boy's phone number. When she rang Damien's mother, the woman was surprised that her son had gone out at such a late hour. Usually, he told her what he was doing, she said. Maybe he'd decided to sleep over at a friend's place and forgotten to call. Gemma got off the line before Mrs Wilcox could ask too many questions.

She was exhausted by the long day, but sleep was out of the question. Gemma couldn't get Claudia out of her mind. How could the girl just vanish like that? If anything happens to her, Gemma thought, how will I ever forgive myself?

She tried to distract herself with television then went to Mike's laptop, switched it on, logged on and waited. Into view came the interior of Mrs Dunlop's living room. She could see the small figure, dwarfed by the large armchair, either dozing or watching the television screen. Nothing doing there. No animals in view. It was late but Gemma wasn't sleepy. She went round switching lights off.

THIRTEEN

In the morning, Gemma was again checking on the Annie Dunlop feed when Angie rang. 'It's panic stations around here,' she said. Claudia Page had not come home that night and Damien Wilcox was also still missing. 'Claudia must have been feeling like the last clay pigeon in the box.'

Gemma, her eyes still on the laptop screen with the view of Mrs Dunlop's flat, thought of something else. 'Has anything been done about the warning of that contract out on me?'

'You know how it is. G-for-Gross is still off with his goddam ear. I took it to the big boss,' said Angie.

'And?'

'And he said leave it with him. He'd take appropriate action.'

Gemma hadn't expected anything more.

Mike arrived and she let him in, thinking it was getting easier every time and soon relations between them would be normal again.

'Forever Diamonds is still looking for a receptionist,' he said. 'I went past last night and they've
added "urgent" to the sign.'

'They know my face,' said Gemma. 'Otherwise
I'd do it myself. I'll have to pay another professional to go in there.' She gathered up the
completed jobs that Spinner had left in folders in
the out tray on his desk. 'But I'll need to talk to
Mr Dowling first before incurring such an extra
expense.'

She was about to go to her own office when
something caught her eye—a movement in the
monochrome picture on the laptop screen. In Mrs
Dunlop's flat, something low and ill-defined was
definitely moving. Gemma peered closer, trying to
work out what it was. Had it just been a breeze
lifting the skirts of the big square armchair? The
lighting wasn't very good but she would have
sworn she'd seen something that was separate from
the chair move and vanish down the side hidden
from the camera. 'Damn,' she muttered.

With one eye on the screen, she called Mrs
Dunlop. No one answered. Gemma put the phone
down.

'What?' Mike swivelled round on his chair.

'I thought I saw something move in Mrs
Dunlop's flat.'

'Her animal?'

They both stared at the screen, but nothing
moved in the grainy picture.

'I did see something. On the other side of that big
armchair of hers.'

Again, they stood and watched the time-lapse frames. Nothing.

'I'm going over there,' said Gemma. 'There is definitely something in that woman's flat.'

'Didn't her daughters say they'd searched the place thoroughly?' Mike said.

'They did,' she said. 'But I haven't.'

Gemma grabbed her bag, camera and notebook.

'I'll come with you,' Mike said. 'One to search, one to record.'

With all the pressures she was under right now, it felt good to have Mike's support. 'You're on,' she said.

Mrs Dunlop didn't seem in the least surprised when they arrived at her place. 'So,' she said, 'you've seen that animal on your camera, have you?'

'Maybe,' said Gemma. 'What we plan to do, with your permission, is a full-scale search.'

'It was at me again last night,' said the old lady. 'I could feel it tickling my legs. It's a big creature, whatever it is.'

'Peripheral neuritis,' Mike whispered to Gemma as Mrs Dunlop made her way to the tiny kitchen to put the kettle on. 'Nerve damage. Sometimes people get pins and needles in their extremities. It could feel as if something was touching her legs.'

They divided up the small rooms, starting floor to mid-height in the bedroom, checking under everything, the undersides of all the fittings and the contents of every drawer and container, turning the brilliant beam of Mike's flashlight into any ill-lit areas. It was a fairly recent building with plain square rooms, easy to search. Then they moved higher, from mid-height right up to the ceiling— searching through built-in wardrobes, shelves, furnishings and the storage cupboards.

When they'd cleared the bedroom Mrs Dunlop brought the tray of tea things out and put them on the table near her big square armchair.

Mike and Gemma searched the bathroom, a tiny space with a small, partly opened window. Gemma stood in the bath to open it fully and peered out. She was looking down into a narrow walkway that ran between Mrs Dunlop's building and the block of flats next door. There was nothing down there except a grille-covered drain near the basement wall. No cover of any sort for an animal to hide in. She looked either side. Again, nothing, no balconies or footholds. Just the external pipes of the plumbing.

She pulled the window down to the level it had been at and climbed out of the bath to check the tiny cabinet, closing its mirrored door when she'd finished.

Mrs Dunlop poured three cups of tea and sat herself down in her ancient armchair. She looked tiny in it, dwarfed by its huge, old-fashioned structure.

Gemma and Mike checked the small kitchen, searching every nook and cranny, pulling the fridge out, checking the stove and its housing, the cupboards and shelves.

'Here's an ant,' said Mike, pointing to one that was wandering near the windowsill. 'That's the biggest animal in here so far.'

They started the systematic search of the lounge room while Mrs Dunlop watched them from her chair. Gemma turned her attention to the section behind the old lady, pulling out an art deco cocktail cabinet filled with photographs of Mrs Dunlop's grandchildren. It didn't take long.

'There's nothing here,' Mike said, shaking his head, talking over Mrs Dunlop's head to Gemma who was standing behind the armchair.

'I'm not deaf!' said Mrs Dunlop, catching him at it.

'I'm sorry,' he said. 'But really, Mrs Dunlop, there's nothing in here except us three.'

Gemma put her hand on the back of the armchair and looked down at the top of the old lady's grey hair, feeling sad. Now, she thought, they'll take her away from her familiar surroundings and put her in some nursing home where she won't know her way around and where she'll die among strangers. Then she felt something and stepped back, curious. Her fingers had found a frayed hole, the size of a man's fist, in the fabric stretched across the back of the old chair. She looked more closely at the grimy ring around the edges of the hole. It put her in mind of the dirty grease marks left along rat runs, yet there hadn't been the slightest sign of rats or vermin in the place—no droppings or chewed edges of any kind.

'Mike,' she said. 'Just bring the flashlight over here, will you?'

He handed the powerful light to her and, switching it on, she shone it through the hole in the back of the lounge chair. She peered in. The beam of light revealed springs and cotton-waste padding.

Something moved and it wasn't Mrs Dunlop stirring. Gemma jumped back.

'There's something in there!'

Mike frowned. 'Let's see.'

Gemma handed him the torch.

'What is it?' Mrs Dunlop struggled to stand up. 'What are you whispering about?'

'We want to have a look inside your armchair,' said Mike. 'We think there might be something inside it.'

Mrs Dunlop stood to one side while Mike and Gemma slowly turned the armchair upside down.

'It's very heavy,' said Gemma.

'They knew how to build things in the old days,' said Mrs Dunlop, straining to see what they were doing.

Now that they had the armchair on its head, the heavy canvas that covered the bottom of the frame was in clear view. It was stained and Gemma drew back from the smell. Something rattled inside, sounding like old dry bones.

'What the hell is it?' said Gemma.

'I think we need to have a real good look in there,' said Mike, turning to the old lady. 'Mrs Dunlop, I want to take this chair outside and—'

'Mike! Look! It's coming out!'

Gemma's shout made him let go of the armchair and it tipped over. As it did, the stained canvas bottom tore right open, revealing the pulsing coils of a huge python that was sliding out of the hole in the back of the chair, flowing along the carpet and heading for the bedroom.

'Jesus Christ!' said Mike, looking round for some way to catch the snake.

The python flowed into the bedroom and Gemma sprang to shut the door after it.

'What was it?' asked Mrs Dunlop, hearing the excitement and aware of something moving low along her carpet.

Gemma and Mike noticed for the first time the pile of debris and bones that had spilled out of the rotted canvas bottom of the chair. Gemma poked at a small flat skull with the end of the torch— needle-sharp carnivore's teeth, huge round eye-sockets, then fine vertebrae.

'Oh dear,' she said. 'Pusskin.'

After Mrs Snellgrove had taken her mother to stay at her place for a while and WIRES had taken the python, Gemma and Mike dismantled the camera installation and headed for home.

'That's one case wrapped,' said Mike. But it brought Gemma no satisfaction. All she could think of was Claudia Page. She'd let the girl down. Claudia had tried to help her and she'd failed her completely. I will find you, Gemma vowed. I swear it.

'What would you do if you were Claudia Page's boyfriend,' she asked, turning to Mike, 'and you were scared for your girlfriend's life?'

'I'd be a hero,' said Mike. 'I'd run away with her and hide out somewhere.'

'Where do you think they'd go?'

Mike shrugged his broad shoulders. 'Friends, rellies. It's a big country.'

'And all we've got is a thief knot,' she said.

Mike asked the question she'd been trying to avoid. 'What if they haven't run away? What if they've been taken?'

She asked him to deviate at New South Head Road and they drove to the Cross, Gemma refreshing her memory from her notebook about the youth refuge where Sandra Samuels worked.

Situated in one of the back streets, opposite the rear of the church across the road, the refuge seemed to be little more than a long hangar with a small kitchen area at one end, some plastic tables and chairs, a partitioned room where sleeping bags and foam mattresses were piled and, next to it, a small office area. In a corner, a television flashed with the sound turned down and the scent of roses sweetened the spare surroundings. A young man sat at a table reading. Gemma immediately thought of the Ratbag, but couldn't picture him settling for a church-run refuge.

'I'm looking for Sandra Samuels,' said Gemma, approaching the youth. He cocked his head on one side, indicating an ear and shaking his head. He can't hear, Gemma realised. She pulled out her pen and wrote the name 'Sandra Samuels' with a big question mark beside it in the margin of a discarded newspaper. Again, the youth shrugged. She was about to go and ask at the church when a slight woman in her thirties appeared at the door.

'Looking for someone?' she called, her head lifted in an enquiring, even aggressive way.

'I think I'm looking for you,' Gemma said, turning her attention to the woman and showing her ID, 'if you're Sandra Samuels.'

'What do you want?' said the woman, immediately defensive as Gemma dropped her gaze to confirm the name tag in a plastic sleeve clipped onto Sandra's T-shirt. 'Who are you?'

'I'm Gemma Lincoln and I need your help,' she said.

Sandra flashed Gemma a hard look. 'People like you don't need my help.' She glanced across the room at the reading youth. 'We're due to be kicked out of this place unless we can find next month's rent.'

'A young girl called Claudia Page has gone missing,' Gemma pressed on. 'Her two best friends went the same way. They're both dead and I've been employed by the college they attended to investigate.'

'I read about those girls.' Her manner softened a little. 'But how can I help you with that?'

Gemma searched for a gentle way to bring the gang rapes of twenty years ago into the conversation. 'When you were a fifteen-year-old schoolgirl,' she said, 'you were involved in a very serious incident.'

The change in Sandra was electric. Before Gemma could say another word, the woman had grabbed her arm. 'Get out of here!' she said, eyes blazing, her whole body shaking. 'Just get out of here right now!'

Gemma pulled her arm away from the other woman's grip. 'I need to know the answers to some questions, Sandra. This young girl could be in terrible danger. She needs your help! My help! She—'

'I said, get out! Now!' Sandra's voice had hardened. 'Or I'll get you charged for trespass.'

Gemma backed away. This was not going well. 'Okay, okay,' she said, hands up in a placatory position. 'I'm sorry if I've distressed you.'

She managed to pull one of her business cards out of her briefcase and tried to give it to the woman. But she wouldn't take it and it fell to the floor.

'Please,' Gemma begged. 'I can understand that you'd be reluctant to revisit those memories—'

But it was as if she no longer existed. Sandra Samuels had turned her back and hurried away, almost breaking into a run. Gemma heard a door slam. Interview terminated. She picked up her business card and took it over to the table where the youth was still lost in his book, leaving it propped up against the vase of roses.

Slowly, she walked back to where Mike waited in the car. He saw her face as she slid in beside him. She shook her head.

Back in her office, Gemma tried ringing Mr Dowling to discuss hiring the services of an outside undercover operator but he wasn't answering his phone.

She gathered up the folder in which she'd put the expenses incurred so far by Daria Reynolds, plus the summaries and charges for the long hours spent watching the Reynolds's house for a phantom who never came, and went outside to her car. At the top of the steps leading up to the roadway, she turned and saw the new tenant had finally put up plain white curtains. She hoped they meant the tenant would be a plain, quiet soul.

She climbed into her car and rang Angie. 'Any news yet on Claudia?'

'Negative,' Angie said. 'But Francie rang me to say they'd found a pile of polystyrene boxes near where all those bone fragments and teeth turned up. That's news.'

The curious case of the multiple remains didn't interest Gemma right now. 'All I can think of is Claudia Page,' she said.

'Today's papers are already on the case,' said Angie. 'Listen to this front page: *Murder College: Third girl vanishes!* And the *Herald* is almost as hysterical. *Police always too late says neighbour.*' Gemma could hear newspapers rustling at the other end of the line. 'And guess what?' Angie continued. 'The principal of Netherleigh Park Ladies' College has resigned.'

Was it because of the disgrace, Gemma wondered, or was Beatrice de Berigny on the run because the truth was slowly revealing itself?

'We're going to talk to the Wilcox boy's family,' Angie said. 'They might have some idea where he and Claudia have got to.'

'That's if they went somewhere voluntarily,' said Gemma.

'I'm still waiting on toxicology and other results on Tasmin Summers,' Angie sighed. 'Anything comes up you should know, I'll call you.'

Gemma drove to Daria Reynolds's house and parked outside. She swung her briefcase with the account in it over from the back seat and got out of the car, went up the path and banged on the door. She sniffed. Something was different—no incense. She knocked again and could hear it echoing through the house. As she peered through the front window, Gemma could sense that the place was uninhabited. A voice interrupted her investigation.

'No use knocking on that door, love. She's gone.'

Gemma swung round. A woman in next-door's front garden pushed hair out of her face with a gloved hand. A wheelbarrow piled with trimmings from camellia bushes stood nearby.

'She hasn't been around for a couple of days.' The woman picked up a pair of secateurs and continued with her snipping. 'Does she owe you money too? There were debt collectors round earlier.'

'Do you know where she's gone?'

The woman shook her head. 'She never spoke to me.'

Damn and blast, thought Gemma. She went down the side of the house and looked in through a side window. The place was bare. All the saints, statues and candles gone.

Even though she felt it was hopeless, she shoved her account under the front door. Now she'd have to do more work tracing a missing person if she wanted to be paid. And even then there'd be no guarantees. Her instincts had been right all along. The woman was a nutter.

Gemma hurried back to the car and drove to the Cross considering her position. Now that Miss de Berigny had resigned, did that mean Gemma was no longer required by the school as an investigator? She recalled the tally of hours she'd kept on this investigation. Netherleigh Park owed her a substantial amount of money even if they paid her off right now.

She dialled Miss de Berigny's number again, leaving a message asking her to return the call as soon as possible. She stowed the mobile feeling miserable. Business was not going well. She'd taken on a case that made no sense and now Daria Reynolds had skipped without paying. And she might be just about to lose the Netherleigh Park contract. Even so, she knew she would never be off this case until those responsible for the deaths of the girls were brought to justice. She needed to find out all she could about Eddie and the sleazebag, Vernon, who'd interviewed Claudia.

She narrowly avoided a car that cut in too close, leaning on the horn to advise him of his bad manners. He gave her the finger. She decided to ignore it and turned her attention to the traffic again.

Gemma parked near Kellett Street and walked down to Baroque Occasions. Beyond the open door, a new minder, long and thin and looking as if a gust of wind would blow him over, lounged in an armchair in the front room, half-dozing in front of a small screen showing a porn flick.

'Naomi in?' she asked.

'Who are you?'

'Girlfriend. Who are you?'

He pointed upstairs, giving Gemma an appraising look. She climbed the stairs, calling out, and found Naomi in the bathroom.

'Come in, Gemma,' said Naomi. 'I heard you from downstairs. I'm having a lovely soak—a break between the mugs.'

Naomi, hair tied up in a gold lamé turban she'd inherited from her mother, lay back in the suds of a bubble bath, painted toenails showing through at the opposite end of the bath. 'Schwarzenegger down there is supposed to be keeping cocky.'

'He doesn't inspire much confidence,' Gemma replied. 'Even I'd beat him in a fight.'

'You'd beat most people in a fight,' said Naomi. 'Sit down. You look awful. What's up?'

Gemma sat on the toilet lid. 'A heap of things. Overworked, underpaid.' She thought of Claudia. 'I've let someone down. She might be in terrible danger because I wasn't vigilant.'

'You can't save everyone, Gemma. Steve should look after you better,' said Naomi.

Gemma put her head in her hands. 'There's no Steve anymore, Naomi. We're finished.'

As she said this, a wave of grief rolled over her and she let it have its way for a few seconds, covering her face with her hand, sobbing.

'Men,' said Naomi. She wrung out the washer and passed it to Gemma who wiped her eyes.

'Thanks,' she said. It was hard to remember that Naomi was only a few years older than the Ratbag. She was decades older in experience. 'I sometimes wonder if I'm ready for a grown-up relationship. I just couldn't stop punishing him for being unfaithful.' She still couldn't bear to recall the scene with Lorraine Litchfield and the Colt M1911—her terror, Lorraine Litchfield's triumph. 'It was part of his work, his script. And when *I* strayed, he just forgave me.'

Naomi shrugged. 'We've got to get over that stuff,' she said, sitting up in the bath. 'You straight girls don't look after your men. You keep pushing them around, trying to make them different. Us workers, we take men the way we find them.'

Gemma listened. The people skills of a modern courtesan were not to be sneezed at.

'Tell him he's wonderful, that he's got a big cock, that he's the best in the world.' Naomi paused in her soaping. 'And you know something Mum used to say? If you love a man, all of that's true anyway.'

Shelly, thought Gemma. Where were you when I needed you?

'But you didn't come here to talk about men with me,' said Naomi.

'Couple of things,' said Gemma, reaching for a box of tissues and blowing her nose. 'Can you keep an eye out for young Hugo? He seems to have gone back out there.'

'The Ratbag? Sure. What else?'

'A young couple.' Gemma described Claudia Page and Damien Wilcox. 'I'm hoping they've gone underground.'

'But if they haven't?'

'They could be in real shit.' Gemma thought of Claudia and her fears. *I'm the last one*, she'd said.

'I'll ask around,' said Naomi. 'The street girls know what's going on out there.'

Gemma leaned forward and tucked the tissue into the toilet. 'Thanks. I'd do it myself, but I want to stay out of sight.'

Naomi subsided under her covering of bubbles again and Gemma thought of the man whose name had come up twice—with Hugo and also with Claudia. 'Have you heard of someone called Eddie?'

'The guy who works at Deliverance? I was there last night with my girlfriend. Eddie's built like a tank.'

'That sounds like him,' said Gemma. 'What do you know about him?'

Naomi shrugged, pink nipples moving in the soapsuds. 'He's just a heavy who works there. King of the bouncers.'

'Maybe Kosta might know more?' Gemma asked.

'He's got problems of his own,' said Naomi.

'Business going bad?' Gemma handed Naomi the washer from the end of the bath that she'd been trying to pick up with clenched toes.

'Worse than that. There've been break-ins at Indigo Ice, damage done to the building. He reckons it's the people from Deliverance. Reckons they're trying to put him out of business.' She washed her neck and ears.

'Kosta has always been a bit of a misery guts though,' Gemma said. 'Always paranoid.'

'Maybe he's got a reason this time.' Naomi used her toes more successfully this time to add hot water. 'Deliverance is the only place doing all right at the moment, if you believe what everyone's saying. Most of the businesses reckon they're struggling. Deliverance is a dealers' paradise. It's always full of celebs too. Stacks of coke get moved there.'

Gemma remembered the stoned girl with the glued-on glitter dress who'd staggered past her the night she'd visited the club.

'Very discreet,' Naomi was saying. 'All done on mobiles. A punter moves his money electronically into the dealer's account. The dealer checks his account and then sends a delivery boy round. And there's never any trouble. The bouncers are very professional. Slightest hint of trouble and out you go.' Naomi washed an elegant foot, splendid with scarlet nails. 'Which reminds me. Remember those two regular mugs I was grizzling about losing? The one who fucked and the one who watched?'

The guys with the sports trophies, Gemma remembered. 'Don't tell me they've come back to the fold?'

'Last night me and Rob took the night off.' Naomi washed the other foot and squeezed out the washer, delicately wiping the skin under her eyes, removing mascara. Under the glitzy golden turban her face shone like the kid she was. 'We try doing that every week if we can manage it. Go out, get a meal. Go dancing. Go to the flicks. Sometimes together, sometimes with a boyfriend. And like I said, last night we went to Deliverance.'

Gemma leaned forward, listening intently.

'I was on my way to the Ladies,' Naomi continued, 'a little worse for wear I have to say, and I opened a couple of doors before I got the right one. Behind the second door—what a surprise. There's one of them—the watcher—sitting up in the office behind this big desk like Jacky. No wonder I haven't had any outcalls to him in ages. If he's working at that place, he gets all the free pussy he can handle. And so would his big mate.'

She lay back in the suds, ten painted toes in a line along the end of the bath. 'He's put on a lot of weight. I don't remember him being that fat when he was watching me doing the business with his mate. And then, just as I was backing out, up behind me comes the other one! He didn't notice me. And he was all over this kid. I mean really. She couldn't have been more than fourteen. And he said, "Vernon, look what I've got."'

'Vernon? He called the fat man Vernon?' Another connection jumped a gap and sparked.

'What are you so excited about?'

'Can you describe the girl?'

'She's a new girl. Only been working round here a few weeks. Very thin. A user. I feel sorry for her, really. She's not going to last much longer. She could hardly stand up that night.'

'Someone called Vernon has been mentioned in

a case I'm working on, Naomi.' A real sleaze, Claudia had said. 'So Vernon was one of the guys you told me about earlier—the ritzy house with the GPS trophies?'

Naomi shook her golden turban. She lathered up her legs, prior to shaving. 'I'm sure it was GBS. That mean anything?'

'George Bernard Shaw? Gilbert and Sullivan? Grievous bodily something?' Gemma ran out of ideas.

'But I haven't told you the really interesting thing,' said Naomi, pulling the washer over her face. 'The guy with the little worker didn't recognise me. The mugs never do when they meet us socially. And I'm just one among hundreds, probably. But I sure recognised him.'

'Who?' asked Gemma.

'Now that his face has been all over the news,' Naomi said. 'It was that footie legend. The one who's suing the woman. Scott Brissett.'

Back home after a smoked salmon sandwich, Gemma left a message for Angie, passing on the gist of her conversation with Naomi, then wrote up her notes. That done, she went into the operatives' office and from the hanging space where Spinner kept his working wardrobe chose a Lightning Couriers black and lime-green lycra outfit. She checked the velcroed back pocket and found a Lightning Couriers receipt pad and Spinner's fake ID card which she jettisoned. Digging through a box of bits and pieces in the corner she found a spare video cassette. After she'd stuck a label down the spine she paused for a second to think, then scribbled a title in black pen, wrapped the cassette in bubble-wrap, changed into the form-fitting outfit and, with the package, drove back to the Cross, having remembered to throw Spinner's bike helmet into the backseat.

Twenty minutes later, with the helmet in place and feeling strange in the hot clingy outfit, Gemma presented herself at the front entrance of Deliverance. One side of the black double doors was open and she slipped in, getting her bearings while her eyes adjusted to the dim light.

The security wouldn't be far away, she thought, and there'd be a camera watching her every move. It was only a matter of time before her presence was discovered. With the packaged cassette ready in her hand, Gemma hurried along. Turning a corner she noticed the Ladies sign at the far end of the hall. Naomi had mentioned opening a wrong door on the way to the toilets the other night, Gemma recalled.

The first door on her left, marked 'Private: Do not enter', was locked. Too early for the management to be here, she thought. That must be the room Vernon was sitting in. She moved to the next door and found it standing slightly ajar. She felt around for a light switch in the windowless, airless environment. As her fingers groped, the light suddenly came on and she jumped back, startled.

'Who are you? What do you want?'

Someone was already in here. Gemma blinked, momentarily blinded by the brilliance of the chandelier in the centre of the room. A big Polynesian with bleached blond hair and a white shirt that stretched across his chest for a metre or so, blocked her way, chewing gum and gazing down at her from a great height, exuding a strange mix of peppermint and body odour.

'Lightning Couriers,' she said with a smile, tilting her bicycle helmet back a little and waving the package. 'Got a delivery here for Scott Brissett. He'll need to sign for it.' She whipped the receipt pad and a pen out of her back pocket then thrust the cassette and the paperwork in his direction.

The big man took the package and ripped the bubble-wrap off, checking the cassette. Gemma peered around his bulk and saw a huge bed covered in black satin and fake bearskin rugs, lit by the glittering jet and black diamonds of the central chandelier.

'I'll sign for this,' he said, inclining his bleached head. He scribbled something on her receipt pad and shoved it at her. 'Okay,' he said. 'You can go now.'

'You'll make sure Mr Brissett gets it?' she asked. 'I was hoping he'd sign in person. He does come here a fair bit, doesn't he?'

'I think you'd better go now,' he said, switching off the light and closing the door.

Gemma hurried back outside, aware of the big Polynesian following her to the main entrance doors. Her failure to connect with Scott Brissett was compensated for by what she'd seen. The room featured in the video streaming teaser—the Black Diamond Room. Angie could get a warrant and raid the place, she thought. Maybe they'd find the necessary physical evidence to link that room with Amy Bernhard. She left another message for Angie on the drive back.

She couldn't wait to get the hot lycra suit off and was almost home when her mobile rang. 'Angie?' she started as she answered. But there was a long silence. 'Hullo?' she said again. She started to wonder if it was a prank call. Then felt a clutch of fear.

'It's Sandra Samuels,' said the caller and Gemma relaxed. 'I've thought about what you said.' There was another long silence. 'And I know that the time has come for me to do something about the men who raped me. Especially now.'

Gemma felt a surge of relief and gratitude. 'Thank you so much for changing your mind. I'm not all that far away.' In the excitement of having Sandra call, she forgot the tightness of the bike outfit. 'I can be back at the refuge really quickly.'

'No need,' said Sandra. 'I've got a part-time job at Coogee. I can call in at your place on the way. I've got your card here. See you in a little while?'

Finally, Gemma felt she was getting somewhere. She tried ringing Angie again but went through to voice mail. She didn't leave another message; just rang off, praying that Claudia was safe.

•

The minute she was home, Gemma went online to the Australian Securities website and typed in the registered business name of Deliverance, copying the ACN from the card Kosta had given her. Soon she was hopelessly lost in a maze of subsidiary companies and offshoots.

She was still trying to trace her way through when she heard someone at the front door. Sandra Samuels.

Gemma ushered Sandra, now wearing a pretty summer suit, down the hall and into the living area. 'Thank you so much for coming over,' Gemma said, curious to know what Sandra had meant when she'd said, 'Especially now'. But she didn't want to push things too hard. Instead, she indicated a chair. 'Coffee?' she asked.

Sandra hesitated. 'This sounds rude, but could I have something stronger? A scotch if you've got one?'

Gemma obliged, going to the crystal decanters on the tray and the four cut-glass tumblers standing in a row next to the little fence around the tray. She picked one up, poured in what she hoped was a decent measure and put the stopper back. 'Ice or water?'

'Water. I don't usually do this. Not at this hour.'

'You look like you could do with it,' said Gemma. She poured a little cold water from the fridge into the glass and brought it out to Sandra.

'Thanks. I was so angry at first,' said Sandra, after a drink, 'at the way you were dragging up the past again. I just wanted you to go away. Then after you'd gone, I couldn't help thinking about that missing girl. I'm a youth worker, for God's sake! I've devoted my life to kids in strife. This girl needs me.' She paused. 'If she's still alive.'

Sandra took another swig of the scotch. 'I need to talk about what happened to me,' she continued. 'It's time for me to do it.'

'You said that on the phone,' said Gemma, studying the square-jawed face; the lines of anger and bitterness etched around her mouth. Sandra turned away, tears starting in her eyes.

'Why don't you go out to the deck and sit down and I'll make us some coffee,' said Gemma gently, leaving the woman alone to collect herself.

When Gemma came out with the tray, she noticed some colour had returned to Sandra's face. Nothing like the sea to restore a woman, Gemma thought, deciding she'd go for a swim later, hoping it might relieve the discomfort in her belly.

'You're lucky to have this place,' Sandra said, putting her empty glass down. 'I feel safe here. It's so quiet and out of the way.'

Gemma poured two coffees and pushed the milk jug towards Sandra, who sat with her back to the table, still staring out to sea. Gemma's instincts were working overtime. Sandra's breathing was audible and her struggle to contain an explosion of emotions was visible on her face.

'I find it very hard to talk about,' she said eventually. 'To anyone. Especially a stranger. But if there's any way I can help another girl . . .'

There was another long pause before she spoke

again, her voice almost a whisper. 'You can't imagine what it's like waiting at the hospital for the police to arrive, wearing one of those stupid, stupid hospital gowns that open down the back. They took all my clothes.'

Gemma put a hand out and touched Sandra's fingers briefly, just a tiny pat. 'Sandra,' she said. 'I'm so sorry.'

'I could hardly walk,' Sandra continued. 'I was all torn and swollen from the rapes. And I was filthy. I just wanted to get cleaned up. The cops talked to me and took down my statement. They wanted to photograph me, get the nurses to take swabs. I couldn't stand the thought of any more pulling around. The policewoman there was worse than the guys.' A tear rolled down her face, hanging from her jaw, catching the light behind it. 'They photographed the bruises and the cuts. Because I'd gone willingly with John, and that wasn't even his name, I got the feeling they thought I was really dumb and just asking for trouble.'

She paused, dashing the tear away as if angry that these events could cause her grief nearly a quarter of a century later. 'I ran away from the hospital. I borrowed some clothing and some money from another girl in the ward and got the train home. I couldn't tell Mum what had happened. I tried to put it behind me. Then after I left school, I went up to Queensland to live. I pretended it had never happened.'

'When did it happen?'

'The eighteenth of November, 1983. It was the

night of the Picton Show. We walked through the stalls and he'd won a snake on a rubber band at one of those shooting galleries. I was wearing a new silk scarf. I was so proud of that scarf.' She put her head in her hands. 'I was just a kid of fifteen.'

'I've seen the case notes, Sandra. I've read your statement. That's why I wanted to talk to you. Why I came round to the youth refuge.' A case that had seemed impenetrably locked down started to creak in its bonds.

Sandra looked bewildered. 'What do you mean? I didn't *have* a case—that was the whole problem. I was betrayed by the man I thought of as my boyfriend. And I ran away.' Tears continued to spill from her eyes. 'It's the most terrible thing that has ever happened to me.'

Gemma remembered the vicious details she'd read, the photographs of the seared young body. 'He tied your hands with your own scarf. But you still managed to start the car. You even ran over one of them getting away.'

Sandra looked at Gemma with disbelief. 'There's a record of that somewhere?' she asked.

'Yes,' said Gemma. 'You made a statement and I've read it. But there was no further contact with you because you left the hospital.'

Sandra's face paled as she relived the fear and horror of the past.

'They brought one of the rapists into the ward next to mine,' she said. 'I heard him—I saw him. It was the one I'd run over when I was escaping. I panicked and left. Nowhere was safe.'

No wonder, Gemma thought, that the young girl hadn't left a forwarding address. She put out her hand and covered Sandra's cold fingers again as the woman struggled to speak.

'So you know the details of what happened to me?' Sandra whispered eventually.

'Yes,' said Gemma. 'I was desperate for a break-through in two murders and I was reading through old cases looking for some connection with them. I've only just read through the file that held your statement and a few case notes.'

'I tried to make a new life,' said Sandra. 'I was terrified they'd come after me again. Especially as I'd injured one of them.

'You asked me why now,' she said eventually. 'Why, after all these years, I want to talk about it. More than that—I want to get this man.'

'It was a long time ago,' said Gemma. 'It's not going to be easy.'

Sandra stood up and went to the rail, turning to face inside, her back against the bar. 'It's as easy as saying a name,' she said. 'Gemma, I know who John is. I've seen him on television. Just recently.'

Gemma held her breath.

'I'll never forget that face,' Sandra continued. 'That scar on his eyebrow and nose. Those eyes. The others' faces are a blur now, because I couldn't bear to look. I had my eyes closed most of the time. But I've never forgotten the one who called himself John. The one who pretended to be a gentleman.'

This could break the case right open, thought Gemma. Question this man, find out who his friends are, where they were, what they and he were doing when the girls went missing. Look in the right places for the necessary physical evidence.

'I saw him on television a few weeks ago,' Sandra repeated. 'And I've had nightmares every night since. There he is, rich and famous, with people falling all over themselves wanting his autograph, his football jersey. Kids looking up to him. Now he's just destroyed another woman who had the courage to come forward and name him as a rapist.'

'Scott Brissett,' Gemma said. 'That's who you're talking about. Sandra, you're the second woman to name him. Now that there are two women willing to tell their story, we've got a case. We can get in touch with the woman who's withdrawn the accusation.' Otherwise, it would just be oath against oath. 'Once you tell your story,' Gemma continued, 'she'll have to reconsider.'

Sandra looked at her. 'Then you haven't heard?'

'Heard what?'

'She suicided two days ago,' said Sandra. 'It was in the papers.'

Gemma felt it like a body blow. She remembered what Naomi had said. *He'll get away with it.* She felt the fighter in her come up. Not if she could help it.

'What about the man you ran over?' Gemma asked. 'We could work on him. There'll be old hospital records with his name and details.'

This old case could shed light on the mystery of what had happened to two dead and one missing schoolgirls. It could lead straight to the thief-knot killer.

'We can chase him up,' Gemma continued. 'Lean on him. Make a deal.'

Sandra shook her head. 'The hospital closed down long ago. There are town houses built on the site. The old records ended up at the tip.' She looked at Gemma. 'So I haven't really got anything except my memories. The car they'd used was a stolen one.'

Gemma recalled the unfinished brief. There'd been no certificates of analysis of physical evidence.

Twenty years ago, the police weren't so conscious of collecting trace evidence. In those days, there was even more of a tendency to see an incident like the attack on Sandra as just another example of a silly girl who'd made a couple of bad choices one night.

'For a long time I kept waiting for him to rape someone else,' Sandra was saying. 'And get caught. But he's settled down. He's got a wife and family.' Her voice darkened with anger. 'He's the sort of man who gets Father of the Year awards now. His raping days are behind him. He's Australia's favourite sports legend now.'

Gemma went to the kitchen and brought out two forks and a perfect mango. She cut it into dainty squares, pressing them out onto a plate. Beyond the timber deck and the end of her scrubby garden, seagulls wheeled on a light southerly breeze.

After they'd eaten the fruit, Sandra stirred a lot of sugar into another strong black coffee.

'What would you say to talking to a journalist I know?' Gemma asked. 'It'd make a great story and you can bet it'll stir up some other victims. Maybe they'll come forward.'

Sandra looked unsure. 'I think I could do that.'

'And you must ring my girlfriend, Angie McDonald,' said Gemma passing Angie's details over to Sandra, 'and tell her everything you've told me. You must make this official. I'll call her too.'

Sandra took the card, nodded, then glanced down at her watch. 'I have to go,' she said. 'I'll be late for work.' She stood up.

'Where's that?' Gemma asked.

'I'm working at a medical practice,' Sandra said. 'It's only part-time, but it leaves me free for my refuge work.'

'Have you got good references?' Gemma asked.

'The best. Why? Are you offering me a job?'

'Actually, yes,' said Gemma. 'There's a part-time receptionist's job going at Newtown. With a firm of memorial merchants.'

She explained what she had in mind and the puzzled expression left Sandra's face.

'And I'd also pay you,' said Gemma, after giving her more details about Forever Diamonds. 'So you'd be earning extra if you could do a simple little job or two for me while you're there.'

'I'll call them,' Sandra said when Gemma finished talking. 'At this stage, I'm willing to do as much work as possible. I don't know what will become of my kids if we can't raise next month's rent.'

'Let me know,' Gemma said, 'if you get the job.'

She rang Angie and briefed her on the conversation she'd just had with Sandra.

'She'll have to come in and make it official,' said Angie. 'I can't do much until I hear from her.'

'I'm sure you will,' said Gemma. 'She's ready to move.'

'I've never liked football much,' said Angie, ringing off.

Later, Gemma made a couple of crackers with cheese and flicked on the early news broadcast. She watched the footage of a huge white pointer in its sea cradle lashed to the side of a Fisheries launch. Injured while tangled in fishing nets, the shark was on its way to the Sydney Aquarium for a full-scale physical check-up before being released. The next news story concerned Netherleigh Park Ladies' College and the resignation of its principal. Gemma rang Miss de Berigny's number but all she heard was the voice mail message.

She'd been avoiding the next step. She went to the pocket of the jacket she'd worn last night, now hanging in her wardrobe, and pulled out the envelope that Mrs Snellgrove had given her. For a few moments, she just looked at it, feeling like she was standing at a huge choice point. She could drop it in the recycle bin and that would be the end of it. Or she could open it. Once she read the information she guessed this envelope contained, it would be almost impossible to ignore. Huge invisible gears would shift, twisting her in a new direction, landing her in some new world. Would she regret it if she did open it? But, just as surely, wouldn't she regret it if she didn't?

Gemma ripped the envelope open and read the short note from her music teacher.

I've asked a few people who knew the Kingston family in the old days and I've found out that the family moved to the country not long after the baby was born. The baby was called Grace and I should imagine her surname was Kingston. Beverley or her daughter may have married of course, and that will make it difficult to find her. I hope this helps.

Gemma went straight to her ICQ program and typed in her details. Then, in the spaces provided, she typed 'Grace Kingston' and entered the year of her birth. Who knows, she thought. Grace might be looking for her. Gemma put out an email message: *Someone from your father's family would love to get in touch with you.*

That's all I'll do, she decided. If Grace was out there, and looking, they'd find each other. All she had to do was hit 'Reply' and her message would come straight to Gemma's inbox. If Grace wasn't looking for her, then she'd let the search for her half-sister go for now. She had more than enough to deal with at the moment.

FOURTEEN

While her email was loading, Gemma checked her mobile for voice mail. There was a quick hello from Spinner with his address at a motel in Bathurst which she scribbled down. The next message started halfway through—a high young voice, desperate with fear, which caused Gemma's veins to ice over even before she took in the words.

' . . . is where they've taken me. I can't get away. Please help me!' Gemma jumped up, startled. 'Someone's coming. They're—'

The voice was abruptly cut short. On the replay, Gemma identified it as Claudia Page. Almost in the same second, her email program sounded and she saw Claudia's name in the sender field. The girl was sending attachments from her mobile. Gemma opened them and waited while three blurred images unfolded. The first two were muddy shots of a male figure looming through a doorway, far too shadowed and blurred to identify. But it was the last shot that really caught Gemma's attention. It showed a dark room, a chandelier, a huge bed strewn with black cushions and, in the foreground, a small trolley or movable bar stocked with glasses and bottles. Gemma hadn't noticed those earlier today, probably because the huge Polynesian had been blocking her way, she thought.

Gemma grabbed her mobile and rang Angie. Be there she prayed silently. But Angie still wasn't in. Gemma forwarded the images to Angie's email with a message describing how she came to have them and an urgent plea to get in contact as soon as possible. Just for good measure, she left another message on Angie's mobile. 'Get a warrant and search the nightclub Deliverance. I've just had a call from Claudia Page. She's in trouble. I think she could be there. I found the Black Diamond Room there. You've got to bust that club right now. Call me!'

The last girl Gemma had seen in that room was dead. So was Tasmin Summers. Had she been there too? And was that where Claudia had ended up?

As she rushed out to her car, she rang Sean Wright and told him what she'd told Angie. 'Sean, remember what happened to the last two girls! I'm really fearful for Claudia. I'm heading to Deliverance now.'

Gemma drove to the Cross, cursing the hopeless drivers and the traffic lights. After a torturous twenty minutes of weaving in and out of traffic she reached one of the back streets near Deliverance and was looking for a parking spot when Angie rang. 'Got your message. The raid's being set up right now,' she said. 'We want to go in as soon as Sean's organised everyone. If Claudia Page is being held there, we'll get her.' It was what Gemma wanted to hear.

'Claudia was interrupted,' said Gemma. 'She just had time to send off three fast photos before—' Her voice faltered. Before what? Before she'd been discovered on a phone and had it ripped away from her? Before she'd been drugged and subjected to the sexual violence that had killed Amy and Tasmin?

Angie's voice broke into her thoughts. 'Gems? Vernon Kodaly—he's the man Naomi saw at the club behind the desk. He married his nurse.'

'Nice,' said Gemma. 'See you there.'

'No!' shrieked Angie. 'You stay right out of it!'

Gemma called off.

Grabbing the 'visitor' card from the Western Australian Police Academy out of her glove box, she tucked it in her pocket and then sprinted to Darlinghurst Road. She found a window seat in the café diagonally across the road from Deliverance and ordered nachos and coffee. Not exactly health food, but she needed some fast carbs.

Gemma was dipping the first corn chip into the guacamole when she saw the unmarked car pulling up. Immediately, the street changed. People who'd been standing in doorways or on corners suddenly disappeared as Angie, Sean and two others got out of the car. Angie and Sean hurried towards the club's entrance, while the others, also in plain-clothes, disappeared into the shopfronts on either side of the club, working towards covering any back exit.

Gemma grabbed another corn chip, loaded it up, popped it into her mouth, left a twenty-dollar bill on the counter and bolted out the door. She ran across the road, ducking between cars, and pushed in behind Angie and Sean as they raced past the huge Polynesian.

Gemma followed Angie down the same hallway she'd been in only a little while earlier, running to the right of the foyer area. When she glanced behind, she met the eyes of the big Polynesian. Had he recognised her? He was yelling into his mobile, warning someone of the arrival of the police. But it was too late. Already she could hear raised voices around the corner. She ran, following the noise, hurrying towards the room she'd found locked previously.

This time, the door was open and Gemma looked in to see Angie holding a warrant in front of a heavy man seated at a desk. Vernon Kodaly, Gemma remembered. Sean was snooping restlessly around the office, lifting things up, opening drawers, already gloved.

'Vernon Kodaly? I have a warrant here to search these premises,' said Angie, shoving the warrant under his nose.

Kodaly pursed his lips in an odd grimace, but made no effort to get up or take the warrant. He waved it away with disdain. 'Do what you need to do. I'm busy.'

Why isn't he jumping up and down, Gemma wondered. It's almost like he's expected this.

'Mr Kodaly, you don't seem to understand the seriousness of this matter. We have reason to believe that a young woman has been abducted and is being held on the premises. We've also seen video footage of a young woman, Amy Bernhard, with several men. Amy Bernhard was murdered a year ago and we have reason to believe the video of her was shot here in this club.' Angie moved in even closer and Gemma wondered why Kodaly still didn't get out of his seat.

'A year ago? You believe?' Kodaly feigned shock. 'You're making a lot of suppositions, Sergeant. You're not going to find this missing girl here, I can tell you that now and save you a lot of time. So what exactly do you think you can charge me with?'

Angie, sensing a presence behind her, suddenly turned. 'Gemma? What the bloody hell are you doing in here? I warned you!'

'You'll excuse me if I don't get up,' Kodaly was saying. It was then that Gemma noticed the wheel-chair.

Angie beckoned Gemma to come with her and, leaving Sean to mind Kodaly, the two women left the manager's office and hurried down the hall. 'This is it,' said Gemma, pausing at the door. 'The Black Diamond Room.'

Angie tried it but it was locked.

'It was open when I was here,' said Gemma.

'I need a key for the next room,' Angie called, hurrying back to Kodaly's office.

He wheeled himself around from behind his desk. 'You'll have to wait,' he said. 'My partner has the key to that room. I don't seem to have a spare with me.'

'I'm not waiting for anyone,' said Angie. 'Sean? Come and give this door a nudge for me?'

Sean moved outside and took a running jump at the door, kicked it hard, then backed off, this time using the weight of his body to shoulder the door jamb. Weakened by the first kick, the timber around the jamb split and Sean's third assault caused it to fly open. Sean felt around for the light and switched it on. The three of them stared at an empty room. A huge bed covered in fake black bearskin, illuminated by the light of a chandelier, practically filled all available space. Black satin sheets, black cushions. 'This is it!' said Angie. 'The room Claudia captured on her mobile phone!'

Gemma looked over their shoulders. The only thing missing was the drinks trolley. And Claudia.

Even though there was nowhere for anyone to hide, just to be sure Gemma looked under the bed, fearing what she might see. But there was nothing there either.

'Search the damn place,' said Angie to Sean. Then, pointing to Gemma, she barked, 'You wait over there. I'll deal with you later. I don't want anything we find thrown out because we had a student visitor on the team.'

Gemma nodded but she had no intention of

obeying. Instead, she went right through the place behind Sean, as he opened every door and turned over every room looking for Claudia. When they'd finished it was clear the place was empty apart from Kodaly and the police.

Back in the Black Diamond Room, Sean squatted to be at eye level with traces of white powder on a cushion. 'It's coke,' he said, running a gloved finger over and tasting it.

'Hey!' Angie objected. 'That's not your job. And how come you're so sure it's coke?'

'Don't ask,' he said.

'I didn't hear that,' said Angie. 'Get Crime Scene down here straightaway. Stop eating the evidence and wait here till they come. I want this place picked over. Every room—walls, floors, ceilings. Carpets, hangings, windows, bathrooms, offices. I want every stitch examined. Every fucking speck. Got it?'

She turned round to Vernon Kodaly who had silently wheeled up behind them.

'If I find one cell from Amy Bernhard or Claudia Page in this place,' she said, 'I'm arresting you.'

Kodaly smiled. 'You'll have to do better than that, Sergeant. Claudia Page has been to this club from time to time. I wouldn't be surprised to find that the other girl you mentioned, the dead one, had also been here. There are probably traces of both of them all over the place.'

Gemma couldn't help herself. 'She asked me for help! What have you done with her?'

Kodaly affected mock surprise. 'Me? Why do

you think I know anything about her? Shouldn't she be at school? Or with her family? Shouldn't you be asking those people these questions?'

'We've found traces of cocaine, Mr Kodaly. We think you'd better come with us and tell us what really goes on in these premises.'

Kodaly shrugged. 'Some of our clients may be a little free interpreting the law. I can't be held responsible for the behaviour, the infelicities, of the club's patrons.'

'What's your partner's name?'

'He's a sleeping partner,' said Kodaly. 'He wants to remain anonymous. His name's not even on the business registration certificate.'

'Doesn't he want to be associated with this place?'

Kodaly ignored Angie's barb. 'I'll ask him to contact you. More than that I cannot do.' He wheeled himself towards the foyer area. 'You can find him yourself any time you wish.'

'Why won't you give me his name? Is it because he's hiding Claudia somewhere?'

Kodaly turned his head and laughed. 'You've got this obsession that she's here somewhere. Or has been removed from here. I've been here all the time and I'd know.'

'How do you explain that she sent off a photo of your Black Diamond Room before she was interrupted?'

Kodaly shook his head. 'Maybe she took the picture sometime she was here as a patron, and it got sent off accidentally from the memory. I've heard of very embarrassing incidents with unintentional sendings.'

'You interviewed Claudia Page. Tried to get her to do some "modelling" for you,' said Angie.

'That's a crime? I was trying to help the girl.' He turned the chair round to face them. The situation reminded Gemma of a duel and she could see the colour rising on Angie's neck. It was taking all her friend's professional cool to stay in control of this interview. Kodaly was needling Angie with the sang-froid of a man who knows that there's just no way he'll ever be caught, thought Gemma.

'This place isn't just a nightclub,' Angie said. 'You deal coke here.'

'I deny that absolutely. You have no proof.'

'And make porn videos!'

'I'm a businessman.' Kodaly looked at her with pity. 'Eighty per cent of the internet is devoted to porn. Where there's such a strong demand, it's my business to supply it. I'm not aware of a law against that.'

'When the girls are under age, there is,' said Gemma, thinking of Naomi's account of Kodaly's partner with a fourteen-year-old.

Angie's mobile rang. She took the call, listened and rang off. 'That was the toxicology report on Tasmin Summers. Our chemists found a lot of Valium and Zanax as well as alcohol in urine samples. Sounds like someone spiked Tasmin's drinks. Stupefied her.'

Kodaly shook his head. 'It's too bad. These days,

young girls will experiment with everything and anything.'

'Including asphyxiation by some strange man's penis in their throats?'

Kodaly didn't miss a beat. 'They're very playful too, the young girls these days. They enjoy all sorts of liberal sex games.'

'You call being choked by someone's dick a sex game?' Angie's voice was soft and menacing, a low decibel growl as she put the questions. 'Being anally raped your idea of fun?' Kodaly shifted in the wheel-chair and Angie decided to stick it to him. 'You'll get to experience all that fun yourself,' she said, 'when we've got you charged, convicted and locked up. The heavies in maximum security are very liberal too. Love a good sex game. Remind me to tell you some of the stories I've heard from inside about barbed-wire sex toys.'

'I really don't know,' said Kodaly, the injured innocent, 'why you're taking this line of question-ing with me. And making these unpleasant threats.'

Gemma pulled out the business card that Kosta had given her and passed it to Angie who looked at it.

'What's this then?' Angie jabbed at the art work, the stylised blade and the powder. 'That's an adver-tisement for what you do here. This graphic shows a blade separating cocaine into a line.'

'One has to be cutting edge,' Kodaly said. 'It's a very competitive business I'm in. That's what's denoted in that graphic. Cutting edge, Sergeant.' He smiled, revealing gold. 'Merely a symbol.'

'You have an employee called Eddie,' Gemma said. 'We'd like a chat with him.'

Angie's bewildered expression changed to anger, reminding Gemma that she'd failed to tell her friend about this. 'I have some inside information about this Eddie,' she added.

'Eddie?' At least Kodaly was engaged now, Gemma thought. Engaged and even just a little rattled. 'He's got nothing to do with this. Anyway, he doesn't work for me anymore.'

Angie took her cue from Gemma. 'How can we get in touch with him?'

Kodaly shrugged. 'Your guess is as good as mine.'

Obstruction and contempt, Gemma thought. Kodaly was master of both. Sean came up with rolls of plastic in his gloved hands. 'We found this,' he said. 'And a hot press. For sealing plastic packets.'

'The use of cling wrap is a crime?' Kodaly was enjoying himself.

'When it's part of a cocaine packaging operation, yes,' said Angie. 'You deal in prohibited substances here, don't you?'

Kodaly spread his hands. 'What can I say, Sergeant?' he begged. 'I run a nightclub. That's what I do. I don't know what you're going on about. Plastic? Criminal cling wrap? Really.'

Angie and Gemma stood outside near the Forensic Services station wagon. Crime Scene had arrived and were working inside. Meanwhile, while outside, a small crowd of people—those who hadn't vanished at the arrival of the first car—hung around on the footpath.

'You should have told me about this Eddie character! I felt like a fool in there. I didn't know what the hell you were talking about!' said Angie, angry eyes flashing.

'Sorry, Ange. I forgot to pass it on to you. It slipped my mind.'

'Slipped your mind? This isn't the Royal Commission. This is a murder investigation!'

'There's been a lot going on.'

'You reckon you've had a lot going on! What about me?' Angie walked a little distance away, trying to recover her poise.

Gemma followed. 'Where is she?' she said. 'That girl is being held somewhere against her will. Scared, terrified. Or worse.'

'We'll find her. If they've moved her, someone must have seen something. I'll get the local boys to do a doorknock along the street.' Angie threw her mobile into her car. 'Bloody fucking hell!' She opened the door and slammed it. 'That was a waste of time. All we've done is put them on notice. We didn't find a damn thing that was helpful.'

'It won't take you long to get the partner's name,' Gemma reminded her.

'But they know now that we'll be searching and that gives them a chance to reorganise, regroup. If they're holding Claudia somewhere, it gives them the chance to move her,' said Angie.

If Claudia was already dead it didn't matter how long it took them to track down the elusive sleeping partner. Gemma didn't want to think about that. 'I was so sure she'd be there,' she said.

Another unmarked car skidded to a halt on the opposite side of the road and Bruno, one ear heavily bandaged, jumped out of it and raced across the road, dodging traffic.

'What's going on here?' he demanded of Angie. 'Why wasn't I told about this?' Then he caught sight of Gemma. 'What the fuck is she doing here?'

Angie started to explain, but he cut her off.

'This is deliberate white-anting! Why wasn't I informed about this raid?'

'You were off sick!'

'I was back today. It's on the day roster! I should have been informed!'

'Claudia Page emailed an image of a room in this club and a message saying she was being held here. We went to the boss and got moving as fast as possible. I didn't have time to look at any roster! You're never around anyway!'

'Out of order, Sergeant!'

'I don't believe you've been sick!' Angie yelled, coming up, toe to toe. 'I'll bet you're moonlighting!'

Bruno looked startled but rallied fast. 'You'd better back that up, Sergeant. That's a serious allegation!'

'You're never bloody here when you're needed!'

'I'm putting you on paper, McDonald!'

'You do that, you bastard, and I'll make it my business to find out why Jim Buisman took you off the original investigation! And wherever your second job is, they'd better be happy with you, because by the time I'm finished with you it'll be the only job you'll have!'

'Angie,' said Gemma as a crowd gathered, 'this is not getting anywhere. Leave it.'

Bruno swung on Gemma. 'And as for you, you bloody interfering bitch—'

'Chill, Bruno,' said Gemma. 'Or you'll bust your bandages or your infected ear.' Toes clutched tight and with racing heart, she practised professional poise. Every fibre of her body wanted to let him have it; instead, keeping her voice low and steady, she continued. 'Claudia Page contacted me. Not the police, certainly not you! She sent break-through information to me! I've got more right to be here than you!'

Bruno seethed a moment longer. Then he hurried back to his car, slammed the door closed and wound down the window. 'So help me God,' he yelled out, 'you'll never get your PI licence renewed again! Never! That's a fucking promise!'

He screeched off, causing the nearby pedestrians to scatter.

Angie and Gemma retreated into a coffee lounge for an informal debrief. In the cool, dark interior, a television screen flickered with a program no one was watching. Angie threw herself into a chair. 'That prick! I can negotiate with psychopaths but not someone like Bruno Gross!'

'Men like Bruno are always going to be there,' Gemma said, as much for her own sake as for her friend. 'And they'll always underestimate you because you're a smart, good-looking woman. And then, when they realise they've done that, instead of you going up in their estimation, they'll just hate you more, because you've shown them up again for the mediocre arseholes they are.'

'I hope he doesn't make your life impossible,' Angie said. 'I don't know how much influence he might have.'

'I don't want to have to change my career just now,' said Gemma. 'What's our next move?' she asked. Then she noticed something on the television. 'There's that shark again.' She'd seen it in the earlier newsflash, being taken to the Aquarium.

'What shark?'

'*A white pointer shark,*' the newsreader announced, '*taken to the Sydney Aquarium for veterinary attention has proved costly. The shark smashed its way through a holding tank and bit a large chunk out of a display item in its enclosure before vomiting the contents of its stomach. Veterinarians finally had to sedate the shark with a tranquilliser. And a warning,*' the newsreader added, '*this report contains images from an amateur video that may distress some viewers.*'

Gemma leaned forward to see the items in the cloudy water surrounding the doped-up shark— the artificial coral with a huge bite mark through it, the front half of a dog, a partly inflated sex doll, and a diver's weight belt. She grabbed Angie's arm. 'Look at what's attached to that belt. See what's round it?'

The heavy belt lay along the bottom of the enclosure and from it a length of cord trailed in the water. Angie, still stewing over the fight with Bruno, took a moment to comprehend.

'Quick!' said Gemma. 'Ring the Aquarium. Tell them under no circumstances must they discard anything from that shark's belly.'

Angie downed the other half of her coffee and was already out of her seat and pulling out her mobile.

Less than an hour later Gemma and Angie, along with one of the marine biologists and the assistant manager of the Aquarium, watched while Nicole from Crime Scene turned the heavy belt and attached cord over in her gloved hands. 'This end looks like it's been cut,' she said, indicating the end tied to the belt, 'with a very sharp knife. But if you look at this end,' she pointed to the trailing end, 'there's fraying. This doesn't look like a knife's been used on it.'

'Could it have been bitten?' Gemma asked.

Nicole carefully bagged and labelled the green and white Vectran cord. 'Maybe,' she said. 'Mr Roper will give it the once-over.' A systematic search of the rest of the debris from the shark's belly had failed to turn up anything else of interest. 'Looks like the belt was used to weigh something down,' said Nicole. 'Maybe that dog's corpse?'

With these words, an idea flashed into Gemma's mind. 'Ring Dr Chang,' she suggested. 'Ask her if those post-mortem injuries on Tasmin's wrist could have been made by the drag of a heavy object.'

Angie pulled out her phone. 'You're thinking the shark went for the wrong end of the rope?'

'Imagine it,' said Gemma. 'There's this nice body

drifting down through the depths, with a diver's belt for weight, and the white pointer snaps the line in half but swallows the wrong end.'

'They don't have good eyesight,' said the marine biologist.

'And huge forces tug as the shark bites down on the cord, causing those injuries on the dead girl's wrist.'

For a moment, this new information seemed like a breakthrough. But then Gemma thought of all the places along the coast from where a body could be disposed. All it needed was a dark night, and over the cliff or off the bridge with the body and the diver's belt.

'We really haven't learned anything new,' said Angie. 'Except for a plausible explanation of that post-mortem tear in Tasmin's wrist. The Australian Oceanographic Data Centre supplied an assessment of conditions for the period Tasmin was missing,' she added, 'and the best they could offer was that she could have been put in the water anywhere between Port Jackson and Botany Bay.'

'Any result on the positive semen swabs?'

'We have to wait till the lab lets us know.'

'I am so over men,' said Angie on the drive back. 'The only thing that's keeping me going is what's going to happen to that bastard, Trevor Dawson, at Graingers. If it all goes according to plan, he'll be stripped down and just about to get stuck into it when Mrs Trevor,' she threw a glance at Gemma, 'for whom, by the way, I have nothing but sympathy, walks in.'

'I'd give anything to be a fly on the wall.'

'It's not going to be pretty.' She checked the rear-vision mirror. 'Melissa Grey told me Mrs Trevor shot her first husband eight years ago. She was never even charged. Claimed it was an accident.'

'Maybe it was,' said Gemma.

Angie snorted. 'Melissa said the investigating team found a target in her basement with his photograph and nine beautifully grouped head shots.'

'Sounds like cops' gossip to me.'

'Deadset it's true.'

'You're a devil woman, Angie.'

'Only when I'm treated bad. Basically I'm just a sweet country girl.'

'You can take the girl out of the country,' Gemma started quoting.

'Right. But you can't take the—'

Their old two-hander was interrupted by Angie's phone. She plugged in her earpiece, grunted and then rang off.

'That was Julie,' she said. 'They've been given a couple of extra people. She and Sean are going through ASIC files—trying to get names for the owners of Deliverance. The sleeping partner.'

'What do we do next?' Gemma repeated her unanswered question from the coffee lounge.

'The usual doorknocks, talk to our integrated corporate resources. Keep on the track of that sleeping partner, the ex-bodyguard Eddie, anything they might know about the club. And once I have something official to go on, once Sandra Samuels talks to me, I'll go and have a chat with the footie legend. Once we've done *that*,' she continued, 'we sit and wait. That's always the hardest time of an investigation.'

Gemma knew what she meant.

'Do you think Claudia is still alive?'

Angie didn't answer.

Next morning Gemma checked in with Angie but there was still no news on Claudia Page. 'I slept in here surrounded by VMO files,' said Angie. 'No wonder I had nightmares. If I was the boss and I had the resources,' she went on, 'I'd get Deliverance put on around-the-clock surveillance.'

'If the public and the press make enough fuss you just might get them. They've already put extra people on the ASIC search,' she said, remembering Julie's call. 'When Spinner gets back from the country,' she continued, 'the three of us here could manage a bit of surveillance. Build up some mosaic intelligence.'

'You've got your own business to consider,' said Angie. 'You can't afford to take time off that.'

'I feel responsible. Claudia went missing while I was talking to her,' said Gemma, feeling helpless.

Angie yawned. 'Your friend Sandra Samuels still hasn't contacted me.'

'She will,' said Gemma, and rang off.

She opened her emails, hoping against hope that there was something from Claudia. There wasn't. As she logged off, the radio came to life. It was Spinner, on his way home.

'Spinner! Base here. Good to hear from you. How's it all going?'

'I've got some information about Mr Romero that I know will interest you. Not to mention some pretty interesting video footage of the man whose sex life is finished.'

'What's the information on Romero?' She couldn't have cared less about Mr Pepper just then.

'I got the name of someone who'd been a student at Bathurst High during Romero's last year there and pretended I was his brother. I heard the same thing from three different people. About Mr Romero.'

Gemma pulled out the Romero file and grabbed a pen. 'Okay. Go.'

'Mr Romero didn't leave the public system because of the workload. He left Bathurst High because of an inappropriate relationship with an under-age student.' Spinner paused. 'In fact, they ran away together.'

Gotcha! thought Gemma. 'You're sure of this?'

'You bet. There's no doubt at all. One of the people I spoke to was on the staff at the same time. He's going to look up the records and get back to me with the girl's name. She was only fourteen.'

'Spinner, you really are my ace roadie.'

'Just doing my job, Boss,' he replied, but Gemma could hear he was pleased. 'I should be there in an hour or so.'

The TV technician arrived to sort out the poor reception on the Sky channels. Gemma trusted him from his earlier visits and left him to it, going back into her office to try to call Beatrice de Berigny. Again, all she heard was the cool voice mail instructions. She rang the school office. Miss de Berigny was temporarily out of town, and out of touch, she was told. The secretary promised to pass on Gemma's message if and when the former principal phoned the college. Apart from that, she said regretfully, there was little she could do.

When Gemma went through to the kichen to make a snack, the technician was running through the channels, tuning them. 'I've got them all looking good except one,' he said. 'I'm not sure why there's a problem with it. Are you transmitting anything around here?'

Gemma shook her head.

'There's some sort of interference happening. I'll have to come back later with some gear and try and track it down.'

Although Gemma felt she was now getting somewhere with two of her cases, it was still hard to settle to work. The memory of Claudia in that mausoleum of a house, the girl's guilt and shame about the way she'd covered up her friends' disappearances and her helplessness to make it all better, had touched Gemma deeply. She went over and over the last few minutes with Claudia, desperate for a clue. Damn it. She should have been sharper.

Her desk phone rang and she picked it up. Sandra Samuels.

'I got the job,' said Sandra. 'Receptionist handling

cremains and grieving relatives. In fact, I'm working here now. There's quite a backlog of paperwork so I won't talk for long. Mr Gardiner was knocked out by my references.'

'Congratulations,' said Gemma. She gave Sandra Mike's name and number. 'Someone else on my payroll,' she explained. 'If anything comes up and you need back-up or a helping hand and you can't raise me, ring Mike.' Sandra said she would.

'You still feel okay about having a look around that place?'

'Gemma,' Sandra said, 'I'm really grateful to you. Not just for taking what happened to me seriously, but for everything you're doing. I'm happy to help out. Makes me feel like I'm joining the human race again. I've been in hiding for too long in refuges—one way or another.'

'Don't forget to call Angie McDonald,' Gemma reminded her.

When Sandra rang off, Gemma considered the way the gang of men had organised their attack, using the handsome, outwardly courteous youth as bait to catch their prey. Then, once they'd caught her, they all converged on the wasteland, like hounds tearing apart the quarry.

She glanced out the window and saw Spinner coming down the steps from the road. Gemma opened the front door for her much-valued colleague. 'Welcome back,' she said as he came into the operatives' office and threw down his overnight bag. He slung his computer bag onto the desk looking slightly less miserable than when she'd last seen him.

'Here are the names of the people I spoke to about Mr Romero,' he said, digging a small notebook out of a pocket in the camera bag.

Beatrice de Berigny will faint, Gemma thought, when she hears that the senior History teacher at Netherleigh Park Ladies' College is the sort of man who'd run away with a student half his age.

'Then there's Mr Pepper,' said Spinner. 'Claiming the end of his sex life.'

Gemma came up close and watched while the video fast-forwarded. Spinner stopped it at the relevant section and played it. 'Cop a look at this,' he said. There was Mr Pepper somewhere in bushland, digging furiously around the base of a Gymea lily, the densely packed petals burning like an eternal flame high above him.

'Talk about nimble,' said Gemma as the busy little figure on the camera's tiny screen dug into hard soil around the plant. 'But he wasn't claiming crook back syndrome.'

'Wait,' said Spinner. 'Keep watching.'

Mr Pepper stopped labouring, wiped his brow, scratched his balls and walked towards a large tree, pulling his penis out of his shorts.

'Do I have to watch him taking a leak?'

'He hasn't got it out for a leak,' said Spinner.

Spinner was right. Mr Pepper started fondling his dick and was soon going for his life. After a few seconds Spinner hit the stop button. 'You don't need to see the rest of that,' he said primly. 'You get the picture.'

'Nothing wrong with his sporting gear,' said Gemma.

'You can take my word for it, Boss.' Spinner switched the video camera off. 'Imagine how he's going to feel when the insurers invite him in to discuss his case and then put this on the VCR.'

Gemma almost felt sorry for the cheat.

'Oh,' said Spinner. 'I'll be starting that new Mandate check.' A man, away on business, wanted the marital house watched overnight, certain that his wife was bringing a man there in his absence.

'It's just down the hill at Bronte. I won't be far from you,' he said, grinning. 'You could bring me a nice cup of tea.'

'I might even do that,' said Gemma.

They both fell silent as the radio news began. The first item was the search for Claudia Page and her boyfriend. '*Police now hold grave fears for their safety*,' the newsreader said.

Spinner started to leave then turned back, pulling a small flat gift-wrapped parcel out of his pocket. 'Here,' he said, awkward. 'I thought you might like this.' He hurried away, embarrassed at his own generosity, and Gemma had to chase him to thank him.

She opened the little packet. In spite of everything, the softness and beauty of the purple, aqua and blue painted silk caused her a soft, involuntary 'oh' of pleasure. It would be too hot for summer wear, but the scarf would look stunning draped across a black jumper. She tried it against her skin in the hall mirror. It was perfect for her colouring. As she fiddled with it, her mind empty of everything except the colours and fall of the exquisite silk, something in her mind flashed on. The scarf! Sandra Samuels' scarf. She'd used it to clean herself up; the rapist had used it to tie her hands. Enough of it had been saved for Colin Roper to identify the thief knot. She ran to her office and scrambled to find Sandra's phone number.

'Yes?' The hesitant response at the other end of the line.

'It's me, Gemma. That scarf! What colour was it? The one you wore that night?'

'Pink and red,' she said. 'Why?'

Gemma told her.

At Strawberry Hills, Gemma waited outside for Angie. She'd pulled the crime scene envelope containing the old blood-streaked fabric from where it had sat for years in a plastic sleeve, mixed up with old VMO files. As well as providing them with the thief knot, that scrap of torn fabric could provide evidence of every person at that crime scene—Sandra's blood and epithelial cells together with the rapists' semen. It was better than a photographic record of the crime. And one of those profiles would match the sporting legend, Scott Brissett.

Gemma and Angie drove to the Division of

Analytical Laboratories at Lidcombe. 'We want this yesterday,' said Angie to the clerk at the counter.

'They all say that,' said the clerk as she numbered the job and gave them their receipt. 'You know it takes at least twenty-four hours.'

'If I say the names Amy Bernhard, Tasmin Summers and possibly Claudia Page,' said Angie, 'would that help speed things up?'

It would.

'While I'm here,' Angie said, 'would you mind checking on another job for me? It would have gone through Melissa Grey from Parramatta Crime Scene for the forensic anthropologist, Francie Suskievicz. Multiple human remains out Richmond way. Including a lot of teeth. I'm very curious about that case.'

The clerk raised an eyebrow. 'I remember that job coming in because it was so weird. Hang on. Linda Shipper was doing that one.'

The clerk vanished through a door in the back wall of her office and Gemma and Angie waited. Gemma was halfway through reading a poster about evacuation drill in case of fire when the clerk returned. 'That job was dispatched a little while ago, Angie. The results have been sent back to the investigating police.'

'Good, I'll call Melissa.'

They drove back to Strawberry Hills where Gemma had left her car. Sean was waiting for Angie, having been delayed at ASIC headquarters. 'I've got what you want,' he said to her. 'Guess who's Vernon Kodaly's sleeping partner?'

'Ned Kelly?'

'Scott Brissett.'

He told Angie Brissett's address and Gemma noted it too, working out her plan of action. Angie disappeared upstairs, returning within minutes.

'Okay,' she said. 'Let's go.'

Gemma didn't want to push her luck so she hung back as Angie and Sean got into the car. As Angie buckled her seatbelt, she looked up at Gemma. 'By the way,' she said, 'I had quite a conversation with Sandra Samuels, over the phone. She's pretty convincing.'

'I knew she'd contact you,' said Gemma. She hurried to her car and followed Sean and Angie to Watsons Bay and then in and around a maze of little streets until they found Brissett's house hidden away at the end of a shady driveway. The heat beat down furiously, cicadas shrieking, and a wisp of high cloud visible through the leaves. It was one of those days, Gemma thought, that just keeps getting hotter.

'A few quid here,' said Sean, looking through the wrought-iron gate, taking in the formal front gardens, the pristine beds of summer flowers, the mature cycads in pots moving stiffly in the ocean breeze.

'Okay,' said Angie, looking at Gemma. 'You'd better make yourself scarce.'

'But I want to go in there. See what his place looks like.'

'You *are* joking. This is an official visit. No way.'

'What about my student "visitor" ID?'

'Go home,' said Angie. 'Now. You shouldn't even be here.'

'I'm part of this! You wouldn't have had the Deliverance connection without me. You wouldn't *be* here without me!' Even Gemma was surprised at the passion of her defence.

'I'll fill you in later, okay?' Angie hissed. 'Now go.'

'He was very relaxed,' Angie said later, referring to her visit to Scott Brissett. 'Confident that whatever business the police had with him, it could only work to his benefit.'

'What's his place like?'

'Ritzy. Lots of leather and chrome. Cedar plantation blinds, ceiling fans. Very resort. A huge nude portrait of his wife—she was a model—letting it all hang out. She was posing on a cane chair. Imagine the indentations that'd make on a girl's bum. And beside that, another painting of a million-dollar cruiser.'

'His two trophies,' said Gemma.

'That's exactly what I thought,' said Angie. 'Lots of trophies.'

Naomi had mentioned those, Gemma remembered, sporting trophies with engraved initials.

'He's a pantsman, for sure,' Angie said. 'And he's the sort of man who talks about his wife as "The Missus". His sporting injuries must be coming home to roost,' she went on. 'He's walking with a slight limp and stooping over just a little.

I noticed him wincing a couple of times at sudden movement.'

'Me too,' said Gemma, remembering the TV footage of Brissett getting into a car. It's in the fifth decade, she'd heard someone say, that sportsmen's injuries really start.taking their toll. Especially groin injuries.

'When I told him about the nature of the complaint he went all quiet and wary,' said Angie. 'Then when he heard how old the allegations were, he hit the roof. I told him we were just doing our job—checking it out.'

'So?' asked Gemma. 'His response?'

Angie pulled out her notebook and scrolled down. '*I've never heard such a load of garbage in my life! Who is this little low-life?*'

'Charming,' said Gemma. 'His counsel will have to straighten him out about a few things.'

'When I asked for his official response to my question concerning his whereabouts on the evening of 18 November 1983, he really got pissed off,' said Angie, glancing down at her notebook. 'Listen to this.'

She summarised her notes. 'He reckons this is happening all over Australia—reckons it's becoming like some fashionable blood sport. Decent men, family men, who've made a name for themselves becoming the targets for any emotionally disturbed little scrag—'

'He said "scrag"?'

'You bet he did. Any emotionally disturbed little scrag,' she repeated, 'who needs to draw attention to herself and her pathetic life. Anyway, when I offered to jog his memory and reminded him it was the night of the Picton District Show and mentioned the name of his fifteen-year-old companion, he started to get uncomfortable. He went a bit pale at the mention of that rubber snake at the end of a cane.'

'He remembered that detail,' said Gemma, 'and that night. What happened after the Picton District Show.'

'Then I told him we were in possession of an emailed photograph,' she said, 'transmitted by mobile phone from the Black Diamond Room at the nightclub called Deliverance. I told him we knew he was a partner in the business. And that image was the last contact we've had with another young girl who's gone missing, Claudia Page.'

'And what did he say to that?'

'He went straight into the attack,' said Angie. 'Said he'd be advising his solicitor to sue for damages. Malicious prosecution. I suggested he calm down, that no one was prosecuting him.'

'Yet,' said Gemma.

'Then he clammed up and got on the blower to his legal people,' Angie continued, 'and I invited both him and his lawyer to meet us at Strawberry Hills. I said there were some other matters we wanted to clear up.'

'Did he ever say, "I didn't do it"?' asked Gemma. Angie shook her head.

FIFTEEN

Back home, Gemma was about to ring Sandra to keep her up to date when Angie rang to say that Damien Wilcox had turned up and was this very moment undergoing surgery to relieve subdural bleeding from a fractured skull. He wouldn't be available for conversation for some time, according to the doctors. In fact, he might never speak again.

'It gets worse,' Angie continued. 'Those images from Claudia's mobile—the ones you received— weren't sent from anywhere near Deliverance.'

'So what are you saying?'

'Just that. Wherever she was, she wasn't at the club. Or anywhere near it.'

'But you saw it!'

'In any case, those photographs weren't transmitted from the inner city area. The techies are working on the embedded information, trying to locate the position those images were transmitted from.'

It could be anywhere in Sydney, Gemma thought, with sinking heart.

'It gets even worse, Gemster.'

How could it?

'We can't charge Brissett.'

'Why the hell not?'

'What with? We haven't got anything on him! He's denying everything.'

'Well, of course. It's his job to deny everything!'

'Everything is circumstantial, Gems. There's nothing to lock him in.'

'Naomi saw him with a young girl hanging off him, talking to Kodaly.'

'So? He might have been going to take her to de-tox.'

'Yeah, sure.' Angie was right. 'We need the DNA,' Gemma said.

'Brissett reckons he's going to make life impossible for me,' Angie said. 'He's got mates in the job. You know what the cops are like once they get it in for someone. And if he gets wind of your involvement, you'd better look out. You've got a licence that needs renewing.'

'It's just rumours, Angie. You know what it's like. Bullies' talk.' Gemma wondered why her words sounded unconvincing even to herself. She remembered the vicious, spiteful harassment of people who'd fallen foul of certain police officers. She didn't need that. This year had been painful enough without any threat to her licence.

'But we can still get him,' she reminded them both. 'That old crime scene evidence. The DNA on Sandra's scarf. Once we've got that—'

'And that won't be ready till tomorrow morning,'

said Angie. 'At the earliest. Look, even if we charge him, he'd be bailed in ten seconds flat. And that gives him time to start rounding up support among the old boys' network, the sporting hero circuit. The media will go crazy. Commercial radio gurus and their mob. Newspaper stories. Interviews.' She paused. 'Do you want to get this bastard?'

'You know I do!'

'Okay. So let's not do anything premature that might end up in a media circus and then go on to being no-billed.'

'But, Ange. You let him go and Claudia's still being held somewhere—'

'I know what you're saying. He's got nothing to lose by killing her. And everything to lose if he lets her go.'

Heavy silence on the line.

'We're watching every move he makes and there are warrants out to search all his holdings,' said Angie. 'We're doing everything possible. If he moves, every satellite in the area will be tracking him.'

'Surely there's something!' Gemma felt keen disappointment.

'Gemster. We still have no proof that Brissett's involved in the disappearance and deaths of Amy or Tasmin. He's denying any connection with the club apart from a financial interest.'

'But we already know he's a violent rapist!' shouted Gemma, losing her cool.

'Sandra Samuels *alleges* he's a rapist,' Angie corrected her.

'But the thief knot!' countered Gemma.

'Doesn't prove anything. It's a similarity, that's all,' said Angie.

'We need to find that fancy green and white cord in Brissett's possession, maybe at one of his properties—'

'Even if we do, it still wouldn't prove anything. Just that he has similar cord. This little chat we've just had with him,' said Angie, 'that's going to put the pressure on him.' She paused. 'Gemster. When the DNA results are in we've got a better chance.'

Gemma rang off and a deep unease settled on her. Catching a rapist was always going to be hard work, especially with someone as wily and popular as Brissett. Angie was right. There was nothing to tie him to the two dead schoolgirls. Scott Brissett, footie hero, brilliant in the light projected from the hearts and minds of millions of Australians, had been endowed with god-like stature. Gemma knew her countrymen and women: even if they eventually cut down every other public figure, they canonised their sporting heroes and heroines.

Feeling dejected, she made a snack and found herself worrying about the Ratbag. She should be looking for him. If Eddie found him, God knows what he might do to the poor kid. She turned on the radio and listened to the latest news. Scott Brissett, saying he was considering legal action against those people who were making false and malicious allegations. The search for missing teenager Claudia Page was continuing as her boyfriend lay in an ICU fighting for survival.

Gemma was preparing a salad when she heard someone outside. She glanced up at the CCTV image: Angie was running down the path.

'What is it?' she asked, alarmed, as she opened the door.

Angie pushed past her, threw herself on the sofa, startling Taxi. She looked shocking.

'What is it?' Gemma said again.

'The Assistant Commissioner is good mates with Brissett,' said Angie. 'I've been told that my career in the New South Wales police is as good as finished. Just because I did my job and interviewed Brissett.'

'But that's crazy,' said Gemma. 'They can't just throw you out. Not for having a chat to someone! It's just the bloody rumour machine. It'll blow over.'

'If they want to throw me out, they'll find something. Or they'll send me to places I hate, give me jobs I'm no good at. You know how they can wear someone down.' Angie hunched over. 'I've only ever wanted to be a good cop. What the hell would I do with the rest of my life?'

'Ange, Ange, it'll be okay.' Gemma dropped to sit beside her friend. Angie threw her head back. 'How will it be okay? First Trevor, now this. This is the worst fucking year of my life!'

'Do you want a drink?'

Angie nodded. 'And pour yourself one. You're going to need it.'

Gemma went to the decanters and poured a scotch for Angie and a brandy for herself. 'Why?'

She felt dread clutch at her. What new blow was Angie bringing?

She carried the drinks over to her friend who sniffed and pushed her hair off her damp face, looking up with red-rimmed eyes.

'Tell me,' said Gemma. 'What's going on?'

'The DNA results,' Angie started.

Please, no, Gemma thought. Don't let this be happening. But as she was making the desperate prayer, Angie's words hit her like a kick in the heart.

'Just after we'd been speaking on the phone,' she said, 'Linda Shipper got back to me.'

Gemma could feel her blood pulsing in her ears. 'What? What did Linda say?'

'The genetic material extracted from Samantha's old bits of scarf—'

Gemma held her breath.

'It's UN,' said Angie.

Gemma stared, uncomprehending.

'UN means unsuccessful,' Angie continued. 'No result possible. Degraded to absolute buggery.'

'Oh shit!' Gemma stood there a moment. She couldn't believe all the possibilities were just blowing away like this. 'But what about the vaginal and oral swabs from Tasmin Summers's autopsy? Dr Chang told us about those. The DAL could surely get a match from that. Remember the preliminary report? The doctor got a positive for semen.'

Angie shook her head. 'I thought of that too. I rang Dr Chang. I didn't understand everything she said,' Angie put her drink down, 'but I don't think there's much hope there.'

'Why the hell not?'

'Apparently there were too many shared peaks. Nothing clear to convince a jury.' Angie paused. 'The best they could do would be to use statistics. But the profiles themselves are a nightmare of similarities.'

Gemma wanted to cry. 'I can't believe this! I thought we had him both ways. Now you're telling me we haven't got him at all!'

Angie threw herself back against the leather sofa. 'Can you imagine the damages claim? Scott frigging Brissett is on the cards to score squillions out of this! And I'll be hung out to dry.'

Gemma sank to a seat, the drinks still in her hands. 'What the hell are we going to do?'

The question hung in a long silence. From somewhere beneath the cliffs, a startled plover shrieked.

'We do what we always do.' Angie's voice sounded hopeless.

We start again, Gemma thought. We go right back to square one and we start again. We go over everything one more time.

'I'll go back over the statement Sandra Samuels made when she was fifteen,' said Angie. 'I'll go through those VMOs one more time. I'll check every goddamn thing that Scott Brissett has ever done in his life, everything he's ever owned, ever bought or sold. Anything he's even pissed up against, I'll check out.'

'Bring it all back here,' said Gemma. 'I can help you. And that way, when they come to kick you out, they'll have to track you down.'

Angie left to collect the rest of the VMO files

and Gemma poured away the drinks and went into the kitchen. Strong coffee, she thought. That's what we'll need.

Angie and Gemma sat on either side of the dining table with a pile of files on both sides of them—the one on the left slowly decreasing while the one on the right became taller with every re-reading. Gemma went through her pile thoroughly and slowly—it helped to keep her focused. But there were no more thief knots. No more fancy green and white kite-flying cord.

Angie was looking for anything that might cast light on Scott Brissett. It was so quiet, apart from the gusting westerly flattening the ocean. They worked in silence, each of them depressed by the way things were going. It was late by the time they'd finished.

'There's nothing new here,' Gemma finally said.

'I'm whacked.' Angie stood up and stretched. 'Time to call it a day. Oh, I nearly forgot. Francie Suskievicz faxed over her initial findings on the multiple human remains. Remember those polystyrene boxes in the bush not far from where most of the teeth were. They're trying to find out where they came from. They've got names and dates on them.'

'Are they old file boxes?'

Angie shrugged.

From the rocks below came the thump of a big breaker. Gemma registered it through the soles of her feet. 'No one's come to kick you out yet,' she said.

'No one's awake is why.'

'Go home, Ange. Get some sleep.'

She put Angie out the door and stood awhile in the garden. It was still hot and through the white curtains of the upstairs flat she could see the bluish flashing of a television.

Back inside, she printed off two more copies of the photo of the room Claudia had sent her. She wished she had a picture of the Black Diamond Room at Deliverance so as to compare the two. Apart from the drinks trolley near the black draped bed, they looked to be identical. She felt sad and exhausted and, although dog tired, she couldn't shake the awful images of Tasmin's last moments of life. She'd had blood in her mouth, she remembered Dr Chang saying.

She left the prints of the picture lying on the dining room table, too tired to think. Her mobile rang and she was about to switch it over to voice mail when she saw it was Mike.

'Sandra Samuels rang me. She's got a key to the premises of Forever Diamonds. I suggest we move now. What do you think?'

'Great,' said Gemma, forgetting how tired she was.

'If you want to come along, I'll pick you up,' Mike added.

Gemma hesitated. She should be getting to bed but this was another chance to put things back on a business-like footing between them.

While she waited, she washed her face, cleaned her teeth, changed into jeans and a dark shirt and put on fresh lipstick. Taxi, cranky that she wasn't settled on the lounge or going to bed, sulked around her ankles. When she heard Mike's car up on the road, she grabbed a jacket, her torch from the office, picked up her video camera, locked up and ran up the steps. For a second, she was overcome with the memories of what had happened last time she'd been in this particular vehicle, but she gamely put those thoughts aside and climbed in, slamming the door.

There was little conversation in Mike's car on the way to Newtown. The traffic was light at this hour and they soon turned into the back lane behind Forever Diamonds and parked a little way from the cyclone fencing. Gemma recognised the woman coming towards them as Sandra Samuels. 'I've got a front door key,' she said. 'It's my job to open up in the mornings and sort the mail.'

The side street was deserted, but only a few metres away King Street still buzzed as the three of them walked towards the front entrance. Sandra opened up, disarmed the alarm, switched on the soft floor lighting and Gemma and Mike followed her in. The scent of yellow and white lilies perfumed the small space. Gemma noticed several bills on the counter, including one from Energy Australia. She remembered Raymond Gardiner mentioning the huge costs involved in the transformation process and Kevin too had said it was a costly business. Sandra unlocked the door to the small office to the right of the coffin-like counter, and walked over to a locked key cupboard, unlocked it and selected a security key from its hook.

'What are the kids at the refuge doing while you're here?' Gemma asked, following Sandra as she opened the security door that led to the factory area behind the shopfront.

'Sister Dorothy from Youth Off the Streets said she'd keep an eye on them for me,' said Sandra. 'Most of them don't come in till later anyway.'

Mike switched his torch on, keeping the powerful beam low as the three of them went inside.

'We probably shouldn't be here,' he said.

'We're with a key-holder,' Gemma reminded him.

'What are we looking for?' Sandra asked, as Mike played the torch around the walls and ceilings. The place smelled like a mechanic's shop.

'We're looking for their system,' Gemma explained. 'Not so much computer files, but the way they physically log the different jobs, the different containers of carbon. The way they receipt and track the ashes through the process that changes them into diamonds.' She delivered a short lecture on the manufacture of artificial diamonds.

'I can think of a couple of people I'd like to have transformed,' Mike said. 'And I've got some creative ideas about where I'd like to wear them too.'

'Just as well they have to be dead,' Gemma said. She glanced over at his broad figure. I like you, Mike Moody, she thought.

'I think it's creepy,' said Sandra. 'I wouldn't want

anyone hanging round me like that, even if they were a diamond.'

'So we're looking for the place in the process where a mistake can happen?' Mike poked around with his torch beam, highlighting the corners of the large hangar.

Gemma nodded. 'Just so Mr Dowling feels he's got the beginnings of a case to argue. Even if he can't actually prove anything.'

Mike continued to play the torchlight over counters and workbenches, highlighting a set of tools in an orderly collection on the walls. Sandra had gone a little way ahead of them and they could hear her at the far end of one of the long workbenches opening and closing drawers. 'There's nothing much here,' she called back. 'Jeweller's tools. Clasps, fittings. What you'd expect really.'

Gemma joined her, lighting up the counter ahead of Sandra. She saw jeweller's eyepieces, tiny metal picks and pliers and a rolled-up piece of fabric. A desk in a corner contained nothing except several stacked pastel-coloured crematorium containers for ashes. Curious, Gemma opened one. It was empty but dusty inside. She checked the lid. 'This was Stanley John Cotter,' she read, putting the container down. 'Empty, so he must have been processed.'

'Transformed,' Sandra corrected her. 'Mr Gardiner gets angry if I say anything else.' Gemma glanced at her. Despite the trauma of her girlhood, Sandra was perfectly focused right now, a slight frown of concentration on her face—not at all the vulnerable woman Gemma had seen on an earlier occasion.

'These look like the findings for the finished products.' Mike, pulling out drawer after drawer, indicated boxes and containers filled with gold and silver wires, swivels and other settings. 'I don't see how we can gauge their process, Gemma. Not unless we get someone in here to watch the whole thing from A to B.'

Sandra checked other drawers and boxes under the bench while Gemma flashed her torch around. Apart from the desk and the work tables around the walls, the central space was bare. She frowned.

'Surely there should be something else here,' she said. 'I'm not sure what, but something more than this.'

'I've found some stones here,' Sandra called out. She'd unrolled the piece of fabric and Gemma and Mike peered at the dozen or so stones she'd revealed, laid out in three short lines of four. 'Mr Stanley John Cotter might be among this lot.' She poked them with a small tool. 'And how would you know?'

'If they just mix them up like this once they're cooked, they all look much the same,' said Mike. 'Looks like we got 'em cold on this one. There's no identification for any of them!'

Gemma picked up one of the diamonds lying on the piece of unrolled fabric and, fixing the jeweller's eyepiece in place, squinted at the magnified gem while Sandra held the torch on it.

'Take a look,' Gemma offered. She could see

tiny impurities and lines in its depths. A second-rate stone, even she could see that. 'Are they real?'

Sandra straightened up and handed Gemma back the torch. 'Mr Dowling had his examined by a jeweller, didn't he? And it was genuine.'

Gemma shone her torch on the small glittering stones. No way they could tell one of these stones from its fellows. The old elation at catching a cheat lending her new energy, Gemma tugged her video camera out of its bag and began shooting the area, starting with establishing shots of the Forever Diamonds letterhead and certificate of registration as a business, then turning to take in the workbench and the short rows of uncut diamonds on the piece of fabric. She filmed the interior, as much as she could while Mike and Sandra held the flashlights steadily for her. The lighting wasn't ideal, but it would do. Then she concentrated again on the stones on the unrolled piece of flannel.

She put the camera down, pulled some latex gloves out of her pocket and picked up some of the stones.

'How on earth would they know who was what?' said Sandra, peering at the stone in Gemma's gloved fingers. 'Your client was right. He probably hasn't got his wife in that ring he showed you. God knows who he's got.'

Sandra searched again in the dark space under one of the workbenches, dragging out a small carton. 'What's in that?' Gemma asked.

Sandra opened it and pulled out a small parcel carefully wrapped in twine and brown tape. She held it up. The postal franking looked like Chinese characters and Gemma videotaped the parcel and the characters in close-up.

'What *is* this?' Mike asked. 'Don't tell me the Chinese are exporting their ancestors to be processed.'

'Something here doesn't add up.' Gemma pointed to the dark space in the centre of the factory. 'There should be a huge pressure press here.' She flashed her torch around again. 'Where is the press? What are they doing the transforming in? My engineering expert said it would take a huge furnace or a press that could duplicate natural forces 200 kilometres under the earth's surface.' She turned round to the others. 'What's going on here?'

'I smell a rat,' said Mike. 'A diamond rat. There's no machinery here. This isn't a manufacturing space.'

Gemma surveyed the factory area one more time with her torch beam. The facts flew together in her mind. 'They're not making diamonds here! They're not making diamonds anywhere! Old Mr Dowling was spot on,' she said. 'It's not his wife in that ring. It's not anybody's wife.'

She indicated the short rows of uncut diamonds on the fabric square. 'The only thing Forever Diamonds are manufacturing here is bullshit,' said Gemma. 'They're importing low-grade pre-cut diamonds from China. Probably paying no more than a few hundred bucks apiece. Then a jeweller sets them in gold—there's another couple of hundred. They're charging people thousands of dollars for a diamond ring that's cost them maybe six or seven hundred dollars. Maybe a thousand after they've paid for the jeweller's time.'

'Good profit,' said Mike. 'Way to go.'

'Way to go to a fraud conviction. Put the lights on, Mike. No need for subterfuge now.'

Under the bright lights over the workbenches, Gemma pulled her video camera out and started filming the evidence all over again.

Before they locked up and left the premises, Gemma picked up an Energy Australia bill.

'Get a copy of this,' she said, passing it to Sandra who took it to the photocopier in the corner and ran off several copies. They returned the bill to the counter. The amount of power needed to run Forever Diamonds was smaller than for Gemma's business.

Next morning, Gemma was woken by the uncomfortable pressure in her lower abdomen. Immediately, the shadows came crowding in. Angie's fears about the end of her police career, everyone's fears for Claudia, the pencilled warning note. Gemma listened to the early news in the shower—the search for the missing teenager was still continuing—giving her stomach a good rub, remembering that the first period after the breakup of a relationship was always hard and heavy. She felt a little better after the shower, thinking about the success of last night's raid on the cheats at Forever Diamonds. She prayed for a similar result for Claudia Page.

She ate toast with some of Kit's cumquat marmalade, staring out to sea. She thought of Forever Diamonds and Stanley John Cotter's empty polystyrene box. Into her mind flashed Francie Suskievicz's words to Angie: they'd found a number of little polystyrene boxes near the teeth and bone fragments out in the bush. Gemma jumped up, abandoning her toast.

She rang Francie, thinking of the hot day at Richmond and the annoying little bushflies. 'I've had an idea I think you might find interesting,' she said when Francie answered. 'On the multiple human remains and teeth.'

'If what you're suggesting is true,' Francie said, after Gemma had outlined her suspicions, 'we're going to have to get the names and dates of those involved. DNA reference samples are the way to go.'

'I can help you with that too,' said Gemma, thinking of Sandra Samuels.

'Really? When?'

'As fast as a phone call.'

'Great,' said Francie. 'We wouldn't know where to start otherwise.'

'Put it all through Angie, will you?' Gemma said. 'Just so it goes through normal police channels. There's enough that's weird about this case without unduly provoking the hierarchy.'

'Gotcha,' said Francie.

'And if the DNA testing works out, this could make a client of mine very happy.'

'I'm glad to hear it. Remind me to tell you about the squirting worm I found in a body cavity one day.'

'You guys have all the fun.'

Gemma put the phone down. Although she had to deal with people like Bruno, there were also Francies and Melissas, Mikes and Spinners.

After finishing the cold toast, Gemma gathered last night's results, prepared the video and copies of her notes and totalled the bill for Mr Dowling. He'd been right, after all. Fifty years of living with someone, she thought, must make you very attuned to what that person feels like, even when she's rendered down to pure carbon. Or not.

Another wave of sadness overwhelmed her as she thought of Steve. Fifty years together was something she wouldn't be having with the man she loved. She tried to take comfort from the fact that they'd done well last night, that Mr Dowling had not only been vindicated, but he'd been the instigator in revealing a serious fraud perpetrated on grieving, vulnerable people. There was a very strong chance that if he decided to take the matter further, the courts would overlook the unorthodox way in which his evidence had been gathered. *A Current Affair* would love this story, she thought.

'Mr Dowling,' she said when he answered. 'Is it convenient for you to come in later and get your results?'

'I'll be there in half an hour,' he said.

•

Mr Dowling stared hard at Gemma while she told him the story of last night's raid and what they'd found.

'It's all here,' she said. 'In my video evidence. I've also got two eyewitnesses. You were absolutely right in your suspicions. It is not your wife's remains in that diamond. It's not anybody's.'

Mr Dowling was silent for a long moment. 'Is that for me?' he finally asked, pointing to the large manilla envelope with his name on it, in which Gemma had assembled all the reports and the tape.

'It is.'

She passed it to him and he opened it, glancing down at the account, putting that to one side, briefly skimming through the notes. Finally, he put it all away again, except for the account which he handed back to Gemma together with his credit card. She processed it and he signed the chit.

'The dirty lowdown mongrels,' he finally said. 'The dirty dogs. What a terrible thing to do to people.' He looked away, sniffed and pulled out a large hankie, blowing his nose. 'The worst thing is,' he said, 'that I don't even have anything anymore. Not anything. Nothing to bury. Nothing to put in a nice little wall with a plaque beside it. Those people are worse than grave robbers! At least grave robbers only took the treasures. I've lost every little bit of Shirley now.'

Gemma sat back in her chair, wishing there was something she could say to comfort the old fellow.

'Even if I take these frauds to court, I'll never get my Shirley back.'

It was too early, Gemma thought, to mention her recent conversation with Francie. She didn't want to get the old man's hopes up only to dash them again. Instead, she walked with him to the door, a comforting hand on his shoulder. She watched him go up the steps to the road, his heavy tread, and felt a pang in her heart. In some cases she worked, she wondered if discovering the truth was worth the pain it caused, and this case was one of those.

She rang Linda Shipper at DAL and told her about Mr Dowling and his double loss—with reference to her call to Francie Suskievicz. 'It's possible to do something with mitochondrial DNA,' Linda said. 'We might be able to do it in conjunction with the fraud investigation. But it could be easier for him to go through a private lab. It'll be expensive, but if his children gave samples, the lab might be able to find something for him.'

The heat from yesterday filled the apartment and there was no breeze through the barred windows. Gemma pulled the blinds against the sun and poured a cool drink, then sat at the dining room table staring sightlessly at the printed copies of the image Claudia had sent her from the Black Diamond Room. As she sipped, she went over what she knew about Scott Brissett. She stood up, restless, recalling what Angie had told her about the visit to his house, his two big trophies—his wife and his cruiser. Brissett was a winner—he *had* to win—as testified by all the sporting trophies in his lounge room. And when he was young, Brissett had also liked raping young girls.

Gemma reconsidered her earlier decision and rang Mr Dowling with the news about the possibility of mitochondrial DNA testing. Maybe having some hope for a while was better than not having any at all.

She put her mobile back in her bag. Deep in her mind, something was stirring, something Naomi had said about her work. Gemma searched her memories of their earlier meeting and the discussion of Naomi's continuing education. She felt frustrated. There was something she knew, something vital, but she'd stowed it away in her memory and now she couldn't retrieve it.

Damn, she said under her breath, getting up to take her plates back to the kitchen. That was when she freaked. Her front door was wide open. And someone was standing in the doorway. No chance to go for the Glock; her only weapon was a knife and fork. How had this happened? Had she felt so wretched last night, been so exhausted, that she'd failed to lock up after Angie left? It was hard to credit, and yet that's what she must have done.

'Are you pissed off with me?'

Gemma dropped the plate. 'Hugo! You scared the living daylights out of me!'

'Sorry,' he said, putting the key to the door back in his pocket.

'Give me that key!' she said. 'Did you help yourself to that?'

He handed it back and walked down the hall after her, then helped her pick up the pieces of broken plate. 'You've gone real white,' he said.

She stood there, swallowing hard. Then just made it to the bathroom, flinging up the toilet lid and hurling into it. Hugo followed at a distance, standing about in a useless way while she washed her face and teeth, and cleaned up the splashes.

'You're crook,' he observed helpfully as she came out of the bathroom. 'Have you had anything to eat?'

They sat at the dining table next to the sideboard and while Gemma chewed on some dry toast, the Ratbag ate his way through several days' worth of planned meals.

'I want some answers, Hugo,' Gemma said. 'You told me that this Eddie was after you because he thought you'd ripped off drugs. But I don't believe you. There's no way a dealer would let a courier take the drugs and the money together at the same time.'

The Ratbag looked away.

'So, Hugo. Tell me. What really happened?'

The boy looked around then up, pretending to find something of interest on the ceiling.

'I'm waiting, Hugo. I can wait all day.' God, she thought, where do these horrible lines come from?

'You can't really wait all day,' he said.

'How come you had that money?' she demanded.

He twisted in the chair. 'I told the clients that the system had changed. That they had to give me the correct money from now on instead of doing electronic transfers.'

'And they believed you?'

Hugo looked hurt. 'I said Eddie didn't want to use the credit system anymore and made up a real good story about how the cops were watching bank transactions. That scared them. I told them it was cash only now. I made heaps.'

'But it didn't take long for Eddie to hear about it, did it?' Something like that, she thought, would only have been good for a few hours.

'Yeah. He found out pretty quick.'

Sometimes, Gemma thought, it's tough being thirty years younger than the person you're trying to hoodwink. 'So you really ripped Eddie off?'

'But he was dealing drugs! He's a crim!'

'And you're not?'

'No way! I'm just ... just sort of getting money off him. I wasn't hurting anyone.'

'Hugo, when you steal from people, someone is always hurt.' She paused. Even if, she was thinking, it's only a boy of thirteen.

'But how was I hurting anyone? I was bringing them what they wanted.'

The kid should be a lawyer, she thought. Or a Jesuit.

'Okay,' she said. 'Interrogation over. We'll leave the moral discussion for another time. Do you want a milkshake or something to drink with that?'

'A milkshake would be way cool.'

Gemma went into the kitchen and made him a milkshake, using plenty of the new ice-cream she'd bought. When she got back, Hugo seemed more relaxed.

'I talked to Dad again,' he said. 'He says I can live with him next year. He's promised.'

'Does your mother know that?' she said.

'She's cool with it. But she says I've got to go back and finish the year at school—there's not that much left of it.' He made a face.

'Where have you been? I was worried about you.'

He shrugged. 'Here and there. I stayed with Gerda.'

He'd mentioned that name before, Gemma recalled. 'So who's this Gerda?'

'She's a trannie,' he said in a matter-of-fact way. 'She's saving for the op.'

Whatever schooling the Ratbag might be missing out on, Gemma thought, he was sure getting a liberal education.

'And I got something for you,' he added.

'What? Something you've pinched? Bought with your ill-gotten gains?'

The Ratbag shook his head. 'I got Eddie's full name for you.'

Gemma grabbed her mobile. 'Go!'

'Eddie Borg.' He pulled out a scrap of paper and pushed it towards her.

She dialled Angie with the news. 'He's already being questioned,' said Angie. 'Sean got a break from your Greek mate at Indigo Ice.'

While Gemma cleared the table Hugo pulled the copy of Claudia Page's emailed jpeg image towards him. 'What's this?' he said, flicking the edge of the paper.

'It's a picture someone sent me—someone

who's missing,' said Gemma. 'I thought I knew where she'd sent it from. But I didn't.'

Hugo looked at her curiously. She knew she wasn't making sense. He picked it up and studied it. 'That tray,' he said, pointing to the top of the drinks trolley in the image. 'It's got the same little railings on it, like yours. And the bottles have the same big bums.'

Gemma glanced over and saw that it was so. Something like electricity shot through her body. 'Holy shit! Hugo! Of course it has!'

'Has what? What are you talking about?'

'Has little rails!'

He stared at her as she snatched up her mobile, dialling Angie again..

'Tell Sean,' Gemma said. 'Or go in yourself. Tell Sean to say to Eddie that you know about the boat! The cruiser!'

'What boat?'

'Do a rego check. Not vehicles. Boats.'

Gemma recalled the painting Angie had mentioned—alongside the nude portrait of Brissett's dark-haired wife—his other trophy: the luxury cruiser. She hurried on, before Angie could interrupt.

'I'll take bets Amy and Tasmin were taken to a boat.' She explained the implication of Hugo's observation about the decanters and the drinks trolley. 'That's where Claudia sent her last picture from. That's where you'll find the other Black Diamond Room. And Claudia Page.'

SIXTEEN

Hours later, with the water police going after Brissett's cruiser, Angie and Gemma, wired with caffeine and adrenaline, waited at water police headquarters. Outside, gulls wheeled around the high spotlights, flashing brilliant white before vanishing into outer darkness.

Through the open door of the office, they could hear the radioed voices. Along the horizon, the dark purple ocean separated from the sky. Low-lying cloud shone red-gold as sea and sky lightened. Red sky at dawning, Gemma remembered, is a warning.

She and Angie sat over more coffee.

'It was Hugo,' Gemma explained. 'The Ratbag. He noticed the railings and the wide bases of the decanters on the drinks trolley and then all the things that I'd been trying to put together just went snap! You told me about Brissett's two trophies in his lounge room. Remember, next to the nude portrait of his wife there was a photograph of a big cruiser? And Tasmin's body was dumped at sea,

417

weighed down with something that you'd find on a boat—the diver's belt. Colin Roper's report said that cord was used in kite-flying and fishing.'

A car pulled up nearby. It was Claudia's mother.

By the time the sun was well clear of the sea, Claudia, doped and disoriented, but alive and wrapped in a rug by the police, was brought ashore and restored to her mother.

'We'll talk to her later,' said Angie. 'When she's come down from whatever's in her system.'

On the nearby wharf, the Forensic Services station wagon pulled up with a couple of Crime Scene people.

'What's the name of Brissett's boat?' Gemma asked one of the water police.

'Just initials,' he said. 'GBS.'

She turned to Angie. 'But his initials are SGB. Why the mix-up?'

'Might be some maritime reference. We've got him, that's the main thing.'

'GBS!' Gemma suddenly remembered. 'They're the initials Naomi noticed. On the trophies.'

Gemma went home and found Ratbag watching television with Taxi snuggled on his lap, the remains of a pizza on a plate on the floor.

She tried to have a nap, but after lying restless for half an hour or so, she went back to work in her office. Claudia would identify Scott Brissett and the police would lay charges. It was going to be all right. She checked the latest news on the internet. There was a photo of Bruno in his shiny uniform, preening himself at a press conference as if he'd single-handedly saved Claudia Page. Under his cap she could see the plaster over his left ear lobe. What was the matter with his ear lobe, she wondered. An idea suggested itself to her and she was about to ring Angie with it when her mobile rang.

The noise of traffic made it hard to hear who her caller was until she recognised Angie's voice. 'I'm in the public phone down the street,' Angie explained. 'Bruno was looking for the VMO files and wants to know why some of them are missing from the pile he gave me. For God's sake, bring in anything you've still got at your place now. I'll meet you downstairs.'

Gemma grabbed her keys, stuffed the last remaining files into her briefcase and pulled Taxi off Hugo. 'Come on,' she said. 'Want to do some PI work?'

He was immediately awake and interested. 'What's it worth?' he asked.

'Your continued board and lodgings here,' she said.

'What is it?'

'I want you to ID someone.'

'Cool,' he said. 'Anyone I know?'

She gave him a look.

'Only joking,' he said.

They climbed into her car and she switched the radio on and flicked through the stations. '*The police told him they had physical evidence linking him to the crime and then it turned out they didn't!*' said the talkback guru. '*What is the matter with the New South Wales police? We need a return to old-fashioned policing. Kicking the butts of hood-lums, not harassing innocent family men.*' The footie legend was working his media contacts hard, pulling in favours, lobbying for his case.

At Strawberry Hills, Gemma parked in a side street and hurried to the old post office building with Hugo beside her.

'Where are we going?' he asked.

'Just to the corner here,' she said.

As they approached the building, Angie was already waiting, white-faced, lips in a tight line. Gemma tried not to betray her shock. She'd never seen Angie looking so tense and strung-out.

Angie hurried over and Gemma held out her briefcase. 'Everything's in there,' she said.

'Can you wait round a bit?' Angie asked, taking the briefcase. 'I'll get this stuff back upstairs—before Bruno notices—and come straight down again.'

'Sure,' said Gemma. 'Then I'll run you home.'

'I thought you said you wanted me to ID some-one,' Hugo said.

'I do,' Gemma reassured him. 'But we need to call him down here.'

Angie was turning to go when the door opened and Bruno stepped out. Angie stopped dead in her tracks at the sight of him.

'Where do you think you're going, Sergeant?' he said. 'You won't find those missing files down here.'

'I've got work to do,' said Angie.

Bruno looked from Angie to Gemma and then back at Angie again. His gaze dropped to the briefcase she was carrying. He lunged forward and jerked a folder out of it.

'What's this?' he said.

'A VMO file,' said Angie. 'I'm scanning them into the system. It's a job you were supposed to be doing.'

'*She's* had them, hasn't she!' Bruno said in triumph, thrusting the file in Gemma's direction. 'You'll go a row for this, McDonald. Unauthorised access to official documents. You are dead!' His pager beeped, but the smile of satisfaction remained on his face while he dug it out and attended to it, striding away as he spoke.

'Come on, Hugo,' Gemma said, tugging on his arm. He was staring after Bruno as if he were a ghost. 'Hey!' he said. 'I know him!' He swung round to Gemma. 'He's the guy with the diamond ear stud! From the club!'

Bruno looked up from the pager as Gemma hauled Hugo away.

'That's the man I was telling you about,' Hugo continued. 'The cop! See? I was right! He *is* a cop!'

'Shut up, Hugo,' Gemma said, pulling him down the street.

'Why?' he asked.

'Use your brains,' she said. She was thinking of a whistleblower girlfriend, knocked down one dark night by an accelerating unmarked police car as she crossed the road to her house. She hurried Hugo across the street and they stood near Baccarole, waiting for Angie.

'I thought you said you wanted me to ID someone?' Hugo said.

'You just did, Hugo.'

She looked up to see Angie hurrying towards them. 'You look terrible,' Gemma said.

'I haven't had breakfast. Or dinner last night,' said Angie. 'I need a sugar hit. Right now.'

They ordered iced chocolates that came with piles of whipped cream on top and a long spoon. Angie stirred hers without paying much attention to it.

'Hugo reckons Bruno spent a lot of time at Deliverance,' said Gemma. 'Wearing a diamond ear stud.'

'There's no crime in that,' said Angie. 'Apart from how twentieth century diamond ear studs are. Even cops are allowed to party.'

'But he was always there, talking to Eddie,' said Hugo. 'They were mates. He was there heaps.'

'Okay,' said Gemma to Angie. 'What happened exactly?'

'Not much to say really. The boss hauled me in because when he checked the VMO files I'd signed for, some were missing.' She put her mouth around the straw, took a sip, then stirred the ice-cream around. 'It's so picky and mean. Things are always bloody missing. Especially when they're needed. They're gunning for me.'

'What do you think?' Gemma asked.

'You mean *who* do I think? Bruno would have dobbed me for sure.' She squashed the pile of cream flatter. 'With me out of the way, he can run the investigation any way he wants.'

'Deliverance's way?' Gemma asked.

'Any way at all.'

'Do you think he's connected to Scott Brissett?'

Angie plopped backwards in her chair and sighed. 'Looks like most of Sydney is connected to Scott bloody Brissett.'

Hugo sat staring from one to the other.

'Everything was starting to move with the investigation into the girls' murders,' Angie said. 'We showed Eddie Borg the positive matches we'd got when we matched his DNA sample against Crim-Trac's database. Three serious matters attracting very long gaol sentences. I promised him if he helped us with the Netherleigh Park investigation, we'd help him. He looked at the charges we could bring against him and he just went to water. All this bullshit about honour among thieves!' Angie's words came out with a sharp laugh of contempt. 'He dobbed his crim mates in good and proper. Reckoned that Amy Bernhard's death had been an "accident".' She put her spoon down and looked across at Gemma. 'I suggested "manslaughter" might be more accurate. Filling a young kid up with alcohol and opiates and then using her like a sex doll is not going to do anything for her health and wellbeing.'

'Gerda's got a sex doll,' said Hugo.

Angie frowned at him then looked at Gemma. 'Who the hell is Gerda?'

Gemma shrugged.

'Eddie's admitted that he formed an association with Amy through the club,' Angie continued. 'But he couldn't get anywhere with her because she was involved with someone else—some guy who was obsessed with her. Eddie suspected it might have been Brissett himself. Brissett had been giving her money and making promises and she was dying to start work as a model.'

Dying was the right word, Gemma thought.

'But when he asked her if it was Brissett,' Angie went on, 'Amy laughed at the idea. Said the guy who had the hots for her wasn't *that* old.'

'When you're sixteen,' Gemma said, 'anyone over twenty-five is over the hill.'

'She'd been told the sex video would help her commercially,' Angie added.

'That's Sydney for you,' said Gemma. 'So is that what happened to Tasmin too?'

Angie looked out the door onto the street. 'That was straight-out murder. Eddie told Tasmin what had happened to Amy one night when he was drunk and the poor kid was horrified. Threatened to tell. But Brissett talked her out of it when he heard what had happened. He convinced her that it had simply been a tragic accident, too much partying. Too much fun. That nothing could bring Amy back so why should Tasmin ruin a potentially brilliant career because of a dreadful accident?' Angie brought her attention back to her iced chocolate. 'Though Tasmin seemed convinced by this, Brissett couldn't take the chance that she might change her mind. He knew that Claudia knew about him and Tasmin and if she and Claudia got together they'd be very convincing

witnesses against him—if it ever came to that.'
Angie sipped her drink. 'Anyway,' she continued,
'Brissett picked Tasmin up on her way to school.
He knew she liked to run the five clicks.'

'Tasmin had a crush on some "old" man in his
forties, according to Claudia,' said Gemma.

'Sure sounds like Brissett,' said Angie.

'And Tasmin would go willingly in a car with
him.' Gemma stirred her long spoon around,
scraping cream from the sides of the tall glass. 'But
how did they get hold of Claudia?' she continued.
'There's no way she'd go with Brissett. She was
already wary as hell, scared they'd come after her.'

'Through Eddie,' Angie said. 'He contacted
Damien Wilcox, telling him that he had informa-
tion about Tasmin's death. Said he was a friend of
Tasmin's trying to find out what happened to her.
That he needed proof of Brissett's association with
her. Apparently, Claudia had a photograph of
Tasmin and Brissett that Tasmin asked her to keep
because she didn't want her mother to find it.'

'Claudia said that,' Gemma recalled. 'She was
frightened that Brissett could come after her. She
said Tasmin had given her something to mind.' She
remembered the remorseful, guilty young girl who
had carried a huge burden in isolation. 'And then
Damien rang Claudia,' she said, 'when I was there.
I thought she was talking to her boyfriend. She
must have got the photograph and left the house
to meet him.'

'The two of them went to meet Eddie,' Angie
continued, 'and gave him the photograph, thinking

it would prove Brissett's involvement in Tasmin's disappearance. But instead, Brissett gets back the photo and, at the same time, takes Claudia hostage.'

Gemma thought about this. 'But why? Wouldn't it have been better to leave things be, rather than risk creating the storm he must have known would break out over Claudia's disappearance?'

'My gut feeling is that Brissett believes he's invincible. That he can do what he likes,' Angie said. 'I've met it a couple of times before in some of the big crims, especially the ones with good connections. He wants a girl, he takes her. And nobody can do anything about it. My bet is, he feels there's nothing he can't get away with. Did I tell you he's employing Piers Magnus at Magnus Projections to work on his image?' She mixed a dark layer of chocolate at the bottom of her glass into the remaining milk. 'And if he's got Bruno onside, who knows? He may get away with it.'

'Do you really think that?' Gemma asked. 'That Bruno is a dud?'

Angie scraped the cream off the sides of the glass into the chocolate milk. 'Can't be sure. Incompetence and stupidity aren't criminal matters—unfortunately. Corruption is. Often, they can look the same from the outside.'

'So Damien is bashed and dumped,' Gemma said, 'and Claudia's taken out to the *GBS*.'

'That's what happened,' said Angie. 'Claudia had her wits about her and stashed her mobile in one of her shoes.'

Gemma imagined the scene. 'She's left alone for a moment and that's when she fired off those images of the other Black Diamond Room and whoever it was interrupting her. And emailed it to me. Before they snatched the mobile away from her.'

Angie nodded. 'She told her mother she didn't even realise she was on a boat. She said she was half in and out of it. She doesn't remember transmitting those images or calling you.'

'That's weird,' said Hugo.

'It can happen,' said Angie, 'with the sort of drug mix they'd given her. Victims of drug-assisted sexual assault often report amnesiac episodes. She and Damien had had a couple of drinks with Eddie. God knows what she had in her system.'

'But she can ID Brissett as involved in her abduction?' asked Gemma.

Angie shook her head. 'She didn't ever see him.'

'Then what about the photograph of Brissett with Tasmin?'

''Gemster, do you know how many young people—girls and boys—are in photographs with bloody Scott Brissett? Only about half the adolescents of New South Wales. Eddie's the only person Claudia saw in connection with her kidnapping. Not Brissett. Or Kodaly.'

The Ratbag sucked up the last of his iced chocolate, making a loud noise as he vacuumed the bottom of his glass.

'Eddie's told us about how he was always on the look-out for girls for Brissett and Kodaly,' Angie continued. 'Under-age girls who'd come to the club because it was so cool.'

'And what are Kodaly and Brissett saying?' asked Gemma.

'Just what you'd expect. That Eddie Borg is a thieving employee who wants to bring them down because they sacked him for stealing money from the club. That they're great men brought down by petty jealousy.' She chased the melting lump of ice-cream at the bottom of her glass. 'And Naomi's story—about the outcalls she made for those two men? The reason Kodaly just watched when his big bodyguard had sex with Naomi is because he can't walk. He always hides it behind a desk. According to Eddie, he was injured in a hit-and-run accident years ago. Some drunk ran over him.' She signalled the waiter and asked for a glass of water.

'Some drunk ran over him?' Gemma repeated. 'Sandra Samuels ran over one of the men who raped her. What if that was Kodaly?' She felt a surge of hope. 'Sandra could identify him!'

'How convincing do you think that sort of ID would be in the hands of a good cross-examiner?' Angie said. 'Look, I know how you feel. But twenty years makes a big difference in people's appearances. Throw in the distressed emotional state Sandra would have been in and I think you can forget the idea of a clear eyewitness account.'

Gemma slumped back in her seat. Whatever she put up, Angie batted down. And she knew her friend was right.

'So far, all we've got is a bunch of circumstantial

stuff. Like the vinyl flooring in the galley of the *GBS*. The physical evidence team matched it against the stuff Amy was wrapped in.'

'I want to get these bastards,' said Gemma. She could feel anger, like fire, heating her back.

'You think I don't?' said Angie. 'And there were lengths of that fancy green and white cord on board. It'll be a few days before we get confirmation, but for sure all those girls were held on that cruiser.'

'That's *got* to point to Brissett,' Gemma said. 'It's his boat.'

'Brissett's saying he had no idea of what went on there, that he hasn't been on board for ages,' said Angie. 'He's blaming Kodaly and Eddie—says Eddie had keys to the boat. Kodaly's blaming Brissett and both are dumping on Eddie.'

'They should go in for politics,' said Gemma. 'Or policing.'

'I want to lock Scott Brissett and Vernon Kodaly up for a long time.' Angie spread her hands in a gesture of helplessness. 'But if I'm charged, I could be suspended and then it's going to be hard for me to stay in touch with the investigation. As it is, Bruno will do everything he can to get me out of his way. I know Julie would do her best to keep me informed. Not so sure about Sean, the way Bruno's been sucking up to him lately. Not that there's anything I can do right now. All I can do is watch as the whole case falls to pieces.'

Gemma remembered the searing photographs

of Sandra's abused body in the old file. Her heart sank. These men were going to get away with it.

'Angie,' she said, 'with everything we've talked about, isn't there enough circumstantial evidence to bust Brissett?'

Angie considered. 'I doubt it. Even if we get all the samples back from the cruiser saying that the two dead girls and Claudia have definitely been there, it's still going to be very hard to prove that Brissett had anything to do with it. Especially if he maintains his line that he had nothing to do with the club or that people went out to the cruiser without his knowledge. We haven't got enough to charge him. Even if we did, my feeling is it wouldn't get past committal.'

'What about a search warrant for his house?' asked Gemma.

'That was being organised just before Bruno and I had our run-in. But I'm betting Brissett's too smart to have anything incriminating in his own nest,' said Angie, despondent. Then, 'Oh, I nearly forgot.' She fished around in her navy briefcase and brought out a tiny package. 'I bought something for you. To thank you for your help in this. You made the connection—the tip about the cruiser. Thank you for getting Claudia back safely.'

'It wasn't me really,' said Gemma, glancing at the Ratbag with gratitude.

She took the small package and unwrapped the tissue paper. 'Oh, Angie,' she said, 'it's beautiful.'

'I thought it would be perfect. To replace that black stone you lost from your pendant.'

On Gemma's palm, glowing like a drop of honey in sunlight, lay a small rounded gemstone.

'It's a citrine,' Angie was saying. 'I hope you like it. See if it fits okay.'

Gemma took the pendant off and laid it on top of the smooth drop of light. They could have been made for each other—the golden stone warming the silver serpents of the setting.

She picked the stone up again and rolled it around in the palm of her hand. She kept thinking of Tasmin and her crush on Brissett. And what about Amy, she wondered—the man who'd been obsessed with her wasn't that old, according to what Amy had told Eddie. Rewrapping the stone with a new urgency, she put it in her purse together with the pendant. She wanted to move.

'I think I know,' she said, 'why Jim Buisman took Bruno off the case.'

Gemma dropped Hugo off near Central station, ordering him to go straight home and stay there, then she ran Angie home and headed south again.

Buisman was already installed in his corner at the Kensington Club, his copy of the *Sportsman* and the daily newspaper in a messy pile near his schooner glass. She walked over to him and sat down opposite before he could say anything.

'You took Bruno Gross off the original investigation into Amy Bernhard's disappearance because you discovered there'd been a prior, non-professional relationship between the two of them. Bruno was the "old man" who was obsessed with Amy, hanging around, perving outside her window. I don't know how Bruno's involvement came out. Maybe he talked to you about her and you worked it out? Maybe he's one of the men on the video? Maybe we'll be able to identify him with some fancy technical work. Whatever, you decided he had to come off the investigation.'

Buisman continued to stare at her, eyes blazing contempt and intimidation.

Unmoved, Gemma hardened her own gaze. 'I'm right, aren't I?'

'Who cares if you're right? You're just a little piece of shit who couldn't make it as a cop and now you're running around playing cop games. You're pathetic.'

'You're out of the job now,' Gemma continued, determined not to be needled by him. 'You don't have to worry about a thing. I just want you to confirm the truth.' She stood and pushed the chair back in, resting her hands on the back of it, leaning forward. 'An eyewitness has come forward who can put Bruno outside Amy's window only a short time before she disappeared.'

'Tell someone who gives a shit,' he said.

Gemma continued to stare him down. 'I do,' she said. 'I give a shit that the original investigation was so incompetent, so tainted, so compromised by the unprofessional behaviour of Bruno Gross because he got himself involved with a schoolgirl. Maybe if you had taken over the investigation yourself and followed it up properly, chased up the witness statements, found the webcam and the websites, or at least appointed someone competent to do this, Amy might have been found in time.' She straightened up. 'But instead, Bruno was taken off the case and none of the follow-up work was done properly. If Amy had been found in time, there's a very strong possibility that Tasmin Summers would never have gone missing. I hope you think of that, every day. How two young girls are dead because you didn't do your job properly.'

She walked away back out to the street, heart pounding. As the doors closed behind her, she couldn't help glancing back at Buisman. He hadn't moved. He sat in his corner, staring after her.

She was just pulling up outside her place when her mobile rang. It was Beatrice de Berigny.

The account was already made up, so Gemma picked it up and put it in the glove box and drove to Miss de Berigny's residence at Netherleigh Park. The removalist van was loading a dainty Louis XV-style settee as she parked next to it. Two chairs, covered in the same white and gold brocade, waited in the garden.

'Hullo?' she called through the open doorway.

Beatrice de Berigny appeared from the bedroom. With her hair tied back in a scarf and wearing pale rubber gloves, she looked more like a tea lady than the recent head of one of Sydney's most salubrious colleges.

'Excuse the mess,' she said. Stacks of crockery

stood next to bundles of cutlery and potted plants in cartons, their wandering tendrils wound around and bound with string. A pile of cups and saucers stood near a stack of butcher's paper.

'I was sorry to hear of your resignation,' Gemma said. 'You're an institution at this school. So everyone tells me.'

Beatrice sighed. 'It was time to move on and give someone else the chance to run Netherleigh. This whole dreadful business has made me take a long hard look at myself—the way I was living, the values I was teaching. It's too easy to get caught up in the materialism and rampant socialising in schools like this.' She wrapped a cup and stashed it in one of the cartons.

'Tell me something,' said Gemma. 'You and Mr Romero—'

Beatrice held a cup to her breast. 'He's been released, but he'll never teach again.' She picked up some butcher's paper and wrapped the cup in it. 'You knew there was something between us.'

'From the very first day,' said Gemma. 'From the way he walked into your office without knocking. I even thought you might have been lovers.'

There was a long silence. In the distance, Gemma could hear someone practising scales on a piano and it reminded her of her first visit here and Claudia's melodic minor scales.

'You were right to think that,' Beatrice finally said. 'Mannix Romero and I were lovers. But it was a long time ago.'

Gemma, about to put the account down on a

spare surface, paused. Something was starting to make sense. 'How long ago?'

'Thirty years ago.'

Gemma did some quick calculations. 'But you'd have only been very young then.' She hesitated. 'Fourteen or so.' She thought of the schoolgirl in Bathurst who had eloped with her teacher.

'Fifteen,' said Beatrice. 'When Mannix wanted the job here,' she continued, 'I could hardly refuse him. Especially when he hinted that if I did, he had a marriage certificate that would be very embarrassing if it ever came out. Imagine, the principal of Netherleigh Park eloping as a schoolgirl with her teacher.'

She pulled an empty carton towards her and reached for the stack of saucers.

'When that damned letter turned up in Mannix's desk, I got really scared. I thought he might be up to his old tricks. And that the past would race back and swallow me up.' She put down the saucer she'd started wrapping and Gemma saw tears streaming down her face. 'The past is never over. Not while I was still running from it. Not while someone's alive to remember it.'

SEVENTEEN

By the time she got home, Gemma was past being tired. Hugo was nowhere to be seen. She felt drugged so she tried to nap, but could only doze, worried for the boy. She remembered her missed music lesson yesterday and called Mrs Snellgrove to apologise and make another time. Later, she went for a run when the heat of the day had faded. It was twilight by the time she got back. A sudden hot gust of wind moved the leaves on the young eucalypt on her nature strip then died as she jogged past. Spooked, Gemma trod softly down the steps from the road to the front garden, grateful when the automatic spotlight flooded the area, piercing the evening light. The Ratbag had still not returned and Gemma wished she'd kept him with her.

Taxi uncurled from the lounge and plopped on the floor, rolling inside out and upside down to greet her. She walked all the way through her apartment, checking every room.

Her mobile rang. Naomi. 'I wanted to thank you,' she said.

'Me?' said Gemma. 'What for?'

'I heard the news. Getting that little girl back safe.' Naomi's voice softened. 'One of my friends is screwing a cop and she showed me the website those girls made and then the porn site. From fluffy toys to gang bangs in one hyperlink. You brought the third girl back safely.'

'But it wasn't me, Naomi. I was only part of an investigating team.'

'Mum always used to say you were very special.'

Gemma felt awkward. 'It was kind of your mother to say that. I don't suppose you've seen Hugo?' she asked.

Naomi hadn't. 'That pig Scott Brissett has ordered a twosome tomorrow,' she said 'for him and his partner. Two girls so they can play out his sick fantasy.'

They're celebrating, thought Gemma. Brissett and Kodaly have to lie low for the moment so they're getting their sex in a more usual way until all this blows over.

'But I can't get anyone to go with me,' Naomi went on. 'Rob's turned me down. She says no way is she going to service either of those two. None of the girls want to do it.'

Gemma found herself blinking as she put the phone down; her eyes were sticky and irritated. Everything felt alien and hostile around her, including her own body. This must be what exhaustion can do to a person, she thought. She had a bath, hoping it would relax her for an early night, but she found herself jumping at every sound and wished the Ratbag would come home. She unlocked the gun safe, unpacking the Glock again and assembling it.

It was difficult to settle down for the night. She kept thinking of Tasmin's last moments, and Naomi's phrase 'from fluffy toys to gang bangs' kept resounding through her head, the words compulsively repeating, like an unwanted melody. But finally, with the weapon under her pillow and the cat heavy on her feet, she slept.

Gemma spent most of the next morning tidying away the completed cases. Then she made up a cheque for Sandra Samuels and hoped it would cover part of next month's rent for the youth refuge. She could send Hugo there, she thought, if ever he turned up on her doorstep again.

After lunch, the phone rang. Melissa Grey. 'You want the long version or the short version?' Melissa asked after the initial pleasantries.

'A summary will do,' said Gemma. She focused her attention on what Melissa was saying.

'That block of land where we found the multiple remains—that we thought was a body dump site?'

'It was, really,' said Gemma.

'Raymond Gardiner owns it,' Melissa said.

'So the Forever Diamonds scammers had a nice convenient place to dispose of the cremated remains,' said Gemma. 'And the little boxes they come in.'

'That's right,' said Melissa. 'Those small grave

sites we found were where they stashed them. But they didn't know that they were burying them in a dry creek bed. So when the rain came, it washed most of the boxes out. They emptied their contents over a wide area—and the rest you know.' She paused. 'It didn't take Francie Suskievicz too long to work out that she was dealing with cremated remains.'

'Mr Gardiner thought "cremains" sounded nicer,' said Gemma.

'Gardiner's going to be locked up for a long time,' said Melissa.

'Good,' said Gemma. She told Melissa about Mr Dowling's predicament.

'I know about him,' said Melissa. 'Paradigm Laboratories contacted us requesting the crematorium box that had his wife's remains in it. We couldn't actually release it to them, but we got clearance for someone from Paradigm to come over. Apparently they were able to get enough material from inside the plastic box to get a match for him.'

'So how does my client go about getting back what's left of his wife's remains?'

'I'll deliver them myself,' said Melissa. 'Soon as we can. Just tell me where and when. Always looking for an hour or two off the job.'

Angie phoned in the late afternoon. 'Trevor's missus put him in hospital last night,' she said. 'I had to come back and save him.' Gemma had forgotten Angie's planned revenge. 'We were at Graingers, just starting to get it on. Trevor thought

I was using the love-cuffs on him—they come apart with a little pressure. But I cuffed him with the real thing instead; clipped him to the bed. I was wearing my mistress of discipline outfit and I stripped him. It was when I was taking his jocks off that his wife walked in. She was so shocked that I was able to just grab my coat and walk out. But I could hear it from downstairs. I'd forgotten the whip. I was too worried that she might be carrying her pistol.' Angie paused. 'I even felt sorry for the lying bastard.'

'I can't stop thinking about Tasmin,' said Gemma. 'One of the gang must have hit her in the face. She had blood in her mouth.'

'It was a sport for them,' said Angie.

Gemma recalled Sandra's statement about how she'd been hunted and chased down—almost to the kill. Sporting men.

'You'll feel better when I tell you there is some justice in this world,' Angie continued. 'Your old perv—'

'Hey, he's not *my* old perv!' Gemma interrupted, thinking with a shudder of Alistair Forde.

'He's made a statement identifying the man he saw outside Amy's window that night. Bruno G-for-Gross. Forde was on the blower within minutes of Bruno's televised press release. Naturally, G-for's denying it.'

'I worked out that the man outside Amy's window must have been Bruno,' said Gemma. 'Jim Buisman took him off the original investigation because of his relationship with Amy Bernhard—which caused the whole investigation to fall over.

There was no proper follow-up, no handover to anyone competent.'

She thought of the journalist who'd written the Mandate piece, Amanda Quirk. This could be a big feature in a weekend magazine—the incompetence that had led to the deaths of two young girls. Sometimes, she thought, it seemed as if the media ran the police. Crime and sport: the two things that sell newspapers.

Gemma had a sudden realisation that made her sit up straight. 'Angie! That's it!' she said. 'You said it—it was a sport to them! And they gave each other trophies! Naomi saw them. You saw them when you went to his place. GBS! Gang bang sport! Or gang bang squad!' She remembered the phrase from the banner of the hyperlink to the Black Diamond Room. 'That's what those initials stand for. He named his cruiser after his sport!'

Gemma rang off, something still nagging at the back of her mind—something about the way Brissett had moved in the file footage she'd seen on television. Angie too had remarked on Brissett's limp. But whatever was troubling her didn't reveal itself. She did some music practice before tea and then headed off for her rescheduled music lesson, hoping that the Ratbag would be home by the time she got back.

A ribbon of silver glittered on the sea under the waning moon. Gemma got out of the car and walked down the steps, collecting the mail as she went. She hadn't had a chance to check it for a couple of days so there was a pile of junk mail too. The shadows seemed darker than usual in the front garden when the automatic light came on and she smelled the strong odour of Dior's perfume Poison. A shiver ran through her. Someone she knew used that scent although she couldn't for the life of her remember who it was. All she knew right then was that the association was not a happy one. Some long past senior officer? A difficult client? She glanced up to the second storey. The new tenant must be entertaining, she thought, tracing the scent and seeing the flickering goblin light of television on the white curtaining. Again, she wondered when she'd meet her upstairs neighbour.

There was still no sign of Hugo when she got inside but she found a fax from Angie. *This came through to my home fax—you might find something helpful*, she'd scribbled on the cover page. *I shouldn't be doing this. And I didn't, okay?*

Gemma flipped through pages detailing results from the DAL scientists who'd analysed the physical evidence from Tasmin Summers's post-mortem. She was about to file it away with her other case notes when, on the last page, she found a copy of the profile developed from the blood in Tasmin's mouth. Doctor Chang hadn't been able to say very much about the blood when they'd spoken, Gemma recalled. But now the results were in.

Gemma looked at the blood profile again, noticing the peaks at the first locus on the chart: the sex marker. She frowned and put the fax down, then picked it up, looking again at the DNA profile. Could Scott Brissett's limp be telling her something? She clipped the fax to the relevant file and allowed herself just a little hope. There was a tiny chance, she told herself. And if she was right, there might be a way to nail this bastard.

She rang Naomi. 'Still looking for a girl for the Scott Brissett twosome?' She explained what she had in mind and after overcoming Naomi's initial surprise, organised to meet her later. 'Any sign of Hugo?' she asked; there hadn't been. She rang off and called Spinner.

While she was waiting for him to arrive, Gemma removed the pendant from round her neck and opened the drawer where she'd stowed the micro camera. She matched it against the oval space left by the lost onyx. The tiny domed lens housing was a little smaller than the empty circle of Celtic dragons but with a little adjustment she hoped Spinner could rig something up.

She picked up the mail she'd dropped on the hall table and flicked through it. There was an invitation addressed to her and Steve to attend an engagement party. She binned it, biting her lip. One of the envelopes was handwritten. As she opened it, a cheque for five hundred dollars slipped out. Daria Reynolds.

Dear Miss Lincoln, she read. *My pastor has suggested I send this to you even though I don't feel I owe you any more money.* Bugger you, Gemma thought. She read on. *You were specially recommended by a psychic I visited who said that the best way to stop my ex-husband's harassment of me from the other side was to bless the house in the company of a woman whose mother had been murdered.*

Gemma put the letter down. Anger at Daria Reynolds started building. Why hadn't Daria been honest with her? Told her her ex was dead? Had she feared Gemma wouldn't take the case on if she'd known? *Would* she have taken the case on if she'd known? Probably not. She'd have referred her to Kit. Gemma returned her attention to the rest of the letter. *My new pastor has been successful to a degree in keeping my ex-husband away. Please find enclosed a cheque for five hundred dollars which will bring the total amount paid to you to fifteen hundred dollars.*

Gemma put the cheque in her purse, thinking of the expenses Daria had cost her—the installation of spycams, the hours of physical surveillance. It all came to at least three times the amount Daria had paid. But it wasn't worth pursuing the woman through the small debts courts. Put that one down to experience, she decided.

She glanced up to see movement on the CCTV. 'Spinner,' she said when he came in. 'What are your feelings on ghosts?'

Spinner shrugged. She passed him the tiny camera. 'I want that camera in this pendant,' she said. 'Can you do it?'

He took both items, turning them over in his hands. 'Can't see why not,' he said. 'I might have to cut through the silver though to fix the lens in place.'

'Do whatever you need to do,' she said. 'I'll need the finest lead to the battery pack. How long will it take?'

'I've got all my gear in the ute. Not long.' He looked at her. 'What are you going to photograph?'

'Something,' she said, 'that I'm hoping to find. Something that will otherwise be lost for ever.' He shook his head and sighed.

While Spinner fitted and tested the camera through its automatic range, taking different shots, plugging it into his laptop and downloading the captured images, Gemma got dressed. Last time I dressed for this sort of work, she recalled, the evening had a very nasty outcome.

She chose an orange halter top teamed with a tight black skirt, her impossible diamanté sandals and a pair of blood-red garnet earrings. Around her waist she threaded a smart leather belt. She checked herself in the mirror, smoothing a deep bronze eye pencil around her eyes, finishing her lips in gloss. She pushed her hair back on either side with tortoiseshell combs; thought again, took them out and let her hair fall softly. At the doorway of her bedroom, with her jacket hooked over her shoulder, she looked back at herself to the long mirror on her wardrobe. It all seemed satisfactory.

When she walked into the lounge room, Spinner looked up and nearly dropped his pliers. 'Holy Ghost, look at you!'

'Don't say a bloody word. And didn't you just

blaspheme?' She came up to him. 'Have you got it working?'

Spinner held it up for her to see. The pendant, now fitted with the domed lens, hung innocently at the end of its chain. She took it from him, examining it closely. 'That looks great. Does it work?'

He showed her his laptop. 'It's not bad,' he said, indicating the slide show images on the screen: Gemma's living room, the sideboard with the decanters, Taxi curled up on the lounge. 'It's designed for very good resolution even in poor light.' He turned to her. 'So what's this all for?'

Gemma slipped the pendant around her neck, noticing how Spinner had woven the fine lead in and around the heavy chain. It was almost invisible.

'Scott Brissett's got a limp. And I think I know what might be causing it.'

She held the back of the halter top away from her as Spinner pulled the wire under the fabric down to its port in the small battery pack tucked under her belt at the back. 'I'll tape that in,' he said. 'Just so it stays put.' Gemma waited.

'Okay,' he said. 'How's that?'

She turned around; by craning her neck she could just see the small battery pack nestled against the back of the belt. 'You'd hardly know it was there,' she said.

Spinner started folding up his laptop. 'Okay,' he said. 'What's the job?'

•

The waning moon had sunk lower in the west when Gemma climbed into the Fletcher Brothers van clutching her small beaded purse for the drive to Watsons Bay via Baroque Occasions.

'You sure about this?' Spinner was worried; she could see it in the furrows of his face. 'You know what this man is capable of doing. What if he turns nasty? What if he finds the camera?'

'He's not going to find the camera,' she said.

'You're no hooker. He's going to smell a rat.'

'I'm new to the game,' she said. 'My script is simple because it's the truth. I'm a new girl and Naomi is training me.'

Spinner threw her a look—she could see he was far from convinced. 'This is Scott Brissett,' he reminded her. 'Ugly mug supremo. Murder suspect. Do I have to say more?'

'Spinner, I'm just doing my job,' she said, starting to feel angry.

'But what about the camera? You can't do the business without getting undressed! That's okay on the streets but not in an outcall to a private home.'

'You seem to know a lot about this sort of thing,' she said.

'I did what I did before love came to town,' he said. 'Does Angie know you're doing this?'

'Not exactly.'

'You mean not at all,' he said, shaking his head. 'This is dangerous, Gemma.'

Her mood, elevated by her sense that she was taking action that could put Brissett where he belonged, deflated and she suddenly felt very unsure. She'd based this entire operation on a certain conjecture. What if she was wrong? She might not get the information she needed; and her planned actions would definitely compromise her. If this didn't come off, if it went bad, her future as a licensed investigator was in great jeopardy. What she planned to do was a breach of boundaries, both professional and personal. She was a licensed investigator, not an unlicensed sex worker. She heard her sister's voice warning her about the dangerous situations she seemed to seek and was silent all the way to Baroque Occasions.

Naomi, gorgeous in a scrap of a dress, hair in pigtails, white hoop earrings dangling, legs encased in thigh-high pink leather boots despite the heat, carrying a white straw bag, was keeping an eye out for them and ran outside. Spinner averted his eyes as she climbed into the Rodeo. Turning to Gemma, she patted her pigtails. 'He likes these.' With her skimpy dress and childish hairstyle, Naomi looked fourteen.

'But what about me?' Gemma was alarmed. 'No way I'll pass as an adolescent.'

'That's okay. Rob's a lot older than me and he's cool with that. But you're a real turn-on, honey, because it's your first day on the job.' The way she spoke reminded Gemma of Naomi's late mother, Shelly.

'Hey,' said Naomi. 'What's your working name? We all have a working name. Mine's Carla.'

Gemma thought about the woman who'd

humiliated her last year. 'Lorraine,' she said. 'But you'll have to show me what to do.'

'Sure,' said Naomi. 'Just follow me.'

'But what do I do?' Gemma realised she was very nervous.

'Gemma,' said Naomi, 'I've already told you. You tell him he's wonderful, that he's the best in the world—'

'It's not the talking part that worries me,' said Gemma.

'Relax,' giggled Naomi. 'You'll get the hang of it.'

Spinner refused to drive any further until they'd put the camera through another test run. 'We're not leaving until I'm a thousand per cent sure you're online,' he said.

'But we've gotta go,' said Naomi, concerned. 'He gets really pissed off if we keep them waiting.'

But Spinner insisted, making Gemma activate the micro camera. She heard the tiny beep that indicated it was functioning and watched the jumbled images of the Rodeo's interior: looming close-ups of Naomi or her boots and the upholstery depending on how Gemma and the pendant moved.

'Okay,' said Spinner, satisfied.

In no time they were driving along the dark laneway that ended with the gateposts Gemma remembered from the previous visit. Spinner pulled up near them.

'Off you go. But the second I think anything's going wrong,' he said, 'I'll be bashing on that door.'

His radio crackled and he picked it up, still with the laptop on his knees.

'Mike,' he said. 'Where are you?'

'You've got Mike on this too?' Gemma felt abashed—she hadn't wanted this, although she had to admit to the common sense of it.

'Of course I have,' said Spinner. 'You don't think I'd do this without back-up? I'm not a big bloke. He's on his way.'

'Come on,' said Naomi. 'Don't make him any meaner than he already is.'

Gemma gave Spinner a 'you wait' glare, turned to Naomi, and together they went to the security buzzer on the gate. Gemma realised she was holding her breath. She told herself to breathe, deeply and steadily, and that had a calming effect.

It was then that the first wave of terror shivered through her. She knew Scott Brissett's capabilities. She almost jumped when the door opened and there he was, his heavy body concealed in a terry-towelling bath robe, tied around his waist, feet pushed into scuffs. He stood back in silence, a grim expression on his face, perfectly in command of the situation. The big man, used to having his way in all things.

'Come in, girls,' he said, peering at Gemma. 'You're new,' he added, looking her up and down as she walked past him. He turned to Naomi. 'Where's the other girl who usually works with you?'

Naomi followed Gemma, putting her bag down on a table. 'She's away,' she said. 'This is my friend, Lorraine.'

Gemma, who'd been wondering if Brissett's robe was tied in a thief knot, took a quick look around. Sure enough, there were the two huge paintings on either side of the large hood and flu of an oversized heater that fitted the erstwhile open fireplace: the trophy wife and the trophy cruiser. In front of the fireplace spread a large black bearskin.

'You like boats?' said Brissett, noticing Gemma's gaze. 'We should all go out on her one day. Have some fun.'

'Where's your friend, darling?' Naomi asked. 'Or is it just you tonight?'

Gemma felt nauseous. She couldn't imagine how she was going to go through with this.

'What's up with the new girl?' Brissett asked, going to a cabinet, returning with several chilled bottles of beer. 'Drinks, girls?'

He glanced at Gemma and frowned. 'You're nervous,' he said. 'You're scared. Why are you so frightened of me?'

'This is Lorraine's first time,' said Naomi. 'I guess she's feeling nervous. You okay, darling?'

Brissett put two bottles down, wrenched the top off one. 'Come here,' he said. Gemma walked over. 'You're a bit old to be starting a new career, aren't you?'

He thought that was very funny. Gemma didn't. Maybe I'll be doing just that, she was thinking, if word of this gets out to the wrong parties. She smiled, remained silent, thinking that was wisest.

'It's just not the same without your nice friend here,' cooed Naomi, looking around. 'We can't play our little rape game. Where is he?'

'My friend has other commitments,' Bissett said. 'So it's just us—me and you two.' He lowered himself into his chair, signalling with his beer bottle, like a Roman emperor. 'How would the new girl feel about being raped?'

Gemma froze. Is he just trying to frighten me, she wondered, or does he know who I am?

'Let's sort out the money first,' said Naomi. 'We get that out of the way and then we can relax and enjoy ourselves.'

'Get your gear off first,' said Brissett. 'Put me in the mood.'

'You know the house rules,' said Naomi the professional, wiggling her nose at him. Brissett pulled a roll of notes out of his pocket and dropped it on the table. Naomi picked it up and peeled notes off, all the time keeping an eye on Brissett.

'Hey,' he said, snatching back what was left. 'That's more than last time.'

'You're getting a virgin,' said Naomi. 'Lorraine is fresh. You don't get that every day.'

Naomi recounted the money, turning away and stashing it in her white bag. 'Okay,' she said. 'Let's get in the mood, darling.'

She selected a CD from the pile and, as the music started throbbing, walked straight over to Gemma and seized her in a violent kiss. In Gemma's mind, two ideas collided. The first said, this is Naomi whom I've watched grow up, this is practically incest; the second, this is necessary subterfuge, be professional. It took a long second for her to respond.

'Just pretend it's Steve,' Naomi whispered in her ear, curling her tongue around Gemma's lobe. At those words, Gemma relaxed, closing her eyes, winding her arms around Naomi, trusting that the young woman knew what she was doing, letting her do it, while all the time reminding herself that this was a performance that would put her in the right position to do the job she'd come to do. Imagining and willing it to be Steve in her arms helped to overcome the alien strangeness of a sexual embrace with another woman, of Naomi's female odours and small soft breasts pressing tightly against her. Memories of Steve vanished as she struggled to relax, pretending a passion that she could not feel, pressing herself into Naomi's caresses, watching Brissett through half-closed lids as he lounged on the chair with his robe half open, drinking beer. His eyes were on Naomi as she stepped away from Gemma to wriggle out of her dress, swing it a few times like a stripper then kick it away from her.

'Want some Puss in Boots, darling?' Naomi said, turning to Gemma. 'Take some gear off, darling,' she suggested, 'or I'll take it off for you.'

Knowing she needed to keep her halter top on, Gemma loosened her belt, watching as Naomi dragged the bearskin over and positioned herself on it, rolling round a few times, then, for Brissett's delectation, running her hands up and down her body, her legs in their boots opened wide. It was a gorgeous sight, Gemma thought. If you were a man.

'Come on down, Lorraine darling,' breathed

Naomi, one hand extended towards Gemma, the other between her legs.

'Yeah,' said Brissett. 'Get on down, new girl.' He glared at her, one hand holding his beer, the other rubbing his cock. 'I've paid to see you in action with the kid.'

If only the mums and dads who adore you could see you now, Gemma thought—the great legend Scott Brissett, sucking from a bottle with his dick hanging out. She wanted to get this on camera but she needed to get closer, so, with what she hoped was a sexy smile, she stepped out of her skirt, twirling it the same way as Naomi had, balancing on the diamanté sandals, making as if she were about to pull her knickers down.

She could see his penis was only half erect so instead she moved closer and slid to her knees in front of him, running her hands along her neck and shoulders and over her breasts, activating the camera as she did.

'Let's get acquainted,' she whispered, moving closer still, then bending over as if to take his cock in her mouth. It was rubbery, partly erect, and Gemma prayed the light was good enough for what she needed. The shock when he grabbed her head and shoved her face down against his cock made her almost jump away in disgust. It took everything she had to stay there.

He'd seen her revulsion. 'You want to suck that?' he said, angry. 'Do you? Show me what a dirty little whore you are.' Gemma couldn't speak she thought she was about to vomit. His words sickened her further; the grip round her neck was so vicious she could hardly breathe. There was no escape. 'Suck it and then get on the floor with the other slut.'

Gemma struggled, but he was far stronger. Her head spun and she didn't know if it was because of oxygen deprivation or because of her own nausea. Even the huge strength lent by terror proved useless against him. Suddenly, Naomi's voice.

'It's okay, darling, she's new. Maybe tonight's not your night, Lorraine?'

'You,' Brissett growled, 'are nothing but a dirty little whore.'

'Here's your money back, darling,' said Naomi, but Brissett wasn't listening.

'She thinks she's too good to suck my dick,' said Brissett, tightening his hold around the back of Gemma's neck, forcing her face against his penis, now fully erect and aroused. 'So you can damn well suck it good and hard and long!'

Gemma felt revulsion mixed with icy terror rising in her guts. Anything could happen now and there was no way she could stop it. The terror reached her heart. Could she tear herself away and run on legs that threatened to collapse under her? She was finding it difficult to breathe, every cell in her body pulling away from Brissett, tensing and tightening until she thought she'd faint.

Suddenly the painful grip around her neck was released and the tone of Brissett's voice changed. 'What the fuck?'

Someone was bashing on the front door. Spinner,

thought Gemma. Thank God. Brissett pushed her out of his way, so that she fell. As she did, she executed the best combat roll of her life, ending up as far away from him as possible. She was aware of Naomi slipping her dress back on.

'Come on,' she urged. 'Let's get out of here! Before he wants his money back!'

Gemma scrambled to her feet, grabbing her skirt, skidding and cursing the diamanté sandals, heading for the door that Brissett was pulling open. On the doorstep stood Mike, looking every inch the cop he'd used to be, and Spinner. 'I wonder if we could have a word with you, sir,' said Mike, flashing and closing his ID wallet.

Holding her skirt in front of her, Gemma hurried outside with Naomi. She hobbled around the Rodeo which was idling near the gateposts of the Brissett household and, using it as cover, tugged her skirt back on. She realised she was shaking, that her legs could barely support her as she climbed into the passenger seat with Naomi following her. She prayed the micro camera had worked. It must have, she told herself, for Mike and Spinner to arrive when they did.

It was only a couple of minutes later that the three of them, with Mike following in his car, lurched and swayed in the Rodeo while Spinner executed a three-point turn. Naomi glanced at Gemma who was squashed in the middle seat.

'Did the camera work?' said Gemma, noticing the laptop on the floor near Spinner's feet.

'It worked,' he said. 'I saw what was going on.'

'I meant, did we get the close-ups that I wanted?'

'Geez, Boss,' said Spinner, 'I wasn't real keen on the pictures I was seeing. I mean, I didn't study them.'

Gemma turned to Spinner. 'I don't know what would have happened if you and Mike hadn't interrupted things. You saved me from a fate worse than death.' She was trying to make a joke out of it.

Spinner gunned the motor. 'That bastard will be on the line to the cops right now. He'll know Mike's a phoney.'

'I'm going to be sick!' said Gemma, leaning out and hurling all over Brissett's stone gateposts. The footie legend could have her breakfast and lunch back. And dinner as well.

'I just hope and pray there was enough light,' said Gemma as they drove Naomi back to Darlinghurst.

When they let her out, Naomi pulled the money out of her white basket. 'Here,' she said. 'You take half of this.'

Gemma shook her head. 'No, Naomi. You keep it. I couldn't have done what I did without you.'

'You know,' Naomi said, stepping out of the cabin and closing the door behind her, 'with a bit more practice, I reckon you'd be a really top worker.'

As Spinner set up his laptop in Gemma's office and started running the program again, Gemma felt a surge of hope. If what she was hoping for showed up on this screen, Brissett would be brought to book and Angie would be safe from his malign influence. Her body seethed with adrenaline—some of it left over from the encounter with Brissett, the narrow escape she'd had; the rest excited anticipation of seeing what she'd captured on the tiny camera.

'Okay,' said Spinner. 'Here's what we got.'

On the screen, a series of images appeared one after the other, shadowy, grainy. At first glance, the first half dozen or so could have been mistaken for close-up images of some rare form of sea life, but the later images were quite clear.

'Look at this!' Spinner enlarged one of them so that it filled the screen.

Gemma stared then peered closer, feeling her spirits lift. Her suspicions had been correct. She had made the right choice. She grabbed her mobile and called Angie.

'Wow!' said Angie a little while later, as she stood staring at the same images. 'What is this? Or should I ask *whose* is this?'

'Scott Brissett's virile member,' Gemma said. 'I was wearing a camera.'

'You went down on Scott Brissett with a spycam?' Angie was shocked with admiration. 'I would never have let you do that if I'd known what you were up to.'

'See that?' Spinner said. He touched the screen with a pencil, indicating a crescent-shaped series of marks. 'You done good, Boss,' he said, turning round to her. 'You are the ace operative in this business.'

Gemma felt foolishly elated. If Steve were here, she thought, everything would be perfect.

'Jesus, Gemster. You've done it. This is great stuff!' Angie stared at the marks Spinner was indicating. 'Spinner,' she ordered, 'print them all out. These pics by themselves would be good enough for a physical match.' She straightened up. 'How the hell did you know about this?'

'That report you faxed over—I studied the DNA profile of the blood in Tasmin's mouth,' Gemma replied. 'It couldn't have been hers. The only thing I know about interpreting those profiles is that the first marker is the sex marker. I looked at that and saw twin peaks—'

'A male,' said Angie. 'Tasmin Summers had male blood in her mouth.'

'I couldn't stop imagining how Tasmin had died,' said Gemma. 'And I suddenly understood how the blood might have been there.'

'You'd wonder,' said Angie, 'how he could want more sex if he was sore enough to limp from the injury.'

'I thought about that myself,' said Gemma. 'But a man like Scott Brissett probably doesn't have much sensitivity left. He didn't want sex with me, anyway. He wanted to humiliate me.' And he'd almost succeeded, she thought, shuddering.

'The marks would have faded in a few days,' said Angie. 'And we'd have nothing.'

She picked up one of the printed images from

the small pile. 'Even a non-expert like me can see what this is.' Her face shone. 'This is fantastic. Scott Brissett has a bite mark on his penis.'

EIGHTEEN

The next morning passed for Gemma in frenetic phone calls and chasing loose ends.

Melissa Grey dropped by with a package and a certificate from Paradigm Laboratories. 'I was there picking up a job for DAL and thought I'd collect this for your client, Mr Dowling,' she said. 'Partial remains of Mrs Shirley Dowling—retrieved from the Richmond dump site and identified by mitochondrial DNA testing.' She wouldn't stay for coffee, because she was having a day off and wanted to do some shopping.

Gemma put the package in her office, thinking of the kindness of individual police officers, the way they used their own time for the public good, even if their seniors seemed often to have lost sight of the real goals of policing. She rang Mr Dowling with the good news.

'I've bought a white rose called Shirley,' he told her, 'so now I can bury her somewhere beautiful and mark the place with her rose.'

Next, Gemma rang Sandra Samuels at the youth refuge.

'The police are hoping to build a really strong case,' Gemma said, thinking of Scott Brissett's smirk, his sense of invincibility. 'They want it watertight before they bring him in.'

'I heard Vernon Kodaly's had a heart attack,' said Sandra.

'Natural justice?' said Gemma.

'I can't believe that, after all these years, I might get justice,' said Sandra. 'Then it will be finished.'

'You did a great job at Forever Diamonds.'

Angie rang the moment Gemma had finished speaking to Sandra. 'Bruno's gone. He's off on indefinite stress leave. He'll be out of the way for a while,' she said with great satisfaction. 'When this investigation is nicely filed away, I just might have enough to go after him. The boss is furious that the newspapers did a story on Bruno's connection with Deliverance. He's taped Bruno's locker up as well as the gear he left here, and if there's so much as a trace of coke anywhere, he's in real strife.'

'No wonder he got an infected ear lobe,' said Gemma, 'living two lives. Pulling that ear stud in and out all the time.'

She was suddenly serious. 'What about my spycam photographs? Brissett's defence team might argue that what I did was illegal and disallow them as evidence.'

'Stop worrying,' said Angie. 'You've been watching too much American television. We don't have Miranda out here and the court has power to admit evidence even if it's obtained illegally. Gemster girl, since when has art photography been a crime?'

'I want it all over and finished,' Gemma said. 'I want Sandra Samuels to have her day in court. Even if it's watching him go down for other, more recent crimes.'

'Relax. Your pictures have already gone to the pathologist. The forensic dentist is probably making a cast of Tasmin's teeth right now and she'll match them up with the bite marks. They won't even need to see Brissett's horrible dick if he wants to make things difficult for them.' She laughed. 'I'm thinking of sending Trevor a nice video to watch during his convalescence. Stephen King's *Misery* seems apt. And then I'm taking some leave. Going back home for a while. Remind myself what life's really about. Milk the cow. Do some gardening. Try not to fight with my mother.'

Gemma put the phone down and, thinking of mothers and daughters, hesitantly called the Page household. Mrs Page answered and they chatted for a moment before Mrs Page called her daughter to the phone.

'Good to hear your voice,' said Gemma. 'I just wanted to say hello, see how you were coming along.'

'Pretty good,' said Claudia. 'I've done a whole lot of thinking lately. About life. I mean, *my* life.'

'If you ever want to talk about things . . .' Gemma said.

'I'll call you in a week or two,' said Claudia. 'Could we go to that café again?'

'Sure thing,' said Gemma.

'Every time I think of what could have happened to me—'

'It didn't,' said Gemma. 'You came home.'

'I can't stop thinking of the others,' she said. 'I even wrote to them. But there's nowhere to post letters like that.'

'We'll buy some flowers,' said Gemma 'and you can attach the letters to them and let them float out to sea. Your friends will get the message.'

When she hung up, she had tears in her eyes. She realised she was feeling a whole lot better than she had in days. The winding up of a successful case had a very beneficial effect. In some way, order was restored in her spirit as well. She hoped that the next series of jobs coming into Phoenix Business Services would be plain insurance jobs, not complicated cases like murders, fraudulent synthetic diamonds and violent assaults from another decade. All she needed now was a nice quiet life.

That night, Gemma watched a French movie that made no sense at all, and was thinking of going to bed when a sound at the door had her on her feet within seconds. The CCTV revealed the Ratbag standing on the doorstep and Gemma hurried to let him in.

'Where the hell have you been?' she said flinging the door open. 'I was worried about you!'

Outside, the air was heavy and hot and a wind from nowhere lifted the shrivelled petunias then dropped them again. She looked at him, his worried brow, the smile that never quite arrived, the anxiety he carried. She put her arms out and he came over. They stood in the hallway, hugging.

'Okay,' she said. 'Supper first. Then I want to know what you've been doing and where you've been.'

Over bacon and eggs, Hugo explained. 'I ran into Dad's girlfriend after you dropped me off near Central and went with her to Dad's place.' He pushed a huge forkful into his mouth and chewed. 'I think his girlfriend really likes me.' He grinned.

It was the first time Gemma had seen such a big smile on his face. 'Hugo,' she said, 'lots of people like you. You're a likeable kid.'

He bit into a piece of bacon, tearing away the rind with greasy fingers.

'I don't want to sound unwelcoming, but why did you come back here then?' Gemma asked.

'I wanted to thank you and I left some of my stash here, under your lounge. I want to say goodbye to Gerda and give her some of the money. To help her pay for her operation. She doesn't keep ordinary hours but I know where to find her.'

'I should ring your mother then,' said Gemma. 'Get you on a bus back to Melbourne.' She switched on the television, hoping to get the latest news.

'You don't have to. Mum's coming up tomorrow to pick me up. She needs to sign something about the house with Dad.' He licked his fingers. 'So I'll be going back down with her.'

Gemma took his plate out to the kitchen.

'Hey,' he called. 'They've arrested that old footie dude for murder. You know—that famous guy?'

Gemma hurried in and sat down with him, but the segment was finished. She ran through the other channels, trying to find more news on the arrest. Finally, she passed him the remote. 'See if you can pick up something about it.'

While she rinsed the plates, she could hear the syncopated sounds as Hugo flipped from channel to channel. She remembered that the technician hadn't come back to sort out the channel he hadn't been able to tune properly.

'Hey!' Hugo yelled. 'Here he is again!'

Gemma hurried from the kitchen and watched as Scott Brissett, face pixilated, was escorted from a car surrounded by jostling people. A deep satisfaction filled her. Tonight, she thought, I'll sleep soundly. What a week it had been. So much had happened. Maybe now she could take some time to consider whether or not she wanted to continue with the search for Grace.

She went back to the kitchen to finish cleaning up. When she turned the taps off, she was aware of a strange, pervasive silence. An atmosphere, almost a presence. Something made her go to the kitchen doorway and look through to the lounge room. Hugo was sitting bolt upright on the lounge. Taxi too was staring straight ahead, jet ears swept back.

'What is it?' she asked, spooked.

Hugo pointed at the screen and turned to her, mouth opened. The silence spread, taking on a dark and menacing tone. She hardly dared to look. 'Hugo! What is it? You're frightening me!'

He pointed again. 'Look!' he said. 'How come? We're on TV!'

She followed the path of his entranced stare. To see herself staring at herself, to see Hugo staring at himself, Taxi sitting up alert—all there on the television screen.

Hugo turned to her again. 'Did you do that?'

She had not done that. Someone else had. Someone had set up a spycam. In her house. In her living room. Someone was watching everything that she did in this space, all her comings and goings. Someone was watching them now. Gemma's first impulse was to throw something, destroy the screen. But she knew that somewhere else, in a van not too far away, was another screen and another watcher, and they would see her smash the screen but that wouldn't touch the screen they were watching. The hidden camera would simply keep recording her distress, her fear.

'Help me,' she whispered to Hugo, in case they were stealing audio too. 'Somewhere in this room is a tiny camera. It won't look like a camera, it'll look like anything else. A light switch. The buttons on a radio, a clock. Anything. It'll be tiny. But it's in this room and it's transmitting all the time.'

'Why?'

Because someone wants me under constant surveillance, she thought. Immediately, the pencilled note of warning, all but forgotten in the excitement of recent events, filled her mind again. 'Someone's watching me.' She didn't want to think why.

'We need to switch the lights off,' she hissed. 'And the TV. Make it look like we're going to bed.' She switched off both, then dropped to all fours.

'But how will we find the spycam without light?'

Gemma crept into the bedroom and came back with her torch. 'We'll find it.' If it's the last thing I do, she thought. Then shivered at the expression she'd just used.

She felt weak and helpless. 'Where's my mobile?' she whispered.

Hugo skittered across the floor like a huge crab and snatched it off the dining table. He brought it to her and she dialled Mike's number but her call went straight through to voice mail. 'Mike,' she said. 'I've been going out live to someone. From the lounge room. I need to find the camera. Can you come over when you get this message?'

'But what if Mike put in the camera?' Hugo's question jolted her.

'Why would he?'

Hugo shrugged. 'I don't know. But men spy on women, don't they? There's this place in Macleay Street where there are peepholes drilled in the walls. Gerda told me.'

Gemma dismissed the idea. Mike had been an employee and colleague for over a year now. She trusted him like she trusted Spinner. Despite her bad behaviour towards him, she felt there was no way she could have misread him for so long. And why would he be wanting to watch her? He could check up on her any time in the normal run of his work.

She wished hopelessly that she had Mike or Spinner's electronic know-how. There would be a way, she knew, to tune in to the frequency that the unknown observer was using and use it to work back along his own signal until she found him. But she didn't have that expertise here with her right now.

'Let's find the little sucker,' said Hugo, crawling near her. Taxi, picking up the fearful urgency in the room fled, and hid under the lounge. 'Who do you think did it?'

Hugo's question brought her to earth. That should have been her very first thought. She was more exhausted than she'd realised.

'Someone, some time, who has been in this flat. Someone who had the chance to install a tiny camera lens. It only takes a few minutes if you know what you're doing.'

She reviewed all the people who'd been here. It didn't narrow the field. Spinner, Mike, Sandra Samuels, Angie. It couldn't be any of them, surely?

'The only people who've been in here are my friends. Or a client.'

'That's where you're wrong,' said Hugo. 'You've forgotten someone.'

'Who? You?' The idea of Hugo being suborned by an enemy of hers was unbelievable.

'No, not me.' The boy's voice was reasonable and steady. 'You're forgetting the television technician guy and the gasman.'

She was. She thought about them. The TV guy

had been here a couple of times before, but the gasman was a complete stranger—a quiet, seemingly competent tradesman. He'd gone about his business. He'd run out of fittings. She'd had to explain to Hugo what a bayonet was. He was going to come back. He'd never come back.

The gasman had never come back because he'd achieved his objective.

'I know where it'll be,' she said.

They crouched together to examine the bayonet fitting, Gemma holding her torch in her cupped hand so as not to reveal what they were doing. There it was, innocently fixed inside the housing for the gas pipe, a small beady eye transmitting the events of the room with a wide-angled lens to whomever and wherever it was required.

'There'll be a van,' she said to Hugo. 'If they're watching right now, they'll have seen that I've found their camera. Chances are they don't watch all the time. It's about the most boring job in the world.' She'd done it often enough in her past; sitting in a nondescript vehicle, watching nothing happening on a small screen.

'Let's go up to the road and have a look for it now,' Hugo suggested. 'We could creep up on them and *wham*!'

'Let's not,' she said. 'Not without reinforcements. Not without a whole lot of wham.'

'But we could do it together. You've got the Glock.'

She sat on the floor, out of the spycam's field of view. God, she thought, I'm not thinking. Spinner's on a job just down the road. She groped for her mobile again.

'What was that?' hissed Hugo.

'What was what?' Gemma froze.

'I heard something.'

The torchlight from the floor threw weird shadows on his face. Gemma looked past him to the CCTV. The front garden area showed nothing but darkness. But the automatic front garden light hadn't come on. Maybe the halogen tube needed changing. Or maybe it had been sabotaged. Thankfully, there was no way an intruder could get past the grille on the front door, not without oxy equipment.

'If anyone was going to come in here,' she said, 'they'd either have to come up the cliff from the sea or come through the roof.'

'But the sound didn't come from outside.'

Hugo raised his eyes to the ceiling and that's when she got it. There wasn't a van anywhere down the street. There was no need for a van.

'It came from up there,' Hugo continued.

'Oh Jesus,' she whispered. Upstairs was a new tenant whom she'd never laid eyes on. Someone whose flickering late-night TV she'd seen on several occasions lately through the shroud-like curtains. She jumped in fear when her mobile rang but snatched it up.

'It's me,' said Mike. 'Got your message. I'm on my way.'

'Mike—' she started, but he'd called off. She put the mobile down and that was when the fear really kicked in. What if Mike *is* part of it, a voice in her mind questioned? It wasn't the first time she'd been betrayed by an employee. What if his arrival was the signal? Open the door to Mike and in rushes Death, disguised as a trusted colleague.

'Is he coming now?' Hugo asked.

She picked up the phone again, to tell him to stand by, when it rang again.

'Boss? You're awake?'

'Spinner! I am so glad to hear your voice.'

'What are you transmitting at the moment? What have you got running?'

'You've found it too!'

'I got bored sitting off that house in Bronte. I decided to do a sweep of the area—see what's going on. After I'd sorted through the usual stuff, there was this other signal that intrigued me. When I pinpointed it, it was at your place. What is it?'

'There's a spycam in my living room.'

'Shit,' he said. 'Listen, I'll drive around and take a look. They've got to be somewhere nearby.'

'No, Spinner. Not nearby. They're here. They're in the flat upstairs!'

'Stand by. I'm on my way.'

The cavalry is on its way, she thought. But now her mind was spinning out, betraying her in every direction. What if Spinner had been lying to her? Taking on that new Mandate client just so he could be in the area and keep her under constant surveillance? But why? It didn't make sense. Unless he was in league with someone else. Someone who wanted her dead. This was awful. Suspecting everyone; realising that underneath it all she trusted no one.

'Hugo,' she said. 'This reminds me of last year.'

'That night we were down on the beach,' he said. 'And that man was trying to get us.' In the torchlight, his face filled with fear. 'You don't think he's come back, do you? He could climb up from the sea.'

Until he said that, she hadn't even considered the possible return of last year's cyberstalker. Now, suddenly, every hateful hostility was possible. Coming from all directions. Even familiar faces being pulled away, revealing themselves as masks covering something evil. Last she'd seen of him had been at sea. It wasn't possible he should return.

'No one can get in here,' Hugo reminded her. 'You told me that. We're safe in here.'

Despite the two colleagues heading her way, Gemma felt trapped. Just waiting. What if he was getting down through the ceiling as they sat here? She heard a car pulling in on the road above. Mike?

'Just don't let anyone in,' said Hugo. 'Ring Angie!'

'She's gone away!'

She ran to the bedroom and checked on the Glock under the second pillow on her bed. She came out to rejoin Hugo. Help was on the way. All she had to do was let Mike and Spinner come in and deal with whoever was upstairs. Maybe, said the treacherous voice in Gemma's mind, maybe that's just what they want. To make her believe that she's safe if she stays put. Then what? An earth-mover through the plate glass of the sliding doors to the deck? Don't be so stupid, she scolded herself. She wasn't living in a Hollywood blockbuster.

She went to the curtains and hesitated. She had a strong desire to pull them back, to confront her absurd fear of the earthmover crashing through, show herself how completely stupid she was being, see for herself how nothing moved out there except the stringy bushes at the edge of the cliff. And yet, some atavistic fear immobilised her. She stood irresolute a few seconds, then grabbed the curtains, spreading them wide.

The world exploded. Hugo's scream and the crash of glass breaking. A shower of knives and her own shriek of shock and terror as the looming figure hurtled through the shattering plate glass. Gemma jumped away from him, but stumbled against the edge of the dining table and went down, banging the back of her head sharply on the corner. Before she could regain her feet, he was on top of her, pressing down hard over her lower face and upper body so that she could hardly breathe. His breath stank in her nostrils. Terror charged her body. She kicked out, stifled screams forced backwards into her own throat by the painful blocking of her mouth. The screams rang inside the turmoil of her own head. He'd pinned her right arm awkwardly, painfully, beneath her own body; her left arm tried to engage with him. She flailed, intent on trying to breathe. From somewhere, Hugo's yelling reminded her she needed to live. Desperately, she tried to see who her assailant was, but just as he'd been too close up against the glass for her to see him on the deck, he was now far too close to her face. Memories flooded as the pressure built in her skull. It was the smell that did it. Peppermint and body odour. The big Polynesian from Deliverance. The stench of body odour and her own terror triggered another memory—the scent of Dior's Poison. She knew now who it was who wanted her dead. *You're dead, bitch!* she'd screamed at Gemma last year.

Gemma went limp at the realisation. Lorraine Litchfield. And the grip on her throat loosened sufficiently for her to get a lungful of air. 'Hugo!' she screamed. 'Help me!' The hands closed hard around her neck again. A terrible pressure was bearing down on her throat, her chest. Her ears were filled with explosive humming, then there was a crashing sound and tearing pain. She felt as if her head was being pushed into the floorboards, crushed into the darkness under the floor. Then suddenly, the pressure was gone and pain flooded in after the numbness of shock.

In the corner, either dead or unconscious, lay the huge Polynesian who'd stood in her way at Deliverance and signed for the bodgy courier delivery. With huge, raking gulps, Gemma got some air into her lungs, the oxygen feeling as if it had to be dragged over knives to get down there.

'It's okay, we'll lift you,' said Mike. 'Just relax.'

With Spinner on the other arm, they gently supported her, lifting her over towards the couch. She tried to help by walking, but when she went to stand her legs were jelly. She was aware that someone had turned the lights back on but she could only see as if through a narrow tube, still blind with shock.

'Sit here,' said Spinner, guiding her back onto the cushions.

'Just take it easy,' said Mike. 'Get your breath. Don't try and talk.'

'Hugo?' she gasped.

'He's here.'

She raised her head and looked up at them. She wanted to say thank you but words were impossible. Hugo went over to the decanters and turned up four glasses, then he emptied the brandy bottle with four generous serves. She wanted to say, 'You mustn't drink that', but it seemed a silly thing to even think, let alone say. She sat there, trembling, holding onto a very large brandy, her three friends around her.

NINETEEN

Before the ambulance took the Polynesian away, Mike pulled on a pair of gloves and checked him for ID. All he found was a set of keys, a substantial wad of cash and a mobile phone number on a piece of paper.

Gemma, Mike and Spinner went upstairs to the vacant flat with the keys. None of them fitted.

'How's he been getting in and out then?' Gemma asked, puzzled.

'Who wants to do the lock thing?' Spinner asked, squinting at it. 'It's one of those old-fashioned ones.'

'There's an easier way,' said Mike, and he shouldered then kicked the door, breaking it down.

Inside, they found the monitor with its view of Gemma's living room, now very still and showing only Hugo, overdosed with brandy, sleeping with Taxi on the lounge. The interim lease agreement, with its credit card payment, lay with other bits of paper, including a small spiral notebook. Gemma tried to decipher the signature on the credit card receipt but had no luck.

'I'll take bets,' said Mike, 'that the paper trail will lead straight back to Lorraine Litchfield. Not to mention what that big hulk might have to tell us. Conspiracy to murder is a nasty charge.'

Gemma poked at the notebook, flipping through its pages with a pen. She found a page with a list of starters at Rosehill and the instruction, *Ring beautician*. 'She wrote that note,' she said. 'On the page before this one.' She remembered the beautiful young woman, full of hateful jealousy. 'She couldn't forgive me because Steve chose me.' For a while, at least, she thought sadly. 'But why would she send me a warning? If you're going to murder someone, why alert them? It doesn't make sense.'

'I'll ring your sister,' said Spinner. 'You need her to come over. Look after you a bit.'

Gemma nodded. 'In a minute,' she said.

Spinner, after being reassured there was nothing more he could do, said goodnight.

'I'll stay, Gemma,' said Mike. 'Hugo and I can sort out the sleeping arrangements.'

'But something's not right,' she said. 'Why did he wait until tonight to do it?' Her voice was a rasping whisper, still too painful to push too much energy through her voice box. 'He's been up here for days. He could have crashed through any time. Why tonight? And why doesn't he have a key to the place?' She started looking around the flat.

'Lorraine came here one night. I could smell her perfume from downstairs.'

Gemma picked up one of the glasses in the sink. The lipstick ring was obvious. With the tip of her pen, she lifted the lid of the kitchen tidy and poked through the rubbish. Then she went into the bedroom. A Hawaiian shirt lay on one bed. Gemma had a flash of memory—the man in the white Ford who'd followed her at the car park. A colourful blur with dark hair, she recalled. Not the bleached hair or massive bulk of the Polynesian. She thought of the man who'd abducted her last year, forcing her to go to Lorraine Litchfield's place where Steve had rejected her at gunpoint and Lorraine had lowered the Colt, smiling at Gemma's humiliations.

'I don't think the Polynesian has been living up here,' she said.

'Then who the hell has?' Mike asked.

Later, Mike sorted through the shards with gloved hands and picked up a large section. He examined it closely. 'He used a glass cutter,' he said, 'and then just tapped it in. The whole plate fell inside. You're lucky you didn't sever something important.'

'I've never been so scared in my life,' Gemma whispered. 'I pulled open the curtains and he seemed to fly through the glass.'

Mike reached for her then and took her in his arms. 'Gemma,' he whispered. 'Gemma.'

She stayed there for a few seconds, but pulled away from him.

His arms fell to his sides. 'I've wanted to do that,' he said, 'from the first moment I saw you.'

'It's not the right time,' she said, turning away, surprised to find that in this moment her heart ached for Steve.

Mike peered more closely at her. 'You've gone as white as a sheet!'

Gemma bolted then, and just made it to the bathroom and the toilet, hurling out the fear and terror of the night, the lack of food and too much brandy. When she'd finished, she washed her face and cleaned her teeth, smoothing her hair back. She looked at herself in the mirror. Dark purple-red marks marred the skin of her throat and the sides of her neck and there was a grazing bruise starting to swell and shine over her eyebrow. She hadn't even felt that one. The back of her head was tender where she'd gone down against the corner of the dining table.

She made her way back to the living room where Mike had finished clearing the glass away. 'I'll keep it for the cops,' he said. 'They might get prints off it.' He straightened up and put a parcel of glass on the table. 'Feel better now?'

She shook her head and sank into the lounge. Hugo, as shocked children sometimes do, still lay heavily asleep next to tightly curled-up Taxi cat.

'After an assault like that,' Mike said 'you should get yourself checked out. Especially—' He broke off.

She put a hand to her bruised throat. 'I'll survive.' Her voice was a croak. 'Especially what?'

Mike seemed about to answer her, but changed

his mind. She asked him to bring her a couple of painkillers from the bathroom cabinet because her head was starting to ache. He put the kettle on and made a cup of tea for the two of them.

Gemma went to bed with Mike still hovering around. Finally, he made a bed on the floor using cushions from the lounge, pillows and a cotton throw.

Gemma lay awake for a while before the drugs kicked in, listening to the sound of the sea coming straight through where the sliding door used to be. It was nice having Mike out there, she thought, recalling the feel of his arms around her. And Hugo, sprawled on the lounge with Taxi cat. Her little family, she thought, and then slept.

She woke with the sun high in the sky and wondered for a split second why she felt so terrible. It wasn't just the ache in her head and throat and the dryness caused by the opiate. Her whole body was nauseated. She lay still for a few moments, reviewing the events of last night. Resentment and hatred, Gemma saw, had almost caused her death. She couldn't help realising that her own lack of forgiveness for Steve had destroyed their relationship. She and the widow Litchfield had something in common.

This understanding, unpleasant though it was, energised her and she jumped out of bed, throwing her dressing gown around her and hurrying to her office. Mike had risen and was already in the operatives' office and she greeted him as she passed. Sitting at her desk, she pulled out a piece of paper then sat for a few moments in thought. She picked up her pen.

Dear Steve, she wrote, *I'm so sorry that I destroyed our relationship—our friendship—with my inability to forgive you. I miss you so much. One day, I hope you can forgive me too. I will never stop loving you. Gemma.*

Quickly, so she wouldn't change her mind, and with tears in her eyes, she sealed, stamped and addressed it, slipping it into her briefcase to post later in the day.

She made tea and toast and Mike came down and ate with her out on the timber deck, Gemma wincing as she swallowed.

Later in the morning, and wearing the scarf Spinner had given her to disguise the bruising, Gemma greeted Hugo's mother, pretending bad laryngitis—which, in a way, was true. Gemma watched the lanky kid and his mother disappearing up the steps to the road and felt a pang in her heart. She slowly tidied up, finding bits of Hugo that she put in a box. He'd left a card and a ten-dollar bill under the kitty jar in the kitchen and she realised she'd actually miss him.

Finally, she went back to her office. This was her work and her life. To mount investigations against the cheats. To bring a little justice to an unjust world.

There was a voice mail message for her from Angie that she must have slept through. 'I had to let you know—the forensic dentist got a perfect fit from Tasmin Summers's teeth and the bite mark on Scott Brissett's penis. The guys told me that when he was shown your snapshots, he stopped fighting. And,' she added, 'all the knots he'd tied—apart from the correct nautical lashings—were thief knots.'

Gemma was about to hang up, but the message wasn't quite finished. 'Julie said to tell you that the big thug who tried to kill you is Kenny Rataroa. He's telling everything he knows about Lorraine Litchfield. He was carrying her mobile number. She'd sent one of her other thugs, Murray Boyle, to do the job but, according to Kenny the Rat, Murray had become reluctant to do the job. Watching you day and night like that, he'd got to like you.'

Murray Boyle—Lorraine's henchman who'd forced her to the floor of a car last year and called her 'girlie'. Murray of the Hawaiian shirt whose heart hadn't been black enough for murder. Who'd even tried to warn her with his pencilled note.

'Kenny told us Murray got even more reluctant when Hugo kept coming and going. He'd started bonding with the two of you. Some sort of reverse Stockholm Syndrome. Told Kenny he couldn't do it, but he was too scared of Lorraine. He knew what she was like. Anyway, the Litchfield woman had to call on Kenny Rataroa. The only thing he's ever bonded to is cash. You did well, Gemster. I'll see you before Christmas. Message ends.' Gemma smiled, despite the pain in her throat.

She checked her emails and her heart sank when she saw how many there were. She deleted one after the other, barely glancing at the summaries before hitting the delete button. But she stopped, shocked, as one name registered. Grace Kingston.

Gemma felt faint with excitement. Grace. Her sister had found the ICQ message! With shaking fingers, she undeleted and the message opened up.

> *Dear Gemma, I'll be coming to Sydney next week and will ring you to set up a meeting. I'm looking forward to meeting a member of my father's family. Is that you? Sincerely, Grace Kingston.*

Gemma stood up, dazed. She walked around her office not seeing anything for a moment, vaguely aware of Mike sitting at the desk in the office opposite. Then she picked up her phone and rang Kit.

'Why can't you talk properly?' Kit asked.

'Lost my voice,' Gemma lied. She'd tell Kit about what happened later, when she could face it all. Instead, she told her about the email from Grace. There was a long silence.

'Are you going to reply?'

'Yes,' Gemma croaked. 'Yes. I am.'

She went to the hall table and opened the drawer. The photograph of her father smiled up at her. Would Grace want to know what her father looked like? If she did, Gemma would give her the photograph. But she'd have to tell Grace everything about their father and mother, what had happened. She closed the drawer over her father—their father's—cocky smile.

She went back to her office, aware of Mike across the hall. She would have to make a decision about him, she realised. Either take him up on it or let him go. She felt the beginnings of excitement. A new phase. A new sister. The possibility of a new man.

Yet the nausea, forgotten in the excitement of their sister's email, reasserted itself. She'd been about to sit down at her desk again, but instead she headed back out the door.

Mike was standing in the doorway of the other office, a file in his hand. 'I need to ask you something about this,' he said. Then he looked closer. 'Are you all right?'

'The half-sister I didn't even know we had has just emailed me. And I think I'm going to be sick. Again.'

He followed her careening run down the hall. Gemma just made it to the bathroom. There wasn't much to come up, just the toast and tea. Afterwards, she washed her mouth and face and cleaned her teeth again, and came out, the hair round her face dripping.

Mike stood in the the entrance to her private world. 'Haven't you worked it out yet, Gemma?' he asked.   —

An hour later, after posting the letter to Steve and a visit to the pharmacy, Gemma was back in the bathroom, staring at the kit. She dipped the lower end of it in urine, as instructed. According to the directions and diagrams on the side of the box, a small dark oval would appear in the centre of the sensitised strip if the test were positive. If she wasn't pregnant, no oval shape would appear and the sensitised strip would simply remain as it was—a long, straight pink band. She stared. The pink band remained blank.

Her mobile rang and she hurried up to the office to answer it. It was the glazier. He was running late, he said, and apologised, but he'd definitely be there within the hour to replace the glass in the sliding doors. She still had the strip in her hand and Mike turned round at his desk, an enquiring expression on his face.

Gemma shook her head. 'Nothing,' she said. It was just the nausea of overload. Too much going on, poor sleep, a lethal attack, a new sister. Stress and more stress. She headed back towards the bathroom to throw the test strip away and wash her hands.

But she didn't make it. Something out at sea caught her attention and, still clutching the blank test strip, she stepped onto the deck into the bright sunshine. There was a churning on the surface of the ocean quite close to her and a flock of gulls wheeled in a synchronised swirl. Must be a huge shoal of fish, she thought. As she watched in wonder, the sea broke open and shiny black shapes curved out of the waves like a child's delighted scribble, over and over, stitching themselves through the water. There must have been more than a hundred dolphins. Almost as suddenly they vanished, pulled under by some secret dolphin command, and the sea closed over them, resuming its dark blue chop.

Gemma looked down at the strip in her hand. Her eyes widened and her lips formed the same oval shape as the positive reaction now clearly visible on the sensitised pink band.

'Oh!' said Gemma. 'Oh!'